Western Writers of America

SILVER ANNIVERSARY ANTHOLOGY

Edited by

AUGUST LENNIGER

ace books
A Division of Charter Communications Inc.
A GROSSET & DUNLAP COMPANY
1120 Avenue of the Americas
New York, New York 10036

Acknowledgments

TALL MEN RIDING by S. Omar Barker
Copyright by S. Omar Barker
Reprinted by permission of the author

HELL COMMAND by Clifton Adams
Adventure, Copyright 1950 by Popular Publications, Inc.
Reprinted from A WESTERN BONANZA, Doubleday & Co., 1969
By permission of Mrs. Clifton Adams

BUILDER OF MURDERER'S BAR by Todhunter Ballard
Saturday Evening Post, © 1945 by Curtis Publishing Co.
Reprinted from BRANDED WEST, Houghton Mifflin Co., 1956
By permission of the author

A PLACE FOR DANNY THORPE by Ray Hogan
© 1967 by Western Writers of America, Inc.
Reprinted from THEY OPENED THE WEST, Doubleday & Co., 1967
By permission of the author

THE DEBT OF HARDY BUCKELEW by Elmer Kelton
© 1959 by Western Writers of America, Inc.
Reprinted from FRONTIERS WEST, Doubleday & Co., 1967
By permission of the author

THE MAN WE CALL JONES by T.V. Olsen
Ranch Romances ©1959 by Popular Library, Inc.
Reprinted by permission of the author

WESTWARD RAILS by Giles A. Lutz
© 1977 by Giles A. Lutz
First published in this volume by permission of the author

STEEL TO THE WEST by Wayne D. Overholser
© 1977 by Wayne D. Overholser
First published in this volume by permission of the author

CAPROCK by Nelson Nye
Copyright 1953 by Stadium Publishing Corporation
Reprinted by permission of the author

DOBBS FERRY by Lewis B. Patten
Copyright 1950 by Fiction House, Inc.
Reprinted from RIVERS TO CROSS, Dodd, Mead & Co., 1966
By permission of the author

ONE MORE RIVER TO CROSS by William R. Cox
© 1966 by William R. Cox
Reprinted from RIVERS TO CROSS, Dodd, Mead & Co., 1966
By permission of the author

PEACEFUL JOHN by Kenneth A. Fowler
Zane Grey's Western Magazine, Copyright 1953 by Kenneth A. Fowler
Reprinted from THEY OPENED THE WEST, Doubleday & Co., 1967
By permission of the author

DANGER HOLE by Luke Short
Saturday Evening Post, Copyright 1948 by Curtis Publishing Co., Inc.
Reprinted from WESTERN BONANZA, Doubleday & Co., 1969
By permission of Mrs. Frederick D. Glidden

A COWBOY'S CHRISTMAS PRAYER by S. Omar Barker
Copyright by S. Omar Barker
Reprinted by permission of the author

Published simultaneously in Canada

ISBN: 0-441-87975-6

First Printing

Printed in the United States of America

CONTENTS

INTRODUCTION

Twenty-five years ago about a dozen authors of Western fiction founded Western Writers of America and dedicated their organization to the advancement and promotion of all literature about the American West. As literary agent for three of the founding fathers I was invited to join as their first associate member; later I was appointed to handle the sale of WWA anthologies and honored with full membership.

Today, Western Writers of America has grown into a unique association of over three hundred professional writers and others interested in Western literature, biography, history and cinema; its membership is worldwide, including editors, publishers, reviewers, screen writers, T.V. directors and producers.

One major part of WWA's program has been the publication of anthologies of the best short stories, novelets and articles by its members. The first of these, *Bad Men and Good*, appeared as a hardcover trade edition in 1953; a selection of the best Western short stories that had appeared in magazines during the previous year. As the magazine market declined in the late 1950s, WWA anthologies began to include many originally written short stories and some nonfiction pieces contributed by members for specific volumes. There have been thirty-two anthologies by members of Western Writers of America published in both trade and original paperback editions in the United States; many have also been reprinted in British editions and translated into Spanish, Portuguese, Norwegian, German and other foreign languages.

When Western Writers of America began, scores of Western short stories, novelets and a few serials appeared in periodicals every month. Weeklies like *Colliers, Liberty,* and *Saturday Evening Post,* monthlie's like *American Magazine, Esquire,* and *Argosy,* and even women's magazines like *Good Housekeeping* and *Redbook,* used them. And there were more than twenty pulp-paper magazines—*Adventure, Blue Book, Western Story, Ranch Romances,* and others—that regularly published much of the best Western short fiction ever written.

But by the late 1950s, the competition of television and the increasingly prohibitive cost of paper, printing and distribution resulted in the discontinuation of many magazines. Over the past two decades the classic, uniquely American Western short story has practically disappeared.

As very little short Western fiction is available to present-day readers, Western Writers of America commemorate their Silver Anniversary with this nostalgic selection of novelets and short stories by some of their best known members and a sampling of verse by our poet-laureate S. Omar Barker, honorary president of Western Writers of America.

The contents were chosen to reflect a wide variety of subject, locale and character interest during the years of America's expanding western frontier. The novelet *Hell Command* by Clifton Adams shows the hardships of the U.S. Cavalry in protecting Arizona settlers from marauding hostiles; "The Builder of Murderer's Bar" by Todhunter Ballard engagingly portrays life in a California gold camp; "A Place for Danny Thorpe" by Ray Hogan features a young rider of the Pony Express; "The Debt of Hardy Buckelew" by Elmer Kelton and "The Man We Called Jones" by T. V. Olsen are both unusually fine character studies.

We give you a glimpse of the railroad-building era in the two original short stories written specially for this volume, "Westward Rails" by Giles A. Lutz and "Steel to the West" by Wayne D. Overholser. And Nelson Nye's "Caprock" is a classic that was aired half a dozen times on the *Colt .45* TV program.

"Dobbs Ferry" by Lewis B. Patten depicts an emigrant river-crossing in New Mexico, and "One More River to Cross" by William R. Cox is a realistic epic about the diverse breeds of pioneers who developed Texas. In "Peaceful John," Kenneth A. Fowler presents the saga of a Northern European immigrant, a despised "carpetbagger" who winds up with a "welcome to Texas." And the novelet by Luke Short, *Danger Hole*, is a humorous hard-rock mining story about a reluctant pump!

Western Writers of America thank all of the authors on the contents page for their contributions to this *Silver Anniversary Anthology* and are particularly grateful to the widows of Clifton Adams and Luke Short for permission to reprint *Hell Command* and *Danger Hole*.

We hope you will enjoy this sampling of short

Westerns which in true historical perspective present the intrepid men and women who extended and established America, "from sea to shining sea!"

August Lenniger,
Western Writers of America
January, 1977

TALL MEN RIDING

by S. Omar Barker

This is the song that the night birds sing
As the phantom herds trail by,
Horn by horn where the long plains fling
Flat miles to the Texas sky:

Oh, the high hawk knows where the rabbit goes,
And the buzzard marks the kill,
But few there be with eyes to see
The Tall Men riding still.
We hark in vain on the speeding train
For an echo of hoofbeat thunder,
And the yellow wheat is a winding sheet
For cattle trails plowed under.

Hoofdust flies at the low moon's rise,
And the bullbat's lonesome whir
Is an echoed note from the longhorn throat
Of a steer, in the days that were.
Inch by inch time draws the cinch,
Till the saddle will creak no more,
And they who were lords of the cattle hordes
Have tallied their final score.

This is the song that the night birds wail,
Where the Texas plains lie wide,
Over the dust of a ghostly trail
Where the phantom Tall Men ride!

Hell Command

by Clifton Adams

I

THE BROILING ARIZONA SUN beat down on the sweat-soaked backs of the Calvalry, and the men of D Troop, what was left of them, sagged wearily in their saddles. They were slack-faced men, vacant-eyed from exhaustion and battle, dulled by the monotony of route march, and the screech of saddle leather, and the incessant rattle of loose steel. Once in a while one of them would rise out of the stupor that had grasped them and wonder out loud if maybe, sometime, they would ever reach Carter's Wells.

Up ahead, in front of the column, Senior Sergeant Kirkpatrick and Martin Swain, the hired scout, rode together. They had buried their last officer two days ago back at Morrison's Ranch, after a bad brush with a Cheyenne hunting party. So Sergeant Kirkpatrick was now the acting troop commander.

Which was all right with Swain. The sergeant was a good man—as good a top soldier as was likely to be found, if missing a few of the social graces befitting an officer and a gentleman, as they say. But the sergeant didn't give a damn about social graces as long as he could get a bullet into a red hide now and then. Swain thought he and the sergeant would get on all right.

They had been watching the shimmering blue hills to the north for Indian smoke, but they hadn't seen anything since early morning. Now Sergeant Kirkpatrick spat a heavy stream of brown tobacco juice across his horse's neck and tugged his campaign hat down over one eye.

"It ain't like a batch of redsticks to let well enough alone," he said. He looked at Swain. "You make anything out of it?"

He made something out of it, and so did the sergeant, but neither wanted to admit it. They hadn't seen a sign since early morning, but Swain knew they were being watched. The Cheyennes had taken a beating back at Morrison's, as well as the Cavalry, and they would have headed back to the hills for reinforcements. *If we can get to Carter's Wells,* the scout thought, *we'll have a chance. If we can rest the horses and men, and maybe get a hot feed in our bellies. . .* But he had learned a long time ago that it didn't do to plan too far ahead in this country.

The morning passed and the scorching afternoon beat down on them, and Swain began to wonder if they might make it after all. There hadn't been any more signs, and the Wells lay only two hours, three hours at the most, ahead of them. And, behind him, he began to feel a change in the troopers. They started to show signs of life, roundly cursing the heat and the dust and Army life in general, and in the Cavalry that was a healthy sign.

After an hour one of the riders in the advance

guard came back and reported no trouble up ahead, and Martin Swain and the sergeant looked at each other and wondered if they dared get their hopes up yet. A little farther on they came to the base of a long slope, and on the other side of the slope, in a valley, would be Carter's Wells. The sergeant stood up in his stirrups and raised his hand for a halt.

Sergeant Wellington, Junior Sergeant in the outfit, rode up to the head of the column.

"Dismount the troop, Sergeant," Kirkpatrick said. "Breathe the horses for ten minutes, then bring the column up at a walk. Mr. Swain and myself are going forward."

Wellington started to salute, then realized that Kirkpatrick wasn't an officer and became confused. He settled for a brisk "Yes sir!" pulled his horse around and bellowed, "D Troop, prepare to dismount. Hooo-o!"

Swain and the sergeant rode up the slight incline of the slope near the base, but, as the going got rougher, they got down and led their horses, saving what little strength the animals had for any trouble that might be coming. It took approximately thirty minutes to get to the top—and when they got there Martin Swain wished that they hadn't made it at all.

The two troopers of the advance guard were sprawled rag-doll fashion, one across the other, their sightless eyes staring wide in stark horror, their naked skulls gleaming bright crimson. For a wild moment Swain thought he was going to be sick—but he had seen it worse. At least these men were dead.

He heard Sergeant Kirkpatrick cursing, earnestly, monotonously, and it struck Swain that if he couldn't understand the sergeant's words his cursing would have sounded more like praying. The scout's first thought was Cheyenne, but the closer he got to the bodies the worse it got. Their tongues were gone, and that wasn't all, and the ground was drenched in blood. Part of Geronimo's band must have thrown in with the Cheyenne, for this was the unmistakable work of the Apache.

Even before Swain saw the smoke coming up from the valley below he had already guessed what had happened. The column had been watched all right, but only to make sure that they didn't reach the Wells before Apache made his raid. They must have had a lookout up here on the ridge and had ambushed the advance patrol the minute they reached the top. The two bodies were like pincushions pierced with arrows.

"And we can't even chase the devils!" Kirkpatrick grated between curses. "Our mounts are almost too tired to stand. They're just playin' with us, the . . ." Then the sergeant saw the smoke. The two men mounted silently, and from the crest of the ridge they looked down on what had once been Carter's Wells.

Swain rode down alone, ahead of the Cavalry. It was all over now. Apache was gone—up in the hills probably, looking down on them and laughing.

Carter's Wells had once been a Cavalry outpost, but the outfit had been moved up north on the Gila. Now it was a way station for the Nogales stage, and a general store and meeting place for homesteaders foolish enough to try to settle in this country. Or that was what Carter's Wells had been. It wasn't much of anything now.

There had been a stockade fence around the place,

but most of that was burned down now, and still burning. Inside the fence there was a brush arbor shed for the stage teams, and two corrals, and a deep well hacked out of pure limestone by no telling how many Cavalry misfits and yardbirds. The shed was ashes now, and so were the corrals, and, without looking, Swain knew that the well had been polluted with coal oil and God knew what else. The adobe store building and dwelling had fared a little better, but not much. There was a stagecoach, too, still burning.

Apache must have made a clean sweep of things, Swain thought grimly, by attacking while the south-bound stage was making its rest stop.

Then the scout heard the confused clatter of many hoofs as Sergeant Kirkpatrick brought the Cavalry down, and he thought of all the dime novels he had read and how the Cavalry always came charging in with sabers drawn and guidons flying and bugles sounding, just in the knick of time. But they hadn't this time. Behind him he heard Kirkpatrick bellow, "Two's right into line! Trumpeter, sound the Halt!" And the trumpeter gave his brief, tinny interpretation of "Halt." There was no need of keeping trumpet silence now, but, to Martin Swain, a civilian, it all sounded rather ridiculous and unnecessary, the situation being what it was.

But the wise scout keeps his opinions of the Army to himself. Kirkpatrick turned the command over to Junior Sergeant Wellington, and Swain heard the solid clomp of Cavalry boots come up behind him.

"They played hell, didn't they?" the sergeant said flatly. "Have you been inside?"

Swain shook his head. He knew what he would

find inside, and he wasn't eager to look at it. He could see enough from where he stood, there in the driveway in front of the adobe building. Kirkpatrick nodded at a body sagging across a window sill.

"Is that old man Carter?"

Swain said, "I think so. I saw him once and he was about that size." Size was all there was to go by. "Are you going to keep the troop here tonight?" Swain asked.

"It's better than a desert bivouac if an attack comes, but I don't think it'll come tonight." The darkness was sacred to the Apache, and his gods forbade attack at night. "Anyway, the men are dead on their feet. And so are the animals, for that matter. Did they spoil the well water?"

"What do you think?" the scout said dryly.

Sergeant Wellington had already sent out a firefighting detail, scooping up dust in their hands or hats or whatever they could find, and flinging it on the live flames. Another detail was selected to gather up the bodies—more than a dozen dead Indians were scattered about in the yard, but they attended first to the dead inside the store building. One man in that detail—a youngster by the name of Tobin, on his first mission—came out of the building and was sick on the doorstep, and the older troopers pretended not to notice. Most of them had been through it themselves.

Martin Swain, fondling his Henry rifle, watched the activity without actually seeing it. The hills to the north gained his attention and he wondered vaguely how many of the savages were up there, and how many would be there by tomorrow morning. If Apache and Cheyenne had thrown in together it probably meant that the attack would be led by

Choko, one of Geronimo's bloodier lieutenants, since this was considered to be his favorite territory. And, if Choko was in command, Swain could guess pretty well what the procedure would be. The chieftain's scouts probably had been following them for days, perhaps weeks, and he would know, or could guess, that the troop was headed back to Huachuca to rejoin the regiment. It was a six-day march, even with strong horses, and Choko wouldn't be in any hurry. He would snipe at the outriders and advance patrol and rear guards until he had the troop cut down, and then, around the third day of march, he would move in for the kill. The scout smiled grimly. He and Choko were old "friends." They understood each other.

There was a grind and crunch of wheels on rock as the escort wagons came down from the slope, and, lumbering into the yard, added to the confusion. Swain started to move over to the store building when a young, wide-eyed trooper come running up.

"Mr. Swain! Mr. Swain, for God's sakes, they's some women back there!"

The scout stiffened. At first he thought the youngster had snapped, but then he saw that he was only excited. "Women!" he said again. "So help me God. One anyway. They's a blockhouse behind the store building and that's where she is. You can see her in the window, lookin' over a barrel of an Enfield, and Injuns stacked up like cordwood. But the damnedest thing. I couldn't tell if she was livin' or dead."

II

"TELL SERGEANT KIRKPATRICK," Swain said. "I'll go have a look."

"You can just see her face lookin' over the barrel of that Enfield," the trooper said again, as if he couldn't get over it.

"Tell the sergeant," Swain said again patiently, and started running at an ungainly, horseman's lope back to the rear of the store building.

He hadn't taken much stock in the trooper's story, a man imagines he sees some funny things at times. But when he got to the rear it was like the trooper had said, except that there were only two dead savages. The building must have been a guardhouse when the Cavalry outpost had been here. It was a squat, sturdy affair of adobe and cottonwood logs, and there was one small window about as high as a man's head. That was where the girl was.

She wasn't dead, but Swain could see how the trooper might have got that impression. Her face was as pale as death and dumb with shock.

"Ma'am, are you all right?" Swain called. "Open the door and we'll get you out of there."

She only stared at him.

"Open the door!" Swain said again sharply.

Her eyes wandered for a long moment, then, at last, focused on his face. She started, and Swain thought for a moment she was going to let go at his head with that long-barreled Enfield. She shook her head dumbly, as if not believing what she saw. Suddenly, her face disappeared from the window. And the door opened.

She had gone through something that she would never get over completely, but she didn't go all to pieces, as Swain had expected, now that it was over. She stood there, shaking her head as if to clear it, still clutching that heavy Enfield. An ammunition box had been pulled up under the high window, and that was what she had stood on to do her shooting. The top part of her dress was half-torn away, baring one shoulder, but she didn't seem to notice.

Swain stepped into the small building, and, for the first time, he saw that the girl was not alone. There was the quick clack of boots on the hard ground and Sergeant Kirkpatrick came up behind him.

"Swain, I heard there was a woman back here somewhere!"

"Three of them."

"Joseph and Mary!" The sergeant came inside, looked first at the girl and then at the two other women huddled in the corner. They weren't hurt—none of them were—but the two in the corner were scared to death, clutching each other and sobbing convulsively. The sergeant shifted uncomfortably and turned back to the girl with the rifle.

"You sure played hell with Apache, ma'am," he grinned quickly. "Two of them, by God! I guess that'll learn them."

Swain said, "Are you all right, ma'am?"

She nodded, visibly pulling herself together. "Yes," she said, looking at the sergeant. "Thank you. But would you mind looking after the others?"

It wasn't the sergeant's type of work, gentling women, but the doctor had been buried back at Morrison's Ranch, along with the lieutenant. He walked reluctantly over to the corner of the dark, dank-smelling room.

"See here," he said, "there's no use carryin' on that way. It's all over now."

They didn't even hear him, didn't know he was there. One of them was a heavy, buxom woman whose florid face was streaked with tears and dust and screwed up puckishly with sobbing. The other was young, about the same age of the Apache-killing girl. She was expensively dressed in rustling taffeta, and under ordinary conditions she might have been pretty. But now her face was puckered in an ugly way.

"See here . . ." the sergeant started again. And then they started to scream.

The sergeant knew what to do about that. He knew what to do to men, anyway, and one person was the same as the other now. He lifted a ham-sized hand and slapped them across the face. He brought the hand back, backhanding them quick, and the sound was like two sharp cracks of a whip.

The screaming stopped, but there was a sudden silence in the room that Swain didn't like. He turned to the girl beside him. "Wouldn't you like to come outside, ma'am?" he asked. And she nodded, seeming grateful for the chance to get out of the room.

They went outside and stood beside a charred spring wagon and the girl watched vacantly as the burial detail brought the bodies out of the store building and laid them in a silent row in the yard. He turned and faced the mountains to the north.

"Look this way for a while, ma'am," he said softly. "That won't be very pretty."

She did as he said, turning woodenly. She noticed that her dress was torn and tried dispassionately to pull it into place, but at last she gave up and let it hang again. Martin Swain noticed that a great bruise was beginning to come out on her shoulder—the bare shoulder that had absorbed the jarring recoil of the Enfield. The bruise seemed startlingly dark against the whiteness of her skin.

"We're a troop of Cavalry coming down from Salt River," he said, trying to get her mind on other things. "We escorted a convoy up there a few weeks back. We're headed back to Huachuca now to rejoin the regiment."

She looked up at him then, and Swain felt that she was actually seeing him for the first time. "Thanks," she said after a moment, and her eyes gave the one word meaning. She had needed someone to talk to.

"I was on the Nogales stage," she said. "There were six of us, eight including the driver and guard, but I guess we're the only ones left. Me and the other two back there. The menfolks locked us in that little building and said maybe the savages wouldn't find us there. But they did. I don't know why they left without breaking in."

Swain smiled slightly. "Your shooting helped.

And, too, they knew the Cavalry was just on the other side of the ridge and they didn't have much time."

"But they'll be back," she said.

"What makes you say that?"

"Won't they?"

He looked at her face and those sober eyes and he couldn't lie to her. He could only say, "They won't be back tonight."

The sergeant came out of the block building hurriedly. He saw Swain and the girl and came over to them. "Sweet heaven!" he said, wiping his sweaty face. "Do you know who that woman is? The old one? The sow? She's the Huachuca commandant's wife! Her and her daughter was headed for Nogales and the Old Man was goin' to pick them up there and bring them to the fort. And I slapped them both! With the flat of my hand! Twice!" He wiped his face again. "I'll spend the rest of my days in the guardhouse—if I live to see a guardhouse. Which I won't. None of us will, it looks like— " He stopped abruptly, realizing that he was doing too much talking in front of the girl. "Swain, you want to come to the store building with me?" he said.

The scout looked curiously at Kirkpatrick. There was something on the big man's mind—something more than savages and guardhouses, for the sergeant had plenty of them.

Kirkpatrick said, "If you'll pardon us, Miss . . ."

"Coulter," the girl said. "Reba Coulter."

"If you'll pardon us, Miss Coulter, Mr. Swain and myself will go to the store building and fix a place for you" —he hesitated for just an instant— "for you, and the other ladies."

Reba Coulter looked at the sergeant and smiled slowly, wearily, as though there were some little private joke between them—but not a very funny one. She said, "Thank you, Sergeant."

Swain raised his hat and mumbled something—there was something disturbing about that smile of hers, and he suddenly became thick-tongued and awkward. "Perhaps I'll see you again this evening, Miss Coulter," he managed.

"Perhaps," she said, but her eyes didn't think so.

The burial detail had eight bodies laid out, covered with sheets, as Swain and the sergeant entered the building. The inside of the building was a shambles. Everything that could be broken was broken and what couldn't be broken had been carried away as loot. There were sticky-looking red pools on the floor, and some on the walls, but a detail had been put to work on that too before the ladies were brought in.

Swain said, "All right, Sergeant, let's have it."

Before answering, the sergeant went over to one side of the room where some suitcases had been slit with knives and the contents scattered over the floor. He went through them carefully, but whatever he was looking for, it was gone.

"Well," he said, "there it is. It's bad enough trying to take a column across the desert without three women on your hands. But when you have three women—and two of them are Colonel Ridgley's women . . ."

"Choko won't know they're Colonel Ridgley's women," Swain said.

The sergeant looked at him bleakly. "He will. The fat one—Mrs. Ridgley—had some letters from her husband here in one of her suitcases. They're not here now." And he added dryly, "Who do you guess got them?"

The words hit Swain like a kick in the groin, and he felt sick as he contemplated the future. Choko was nobody's fool. In his youth he had been a mission-school scholar, and so had many of his braves. There would be one brave sitting happily on Choko's right hand, Swain thought. The English-reading warrior who had thought to take those letters to his chieftain, when he might well have been rummaging for the worthless loot that Indians hold so valuable. For Choko would cheerfully sell his soul to the white man's devil to get his hands on Colonel Ridgley's wife and daughter!

The chieftain was well aware of the fraternal nature of senior Army officers. He could use the captives, if he had them, as a bargaining point in Washington, by working through the colonel. That failing, he could work on the colonel directly, decoying the main strength of Huachuca to the north and leaving southern Arizona naked of protection. For all practical purposes, there was nothing Choko couldn't do if he had those two women. Or, looking at it more realistically, *when he got* the women, for, by now, the Apache boss would already be making his plans.

Sergeant Kirkpatrick's face hinted worry now, and those broad shoulders were beginning to feel the weight of responsibility that comes with being a troop commander. "Do you reckon Choko's really behind it?" he asked soberly.

The scout looked at him. "It's Choko, all right.

Who else could bring Cheyenne and Apache together?"

Nobody, and they knew it. Then a corporal and five privates came into the store building, a detail to get a place ready for the women. Kirkpatrick and Swain went to the back of the building with them, to the part of the store that old man Carter had used as living space. There was only one big room. There was a kicked-over stove and a floor littered with dead coals and ashes, and a sturdy marble top dresser had been turned over and all the drawers pulled out and their contents scattered. Apparently, the Apaches had been forced to do their house wrecking in a hurry, for they had missed the heavy brass bed in the corner of the room. They hadn't even slit the fat feathered mattress.

Kirkpatrick said, "Get this room cleaned out, Corporal. When you're finished, notify Mrs. Ridgley and Miss Ridgley that their quarters are in order."

"And Miss Coulter," Swain added.

Kirkpatrick looked at the corporal. "Mrs. Ridgley and Miss Ridgley," he said again. "And them only." He turned and walked back to the front of the building. Swain caught up with the big man, strangely irritated at the tone of the sergeant's voice. He said, "I had an idea that room was big enough for three women. They'll live under worse conditions before they get out of the desert."

The sergeant looked straight ahead. "The situation stinks loud enough as it is. I don't aim to make it worse by throwin' a fancy girl in with the ladies."

The scout was a slow man to catch fire, but the term "fancy girl" had suddenly and unreasonably set a flame of anger in his brain. "That's being pretty hard on a woman, Sergeant," he said coldly. "Unless you're sure."

Kirkpatrick said defensively, "It's written all over her. Look at that gaudy dress she wears, and the indecent way she exposes herself with menfolk around. She probably tore her dress herself, if the truth was known. And her lips. It wouldn't surprise me to learn there was paint on them."

Evidently, the sergeant had forgotten that he had referred to Mrs. Ridgley as "the sow." He had had time to think it over since then. After all, the Ridgley women were Army women, and the sergeant was nothing if not Army.

Swain said, "You've got sharper eyes than I have, Sergeant," which was the same as calling the sergeant a liar. "I didn't notice those things about Miss Coulter."

The sergeant had got in over his head. He and the scout had been friends for a long time, and he wanted to keep it that way, but at the same time he couldn't afford not to stand up for the colonel's wife—and he had plenty of standing up to do, to make up for that slapping. He said stiffly, "I'm goin' by what the colonel's wife said, and the word of a lady is good enough for me. She said Reba Coulter was run out of town up north somewhere, along the Gila I think. She knew because she lived up there and it was a scandal all over the country. She was a soldier's wife. Her husband was killed over in the Tonto country not so long ago."

The scout walked out.

Later, he returned and found a dark, dank-smelling room at the back of the building. It had been used to store the thousand and one pieces of stock that goes into a general merchandise place, among them a barrel of vinegar that had been split open by an Apache hatchet. The smell was almost unbearable, but Swain cleaned it up as well as he could because it was the only place in the building that offered any amount of privacy. When he had finished he had a trooper deliver the news to Reba Coulter that her room was ready.

By then it was almost dusk. He went outside and studied the smoky horizon to the north. He studied it carefully for a long while.

The men had small fires going along what was left of the stockade fence, preparing their first hot rations in three days. Swain got his own bacon, harbred and coffee and went over to one of the fires where troopers were waiting in line to cook. He smiled thinly as Kirkpatrick's striker walked across the yard with two cooked meals in his hands and entered the store building. After Swain had fried his bacon and heated his tin cup of coffee he drew another ration and stood in the cooking line again, eating as he waited to fix another.

Carrying the cooked bacon in one hand, between two slabs of harbred, and the cup of coffee in the other, the scout started toward the store building. He paused for a moment as he saw Sergeant Kirkpatrick squatting with his back to the fence, eating.

"I wouldn't send out any patrols tonight, Sergeant," he said.

The sergeant looked at him. "Why?"

That was one bad thing about scouting for the Army, somebody was always wanting to know the reason for things. And a lot of times there wasn't any reason, except for that vague intangible thing called hunch or intuition that most white men mistrusted blindly, and wild animals and Indians and some few white men, very few, staked their lives on. And a lot of times even the tangible things were ignored, or never seen.

He said, "There was Indian smoke to the north about thirty or forty minutes ago."

The sergeant was incredulous. "I didn't see it."

"It was there just the same."

The sergeant didn't argue. Scouts were hired to detect signs that other men would pass over. He chewed thoughtfully. "What do you think?"

"I think Choko's going to try for the women, and he's going to try like he's never tried for anything before. I also think it would be better if we pulled out as soon as it got dark."

"Tonight?"

The scout nodded.

"That's impossible. The men have got to have a chance to rest. And so have the animals."

The scout shrugged. "You asked me what I thought." He started to walk off, but the sergeant spoke again, worriedly.

"They'd pick us off one at a time on march. We wouldn't have a chance in a million."

"Maybe," Swain said, "unless Choko's gathering all his braves in the hills for one big push."

"Do you think that's what the smoke meant?"

"If I know Choko. He isn't going to spend his warriors on hit or miss skirmishes. He's going to wait until he's got a full force together and then engage the whole troop in a man-sized battle. It's the women he's after. And he knows the only way he'll get them is to kill every damned last bluebelly."

The sergeant took another bite of bacon and harbred. He chewed, and the longer he chewed the harder it seemed to go down.

"And I always wanted to command a troop of Cavalry!" he said.

III

THE GIRL WAS IN THE almost-dark room that Swain had cleaned up, sitting cross-legged on some unburned pieces of quilts that he had found. She was resting her face in her hands and she didn't seem to hear the scout as he paused in the doorway.

He said, "You'd better eat some supper. Here's some harbred and bacon, compliments of the command."

She looked up then and smiled faintly. "I'll bet," she said. But she accepted the thick tough sandwich and bit into it, washing it down with the lukewarm coffee. He watched her eat, glad of the poor light and hoping that he didn't look as dirty and grimy as he felt. It wasn't often that he was bothered by vanity, for he was not a handsome man in any sense of the word. He was short, no taller than the girl, and built somewhat on the lines of a buffalo. Powerful, bulging shoulders and chest, with the lower torso tucking in sharply. His dress was haphazard, but, on Martin Swain, not colorful. He wore the broad-brimmed flat-crowned hat of a Nebraska cattleman, a soiled buckskin shirt, and Army issue pants whose orginal blue color was discernible only in spots and patches. When not actually scouting Indian-held territory he wore heavy brown leather boots with built-up heels, and spurs with fantastic sunburst rowels, near the size of a Mexican vaquero's. Spurs such as those would have meant certain and sudden death if worn in the vicinity of Apache, and perhaps that somehow explained the scout's fondness for them. But he didn't permit his whim to exceed the bounds of common sense—when he meant business he wore moccasins. And, thinking of business, he wondered what Sergeant Kirkpatrick was going to do about moving the troops. And, looking at Reba Coulter, he wondered how much right Mrs. Ridgley had to say the things she had.

The girl had finished eating now and was standing up. "I was hungry," she said, "though I didn't realize it. Please convey my thanks to the commandant for the meal, and the room. It must have been a great deal of trouble."

The last was tinged with irony, but no bitterness. Swain felt his face warm.

"The sergeant thought . . ." he started. "The two other ladies being together . . . There being only one bedroom. . ." He bogged down completely.

"It doesn't matter," she said, and she smiled as she said it, to lessen his discomfort. The room was almost totally dark now, and the store building's adobe walls were naked and somehow dead, and pale sky showed through the burned-out places in the ceiling. Swain felt that he wanted to stay for a while and talk to the girl, but he didn't know what to say.

"I guess I'll get back now," he said finally.

He went outside and saw that the company wagon had been pulled around the stockade to fill in the burned-out places in the wall. Sentries had been posted, and a weary-looking burial detail was coming in from the west end of the stockade. Swain wondered if they had buried the two troopers who had died up on the ridge. He decided that they had, because a body wouldn't keep long enough to take back to the fort.

Sergeant Kirkpatrick, who had been inspecting the horses on the long company picket line, saw Swain in front of the store building and came over. He said, "I want you to take a look around after a while, Swain. To the north especially. And in the hills."

"All right."

"To tell the God's truth, I don't know what to do. I don't know if it would be better to stay here or move out. I don't like moving a column in the dark, I know that. And them women."

"You're the commander," Swain said.

"And don't I damned well know it." The sergeant rubbed his big face. "You take a look around," he said again, "and let me know when you get back."

"Sure," Swain said. He watched the sergeant move off in the direction of the burned corrals, where most of the men had already bedded down, exhausted. The sergeant, Swain guessed, had been doing a lot of thinking in the past few hours. Maybe a little too much thinking. And the women. They were something the Cavalry hadn't counted on.

Swain wandered aimlessly for a few minutes, too tired to sleep, and anyway knowing that he would have to move out before long. He walked down toward the end of the store building, toward the block house, and there he saw the figure of Reba Coulter sitting on the tongue of the charred wagon. She heard the silver sounds of Swain's spurs and looked up. "I couldn't sleep," she said. "I came outside without permission. Do you think the Cavalry will mind?"

"The Cavalry's too tired to mind," Swain said. He leaned against the wagon and faced the north. The stockade was completely dark now, and strangely quiet and peaceful. There was only the swishing sound of the big Cavalry horses along the picket line, and now and then a muted thud as one of the animals pawed the ground nervously with a shod hoof.

He felt her looking at him. "Don't you ever sleep?" she asked.

"I'll sleep after a while maybe. After I take a look at the hills."

"I used to wonder about Indian scouts," she said. "Why would a man take up that kind of work—is it the pay?"

"Some scouts get paid pretty well. It depends on what they're good at."

"Are you an expert at something?"

He looked at her for the first time. She was only a blurred figure in the darkness. "I'm supposed to be an expert on Choko," he said evenly. He turned the name over in his mind. "Choko...devil, and fox, and hyena, and maybe a little bit of a god. I've never seen him, but I've known him for a long time."

"From the way you say his name I can't tell if you hate him or admire him."

He had never thought of it that way, but maybe he did admire the savage chieftain in some ways—because he consistently thought two jumps ahead of the scout, because he had outgeneraled and outmaneuvered the Army on every turn. But his driving force was hate. He said, "We had a ranch up north, several years ago. The ranch is still there, but the cattle are gone, and the house is burned down, and up on a hillside, below a thicket of chaparral, there are three graves where I buried my family after one of Choko's raids." He said it flatly, without much emotion. Emotion had long since been spent, and a cold dogged hate had taken its place.

For a long moment Reba Coulter was silent. But at last she spoke, and her voice was bitter. "If hate is what it takes I guess I would be a scout, if I were a man. You've heard things about me, haven't you? Things that you didn't believe, because you don't like rumors and gossip, and"—she laughed harshly—"maybe because you're old-fashioned and still believe in the sanctity of womanhood. What you heard is true, most of it anyway. But maybe you didn't hear it all."

Somehow, the scout hadn't expected to hear such bitterness. He shifted uneasily, not knowing what to say.

"I'm sorry," she said. "I didn't mean to bring that up."

He said, "It's all right. I don't mind."

"I know something about Indians. I know you've got enough troubles without listening to mine."

He said, "Sometimes it helps to talk about troubles. I'm not much of a talker, but I can listen."

She stood up then, and, for a moment, he thought she would go back to the store building. But she didn't move.

"He was twenty-five when we married," she began, "and I was eighteen. That was two years ago. It seems like a thousand years, or yesterday; somehow time didn't mean anything after that. He'd just got his commission at the Point and was eager to come West because they told him chances of promotion were good out here. He didn't want me to come at first, but then my father died, and he was all the family I had—we lived in Kentucky, and after Lee's surrender he didn't seem to care much about anything; and then came what they called reconstruction and he didn't last long after that. And besides, we were too much in love to be separated.

"Soon we came out here and they stationed him up on the north Gila. It was strange country, and the officers' wives were strange, and I don't think they liked me because I came from the South, and most of them were Northerners. But it wasn't so bad because we had each other. Then one day a detail came in from making a routine patrol, and they had him tied across the saddle. He was limp and dangling like a doll that had been slit open and all the sawdust had spilled out. He didn't look like anyone I had ever seen before.

"Then ugly rumors started. They said he died with a Cavalry carbine bullet in his back. They brought him back and buried him honorably, but that was to save the regiment's name. They made that plain enough. I got away as soon as I could, without thinking what I was going to do or where I was going to go. I made it as far north as the San Juan River, to a place called Herman's Crossing, when I ran out of money."

She paused for a long while. There was only the sound of the horses, and after a while a corporal went over to the corrals where the men were sleeping and woke some troopers up to relieve the guard. Swain wondered if she was through. He tried to think of something to say, but nothing he could think of sounded right in his mind. Then she went on.

"It wasn't much of a place. There were a few ranchers across the border in the Colorado country, and some down south, but the Crossing was mostly a place for hunters and traders and drifters. I'd had an idea that I could sell my jewelry—a ring and a brooch that he had given me—for enough money to get back East on. But they only laughed at me. Jewelry was only good for trading to the Indians, and glass was just as good as diamonds for that. I didn't know what to do, but a hungry stomach can make up your mind. I took the only job I could get. Working in a saloon."

Then she added flatly, "Maybe Mrs. Ridgley and her daughter are right. Maybe I'm not fit to be in the same room with them. I stopped thinking about it a long time ago."

Swain wanted to remind her that if it hadn't been for her, Mrs. Ridgley and her daughter would be dead and their scalps would be flying on some Apache's spear. But somehow, he couldn't get the words formed the way he wanted them. She turned suddenly, as if anxious to get away from him, and walked hurriedly, almost ran, toward the store building.

It was almost midnight when Swain returned from scouting the hills. He rode a sturdy little unshod Indian pony, using a blanket folded on the animal's back in place of a squeaking saddle. The scout had left his broad-brimmed hat behind, as well as his boots and spurs and repeating Henry. Now his weapons were a bowie knife, a hatchet, and, tied near the small of his back by a leather thong, a service revolver to be used only if a situation became desperate. He turned his pony over to the corporal of the guard and padded in moccasined feet over to the escort wagon.

The sergeant was sprawled out with his head on his saddle, but he sat upright suddenly as the scout approached.

"Well?" the sergeant said.

Swain sat down cross-legged and rubbed his eyes. "It looks like the hills are clean," he said. "I went north as far as seemed smart, then around a little to the west. Choko must have pulled his braves away to hell and gone up in the canyons to assemble."

"You didn't find anything?" Kirkpatrick asked.

"I found two old Apache warriors down in the foothills. Or rather they found me. They must have been put there to watch us because they were too old to be much good in a war party."

The sergeant didn't have to ask what had happened. There was a dark wet patch on the leg of the scout's pants, about the place a man would wipe his knife blade.

"And that's all?" Kirkpatrick said.

"That's all I saw. But I keep thinking about that smoke. If Choko's making war medicine he's being damn quiet about it—but you can bet your last ration of harbred he's making it. He's not going to pass up a couple of prizes like the Ridgley women."

The sergeant made worried sounds in the darkness. "God, if I just knew what to do."

"Do you want my advice?"

"I just want to know what to do."

"I'd move the column out as fast as I could get the

animals saddled," Swain said. "There's a chance that those two lookouts were the only ones watching us, and Choko must have moved way back, maybe a day's ride, to assemble his party. Anyway, we can get a night's march on him. The closer we get to the fort the better our chances will be of help from the regiment."

The sergeant shook his head. "But maybe Choko hasn't pulled back. Maybe he's just waiting for us to pull some damn fool stunt like this and then snipe us away one at a time."

"Choko doesn't want to snipe," Swain said patiently. "He wants to get the whole damned column, and to do that he's got to have a lot more braves than he used on this raid today. An Indian, even Choko, is going to figure a lot of angles before he attacks a whole troop of Cavalry."

The sergeant sat for a long minute. He still didn't know. Then, as if suddenly realizing that he was the commander, and a commander's job was to make decisions and make them fast, he stood up and called, "Corporal of the guard!"

Heavy Cavalry boots pounded across the yard.

"Corporal, have the junior sergeant mount the troop immediately. We'll move out in ten minutes under trumpet silence. In columns of fours. I don't want to get strung clear across Arizona Territory, not in this darkness."

"Yes, sir," the corporal snapped, stopping a salute and leaving his hand awkwardly in front of him.

"And the women," the sergeant said, "Wake them up and load the bedding in the escort wagons. And don't take any nonsense. We pull out in ten minutes."

This time the corporal nodded, standing at attention.

"For the love of Mary, get to it!"

Inside the stockade the Cavalry came to life, grumbling and cursing and spitting and coughing. Swain got his own pony, let it away from where the column was forming and saddled, making sure that his rifle was in the boot and plenty of ammunition in the pouches behind the cantle. He changed his moccasins for his high-heeled boots and spurs, and, beating some of the dust from his hat, he waited for the signal to march.

He heard boots come out of the store building on the double. Then the corporal's voice: "Missus Ridgley, Sergeant—she says to tell you she's goin' to report you to the colonel for movin' the column out at a time like this. She says she'll have you busted and locked up. She also says she can't get ready to travel in less than a half an hour."

Then the sergeant's voice angrily: "Go back in there and tell the old sow she can go to blazes! Tell her if she's not ready she gets loaded in her nightgown . . .! No, wait a minute, Corporal. You better not say that. Just ask Mrs. Ridgley if she'll hurry as quick as she can. That's all."

Martin Swain smiled in the darkness and wondered if he would ever understand the Army.

They moved out finally, about twenty minutes after march-time, with a light advance guard taking the lead and followed by a close connecting file that kept contact with the main body. It was the rear guard that Swain was mostly concerned with. He pulled his pony to one side and let the column pass him. The aching screech of the escort wagons made a noise that the scout imagined could be heard all the way to Montana. It seemed impossible that a savage like Choko could miss the noise, if he was anywhere within a hundred miles of the march route. Swain knew it was ridiculous, and anyway it didn't make a lot of difference. When the time came, he knew Choko would be there.

IV

THE ESCORT WAGONS were sandwiched in between the main body and the heavy rear guard. Swain watched them go by, blurred crawling forms in the darkness, and once he heard the quarrelsome voice of the colonel's wife, but he couldn't see any of the women. The night was black, as only desert nights can be at times. As the column moved on the scout fell in the drag, behind the rear guard, riding slack in his saddle but tense inside. He listened for things that ears couldn't hear.

By sunrise the column had made better than twenty miles. The scout checked with the rear guard, rode out on the flanks and checked with the outriders, then he went up to the head of the column to report to the sergeant.

"All men accounted for in the rear," he said, reining up beside Kirkpatrick. "How did it go up here?"

The sergeant nodded. "Black as the door of hell, and the colonel's wife complainin' she couldn't sleep. But no savages." He looked around at the flat bronze-tinted desert. "Where do you reckon we are?"

Swain nodded toward a broken upheaval of land in the distance, deceptively quiet and serene in the morning haze. "That's the Loveall Range. I'd say the fort's about a three-day march from there. How's the water supply?"

The sergeant shrugged. "Enough for about five days, I guess, if we take it easy. I figure we'd take a rest halt around noon and move out again when it gets cooler. You'd better get some sleep."

Swain nodded. He pulled out of march again and waited for the column to go past. The troopers slumped more asleep than awake in their saddles. The horses, he noted, looked better than they had the day before, but they still weren't in any shape to fight a running battle. Up ahead, the sergeant pulled out and watched part of the column go by, and it wasn't long before orders came down to dismount and lead the horses for a spell.

The scout fell in with the escort wagons when they came by. It wasn't just an accident that he cut in behind the wagon Reba Coulter was riding. The tail-gate was down, and she was sitting there on a folded tarp, staring flatly out at the desert.

"Good morning," Swain touched his hat.

She smiled faintly. "Good morning. Doesn't the Cavalry ever sleep?"

"We're taking a rest halt around noon to rest the horses," he said. "Probably about four hours. They'll get some sleep then."

"And you?"

He dismounted and walked behind the wagon, leading his pony. "Me too," he said. She motioned toward the tailgate and Swain felt his face coloring because he had been waiting for the invitation. But he vaulted up beside her, keeping his pony's reins in his hand.

"It won't be too bad," he said. "We ought to be at the fort in five days or less."

She looked at him, smiling that curious smile of hers. "But we won't, will we? Choko wants the Ridgley women, and he won't stop at anything to get them."

"How did you know that?" he asked sharply.

"I heard Mrs. Ridgley talking about the letters. But don't worry, I'm not going to tell anybody."

"Does Mrs. Ridgley know what it means?"

She shook her head. "What will they do to them?" she asked.

Swain sighed wearily and leaned against the slatted side of the wagon. "Nothing," he said. "Choko won't do anything—to them. He can use them as a decoy to draw the colonel's forces out. He can use them as a threat and as instruments for building tactical plans of war, but he wouldn't dare harm them. They are too valuable alive, and anyway he would be afraid of Army retaliation if he actually harmed them."

But that wasn't all of it. Choko would handle the Ridgley women gently. But with a woman like Reba Coulter . . . The scout felt slightly sick when he thought of what would happen to her if the Apache got his hands on her.

He risked a quick glance at her face. She knew what he was thinking. He could see it in her eyes. But it didn't seem to bother her. She looked as though nothing would ever bother her again. He supposed that she was thinking of her husband who had died with the Cavalry carbine bullet in his back; and maybe she was thinking of the shame of that, and of being a saloon girl, and that was the reason she didn't care much what happened to her.

She was leaning back against the wagon bed now, her eyes closed. Curiously, she asked, "Do you expect to come out of this alive, Mr. Swain?"

"I always expect to get out alive," he said.

"And Choko?"

"I'll get him some day. I know it. I think he knows it. I've come close before and some day I'll get him."

"And then you can rest," she said. "Then you can go back to your ranch and know that you've done all that can be done."

He started to tell her that the ranch was an empty place and he didn't think that he would ever go back. But he didn't. She seemed to be asleep. After a moment Swain dropped down from the wagon and walked out to the flank of the column, leading his pony. The sun was high, and broiling hot.

They halted for four hours, through the hottest part of the day, and the troopers found what shade they could and slept the sleep of the dead. Around four o'clock the column mounted and again began its crawling pace to the south. Swain, feeling better for the rest, rode again at the head of the column, keeping his eyes fixed on the distant hills in front of them and behind them.

Here there was no sign that day. No smoke, nothing to make the scout believe they were being watched. But he knew they were. He could tell it by the way the pony's ears pricked up every once in a while for no reason, and he looked out across the desert and saw nothing, but when he reached down and touched his pony's nose it was cold and dry from nervousness.

Sergeant Kirkpatrick said, "If we get through tonight without any trouble I'm goin' to send out runners to the fort."

Swain shook his head. "They'll never make it. Choko's having us watched again. And not by any crippled-up warriors too old for the war trail this time."

The sergeant jerked around to look at him. "Where are they?"

"In the ground, in the air, everywhere. You don't have to see them to know they're around."

The sergeant snorted. His confidence was coming back after the successful night march. "The runners go out," he said. "We'll have reinforcements on the way in less than forty-eight hours. Then let Choko try something."

Swain held his tongue. One thing a man learned by working with the Army was patience. "All right," he said finally. "If you're determined, you'd better let me try it alone. I know this country. I'll have a better chance of getting through than any of your troopers."

The sergeant shook his head. "We'll need you here with the column." That ended it as far as the sergeant was concerned.

Late the next afternoon, as the column crawled wearily off the desert and into the foothills of the Lovealls, a trooper from the advance guard came riding back to make a report.

"We just found the two runners, Sergeant," he said flatly. "Two troopers anyway, so I guess it's them." His face was set in grim, tired lines, and only his eyes showed the fury inside him.

Swain saw the sergeant's confidence vanish, and his shoulders sagged as he again took the heavy load of responsibility.

"All right, Corporal," he said finally. "I'll ride up with you." He turned to the scout. "Swain, you'd better come along too."

They turned the command over to the junior sergeant and Swain and Kirkpatrick followed the hard-eyed trooper up ahead, through the heavy underbrush of chaparral and mesquite, to where four other troopers were waiting.

As Swain looked, he imagined that the screams of the two runners were still floating over the hills; unheard, but still there, and bright with pain. They had been tortured methodically, leisurely. Apache hadn't been in any hurry on this job. The scout looked at the shapeless, swollen hands and saw that the fingernails had been pulled out slowly, one by one. A job like that took time. Swain looked up and saw the sergeant staring at him.

"If Choko didn't know all about us before, he does now," the scout said.

After a certain amount of torture a man will tell anything he knows, just for the privilege of dying. There was no reason to believe that the two runners had been different from other men. But their wide-open mouths, and their broken teeth, and their scalpless, bloody skulls proved that the Apache promise of quick death hadn't been kept.

The sergeant pulled his horse around. "We can't take them with us. We'll have to bury them up here." He rode, cursing, back to the column.

The hills were as hot and as dry as the desert. The only difference being that they were harder on the men and horses. And the night was even blacker, and the sergeant was forced to string the column out in two's because the trails were too narrow to hold more than that.

Leading their horses, Swain and the sergeant struggled side by side up the steep black climb. Up ahead somewhere was the summit, but even Swain couldn't be sure in this blackness just where. But they ought to make it in two hours, three at the most, and then they would be headed down, on the last leg of their journey to the fort. A leg, the scout thought, that they would never make. Choko couldn't allow them to have another day for fear they might get some help from one of the fort's patrols. If he had got his attacking force together he would hit them tomorrow sometime, probably the first thing in the morning, since that was the Apache's favorite time for murder.

By morning, Swain calculated, they should be out of the hills and down on the flats again. And that was exactly the way Choko would have it figured. Carefully, the scout nourished the seed of an idea. And he wondered if the time that he had waited on for so long had come—the time when the Apache chieftain outsmarted himself with his own cleverness.

Anyway, he decided, there would be nothing to lose in looking into it. He started pulling his pony away from the column.

"Where the hell are you going?" the sergeant said.

"I'm going to take a look around. I'll meet you in a couple of hours or so on the summit. If I'm not there when you reach it, wait for me."

He moved toward the back of column before the sergeant could offer an argument. Again he exchanged his boots and spurs for the moccasins, and flung his saddle into the back of a passing escort wagon. His rifle he handed up to the driver to keep for him.

He rode as far as he dared, circling back behind the column and cutting into the hills from the north and east. For perhaps thirty minutes he rode recklessly, for time was the prime element now, but when he felt his pony begin to shy nervoulsy he knew it was time to go on foot. He picketed the animal in a gully and started making his way up a rugged slope. The place was strewn with huge boulders and wild with the smell of mesquite. And, except for a faint brush of wind, it was as still as death.

He lay for a moment, listening. He heard something that might have been the wind, but he didn't think so. An almost silent brushing sound. Maybe a loose tumbleweed bumping boulders. But not likely. He reached for his bowie knife and waited.

Perhaps ten minutes went by—a short wait by Indian standards. On occasion the scout had lain for as long as eight hours without moving, but the element of time hadn't been so important then. He began to inch forward, behind a clump of needle-edged cholla, until he reached a boulder. His progress had been slow and almost silent. But not silent enough. The sound up ahead was beginning to take shape. A quick, soft thud, as quiet as a sparrow's heartbeat; and then nothing. Behind some stand of chaparral, out there in the darkness, an Apache would be squatting, peering into the night.

Swain moved a little more, bringing himself to his

knees, pressing as close to the boulder as he could. The quick brush of moccasined feet came forward again. Then Swain saw him, a frozen figure squatting startlingly close to the boulder. The scout held his knife against his thigh, and there in the darkness he seemed a part of the rock. The Indian came forward again, toward Swain. Suddenly, the dark body jerked upward, his scalping knife held ridiculously high as he plunged forward.

In the split second that the Indian framed himself against the paleness of the sky, the scout saw that he was not Apache, but, judging from his scalp lock, a Sioux. Swain slashed upward with his bowie, at the Indian's throat. A warm gushing over his hand told him that he had hit. He caught the body, slick and rancid-smelling, and lowered it to the ground. Almost instantly there was a second Indian rushing at him—there was always a second—with his arm flashing down to throw his hatchet. Swain dived to one side, heard the hatchet slam against the boulder and saw the resulting shower of sparks. He lunged upward, driving his bowie home again.

After it was over he leaned against the rock, breathing hard, the rancid, sour smell of the bodies almost making him sick. After he got his breath he started up the slope again, not so careful this time, because he doubted that the war party had placed more than two men at this point.

When he reached the crest of the ridge he paused and lay flat on the ground. The land below lay in almost total darkness, but it wasn't so important to see. His ears told him what he wanted to know. He closed his eyes and tried to see this ridge and the valley below him in relation to the column's march route. As near as he could judge, the flatlands ought to begin on the other side of the valley—just about the place the column ought to be by sunrise. He began to work his way down the slope.

The column had reached the summit and had paused for a rest halt when the scout returned. He trotted his tired pony past the long line of resting Cavalry and moved up to the head of the column where the sergeant was waiting.

"Well?" Kirkpatrick said impatiently.

"They're waiting for us, all right," Swain said. "Behind the ridge we have to pass to come into the flatlands. Apache and Sioux and maybe Cheyenne. God knows how he got them all together. I don't know how many, but I'd say it was over a hundred. All I had to go on was the sound of their horses."

"Sweet heaven!" the sergeant groaned. "Sioux fighting with Apache! Are you sure?"

Swain looked at the stain on the sleeve of his buckskin shirt. "I'm sure," he said.

The sergeant rubbed his face. "We can't take the column down in the flats then. Not if they're waiting for us. And we've got the women."

Swain said, "What else can you do? You can't sit here and go without water and get too weak to fight. Anyway, it would only give Choko time to bring more warriors together."

The sergeant shook his head worriedly. "I don't know. I just wish the captain was here. I don't mind fighting, but when you've got women on your hands, and your men and animals are dead beat . . ."

"If I guessed right as to their number," the scout said, "maybe we've got a chance. I know that ridge that Choko plans to attack from. It's got a lip about halfway down from the crest, and that's where he'll probably form his attacking force. If we could form a detail behind him, up on the crest, at least we could make him split his forces and fight on two fronts. And Choko knows as well as anybody that fighting uphill is no party."

The sergeant thought about it. He didn't care much for it.

"I figure the troop has one good battle left in it," Swain said quietly.

The sergeant thought hard, but he couldn't think of anything better. They weren't strong enough to run. They weren't strong enough to wait.

"What about the women?" he said. "And how are we going to pull a detail out of the column without Choko knowing about it? He's having us followed right now, if I know anything about Choko."

Swain said, "The women will have to take their chances. And this is the way I've got it figured. After this rest halt the column will pull out again as it would normally. But on march the detail would drop out, one at a time, behind boulders or brush or anything else they can find, and wait until the column is well past before it forms. We'll have to depend on darkness for cover, and hope that Choko's scouts keep following the column. After the column is well on its way toward the flats, the detail can form—I noticed a dry wash a while back that I think I can lead it through and make the ridge by sunrise."

The sergeant accepted the plan, but grudgingly. "If you guessed wrong on their number," he said, "we're sunk. Our holding force will be overrun before you could bring the detail down to attack. But . . ." he shrugged wearily, "I guess it's a chance we'll have to take."

V

SHORTLY AFTER MIDNIGHT the column moved out again, and at the first chance Swain moved out of line and seemed to melt into the darkness beside the trail. He wore his hat and boots now, the only special notes of caution being the removal of his spurs. And his rifle had a solid, comforting feel in its boot under his left leg. After the screech and rattle of the Cavalry had faded into the night, he dismounted and began making his way north again, toward a big spear-shaped rock—the assembly point for the detail.

It took almost two hours for the detail to form, the men arriving quietly in one's and two's, leading their mounts. Sergeant Wellington, who had charge of the detail, was the last to arrive.

"I guess this is it, Swain," Sergeant Wellington said, "fifteen-man detail, all accounted for."

Fifteen men. Putting them against a hundred or more savages, it didn't seem like much of a force. But Swain had learned long ago that a well-trained Cavalryman, drilled in the the use of his weapons, was more than a match for two or three Indians. Anyway, the bulk of the troop would be at the bottom of the slope with Sergeant Kirkpatrick, and they would keep Choko's warriors busy for a while.

At the order of Mount, the fifteen troopers swung up to their saddles. Then, forming in a column of two's, they followed the scout into the hills . . .

It seemed to Swain that dawn was a long time coming. From his prone position on the ridge he could see nothing but blackness down below. But he could hear the restless scamper of many hoofs down on the lip of the slope, and he knew that Choko had already moved his warriors into attacking position. Behind him, down in the gully where the detail waited, it was as silent as a grave.

Swain noticed the sky in the east begin to pale, and he readied himself for a phenomenon of this wild country that he had never quite gotten used to. One minute it was almost pitch dark, and the next minute a big bloody sun appeared over the edge of the horizon and it was light. He caught his breath as he looked down on the milling Indians below. Apache and Sioux, and he guessed some Cheyenne, for he saw three chieftains standing away a little from the common braves, holding their ponies and standing like cold stone statues. They numbered more than a hundred. Closer to a hundred and fifty—a good-sized party to bring together on short notice, even for a leader like Choko. Then Swain heard the muted clatter and rattle of marching Cavalry, and the head of the column nosed out of the hills and came onto the flats.

He saw Apache scouts lying belly-down on the edge of the lip, watching the Cavalry as it came into view, and he wondered what Choko would think if he knew his own back was being watched. Swain wormed down from the ridge and motioned for the detail to come up.

Sergeant Wellington headed the detail as they came out of the gully. The sergeant was leading Swain's pony, as well as his own big Cavalry mount.

"We heard the column clear down there in the wash," he said. "I never knew before that the Cavalry made such a hell of a racket."

The sergeant was a bearded, gaunt man in his late thirties. He came from Virginia, and it was said that he had been a major in the Confederate Army during the war. He left the horses with a corporal and crawled up the ridge to where the scout was.

"It looks like a convention of all the Indian nations in the Territory," he said, looking down. He bit off a piece of tobacco and chewed thoughtfully. "I wonder which one of them devils is Choko."

Swain said grimly, "So do I."

"Not many rifles," the sergeant observed. "I wish they'd use rifles more. I never saw an Indian that could shoot one worth a damn."

The entire column had come into view now, with Sergeant Kirkpatrick riding in the lead, staring straight ahead.

"Look out now," Wellington said, as one of the chieftains stepped back and gave a hand signal. Immediately the warriors scrambled down the side of the lip and swung up to their ponies. The chieftain gave another signal—*Choko*, Swain thought with cold hate—and the riders began mounting the embankment.

The column of Cavalry halted abruptly as the first

of the Indians appeared on the rise. Sergeant Kirkpatrick's voice bawled out, carrying with parade-ground clearness all the way to the crest where Wellington and Swain were watching.

"One thing about Kirkpatrick," Wellington said dryly, "he sure as hell can holler. There go the wagons. Goodbye, ladies."

The wagons had pulled quickly out of column, under small escort, and were moving back from the firing line. Then Kirkpatrick's voice bellowing again. "Companee-ee . . . Squads . . . Right into line!" And the corporal's voice echoing, "Squads right! . . . Squads right!" all the way down to the end of the column. Kirkpatrick wheeled his horse smartly and rode out front and center before the thin, wavering line of Cavalry, then the trumpeter and guidon bearer cut out of line and took their places.

For a moment an eerie stillness lay cold on the morning. There was no sound from the Cavalry, and the swarm of Indians sat their ponies like so many gilded images, their spears and rifles making a deadly thicket against the sky. Then, suddenly, a spine-chilling whoop that came all the way from the guts of some Apache split the morning wide open, and a great thunder of sound rose up as the savages poured down the steep slope.

Sergeant Wellington stood up and spat. "I guess we'd better get the back door open," he said.

The detail mounted in line formation, but they did not ride toward the ridge immediately. They waited until the whooping rose to screams, and, down below, they knew that Kirkpatrick would be giving orders to prepare to fire. And after a moment it came. A rolling volley of carbine fire. Then another one.

And the detail knew that the men would be loading, aiming, and firing with drilled precision, and from standing mounts. They could no longer hear Kirkpatrick's bellowing, but they heard the thin, piercing Cavalry bugle rapping Charge.

Swain said, "It's up to your detail now, Sergeant."

"Forward!" Sergeant Wellington said. "Ho-oo!"

They rode up to the ridge and dipped down on the other side. The battle had closed now and in the confusion and dust and smoke it was impossible to see how it was going. The battleground was littered with brown, painted bodies, but that was to be expected. Warriors were always brought down on that first charge.

"At the gallop!" Wellington shouted.

They seemed to fly down the hillside now, the thin line of fifteen grim-faced men. They skirted the depression where Choko had hidden his braves, sliding into the battle on the oblique. When they got within a hundred yards of the fray, a group of startled Apaches spotted them and wheeled their ponies to charge.

The sergeant raised himself in his stirrups, signaling a quick halt. "I reckon we'd better shoot us some Indians!" he shouted to the scout. Then to the men, "Fire, dammit!"

Fifteen carbines spoke sharply, and dark gaps showed in the Apache ranks. The gaps filled and the carbines rapped out again.

"Let's cash in these government sabers!" Wellington yelled, shoving his carbine back in the boot and drawing his blade. And the detail moved in on the Apache flank.

The plan worked better than Swain had ever hoped

for. It seemed to him that it was working a little too well—that they were drawing more than their due share of attention from the war party. Anyway, they were giving Kirkpatrick's men a breather. A big bronze painted buck bore in on the scout's right, brandishing a bloody hatchet. Swain snap shot from his hip and the buck faded away. He wheeled his pony and took a Sioux off a trooper's back, clubbing him in the face with the butt of the rifle. There wasn't time to make sure if the Indian was dead. He couldn't finish one job before his hands were full with another.

Part of Kirkpatrick's force had worked its way through to the detail now, and Swain glimpsed the big sergeant slashing like a man possessed, butting a bloody swath in the Indian ranks with the bloody edge of his saber. This was Kirkpatrick's kind of soldiering. Not thinking and making decisions. Fighting. Sergeant Wellington's wheeling mount flashed in front of Swain.

"Look at that Kirkpatrick!" he shouted, grinning. "Lucifer himself, in a blue coat!"

And at that moment the junior sergeant sat up very straight in his saddle surprised, and a little shocked. He went down with a curious, bewildered look on his face, and the feathered tip of a Sioux arrow protruding from the base of his neck.

Swain felt an unreasonable anger at the junior sergeant's death, when there were so many others dying all around him. He saw the Sioux drop down from his running pony and race toward Wellington with a bloody scalping knife. The scout reached for his hatchet. He sent it hurtling over Wellington's body and heard the sickening smash. That's one

Sioux, the scout thought angrily, that won't collect any more scalps!

He booted his Henry and drew his service revolver. Nothing was very clear after that. He fired and watched brown bodies go down. Gaps appeared in the blue ranks, but somehow they were filled. Occasionally he would see an Indian taking a trooper's scalp and be too busy to do anything about it, and he would direct his rage and anger at the first painted grinning face he saw. Once he fell back to reload and saw Sergeant Kirkpatrick holding his pistol with his body against the horn of his saddle, trying to shove cartidges in it with his left hand. His right arm was hanging useless, an Apache arrow having gone all the way through his shoulder.

And a small band of Sioux broke through once and made a pass at the escort wagons, but Swain saw the guard beat them off. Automatically, the scout reloaded his revolver and moved back into the fight, back into the dust and smoke, where the sound of wounded horses was even worse than the cries of wounded men. He fired as long as there was anything to fire at. But at last he realized that the Indians were gone.

For a few moments he was lost, with nothing to shoot at, with nothing to direct his anger at. Dust and black powder smoke lay heavy on the hillside, and an incredible number of dead and dying littered the battleground. He heard a voice call, "Swain!"

He looked around and saw that it was the sergeant. A corporal was reining up beside the big man, holding him in the saddle. Swain pulled his pony around, and the animal stepped daintily, like a fine lady crossing a dusty street, in order to miss stepping on the dead and wounded. For an instant there was a gap in the cloud of dust and smoke, and he saw the last of the war party slip over the ridge.

"What do you think, Swain?" the sergeant said.

"I think you ought to get that arrow out of your shoulder and have it bandaged."

Kirkpatrick snorted. "Will they come back?"

The scout thought about it. He didn't feel like the authority on Indian warfare that he was supposed to be. He said, "God knows. Let's get the wounded back to the wagons. Then we'll see."

The troopers devised makeshift stretchers by using their long carbines and jackets, and they brought the badly wounded down to where the escort wagons were formed. The men who could walk walked. The dead and the Indians stayed on the hillside. A two man detail was given what the Cavalry considered to be the worst job in the Army—that of putting bullets into the brains of the wounded horses. So, as the battered, ragged remains of D Troop made its way toward the flats, there lingered a spattering of pistol shots on the hillside.

Swain heard the high-pitched sobbing before he reached the wagons, but he paid little attention. He thought it was one of the wounded. He picketed his pony out a way from the hospital area—hospital without doctors, and without medicine to speak of—and found Sergeant Kirkpatrick leaning against a wagon wheel with the arrow still in his shoulder.

Swain took out his bowie and said, "Turn around."

The sergeant turned around and the scout clipped off the head of the shaft. He yelled, "Bandage!" and a trooper appeared with an armload of white bandage, some of it almost clean. Then he placed his left hand against the sergeant's shoulder, grasped the feathered tip of the arrow with the other, and jerked.

"Goddammit, Swain!" Kirkpatrick exploded.

Swain flung the shaft away and shouted, "Whiskey!" Presently someone handed him a bottle, and the sergeant shrank involuntarily as the scout splashed the fiery liquid on his wounds. Swain then cut the shirt away, pressed bandages to the shoulder and began to tie it up.

"Here, let me do that," a voice said.

Swain turned and saw that it was Reba Coulter. She had her sleeves pushed up and there was blood on her hands and on her dress—the blood of the wounded. She took the bandages out of the scout's hands and began quickly to bind the sergeant's shoulder.

"There's a man over there with a spearhead in his thigh," she said. "Mr. Swain, will you do what you can?"

"The women!" the sergeant said. "Love of Mary, I forgot about them!"

Reba finished the bandage and fashioned a sling for the sergeant's arm. "There's nothing you can do about them," she said. "The girl's all right. Mrs. Ridgley is dead."

The words were like faulty cannon shells. They hit flatly, lay quietly and unnoticed—then after a while they went off.

The sergeant jerked up, his face white. Then he went in a staggering run down the line of wagons. Swain remembered the high-pitched sobbing he had heard as he came down from the hillside. And now he knew that it had been the Ridgley girl.

"Will you help me with this man?" Reba Coulter asked quietly.

Swain came out of it. "I'm sorry," he said. And he followed the girl down the line of wounded and stopped beside a gray-faced trooper. He gave the man belt leather to bite on and said, "Just hold on, lad. We'll have you fixed up in a few minutes." And he went to work with his bowie.

Reba Coulter stayed beside him, her face almost as gray as the wounded man's. After it was over and they were putting the bandage on, Swain asked, "How did it happen?"

"When the small group of Indians made the pass at the wagons. A rifle ball went through her heart."

VI

WITHIN THIRTY MINUTES the Cavalry was patched up again, the men having taken care of each other as best they could in the absence of a doctor. Swain found the sergeant at the company picket line, inspecting the horses from force of habit. The worry in his eyes had turned to grim bitterness, sharpened with extreme pain.

"Have you taken count?" Swain asked.

"Ten dead," the sergeant said flatly. "Twice that many wounded. Troopers Jones and Stoddard will be dead within an hour. There's not a man or horse fit to stand another skirmish." He turned his face toward the hills, as if looking for something to direct his anger at.

Swain studied the battleground. Now that the dust and smoke had cleared he saw Choko had lost heavily. Those trained volleys of Kirkpatrick's troopers and the surprise fire laid down by the detail had taken more than a score of savages. The hand-to-hand fighting, Swain guessed, had been about even. But even at that, counting the wounded, Choko would have his force cut in half.

"If they come back," the sergeant said, "we're done for."

"They won't come back right away," Swain said. "With half their attacking force gone Choko might have trouble keeping his hold on the Sioux and Cheyenne. They won't be eager to take another beating like that."

"They wouldn't worry about it," the sergeant said dryly, "if they could see us now. And the colonel's wife. There'll be hell if we ever get back to the fort."

If they got back. Swain watched Reba Coulter still working with the wounded, and he listened to the colonel's daughter carrying on and wished to God she would stop. It was beginning to wear on the thin-edged nerves of the troopers, and himself as well.

The sergeant was also watching Reba Coulter. He spat bitterly, and the scout knew what he was thinking. He was wishing that it had been Reba instead of the colonel's wife, if it had to happen to somebody. But Swain could only remember that the Ridgley women would have been dead two days ago if it hadn't been for Reba Coulter. And some troopers would be dead now, if she hadn't taken care of them.

The Army! Swain thought with bitterness of his own.

Later, the sergeant sent out a detail to bring in the dead. The total was twelve now. Troopers Jones and Stoddard having died in the meantime. Swain and Kirkpatrick stood in front of the company area, watching, and the scout wondered what Choko would try next. It wouldn't be another attack right away, he was almost sure. The chieftain would try some other scheme first, and attempt to determine the Cavalry's strength, more than likely.

He got his answer sooner than he had expected, for as the detail brought in the last of the dead an Indian appeared on the right. He sat his horse there for a moment, framed sharply against the sky, and then he started down the slope toward the Cavalry. A tattered white rag flew high on his spear shaft.

The sergeant stared at the Indian, then at Swain.

"He probably wants to see how bad we're hurt," the scout said. "But Choko may be cooking up a scheme of some kind too. If I were you, Sergeant, I'd make a show of strength for his benefit—and, if you can find one, put on an officer's jacket. Choko would like it if he knew all our officers were dead."

In five minutes Kirkpatrick had every man who could sit a horse mounted in company front across the area. The troopers had the dust beat from their jackets, their faces washed—they looked like garrison troops mounted for inspection . . . From a distance.

The scout smiled tightly. He only hoped that the Indian couldn't see the horrible exhaustion in their eyes, or the tight lines around their mouths caused by the pain of their wounds. Swain thought again, *The Army!* But this time without bitterness.

Swain and Kirkpatrick stood in front of the company, watching the Indian come toward them. The sergeant had taken his right arm out of the sling and it hung stiffly at his side. His boots had been rubbed and the dust beaten from his pants and jacket. On his shoulders the two silver bars of a captain glinted in the bright morning sun.

"We'd better start toward him," Swain said. The

two men marched out in quick measured steps to face the Indian about a hundred yards in front of the mounted Cavalry.

He was an Apache warrior, Swain saw, mounted on a rugged little dappled pony, and he was completely naked except for a dirty breechcloth and wore moccasins. The warrior looked at Swain, ignoring the big man with the gleaming captain's bars on his shoulders. Swain kept his silence for a period of time, in the way of Apache—then he spoke to the Indian in his own language.

"Choko has sent you to speak with the white soldiers?"

The Apache looked at Kirkpatrick for the first time, then at the mounted troopers in the distance. He nodded.

"What is Choko's message?"

The thick white paint smeared around the Indian's mouth cracked in what might have been a dry smile. "The Great Warrior of the Apache has sent this message. The Indians of this land are weary of war. Too many brave young warriors have died, and the sands of the desert are glutted with their blood. Choko wants peace. He directs that white soldiers shall move across Apache land without fear of death. Choko's warriors will move into the hills, the hills beyond the hills, and there they will live in peace. That is the message of the Great Warrior."

"What's he saying?" Kirkpatrick asked.

"The usual pack of lies so far. Wait a minute." The scout turned back to the Apache. "Wise men know that peace is not given freely, but often it is bought with the blood of many men. What is Choko's price for this peace he offers?"

The white paint around the Indian's mouth cracked again.

"The two women," he said. "The women of the great white chief to the south." The Apache's eyes looked to either side of him and then to the wagons. Swain had an uneasy feeling that the Indian could see the badly wounded and dead that lay on the other side. "That," he stated flatly, "is the Great Warrior's price. If it is not offered, this land shall know again the pain of war and cry tears of blood. White man's blood."

"What is it now?" Kirkpatrick said.

"Choko wants the Ridgley women. If we turn them over, Choko says he'll let the column move on."

The sergeant stiffened. "Tell him to go to hell! No, wait a minute. Tell him the women are dead. They've been killed."

"The women," Swain said, looking again at the Apache, "are dead. Your warriors killed them as they raided our wagons."

The Indian nodded soberly. "That fat one is dead," he said. "The Great Warrior feared it was so. But the young one, the offspring of the white chief, is not dead."

The scout turned wearily to Kirkpatrick. "Choko has already guessed that Mrs. Ridgley is dead. But he knows the daughter is still alive. There's one thing that the devil must have overlooked though—this Apache has only mentioned two women. I guess they don't know yet that we have three with us."

Abruptly, the warrior pulled his pony around and

rode back toward the hill. About two hundred yards from the wagons he stopped again and turned to face them.

"He's giving us some time to talk it over," Swain said.

The sergeant about-faced sharply and started marching back to the wagons. "He can wait until he rots," he spat. "If Choko gets the Ridgley girl it'll be after he kills every last damned soldier in D Troop."

They went back into the assembly area. "Corporal," the sergeant called, "march the troop back behind the wagons and dismount them. Do what you can for the wounded." As the Cavalry wheeled into squads and marched back, Kirkpatrick sat on a wagon tongue and held his face in his hands.

Swain only stood there. He wasn't running the Army, and even if he were he wouldn't know what to do now. He glanced over at the row of wounded on the ground, and Reba Coulter was still with them. After a moment she saw the scout watching her. She got up and came over to him.

"These men have to have medical attention as soon as possible," she said. "They'll die if they don't get it."

"They'll die anyway," Sergeant Kirkpatrick said harshly.

She looked at the sergeant, and then at Swain. "Choko wants the Ridgley girl, doesn't he? I thought that was it." She brushed an arm across her eyes, and Swain noticed for the first time that her eyes seemed much older than the rest of her. They were eyes that had seen too much and had been hurt too much, and they were incredibly tired.

She said, "Mr. Swain, will you tell Choko's messenger that Miss Ridgley will go with them."

The sergeant's head jerked up. "Swain, take that woman away from here!"

"I think," Reba Coulter said, "that I can wear Miss Ridgley's dresses. That should be enough to fool them for a while—until the column is well on the way to the fort."

Both men stared at her. In this country a woman didn't let herself be taken by Apache—not alive. If a husband found it necessary to leave his wife alone in this country, there was always an unspoken understanding between them. In case of attack the last bullet in her gun would not be for the Indians. It would be for herself. It was a lesson they had learned the hard way, through great pain and sorrow.

Kirkpatrick said angrily, "Swain, the woman's crazy! Get her back to the wagon before her madness touches the rest of us!"

Reba Coulter turned on the sergeant now, her eyes sharp with anger of her own. "The wounded have got to be moved to the fort," she said coldly. "Your troopers are in no condition to fight. We'll all be dead if you try to stand off another attack."

"Soldiers sign up to die," Kirkpatrick answered.

"In battle, yes. With a reason. But they didn't sign up to die because their commander was too bullheaded to save them. And the Ridgley girl—you want to save her, don't you? Do you think you'll save her by sitting here and facing it out with Choko?"

The answer was too obvious to bother putting it into words. The sergeant said wearily, "Swain, are you going to take her away, or shall I call a trooper?"

The scout didn't move. For a moment he wondered if Kirkpatrick was right—if the girl was really crazy. But he didn't wonder long. The anwer was in her eyes, there with the weariness and bitterness. She merely didn't care what happened to her any more. She was just tired.

She still faced the sergeant, but this time she spoke with a strange quietness. "Listen to me, Sergeant. Does it make any difference whether I die here or at some Indian camp? It doesn't to me."

Kirkpatrick looked at her, curiously now. "Why in God's name would you offer to do a thing like this? Don't you know what Choko would do to you when he found out you weren't the Ridgley girl?"

"I think Mr. Swain knows why I want to do it," she said. "He can tell you about it some time. As for what Choko would do to me—I've seen hells that Choko never dreamed of."

Swain knew now that the girl was thinking of her husband who had died running from the enemy, with a Cavalry bullet in his back. Maybe, somehow, she thought that what she was offering to do would make up for that. Maybe it was some other reason, something that a man could not quite understand. Swain took her arm, and she tried to shake it off but he held to it.

He said, "We'd better go back to the wagon. There's no telling what'll happen pretty soon."

She looked at him sharply. "I meant what I said. Can't you make the sergeant see the sense in it?"

"I know you meant it," Swain said. "But you'd better go back now."

He saw the hopelessness in her eyes drown out everything else. She turned abruptly, breaking his grip on her arm, and walked quickly along the line of wagons.

"I'll be damned," Kirkpatrick said wonderingly. "She really meant it, didn't she? She would take the Ridgley girl's place and turn herself over to Choko. And I thought I'd seen everything!"

Swain remembered that hopelessness in her eyes. "Yes," he said, "she meant it."

The sergeant rubbed his big face with both hands. His wound started to bleed again, the red staining and spreading on the almost-white bandages, but he didn't notice. He knew that Choko would not risk an attack with his weakened forces unless he had to. All he wanted now was the Ridgley girl. Would it be better to a stand here and die "honorably" or should they save the Ridgley girl, and what was left of the troop, by letting Reba Coulter go through with her plan?

"If we only had a chance!" the sergeant said hoarsely.

But they didn't have a chance. Choko had beaten them on every turn. He was laughing at them now—laughing at Swain, because the scout was the best the white man had to offer, and he had failed to bring Choko in or defeat him.

Swain stared out across the flats where the Apache messenger was still waiting. Beyond the ridge somewhere, not far away, Choko would be patiently waiting for his anwer. The scout was only glad that he didn't have the sergeant's decision to make, because Kirkpatrick couldn't win. On one hand he stood to lose the entire troop, along with the women. The only way he could save them was by doing the unsoldierly thing—that of turning a white girl over to the savages.

"If only we had more troops!" the sergeant said.

"If there was only some way to trap the devil while he's weak!"

Something in the scout's mind snapped. He said, "Sergeant, what do you figure Choko would do if he got his hands on who he thought was the Ridgley girl?"

Kirkpatrick looked up, frowning. "Head for his home camp, back in the badlands, as fast as he could make it. He wouldn't be anxious to hang around until Cavalry reinforcements could catch him."

Swain nodded. "That's what I figured he would do. And he would take the shortest way possible—straight across the Lovealls, through Dover's Canyon, and then into the mountains where no white man has ever been."

The sergeant's frown deepened. "You've got something on your mind, Swain?"

"Maybe I have," Swain said. He picked up a stick and scratched three wavering lines on the ground. "Here's the Loveall Range. Behind that lies God knows what. Indian country. Choko's home grounds. Now say Choko was making for his home ground as fast as possible. Considering that his horses and warriors are almost as tired as the troopers, they aren't likely to head straight up and over the mountains, but more likely they'll go through here . . ." He cut two of the wavering lines in half. "Through Dover's Canyon."

The scout threw the stick away and said soberly. "I know that ground. I've scouted it. I think I could find the canyon in the dark . . . if I had to."

It took the sergeant a moment to get the idea straight in his mind. And when he did get it straight, he didn't believe it. He said incredulously, "You mean turn the Coulter girl over to Choko—and then try to beat him to the canyon? It's impossible! For one thing our horses are almost too tired to stand, and the men too, what's left of them. And another thing, Choko'll make damn sure we don't follow him."

"It will take the right timing," Swain said. "If we turned the girl over now, Choko could make a half a day's march back into the hills, but he wouldn't have time to reach the canyon. I figure he'll stop at nightfall and make camp, and move on to the canyon tomorrow morning. In the meantime we'll pull the column out and head toward the fort. We'll keep moving until dark, and I don't think Choko will have us watched after that. The rest of it will be up to Army guts and Army horses. We'll have to ride all night to make the canyon."

Kirkpatrick said dryly, "You're as crazy as the girl."

"Do you have a better plan, Sergeant?"

The sergeant was suddenly an old man. Old with worry and responsibility and pain. He stared at his hands for a long while. "All right," he said finally. "We'll try it. If the girl still wants to go through with it."

Swain found Reba Coulter in one of the escort wagons, tightening a bandage on a wounded trooper's leg. He waited until she had finished, and then said, "Miss Coulter?"

She looked at him flatly as he helped her down from the wagon. "Do you still want to go through with it?" he asked.

She nodded.

Swain took a deep breath and let it out slowly. He

had never had much to do with women before. He hadn't known that there were women like this. Then he told her of the plan—as much as he knew of it himself. "The thing is," he said, "to get to the canyon and ambush Choko there as he brings you through. You'll be in danger, but I'll instruct the sergeant to have the best marksmen cover you with fire. You'll have to make a run for it."

She said, "I understand," but her voice told him nothing.

He took a tiny, murderous little derringer from his shirt pocket. "This is loaded," he said. "Hide it on your person somewhere. In case something goes wrong—in case we don't make it to the canyon, or the ambush doesn't work."

"I know what to do with it," she said evenly.

Suddenly, the scout wanted to forget the whole thing. He wanted to stay here in the flats and let Choko attack and be damned. At least he could be with her here. That thought took an amazingly important place in his mind . . . just to be with her.

She said, "I'll change into one of Miss Ridgley's dresses right away. Tell the sergeant I'll do my best to look like a lady."

Then the scout knew a bitterness that he hadn't known since the day that Choko's band had raided the ranch. The feeling wasn't directed at the Army, nor at the sergeant, but at the multitude of intangible circumstances that had hurt this girl in ways she didn't deserve.

He said abruptly, "Miss Coulter, there's something I want to say . . ."

But, almost as if she had looked into his thoughts,

she said, ''Don't you think it had better wait until this is over?''

And he said, ''Yes. I suppose it had.''

VII

IT WAS A LITTLE PAST NOON, as the sun beat mercilessly down, already bringing out the sweetish smell of death along the hillside, that Reba Coulter and Swain walked out on the flats toward the Apache messenger. The Indian brought his pony forward, reining up in front of them.

"The Great Warrior's wish has been honored," the warrior stated flatly.

"Only if I have Choko's word that the girl will not be harmed," Swain said in Apache, knowing that Choko's word was less than no word at all.

The Apache said, "The Great Warrior's word has been given. The girl is hostage and shall not be harmed."

Swain looked at her then, and he wanted to say so many things that the words somehow became jumbled and he could say nothing.

She glanced at him, and her eyes were strange. Then she looked away. "You're worried about me," she said. "But I can't be sorry for it. I suppose every girl needs someone to worry about her."

"It's more than that," Swain said.

She did not answer, except with her eyes, and Swain was not sure that he understood what her eyes were saying.

He was not sure if he dared to understand. Then the Indian pulled his pony around and started back across the flats, with Reba Coulter walking behind.

Swain watched as they reached the base of the hill, making their ways across the bloody battleground. The sure-footed Indian pony took the slope in stride, and the girl had to run at times to keep up. They disappeared over the lip, but after a while they appeared again, the Apache riding slouched and heavy, not giving the girl so much as a backward glance. As they neared the crest of the ridge Swain saw the girl stumble and fall, but she picked herself up and clawed her way up the slope after the pony. Only then did Swain hear the cursing—like the cursing the sergeant had done when they found the two troopers dead and mutilated on the hill overlooking Carter's Wells—cursing that was almost the same as praying. The scout clamped his jaws together, hard, and the cursing stopped.

Within an hour the sergeant had the column on the march again. Kirkpatrick and Swain rode in the van, not looking at each other, not wanting to see what the other was thinking. They moved slowly, but not too slowly, because it had to look like a real march. Choko's warriors—God knew how many—were up on the ridge watching.

When they got out of sight of the ridge the sergeant called a rest halt and broke out half of the remaining forage and gave it to the horses. The horses—they were the main thing. Men came after horses in the Cavalry.

"All right," the sergeant bellowed, "them that's hurt bad can ride in the escort wagons and lead their mounts."

Half the troop started to dismount.

"That don't mean every mother's son that happens to have a sore tokas. Just the bad ones."

Four gray-faced troopers dismounted and staggered to the wagons.

The rest of the Cavalry walked—men stupid with fatigue and sick with wounds logged in the blazing sun to save their horses. And every step was taking them farther away from the canyon, farther to ride back if they wanted to stop Choko.

Then—when it seemed the day would never end, and all the world was desert and heat and endless walking—they stopped marching. And the sun lay red and bloated on the western horizon. Kirkpatrick called a dirty, red-eyed corporal up to the head of the column.

"Corporal, we'll make a short camp here. Issue double rations of bacon and harbred to the men, and feed the rest of the forage to the horses. Did we load any water at Carter's Wells?"

"We loaded some," the corporal said, "but it's not fit to drink."

"Break it out for the men to wash their faces in," Kirkpatrick said, "and their feet. They can build fires and boil coffee, if they have any coffee. Tell them to get all the rest they can. After they take care of their horses."

"All right," the corporal said. "Is that all?"

Kirkpatrick nodded wearily.

The sergeant turned his horse over to his striker—the striker he had inherited along with the command—and turned to Swain.

"Well, are they still following us?"

"I don't think so. They watched us from the hills, but I haven't seen any sign for the past hour or so. I'll go out after dark and see what I can find."

A quick succession of colors fell over the desert; yellow, orange, blood-red, and then blackness. Swain saw to his own pony, then built a small, wild-smelling fire from dried mesquite and chaparral and cooked his bacon. The night was pinpointed with the small fires, which was all right if they were being watched from a distance. The sergeant came over to the scout's fire. His face was gray-cast and tight from the pain in his shoulder. Swain wondered absently how the man could stay on his feet.

But that was in the back of his mind where thoughts flowed in and out without direction or purpose. With the front of his mind he thought of Reba Coulter and the things that could be happening to her. He thought of it, and the heavy smell of frying bacon became nauseating.

"When do you think we ought to pull out?" the sergeant said.

"Let the men get a little rest first. About nine o'clock would be about right I guess."

The sergeant fished out a big pocket turnip and studied it in the firelight. "That gives us two hours. The horses don't look so good. Stone bruises mostly. But maybe they'll be good enough."

"They'd better be," Swain said grimly.

The scout allowed himself an hour's sleep. He made a short scout of the desert, and the sleep-drugged, exhausted men of D Troop were already forming when he got back. They moved their horses one and two at a time away from the picket line and stumbled out into the darkness away from the company area and the fires. The sergeant left the wagons and a four-trooper escort where they were, with orders to start moving toward the fort at dawn. In the meantime they were to keep the fires going and make the camp look as natural as possible to eyes that might be watching from the hills.

At nine o'clock sharp the column started moving—twenty-eight men and twenty-eight horses—all that was left of D Troop's combat element. And most of them, both horses and men, had wounds of one kind or another. Only the badly wounded and the Ridgley girl stayed behind with the wagons.

The column reached the foothills in about an hour, and by midnight they were well into the mountains. Three hours, that was about the edge they had on Choko, but the night riding would cut that down somewhat, and the extra distance they had to travel.

The night was black as only a desert night can be, and the thin pale slice of moon hanging high in the east seemed to give off no light at all. They stumbled over the rugged hill country, slashing through unseen clumps of cholla, and sometimes running headlong into the towering mescal plants. D Troop rode when it could, but at times when the going was too rough they walked, leading the horses. Hands were kept on the horses' nostrils at all times, ready to squeeze out any sudden unexpected sounds.

They stopped once after a hard climb to breathe

the animals. The sergeant stood staring flatly into the darkness.

"I hope to God you know where we are," he said. "Because I sure as hell don't."

"I've been through here before," Swain said. "We'd better be moving."

But one hill was much like another, and even more so here in the darkness. It was possible for any man to get lost here, under these conditions. Even a trained scout. Swain forced the thought from his mind. Things were bad enough without making them worse with crazy notions.

They came onto the canyon suddenly, a great ragged tear in the land that, in the darkness, seemed as dimensionless as space. The sergeant passed the word back to halt the column. Swain said, "Hold on here while I take a look."

Swain scouted to the column's right until he found a narrow gap in the canyon wall. He stayed long enough to assure himself that he was not being watched, and then started making his way back to where the sergeant was waiting.

"About a hundred yards down," the scout said, "there's a gap in the wall where the men can squeeze through. The horses will have to stay over here."

The sergeant said, "All right, you take half the troop and station it on the other side. I'll keep half the men here. Then we'll wait. And see."

Swain said softly. "I guess that's it."

Kirkpatrick detailed three men as horseholders. "And for the love of Mary, keep them quiet!" Swain took twelve men and began squeezing his way through the gap, down to the canyon floor.

By the time the sky began to pale, D Troop was settled. Looking across the canyon, Swain could see the sergeant and his thirteen men lying on their bellies across their carbines. And down below, the canyon floor was beginning to take shape, boulders and rubble and flowering weeds developing in the darkness. Swain motioned to the corporal in command of the detail, and the bearded, red-eyed man came crawling over on his belly.

"When they show up," Swain said, "the sergeant wants Miss Coulter covered with fire. Heavy fire, until she can reach some kind of cover."

The corporal said, "All right. Say, have you got any chewin'?"

Swain found a raveled cigar in his shirt pocket. The corporal bit off half of it and pocketed the rest. "Thanks," he said, "I'll tell them." And he crawled away again, pausing behind rocks and boulders, speaking to the men.

Suddenly the chilled darkness of the night was gone, and a fiery sun reared angrily in the east and beat on the backs of the Cavalry. For a time Swain dwelled on the sickening thought that perhaps Choko had made a night ride, the same as the Cavalry, and he had already passed the canyon. He strained his eyes, searching the canyon floor for sign, but it was too far away.

It was then that all the things he knew about Reba Coulter converged on one point in his mind, and he saw the whole woman. She wasn't the woman Mrs. Ridgley had seen with her narrow, self-centered little mind—nor was she the incomplete woman that the sergeant's straight-laced Army mind had made her.

Swain had known that before, but it had never been as sharp as it was now.

And he knew fear. Not for himself, but for her. But he wasn't fooling himself—Reba Coulter wasn't the "pure as driven snow" creature that the convention-bound and lonesome minds of soldiers and frontiermen wanted their women to be. But she was hard and soft at the same time, and hot and cold. And Swain kept seeing her with that murderous old Enfield in her hands, and the bruise on her white shoulder, and the dead Apaches sprawled in front of the hot muzzle. He wondered what kind of special hells the proud milk-skinned Army wives had devised for the outcast—the young wife who had been foolish enough to marry a coward.

From many thoughts a single dominating thought emerged. He admitted to himself that he loved this good-bad hard-soft woman, Reba Coulter. And he admitted that there wouldn't be much point in anything—not even in outsmarting and killing Choko—if he never got to tell her that.

Then his thoughts became mingled with the faraway sound of many hoofs, the solid plumping thud of unshod hoofs of Indian ponies. He felt himself tighten with suspense, then he glanced quickly at the slack faces of troopers on either side of him, and he knew that they had heard it too. He rested on his elbows, peering down, his cocked Henry ready in the crook of his arm.

The sound got steadily closer, and up on the canyon rim there were small clicks as hammers came back on carbines. The scout had a strange mixture of feelings—anxious for action, but at the same time dreading what it might bring. Then, abruptly, around a bend in the canyon wall, the first Indian appeared.

A strange silence set off the morning. Even the thud of hoofs seemed not to have the solid quality of sound. Swain darted a glance across the canyon to where Kirkpatrick was waiting. The plan was for the sergeant to give the signal when the Indian column was in full sight.

Swain dragged in a quick gulp of air as the head of the column came into view, old Choko himself riding in the van. Bitterly, the scout studied this man who was either god or devil, depending on whether you fought for him or against him. He was a small man, much smaller than Swain had imagined. His bony face was warty and streaked with red and yellow war paint. His toothless gums were pressed together, giving his brown Punch-like face an eternal scowl, and his great hooked nose flared like some wild animal's, almost touching his chin. The two other tribal chieftains rode to the right and to the left of the Apache leader, lagging a few inches behind—perhaps unconsciously, but giving Choko the undisputed position of honor.

The warriors that followed sagged heavily on their ponies, chins on chest and weary-looking. Choko alone rode with his head high, his dark little eyes darting this way and that, missing nothing.

And last of all, behind the old warriors and the wounded, was the girl. The scout clamped his jaws hard to keep from cursing aloud. There was a choking buckskin line around her throat on which an old warrior kept jerking angrily. She came running, stumbling, in the wake of the war party—in the choking dust and the stench of hot bodies. Her dress—the

Ridgley girl's dress of fine crinolines—was nothing but rags and tatters now, from being pulled through thorn-daggered cholla and falling on sharp rocks. Bitterly, Swain wondered if Sergeant Kirkpatrick's sensibilities were outraged now by the way she exposed herself.

All the column was in view now and Swain waited tensely for the sergeant to give the signal to open fire. He caught the corporal's eye and made push-out motions with his hand, wanting him to move in Choko's direction as soon as the fight started. The corporal nodded, spat cigar juice on a flat rock, and sighted over the barrel of his carbine.

Abruptly, the signal came. But not from the sergeant. Choko suddenly spotted something, or maybe he only sensed that something was wrong. He let out a blood-chilling screech that startled the warriors awake and sent them plummeting down from their ponies and up the sides of the canyon. Almost immediately the troopers' carbines roared to life, and Swain glimpsed the Apache chieftain as he was literally lifted from his pony's back by the terrific impact of bullets. Every gun in the troop, Swain guessed wryly, had been trained on Choko despite orders to cover the girl.

The old warrior who had been holding the lead line scrambled down from his pony, dragging the girl toward the rocks. Swain's Henry crashed twice and the old man dropped to his knees. Reba Coulter broke away and ran toward the canyon wall, and the Indian's attempt to stop her with his hatchet ended with a carbine bullet in the face.

Swain began scrambling down the side of the canyon wall toward the girl. Up toward the head of the column he saw the troopers doing the same. The first volleys had been effective, but they were over now and the fight was closing to hand-to-hand.

Reba, Swain saw, had made it to a boulder at the base of the sheer drop, with the little derringer that he had given her in her hand. Above her he saw three Apache who had made their way up the side of the wall. He yelled, trying to tell her that the Apache were closing in on her, but she didn't hear. Swain turned loose from his hold on the cliff and dropped.

He went sprawling, losing his Henry somewhere and grabbing for his knife. One of the Apache saw him and grinned. He reached for his hatchet and brought his arm back to throw. But the scout's arm was faster. His long bowie streaked out, turning once in the air and plunging hilt-deep beneath the Apache's ribs. Swain retrieved his knife and leaped down to where the girl was standing, as the two remaining Indians came swarming in. "Get behind me!" Swain yelled. "Get cover behind the boulder!"

But instead she coolly stepped to one side and fired the derringer's one bullet into the first Apache's face. The Indian went down soddenly. Swain met the next one full on, and when the warrior missed with his first lunge the scout buried his bowie beneath the shoulder blade, driving it upward. The Apache died without making a sound.

Swain stepped back and leaned against the boulder, breathing hard. At last he realized that the noise had stopped. His ears missed the barking of carbines and the yells of the Indians. He turned around and looked up the canyon. The troopers were coming down the canyon walls now, carefully, their carbines at the ready. But the fight had gone out of the war party. They dropped their arms and stood in a sullen huddled group on the canyon floor.

Reba Coulter leaned against the boulder. "Is it over?" she asked at last. "Is it really over?"

"Yes," Swain said. "There's no fight in them now that Choko's dead."

Sergeant Kirkpatrick called from up above somewhere and wanted to know if they were all right, and Swain answered yes.

"You'd better sit down," he said to Reba. "You don't know yet how tired you really are."

She sat beside the boulder, numb with fatigue. "So he's finally dead," she said at last. "Maybe the killing and murder will be over now for a little while."

He said, "Yes, it's over now. This country will be safe to live in, and travel in, and people will have you to thank for it. We never would have got him if it hadn't been for you."

She smiled faintly. Then she spoke suddenly, as if the thought had been in her mind for a long while. "I suppose you will be going back to your ranch, won't you?"

Swain didn't know how to say what was in his mind. He wasn't any hand with pretty words, or fancy phrases.

He merely said, "Yes, I'll be going back to the ranch now . . . But I hope I won't be going alone."

From the way she looked up at him then, he guessed he'd said it all right.

The Builder of Murderer's Bar

by Todhunter Ballard

I REMEMBER THE DAY that Lisbeth Peyton announced herself promised to Lysander Cox. Along the American, where miners outnumbered women a thousand to one, this was an event of importance. I also remember how Edmond Jones took the news. The camp expected him to get drunk. He didn't. He went to work.

In a sense, Lysander Cox and Edmond Jones were friends, although they had nothing in common except their feeling for Lisbeth. They arrived at the Bar together, having met on shipboard, tramped across the Isthmus and shared a pack mule from San Francisco.

Cox was big and steady, a State-of-Maine man who had no time for foolishness; a strong man who could lift a two-hundred-pound boulder from a six-foot hole without assistance. But to a boy, Edmond Jones was far more interesting. He was small and dark and handsome, with a ready smile and a quick song on his lips. He built a Chinese water wheel, the first I saw along the river, and wasted half a day to show me how the blades turning with the current would raise the cups and dump the water into the board trough which led to his rocker, and how the rocker worked alone from the force of the water.

He built the first windlass on the Bar, to raise the bucket without carrying it up the crude ladder as the other miners did. To me, he assigned the problem of building a self-filling bucket, so that it would not be necessary to descend into the mud-choked hole, a problem which I never solved. The way he spent his time, lying in the sun, thinking up new gadgets to get more gold with less human effort, was a source of much laughter among the half dozen families and thousand miners along the mile of canyon floor. And since Peyton's driftwood-and-canvas store was the only supply point within thirty miles, and headquarters for the camp, Lisbeth Peyton and I heard the laughter.

I liked to loaf in the store that spring, and watch Lisbeth, and let the heat from the potbellied stove warm my bare legs. The store was very clean with its swept earth floor and its board counters resting on whisky barrels. The stock was far from large, and at times the flour ran low and the meal got wormy, but there was always the sharp smell of coffee from the bright red grinder.

Lisbeth ran the store for her father. She doled out supplies, weighed the miners' dust, mothered and scolded them.

"The wedding," I asked Lisbeth. "When will it be?"

She answered asbsently as she made a list for Pete Barton's pact train which left that night for Hangtown and Sacramento City. "In the fall, I think. After the breakup. If the color holds, Lysander will have his stake by then and we'll ship East."

"I'll never go East," I told her, digging at the packed earth with my heels. "This is a country to grow great in, to develop. The East is too crowded. People there have no imagination."

She stopped her work, placing her hands upon her hips, a patch of color glowing in each cheek. "Austin Garner, you're nothing but a copy cat. Every word that fool Edmond Jones utters you mimic like a magpie. How old are you?"

I scrubbed at my cowlick, embarrassed to have been found out. "Twelve," I said, "going on thirteen."

"You've time to grow up with the country," she said, and her mouth had a tight-lipped look. "I'm getting old. I'm almost twenty-two."

"Is that why you're marrying Lysander?"

She flushed and an edge of temper showed in her voice. "It is not. He needs a woman to look ahead. He'll share his life with me and let me have a part."

"Edmond Jones needs you," I said. "He told me so himself."

"I'll thank him not to discuss me with the neighbors." She sounded really angry now. "He doesn't need anyone. Whatever happens he'll rig a little wheel so the river can do his work. He's lazy and—"

"He's not lazy," I objected. "Only a fool works when he doesn't have to; a wise man thinks of ways to make things easy."

She came toward me around the store. "If you don't stop repeating all that nonsense—"

I knew she meant to box my ears and ducked out through the little rear door. I wasn't a minute too soon, for her fingers grazed my jacket as I fled, but once outside I knew I was safe enough. I could run faster than she could.

On my way down the Bar, I stopped at Lysander's claim. The sand here was only six feet to bedrock, but seepage water was bad and he had trouble cleaning the rough limestone thoroughly. He was bringing up a gravel-filled bucket as I arrived. I watched him empty it into the rocker and go to the river for water.

"Why don't you build a water wheel like Edmond's?" I asked.

He spoke without stopping, his tone slow and considered. "Well, now, it would take two days to build a wheel. In a good day I can make three ounces. Six ounces lost. I don't think a wheel would be worth six ounces."

I went on, for I had seen Edmond Jones in his favorite spot at the lower end of the Bar, close to the natural dam the rock slide made. He was on his back, his hat over his eyes. "Hi!" he said without moving. "What news do you bring today?"

"Well," I said, for I did not know quite how to tell him, "Lisbeth told my Aunt Emmaline this morning. She's—she's promised herself to Lysander."

He did not stir, and for a minute I thought he had not heard. "Now has she?" he said finally. "Well, she got a good man."

I was disappointed. I don't know exactly what I'd expected, but I'd heard my aunt tell about a cousin who had gone off to fight in the Mexican War after he was unlucky in love.

"She said you were lazy," I added. "Said you

didn't need anyone because you could always get the river to do your work."

He moved his hat then and surveyed me with one brown, thoughtful eye. Finally he sat up, put his hat on his head and sat staring at the rock dam which backed the river into a small lake.

"Why, yes," he said suddenly. "She's right, Austin. When a man sees a job, he ought to do it, and I've sat here for weeks, looking at the rock pile. It's time, I think, to go to work."

I looked at him doubtfully. "I could help you with the windlass," I offered.

His face lost the dark brooding look and he smiled, a smile so kind, so full of real friendliness it made you feel warm and pleasant inside. "That rock pile," he said. "It's probably been there a thousand years. You've been swimming here, Austin. How deep is the water above those rocks?"

I was used to his mind switching in the middle of our talks.

"Just over my head," I said. "You going to go swimming?"

He turned to look at me. "Less than six feet, and yet the dam's a good twelve feet high on the lower side. You know why?"

I didn't know, but I knew that he would tell me if I waited, so I stayed silent until he said, "Those rocks fell down a long time ago, making that still water behind the dam. Since then, the river has been washing down sand until the lake is only six feet deep instead of twelve. That means a layer of sand six feet thick; sand and gold, and mostly gold, since it is heavier. . . . Why, Austin"—his voice took on an edge of excitement—"that pool's paved with gold!"

I knew he didn't mean exactly that, but my voice trembled just the same.

"They tried to work the river bed, but the water's been too high. They're praying for low water, come August."

"It will never get low enough to work that channel." He was talking to himself. "The thing to do is to move the river."

I looked to see if he was smiling, but his dark face was serious. "To move the river, there's a job to challenge the caliber of a man." He turned, smiling again, his hand coming out to clasp my shoulder. "What about it? Shall we move the river, you and I?"

I gaped at him. "But how, where would we put it? There's no room for a new channel, unless we took it through the air."

"That's an idea," he said. "I knew the first time I saw you that you had ideas." He studied the far canyon wall with thoughtful eyes. "I think there's room. Come, Austin, we have work to do."

I heard my uncle discussing it that evening. Edmond Jones had been busy.

"He wants to build an earth-fill dam at the head of still water above Buckner's Bar," my uncle said, "and carry the river along the far canyon wall in a twelve-foot flume."

My aunt sniffed. "And how far will this flume extend?"

"For a full mile at least." He sighed. "A tremendous undertaking without proper machinery. Still, for centuries the river's been piling up gold behind that natural dam. The only thing to keep us from taking it is the water, and if we're rid of that—"

"You aren't for it?" There was alarm in my aunt's voice.

"I'm not sure," he said slowly. "It takes a deal of thinking. The cost will be very large. It will take all the dust the men have, perhaps more, but it's something to dream about, something only a big man could conceive. Jones is a builder, Emmaline. It's his kind that make a country grow."

"A dreamer is more like it. A lazy dreamer with a smile to charm wiser men to his folly. I'm glad Lisbeth is clear of him."

Apparently my uncle failed to hear her, for he went on as if she had not spoken. "There'll be a miners' meeting Monday. There are shrewd men along the river who were trained builders in the East. I'm interested in hearing their opinions."

I loved miners' meetings, loved the feeling of the crowd, the excitement and the speeches. I crept behind the stove where I could see and hear. It was the largest meeting the Bar had ever had. The crowd filled the store and fanned out through the open front to jam the level ground almost to the river. Lisbeth joined me, sinking down at my side so that she was out of sight.

We had no alcalde, since the camp was not yet formally organized, but my uncle, as temporary chairman, called the meeting to order and told why they were gathered. This was unnecessary, since Edmond had talked to many, who had told the rest, but in miners' meetings the formalities were strictly adhered to.

The laughter and talk quieted as Edmond Jones stepped onto the board counter. They liked him whether or not they approved.

"This is business which concerns us all," he told them. "This camp is wet. We've been working in water up to our waists all spring. That's seepage water from the river, and under the river is a channel filled with six feet of solid gold. I mean it. Sand and gold come downriver together, but at flood time the sand washes over the natural dam, while the heavier gold sinks. It's all there, ours for the taking, in Nature's catch basin, waiting for men with strength and daring enough to wrest if from her.

"I believe that sand will run five hundred dollars to the ton, perhaps a thousand, against what you're taking from your shafts, and there's a whole lake bottom waiting. Lysander Cox has a good hole, and there's not a better worker on the Bar. He handles perhaps a ton and a half a day and makes three ounces—twenty-five dollars. Think what he would make if his sand ran five hundred to the ton.

"Now, I'm no engineer, but I've talked with men who are builders and mechanics. They say my plan is possible, and the plan is simply this: to build a dam of earth and logs at the head of still water and carry the river in a flume along the far canyon wall to the curve below the rock slide. In that way we can work the stream bed without so much as wetting our feet."

He jumped down and a buzz of voices swelled across the closely packed store. I saw a disturbance to the right as someone pushed forward, and realized that it was Lysander Cox. I stole a look at Lisbeth. Her eyes were fastened on the big State-of-Maine man as he unhurriedly lumbered up to the place on the counter.

"I'm not one to deny that there may be merit in

Edmond's plan," he said, "but it isn't worth the risk. It would cost too much. It would take a big flume, twelve feet, they say, with three-foot sides. The canyon wall is rough, and a shelf would have to be graded. At one place it's all rock, straight up above the stream. How would you bridge that? It's a gamble, and for myself I'm not a gambler."

A hundred voices agreed, but there were others to support the flume.

Major Harry Love jumped to the counter.

"I'll build the dam," he cried, "and not one drop of water will come down the channel! Let those agreeable form on the right, the others on the left, then we can organize."

There was movement in the crowd, but my uncle held up his hands for silence. "No, not tonight. We'll now adjourn, so that you can have time to talk this over properly. Another meeting is called for Wednesday afternoon. We'll make our decision then."

By Wednesday everyone knew that enough men sided with Edmond Jones to assure that the immense project would be tried. But Lisbeth was angry, and she spoke her mind.

"You've a right to foolishness," she told him as he came into the store, "but you've no business to drag others down with your folly."

I was with him and unconsciously backed a step, but Edmond Jones did not retreat. "Why, as to that," he said, "the very act of living is a gamble. Where nothing's risked, there's very little gained, but even the gain is not the important thing. It's the doing that counts, to battle Nature on her own field, to change the river and win the treasure. I'd hoped that you would understand."

There was a note of sadness in his voice I had not heard before, but if it reached the girl, she gave no sign. "Words!" she cried. "Words to make men waste their dust and labor on your schemes!"

But her opposition had no effect. The meeting formed a company to build the flume. Harry Love contracted to build the dam and Otis Nichols to oversee the grading and leveling of the right of way.

For the construction of the flume itself, each of the five Bars formed its own subcompany, the men on New York Bar to be responsible for their section, we on Murderer's responsible for ours, with Edmond Jones as general chairman, his word to be final in case of arguments. After hours of debate, Samuel Tyler, who had been a builder in the East, in association with Ed Lefingwell, offered to build the Murderer's Bar section at six dollars the lineal foot.

When my aunt heard this price, she gasped and almost dropped the skillet full of dried meat.

"Six dollars the foot. And how many feet in a mile?"

"Over five thousand," my uncle said.

My aunt did some arithmetic in the sand beside the oven. "Thirty thousand dollars. Four thousand ounces!" She was horrified. "And that for the flume alone. What will the dam and grading cost?"

My uncle did not want to discuss it with a woman. "A lot," he said shortly, and went to wash.

But my aunt was not to be denied. "And how much would a lot be?" she demanded, following him, still carrying the iron spider.

His hands were deep in soapy water. He turned to glance in my direction, but I could offer him no help. "Well," he said slowly, "perhaps as much. I mean the dam."

"And the grading?"

He gave it up. "There are a thousand men in the five companies," he said, "and each has pledged fifteen ounces. I make that better than one hundred thousand."

My aunt sat down from necessity. "All to be buried in this canyon," she sighed when she had breath to speak. "That man's worse than a fool. He's positively dangerous."

My uncle did not answer this, and supper was eaten in silence. When the dishes were done, my aunt returned to the attack. "And what will this flume be made of that it costs its weight in gold?"

"Lumber," my uncle told her. He seemed relieved to be off the subject of finance. "Tyler and Ed Lefingwell left for Sacramento City this evening. They're after a sawmill, whatever they can find. They'll cut pine on the canyon sides. Harry Love's already getting his dam crew together. At the rate things are moving, we'll be working the stream bed by the first of August."

But they weren't working the stream bed by the middle of August. Building seemed to grow more difficult day by day. Tyler and Lefingwell came back from Sacramento City, bringing with them a circular saw, a shaft and an ordinary "horsepower" which had been shipped into the country with a threshing rig by some fool who thought that grain grew on these wooded hills.

Also, they brought a hundred bronco horses, and

Mexicans to drive them, and it was wonderful to sit and watch the horses on their treadmill track, to hear the high-pitched calls of the drivers, to smell the dust and watch the gleaming saw eat its way through the soft pine.

I had no time to loaf in the store. There was too much to see. Harry Love cut logs and dragged them to the dam. Otis Nichols drove his crew, hacking out the twelve-foot shelf along the canyon wall. Ahead of them was the sheer rock face, and I could not see how it would ever be crossed, but if Edmond Jones was worried, he gave no sign. And he had plenty to worry him for, although Tyler's mill had sawed out almost three thousand feet of lumber, they found when they came to use it that there were two- and three-inch cracks between the boards, due to warping and roughness of the lumber. A flume built of this would never carry water.

Tyler was ready to throw up his contract, taking his loss. Tempers and dust were growing short. Summer was passing and the miners who had not joined the company snickered at Jones' folly, and reminded their friends that they had been warned.

But Edmond Jones was not through. He called a meeting and outlined a new plan. Tyler and Lefingwell were to rout out puncheons with their mill, the flume would be built of these and lined with canvas.

Jerome Howe objected that canvas cost a dollar the yard and that anyway there was probably not enough on the whole coast. But Edmond Jones went to San Francisco and bought sails from the vessels rotting in the bay because their sailors had run off to the mines. Then Edmond sent me from claim to claim to find ex-seamen or any other who could use the palm. These he offered half an ounce per day as wages and set them sewing up the canvas lining.

This was barely done before the grading crew reached the sheer rock wall that dropped straight into deep water. Otis Nichols tried driving piles for his bridge, but the soft pine struck boulders and splintered. He had to build crib dams and scoop out the sand at the bottom, then wedge the piles, a slow and tedious job. But good came of it, for Bert Davis panned some of the sand from the holes. It ran two hundred dollars the yard. Enthusiasm leaped alive again and men worked at fever pitch, certain now that a fortune was theirs.

"We're rich," announced my uncle, coming to the wagon for supper. He was wet, caked with mud and unshaven. A man little given to excitement, he was excited now. "We'll have a town here that will not be second to San Francisco."

"You'll kill yourself," said my aunt tartly. "You're working twenty hours a day."

"Not half as much as that Jones," my uncle said happily. "Why, I'll venture he hasn't slept this week, and when he stops to eat, I don't know. He's down to skin and bones, but nothing stops him—trouble, nothing. I think by Saturday he'll turn the river, if Harry Love has the dam done in time."

Nor was my uncle the only one to appreciate Edmond Jones. Men from other Bars, other camps, from Sacramento City and San Francisco came to see Jones' flume and Jones' dam; they came to see and to ask advice, for other camps were planning flumes.

"You see," I told Lisbeth Peyton as I got some

flour. "I said that he wasn't lazy."

"No," she granted. "I guess he isn't lazy."

"You should let him know," I said. "He'll be a great man in this country. Harry Love says we should run him for Congress when the state gets organized. If you were his wife—"

"I'm satisfied," she told me sharply. "I have Lysander."

I couldn't understand her, but then Lisbeth had always puzzled me. Maybe I just didn't understand women. I left the store, conscious that I had done my best.

My uncle proved an excellent prophet. The flume was completed in that week and the river turned on Saturday as Harry Love closed the last gap in the dam. The shallow lake behind it filled slowly, and just before darkness the brown waves lapped along the canvas channel. The river had been turned.

The news ran through the camps like wildfire and men thronged to watch. The whisky at Peyton's store was low, but these men needed no spirits now. They were all millionaires, laughing and shouting to one another, betting on what the first day's cleanups would run. But the cooler heads, led by my uncle, pointed out that there was still work to be done. Part of the rock slide had to be blasted so the sand bed would drain, and the following day was Sunday. No one on the Bars worked on the Sabbath. Sunday was the miners' day to wash their clothes and clean their camps.

The rule, my uncle decided, would be observed. They blasted the rock slide that evening, but the channel would still be wet the next day. It would not be fair for company members holding drier claims to begin work ahead of their fellows.

The men agreed. All they wanted now was to celebrate. The call went out for Edmond Jones, and he was finally found, curled up in his blankets. They dragged him forth. They carried him upon their shoulders in a torchlight procession lighted by burning fagots from their fires. They wound up and down the Bars, gathering men at every camp, until they finally halted at Peyton's store. I wanted to follow, but my aunt stopped me.

Sunday morning, though, I was up early. The flume was running almost half full, and three miners, disregarding my uncle's edict, were working in the upper channel. I watched until they quit and cleaned the box beneath their rocker. Their faces were pale as they carried the dust to the store and weighed it on Peyton's scales. Nine and one half pounds of gold for three hours' work. It seemed impossible, but—I raced away to spread the news.

Men came awake with my shouts ringing in their ears. It was true. This was the richest strike in the foothills. The celebration started all over again. A few ran with pans to sample for themselves, but the majority gathered at the store.

My aunt came and got me about dusk, and, with Lisbeth, we retired to our wagon.

I went to sleep with the sound of singing in my ears, and the picture of miners dancing like so many bears on the flat before the store.

I awoke on Monday morning and I could still hear voices. I looked out at the lightened sky above the canyon's rim, then at the dark knot of men beside the river. I sensed trouble before I got close enough to hear their words, then I saw the flume and knew what had happened. It was spilling water over the sides for as far as I could see.

I heard ". . . a cloudburst in the hills," and felt the dread of those words. Flash floods were not uncommon in the country, and many a miner had scrambled to safety ahead of a thirty-foot wall of water. The American River was bigger than most, its canyon wider. There would be no thirty-foot flood, but the river was still rising rapidly; the flume, the summer's work, might be torn away.

A man ran past me with a wrecking bar, and I realized that it was Edmond Jones. Others went after him up the canyon, to break the dam, to save the flume. Excitement and fear clutched at my throat and cut my breath as I ran with them. They piled out onto the dam, prying desperately with their bars, and the river seemed trying to help. Already, in a low spot, it was eating into the earth fill.

It was close, but they found the key log and broke the dam, jumping wildly for safety as the brown flood poured through the breach, widening it by the instant, filling the old channel with churning, broken water. The miners dropped exhausted, but they did not rest long, for the danger was not past. The flood struck the rock slide with tremendous force, widening the cleft we had blown, rolling rocks as big as a house from its charging way, tearing out the golden sand which had filled the channel and sucking at the piles which supported the flume bridge. One gave, a second and then a third, until, with a shriek of splitting timber, the whole bridge section splashed into the river.

I expected the flume to break in two, but the stout canvas lining held. Instead, the weight of the sagging section dragged more and more of the mile-long box sidewise from its shelf, into the water, until it floated like a serpent, its whole length dragging at the fastenings on the dam end. It hung for one awful, eternal moment; then, with a rending, tearing sound which reached us all above the noise of the raging water, it wrenched free and went writhing down the flood, past the natural dam and on around the bend.

For years afterwards, miners making camp along the river would search the driftwood piles, come up with a torn scrap of canvas, and roof their shelter with a piece of Jones' flume.

You could laugh at the majestic gaiety of the flume bouncing over the torrent that morning or you could cry. No one on the Bar had time to do either. The water was still rising. Peyton struggled to get his goods up the canyon side. Miners fought to save their rockers. My uncle tied our oxen to the wagon and dragged our household to safety. Not until everything was on higher ground did we pause to take stock.

The camp was ruined, and winter less than a month away. The extra pressure of water released from the log dam had torn out the rock slide, and the swift current was sweeping the golden sand down the river to a thousand bars below, leaving the channel clean.

I found Edmond Jones seated by himself, staring emptily at the river. He had helped move Peyton's goods, helped yoke our oxen, helped a dozen miners, and lost his own meager possessions.

"Some flood," I said, and settled at his side.

"Why, yes." There was bitterness in his voice. "And to think as smart a man as I'm supposed to be would overlook the possibility. In my stupidity I never thought what a flood might do."

"It's not your fault. You shouldn't have to think for all of them."

"Yes, I should, Austin. Yes, I should." He wasn't looking at me. "I talked them into risking everything. They trusted me, and I didn't know enough. I'll never build anything again. I'm through with schemes to try and lighten work. From now on, I get down into the mud of the hole. I'll not even use a windlass."

"That would be a mistake." Lisbeth Peyton was standing close to us. We did not know how long she'd been there. Edmond Jones jumped up, and I rose more slowly, noticing the flush on her cheeks as she went on breathlessly, "You can't quit because of one setback. The men still need a leader."

"No," he said. "You were right. A man is privileged to make a fool of himself, but not of a thousand others. Look at the Bar. The miners have lost everything and I've lost their respect."

She shook her head. "I think you take too serious a view. They've lost money, yes, but they've found out what can be done to make more. There'll be a hundred flumes because of yours."

"Kind, sweet Lisbeth," he said. "You take some of the soreness out. I'm glad you and Lysander didn't lose. You and he—"

She looked straight at him. "There's your proof that anyone can make a mistake. I thought Lysander needed me, that I could be a partner to help him, but he doesn't want a partner. He wants a house with the best horsehair furniture, and me to sit in it. I'm not much good at sitting in parlors, Edmond. I'd rather help you build things."

My eyes went wide, but Edmond Jones missed her meaning. He was still too deep in the misery of his failure. "I'll never build anything again," he repeated.

She watched him a moment in silence, then her eyebrows went up. "Well then," she said, "we'll just stay here and work a claim. There's still sand on the Bar, even if it isn't as rich as the stream bed was. We'll have a little cabin here on the rocks, and you can rig a wheel to bring water from the river to the cabin in a trough, so we won't have to carry it."

He raised his head then and looked at her, and for a long while words flowed between them, although neither spoke. Suddenly, he smiled. "Why, yes, partner, a trough, or, better yet, a pipe of logs. We can hollow them out with a heated rod. We can run the water into a tub, and we might mount the tub on a shaft, so that the force of the water will make it turn. You could put clothes into the tub, and we'll build paddles on the sides to pound the clothes. Here, look. Like this." He dropped to his knees and drew a diagram in the sand.

As Edmond stooped, I started to say, "I thought you weren't going to build—" Then didn't speak, for Lisbeth was solemnly winking at me, with her finger pressed against her lips for silence, her shoulders shaking with suppressed laughter. I turned and fled.

A Place For Danny Thorpe

by Ray Hogan

HE CAME FROM THE blue-shadowed mountain and deep-valleyed country of New Mexico; from the long, glittering flats of Arizona, from Texas, from Kansas—from everywhere almost and had yet to find his place in the scheme of things. In San Francisco he thought the search had ended but again failure, in the shape of Nate Tobin—Nugget Nate Tobin, the gambling king—had overtaken him. Now he was on the run, fearing for his life.

In the black corridor of Montgomery Street, he flattened himself against the clammy wall of a building and peered into the misty darkness. Newton and Stanger, two of Tobin's plug-uglies, were out there somewhere, silent, vengeful figures still dogging his steps, still thirsting for his blood. Scarcely breathing, he waited, listened. Off in the direction of the bay a ship hooted, a lost, lonely sound in the fogbound night.

In the beginning Danny Thorpe had dreamed of being a rancher. Since he was Texas born and raised, it was a natural desire, but in that broad land of tall and powerful men it soon became apparent to him that he was a misfit, a boy-man no one ever took seriously.

Eventually it set him to drifting and he moved from one territory and state to another, astray in a heedless world where his diminutive stature was continually a handicap that denied him the opportunities for which he so eagerly hungered.

Finally San Francisco, where he had heard jockeys were in demand and there was good money to be made at the race tracks. . . . It had started well. He had a way with horses that brought out the best in them. In a few weeks he was recognized as one of the peers—and then Nate Tobin had stepped in. He ordered Danny to lose a certain race, voiced dire threats if he did not. Danny played it straight and his mount won easily. Tobin dropped a small fortune and quickly sent Pete Newton and Bill Stanger, two of his prize killers, to make an example of the little man who dared defy him. Danny Thorpe fled, aware of his great danger, aware, too, of another failure. He was . . .

"Got to be right along here somewheres."

Stanger's low voice cut through the muffled night. Danny drew closer to the wall, his nerves taut, heart racing. They were moving in and there was nothing he could do but wait—and hope. He had no weapon of any kind with which to defend himself, not even a pocketknife. The pistol he had once owned had been sold long ago when cash ran low.

"Ain't so sure," Newton's reply was couched in doubt. "Could've turned the other way. Sure ain't seeing no signs of him."

"He's here," Stanger said stubbornly. "Just stand quiet for a spell and listen."

Guarding his breath, Danny rode out the dragging moments. The ship in the harbor hooted again and somewhere a horse trotted over cobblestone pavement, the hoofbeats faint and hollow sounding. Saliva gathered in his mouth and he swallowed hard. Despite the coolness of the night sweat lay thick on his brow and he fought the urge to wipe it off.

A wave of frustation and anger surged through him. Why did such things always have to happen to him? Why could he never find a decent job, live an ordinary life as did other men? Why did something always happen to upset things just as he was getting set? He was finished in San Francisco, and in horse racing, thanks to Nate Tobin, whose tentacles reached far to touch and encircle the sport. He would have to move on, look for a different way to live. But what—and where?

He groaned silently at the prospect; he had tried about everything. There was little, if anything, left. And then, suddenly, he recalled a newspaper advertisement he had read. At the time he had thought little of it; now he brought it back to mind:

WANTED

Young, skinny, wiry fellows. Not over 18. Must be expert riders willing to risk death daily. Orphans preferred. Wages $25 per week. Apply Central Overland Express.

The Pony Express! It had begun operation just that spring, carrying mail between Sacramento and St. Joseph, Missouri. Maybe he could get on with them.

His spirits lifted as this ray of hope broke through his despair. There was a company office in San Francisco but that, of course, was out; he could not risk being spotted by Tobin's thugs. The division point was Sacramento, he had heard. He could go there, apply for a job. Sacramento was a good ninety miles away, but there were always freight wagons on the road and if a man worked it right he could always hitch a ride.

He could do all that, he thought grimly, if he could stay alive—could give Stanger and Newton the slip. Desperately he began to search his mind for an idea, for some means of escape. There must be a way—there had to be.

"I'm telling you, he ain't here," Newton's words came unexpectedly from the darkness a dozen paces to his right. "He headed the other way. I'm betting on it."

"You're betting on it," Stanger said mockingly. "Man needs a reason to bet—"

"Heard a noise over there a bit ago. Could've been him."

"Could've been you dreaming."

"Naw. Reckon I know what I heard."

A small tremor raced up Danny Thorpe's spine as an idea lodged in his mind. Pete Newton thought he had detected a sound down the street in the opposite direction; perhaps, if he made it definite, proved him right . . . Danny reached for his hat, moving his arm carefully to avoid the rustle of cloth. He took the small-brimmed headpiece in his hand, raised it high, and sent it sailing off into the night. It struck against some obstacle, set up a soft disturbance.

"There!" Newton said instantly. "You hear that?"

"I did," Stanger admitted grudgingly. "Come on. Let's have a look."

Danny listened to the soft scraping of the men's boots as they turned, walked toward the source of the sound. Waiting no longer, he wheeled, and resisting the urge to run, he move carefully and quietly to the far corner of the block. Once there, he gave in to the need to hurry. With luck he would find a freighter rolling north before he reached the edge of town.

Four weeks later, astride a horse lent him by bitter-tongued old Pat McCoskey, Express-line superintendent at Sacramento, he was on the way to Smith's Crossing, in mid-Nevada. In his pocket was his assignment to the post which would be his home station; behind him lay seventeen days of intensive training in the art of being a Pony Express rider. And further in the past were Nate Tobin and all the other symbols of failure that had haunted him. That was all over now for at last he had found himself, his place. It remained only for him to prove his abilities to McCoskey and the job was his permanent property.

It had not been easy to endure the lash of the superintendent's haranguing, but he had stayed with it, stubbornly refusing to lose heart. After taking the oath required of all riders—not to swear or drink liquor while on duty, always to conduct himself as a gentleman and never abuse the horseflesh—he gave himself over to McCoskey, who hammered relentlessly at him day and night.

"Bend your knees, goddammit!" the old man shouted at him time after time when he was having difficulty dismounting from a running horse. "You'll be breaking your legs first out, if'n you don't!"

And Danny Thorpe had learned, just as he had become proficient in handling the *mochila*, an ingenious leather blanket designed to fit over the saddle and upon which four mail pouches had been stitched. It was loaded at each end of the run, was then passed from rider to rider, the trick being to make the exchange without loss of time.

"Nine days from here to St. Joe!" McCoskey had told him. "That's what we're shooting for. We're doing it in ten now—and that's less than half what it takes a letter to come by boat or stagecoach. But we want it done in nine—and we sure as hell can do it if you blasted saddle-warmers'll work at it!"

"Be doing my best," Danny had replied, continually awed by McCoskey's enthusiasm and utter devotion to the cause. "I'll try—"

"Best ain't always good enough. Got to do better. And time's not the only thing important, either. That mail's got to get through; come perdition, it's got to get through! You understand that? No matter what—you get your *mochila* to the next station so's the link rider can keep it moving. We don't take no excuses—none."

"Yes, sir. All I'm asking is a little luck—"

"Luck!" McCoskey exploded. "Man makes his own luck, and don't you forget it! You just mind what I've been telling you and you won't need to depend on something like luck."

And thus it had gone until McCoskey, finally satisfied although frank in declaring himself unconvinced, sent him on his way. Now, with a warm, late fall sun caressing his shoulder, he gained the last rise and looked down on what he hoped would be his new home, Smith's Crossing.

In appearance it left much to be desired. It was no more than a thin scatter of gray, sun- and wind-scoured buildings and pole corrals, completely devoid of vegetation except for a lone tree which stood in solitary dejection in front of the largest structure.

The past was far behind Danny Thorpe when he pulled to a halt at the hitch rack in front of the mud-chinked log-cabin office of the Pony Express and dismounted. He paused for a time, studying the sign above the doorway, a serious-faced miniature of a man dressed in black cord pants, knee-high boots, fringed buckskin coat, and rumpled pork-pie hat. Heavier woolen clothing, suggested by Pat McCoskey, was rolled inside the poncho tied behind the cantle of his saddle.

Hitching at the holstered gun—also borrowed from the line's superintendent—slung at his hip, he crossed to the doorway and entered. Again he halted, allowed his eyes to adjust to the abrupt change of light. It was a large room, he saw, with little furniture that was covered with a thin veneer of yellow dust. Someone was rattling dishes in a room that turned off the primary area and the good, inviting odor of coffee hung in the still, warm air like tantalizing perfume.

"Reckon you're Thorpe, the new rider," a voice said from the left.

Danny wheeled, confronted a squat, dark man with close-set eyes and a friendly grin. "That's me," he said and produced the letter McCoskey had given him. "You'd be Wylie Courtright, the station agent."

Courtright nodded. He opened the letter, glanced at it, thrust it into his pocket. "Had word from Mac that you'd be here today. Good thing. You'll have to make the run in the morning."

"Suits me," Danny said, glancing involuntarily toward the kitchen.

"Expect you're a mite hungry," the agent said, missing nothing. "Sit yourself down and I'll see what I can rustle up. Then we'll talk."

Danny settled himself at a table near a window. From there he could see the corral in which a dozen or so horses stood, hipshot in the pleasant sunlight. All were tough, hard-planed little animals that looked as though they could withstand any amount of punishment heaped upon them. Farther on was the blacksmith shop. The double doors were open and red coals glowed in the forge like evil eyes. Presently the smithy began to work his anvil, the ringing of his hammer clean and clear in the long-reaching quiet.

Courtright reappeared bringing a sandwich of bread and cold beef, cups and a small granite pot of coffee. "Ought to hold you till supper," he said, and sat down opposite. "How's things in Sacramento? Old Mac still pawing the earth like always?"

Danny grinned between bites. "He's sure one for the book, all right."

"Don't think he'd be satisfied even with that feller on the winged horse," the agent said, wagging his head. "But he's got the right idea. Training he gives you boys is what's making this mail-line work."

"Thought I was a pretty fair hand with a horse until I come up against him," Danny said. "What's my other home station and how far is it?"

"Red Valley—and it's about a hundred and seventy miles off. You got eleven relay stations in between."

"A hundred and seventy miles," Danny murmured. "Quite a piece."

"For a fact. Most home stations are about a hundred, more or less. This stretch's the longest on the line. That's why we have trouble keeping a man on it. But it ain't too bad. Mostly flat country and easy going."

"Any Indian trouble?"

"Not lately. Country's too dang Godforsaken even for them I expect. Personally, I don't blame a man for quitting it."

"I'll stick," Danny said, "if I make the grade."

Courtright was silent for a moment. Then, "Don't think you'll have any trouble doing that. Just keep remembering that mail's got to come through on time—but mostly it's got to come through. But I reckon Mac told you all that."

"He sure did—plenty loud and often."

"That's sort of extra special now. You're going to be carrying some mighty important mail in your *mochila* on your return trip."

Danny frowned, poured himself a second cup of coffee. "Important?"

"Yeh, the election returns. People'll be real anxious to know who won—Lincoln or that feller Douglas."

Danny had forgotten all about the national election, not that it meant anything particular to him. A man had to keep on living and working no matter who sat in the White House.

"People like us maybe don't pay much attention to things like that," Courtright said, reading his thoughts, "but these here big businessmen set a pile by who gets the job. Heard some of them say they're mighty certain we'll go to war if Lincoln wins."

Danny showed his surprise. "Pshaw!" he scoffed. "War with who? We licked the Mexicans—"

"War with the South," the agent said quietly. "Sure does seem trouble's brewing down there. Be a terrible thing was we to get to fightin' betwixt ourselves."

"For certain," Danny agreed. "What time in the morning do I start this run?"

"Three-thirty. You can figure on old Bob being here right on the nose. You're allowed two minutes to make the change and get going."

"Won't need it."

"Don't expect you will. And be wearing that gun. Some of the boys don't pack a weapon but you ought to on this stretch."

"Thought you said—"

"Ain't thinking so much about Indians, I'm just thinking you ought to go armed. Been more strangers moseying through here lately. Duded-up city fellers. Was three here only a couple of days ago. Ain't got no idea what they're up to—maybe nothing. But just as well you keep your eyes peeled."

"I'll do it," Danny said. He glanced about the room. "Now, if you'll point out my bunk quarters, I think I'll get me some sleep. Three-thirty comes powerful early."

"Right over there," Courtright said, waving at a door in the opposite wall. "I'll wake you for supper. You can meet the rest of the folks then."

"Fine," Danny murmured, rising and starting across the floor. "That'll be fine."

Excitement was having its strong way with him that next morning as he stood before the crackling fire in the rock fireplace and sipped at his coffee. He was eager to be in the saddle and gone, impatient to open up this new life that lay before him. He grinned at Courtright, who winked back knowingly. Only the agent and the two hostlers were up and about at that early hour. He had met the blacksmith, his helper, the cook, and two or three other employees the evening before. Theirs were the routine jobs about the place and there was no need for them to be abroad now.

Courtright, his easygoing shape slouched in the doorway, consulted the thick, nickel-silver watch he carried. "About due," he said and crossed to where Danny stood. "When you get going, just leave things up to the horses," he said. "They know this here route better'n any man."

Danny nodded. He finished his coffee, placed the empty cup on the mantel, and walked to the window. It was a clear night, silvered by a star-studded sky. Opening the hinged sash he listened into the deep silence. The distant, fast beat of a running horse was a faint drumming in the quiet.

"He's coming," he said and started for the door.

"No hurry," Courtright replied, shaking his head. "Be another five, six minutes."

Danny did not pause, impatience now prodding him mercilessly. "Want to be ready," he said, and stepped out into the yard.

The station agent grinned understandingly. He reached for his sheepskin-lined jacket, drew it on. Picking up the three letters that were to be added to the mail pouch, he followed Thorpe into the brisk night. He halted where Danny was inspecting the gear on the horse readied for him by the hostlers.

"Eastern stuff," he said, thrusting the letters at Thorpe. "Goes in the right front pocket."

Danny bucked his head. Three of the compartments in the *mochila* were padlocked, contained the important mail placed in them at the beginning of the run, and could not be opened until the agent or proper official at the finish of the line—in this case St. Joe—produced the key. The fourth pocket, at the rider's right knee, was left open for pickup and delivery along the way.

Danny tucked the letters inside his shirt. He would put them in their proper pocket after he was in the saddle, not waste time doing it before he mounted. It was another of the small, seemingly insignificant things Pat McCoskey had taught him to do, all of which, added together, meant several minutes of time saved in the over-all run.

Satisfied his horse was ready, Danny walked deeper into the yard. The hoofbeats were louder now and throwing his glance down the road, he caught sight of the oncoming rider.

A thrill of pride raced through him. The man was hunched forward over his mount. A scarf about his neck whipped out behind him, like some brave banner, waving its defiance to all who would see. The horse was running full tilt, head extended, mane and tail flowing in shimmering waves. His legs were no more than a blur in the semidarkness. Danny's heart bulged; this was for him—this was the sort of life he sought, must have. A man could be proud of being a Pony Express rider; and one he would be—or die trying.

The waiting horse began to prance nervously, anxious to pick up the race. One of the hostlers swore softly, affectionately, began to lead the animal about in a tight circle to relieve the tension. Suddenly the rider was thundering into the yard. Danny had a glimpse of the man's taut features as he came off his horse; he saw the oblong shape of the *mochila* as it was tossed to him. He caught it neatly, flung it over his saddle with practiced accuracy, and vaulted into place. In the next instant he was surging off into the night.

It had been a good exchange, a fast one, and Pat McCoskey would have been proud of him, he thought as he rushed on. And then he grinned wryly. He doubted if anything would ever completely satisfy the old superintendent. To him perfection was merely a step to an even higher goal.

Jamming the three letters Wylie Courtright had given him into the *mochila's* pocket and closing the spring snap, Danny looked ahead. The road was a faint white ribbon curving off through a dark border of weeds, grass, and other growth. A great wave of happiness rolled through him and he took a long, deep breath, of the sharp, clean air. He was in the saddle—on his way; it was real now—he was a Pony Express rider.

Or . . . almost, he thought soberly, cautioning his soaring spirits. He still must prove himself to McCoskey. He must make the run over and over again—do it right. He must heed the superintendent's instructions, remember his own oath, not forget the things Courtright had told him. He must be on time, get the mail through—and make no mistakes. It was a big order, but he would do it. Nothing must prevent his making good.

He settled lower on the saddle as the buckskin

pounded on through the night. Miles fled by. Stars overhead began to fade. The scraggly growth and irregular-shaped rock formations grew more distant. A jack rabbit scurried across the road, was quickly lost in the brush. They rounded a turn and abruptly the first relay station lay before him, a small weathered scar in the wide emptiness. It seemed hardly possible they had covered so much ground or that he had been riding for almost two hours.

He swept into the yard, the face of the hostler standing ready with his fresh mount only a soft-edged blur in the half light. Grasping the *mochila* in the manner Pat McCoskey had taught him, he prepared to make the change. It went off smoothly, without lost motion, as he had hoped, and in fleeting seconds he was again on the road, this time astride a barrel-bodied pinto gelding that ran as though all hell and its proprietor were at his heels.

An hour later, as he began to climb a long, gentle slope, sunrise caught him, bringing with it a brisk, cutting wind that struck deep into his bones and made him wish for heavier clothing. But the wind had died by the time he made the next relay point, and when the third change had been accomplished, and without incident, he found himself unreasonably warm and removed his jacket.

Noon passed but he felt no hunger, just a gradually increasing stiffness that claimed his muscles, sent shooting pains up his back and through his shoulders. He had thought himself accustomed to hard riding, hours upon end; he was realizing now, as McCoskey had warned him, that a great difference lay between just riding a horse and forking a Pony Express mount steadily, hour after hour, at a dead run.

The country became more desolate and the loneliness of the land began to weigh on him. He tried not to think of that, to dwell only upon the good fortune that had come his way—that would remain his if he could successfully prove his worth and ability. It was all like a dream, a vague, happy dream—one he hoped would never end.

He received a surprise near dark when he reached the final relay station, found a girl waiting with his remount. She smiled sweetly at him as he lunged past her and leaped onto the saddle. Later he could not recall whether he had smiled back or not. He would make a point of doing so on the return trip, he told himself. She had been pretty and it would be nice to know someone along the trail.

Immediately he remembered that Pony Express riders were supposed to remain unmarried, and he guessed he'd better forget about her. It could lead to problems and nothing—*nothing*—was going to interfere with his job.

It was shortly after seven-thirty when he pulled into Red Valley station and flung the *mochila* to the waiting link rider. Every bone and muscle in his body was crying, and he staggered uncertainly as he started toward the door. He scarely heard the greeting of the agent, and shook the man's hand woodenly. He was hungry, too, but that would have to wait; first he wanted only to stretch out on a bed for a few minutes.

And then as he passed through the doorway into the main room where an evening meal was being placed on a table for him by the agent's wife, he came to a stunned halt. Standing before the fireplace, watching him narrowed eyes, were two men. Danny Thorpe's heart skipped a beat. It was Pete Newton and Bill Stanger. Nugget Nate Tobin's avengers had found him after all.

Weariness dropped from Danny's shoulders, was forgotten. Worry and the old familiar feeling of hopelessness stiffened him. He stared at the pair, incongruous in the rough surroundings in their tight-fitting suits, derby hats, and button shoes.

"What do you want?"

His voice sounded strange to his own ears. It was tight, oddly husky. He watched Bill Stanger take a step forward, lift his hands, palms outward, in a conciliatory gesture.

"Want? Why, nothing, Shorty. We're just passing through, a couple of pilgrims on our way east."

"That's right," Newton chimed in. "Pilgrims, that's us."

"You're not looking for me?" Danny asked, bluntly.

Stanger appeared surprised. "For you—oh, you mean on account of that race-track business? Nate's done forgot that. All he wanted was to learn you a lesson. When you hightailed it, I reckon it satisfied him."

Danny considered that for several moments. It did seem unlikely Tobin would go to such lengths to even the score with him. And how could he and his thugs have known he was working for the Pony Express, or, more particularly, that he was on that exact run?

Stanger said: "How long you been carrying the mail?"

"First time out," Danny replied, his anxiety beginning to ease. Apparently the two men had no interest in him.

"Like it?"

"Real fine," Danny replied and turned to the table. He had changed his mind; he would have something to eat before he climbed into bed.

"Beats whacking them broomtails around a track, eh?"

"Sure does," Danny said, and settled onto his chair. He raised a cup of coffee to his lips, drank gratefully. Newton spoke from across the room.

"You heading back west in the morning?"

Danny nodded. A vague doubt concerning the presence of the two men was seeping into his mind. Perhaps they were no longer interested in exacting vengeance upon him for what Tobin considered a double-cross, but there could be something else. They were much too friendly, and they were asking a lot of questions.

He puzzled over the problem while he ate, now and then casting covert glances at the pair, still standing before the fireplace. What could they be planning? The Pony Express carried little, if any, money; robbery would not be the motive, especially where a big-time gambler like Nate Tobin was involved. It had to be something else—if there were reasons for his suspicion. He finally concluded it best to simply remain quiet but keep his eyes open.

The station agent came in, sat down across the table. "Name's Ruskin. Charlie Ruskin," he said. "Didn't get much chance to introduce myself because of your friends. You'd be Danny Thorpe?"

"Right. And they're not what I'd call my friends."

Ruskin smiled, not exactly understanding. "Just figured they was from the way you were talking. Anyway, thought you'd like knowing you made the run in sixteen hours, assuming you got off on time."

"On the nose," Danny said, then added: "Is that good?"

"Just what it's figured for—sixteen hours. Has been done in less, and a few times when it took longer." The agent rose to his feet, a tall, friendly man with deep lines in his face. "Expect you're ready to hit the hay. First time out a rider learns he has muscles he never dreamed of."

Danny nodded and got to his feet. "What time do I leave in the morning?"

"Six o'clock, if nothing goes wrong. Door to the left is your room. Anything you need?"

"Only sleep," Thorpe said and moved to his quarters.

It seemed to him that he had scarcely pulled the quilts about his neck when Charlie Ruskin was shaking his shoulder.

"Five o'clock. Time you were up and around."

Danny got to his feet groggily, and then as the sharp, cold air sliced through the fog in his brain, he dressed hurriedly and went into the lobby. He ate quickly, gulping two cups of steaming black coffee, then hastened outside to inspect his horse. The hostler had just finished saddling the animal, a half-wild little sorrel that nipped ferociously at the stableman each time he came within range.

"He's a bad one," the hostler said, "but faster'n a turpentined cat on the road. Figured that's the kind you'd be wanting."

Danny said, "What I like," then paused, realizing there was deeper meaning to the man's words. "Some reason why I ought to have a fast horse?"

The hostler glanced up. "Sure. Every rider on the

line'll be pouring it on. We'll be carrying the 'lection returns."

There was pride in the man's tone. Danny grinned at him. "Danged if I hadn't forgot that!"

"Be a big feather in the company's cap, was we to get the news to Frisco in record time."

And in mine, Danny thought and walked away. The sky to the east was dull pearl gray. It looked like he would have good weather. He swung his eyes about the yard, back to the station. There was no sign of Newton or Bill Stanger. Wondering about them, he retreated to the main room. Charlie Ruskin was at his desk.

"Nothing for you to carry on," he said, looking up. "Probably a good thing. Likely you'll be loaded."

"Probably," Danny said. "That pair—the ones you called my friends—what happened to them?"

"Rode out. About an hour ago."

"Which way?"

"Headed east, I reckon. Leastwise, that's what they said. Never paid them no mind. Why?"

He guessed he had figured them wrong. Danny sighed. Whatever it was they were up to evidently had nothing to do with him. He shrugged. "No reason. Was just asking."

He went back to the yard, crossed to where the hostler stood with the sorrel. His mind was now on the job that lay before him. He wondered if he could better the time usually required to cover the distance between the two home stations. Sixteen hours was standard, Ruskin had said. Maybe if he worked at it he could trim it down to fifteen. He would be on a good horse at the start. If he pushed him and his successive remounts hard, he just might turn the trick. A fast time record could go far in cinching the job for him.

He checked the sorrel's gear again, found it to his liking. A few minutes later the pound of hoofs announced the coming of the link rider. Tension gripping him as before, Danny took his position, made ready to receive the *mochila* and continue the relay.

The rider entered the yard in a rush. He left his saddle in a long leap, sent the leather blanket with its bulging pockets sailing through the fading darkness at Danny.

"Lincoln won!" he shouted. "Pass it along!"

Danny spun to the sorrel, already moving out. He flung the *mochila* across the saddle, lost precious moments yanking it into position because of the fractious horse, and vaulted aboard. The sorrel was at top speed before he reached the trail.

Danny swore softly to himself. It had been a poor changeover; the horse had been jumpy and too anxious. He would remember that the next time the fiery little red was given him. But actually the time loss was small and the horse, seemingly to know he was at fault, was doing all in his power to make up for his error. He was running hard, his hoofs beating so rapid a tattoo that the sound blended into a steady drum roll.

He gained the first relay station without the sorrel breaking stride, and he left the horse regretfully, wishing he might have him or his equal to ride the rest of the long journey. The girl was not in the yard as he made the exchange and he yelled, "Lincoln got elected!" at the old man who stood ready with his fresh mount. The man called back: "How's that?"

but Danny was surging away and there was no time in which to repeat the news.

He was in the low-foothill country now, an area where the trail wound through a maze of bubble-like formations covered by thin brush and rock. It was the slowest section of the route and as the buckskin hammered his way up and down the grades and around the numberless curves, Danny saw the lead the sorrel had given him melt away.

He raised his eyes. A long slope faced him. It was one of the few straight stretches to be found in the hills and it led to a naked summit that rose several hundred feet above the surrounding land. Beyond it, he recalled, lay a wide swale. Once over the rim the buckskin could do better.

Suddenly the horse paused in stride. Danny saw first a puff of white smoke off to the side of the road. Then came the dry slap of a gunshot. The buckskin's head went down, then snapped up as his legs folded beneath him. Danny felt himself soaring through space. Abruptly the ground came up and met him with solid, sickening force.

He fought his way back to consciousness slowly. His head ached and there was a stabbing pain in his left shoulder. He became aware of voices and opened his eyes. He lay full length in a sandy wash a few yards from the road. The luckless buckskin, dead, was just beyond. The *mochila*, the contents of its unlocked pocket strewn about, was close by. A newspaper, unfolded, its bold black headlines proclaiming the election of Abraham Lincoln to the Presidency, had been examined and tossed aside.

"How long you stalling around here?"

Danny started. Pete Newton's voice! Ignoring the

pain that raced through him, he twisted about to where he could see better. The two men were a dozen paces to the right. They had shed their city clothing, were now dressed for hard riding. Newton was tightening the cinch of his saddle.

"Not long. Got to get rid of him and that mail. Then I'll be coming."

Newton hesitated. "Could lend you a hand."

"Better not take the time. Sooner we get the word passed to Nate, the better. Shape that nag of mine's in, I'd slow you down, anyway."

Pete Newton finished his chore, swung onto his horse. "Maybe you ought to just leave things as they are. Ain't so sure it's smart to go fooling around with the U.S. mail—"

Stanger swore impatiently. "Quit fretting about it! Let me take care of my end. You get the word to Tobin. He stands to make a pile of cash on this deal and I sure wouldn't want to be the one who knocked him out of it."

Newton muttered something and pulled his horse about, headed for the road. "So long," he called back over his shoulder. Stanger only nodded.

Understanding came quickly to Danny Thorpe. Tobin was gambling heavily on the election. By knowing the results in advance and also delaying the delivery of that information, he stood to make a fortune. Stanger and Newton had been dispatched to accomplish that end.

A hopelessness settled over Danny as frustration gripped him. Why did it have to happen to him? Why did Tobin's thugs have to choose the very run he was on? Was it because he was a green rider on the job?

Or was it that such things always seem to come his way?

That was it, he concluded bitterly. That—and the fact that the run he was on was the longest, most forsaken and desolate stretch in the entire line. Such made it easy for them to work their plan. *Let something go haywire—and it'll end up in my lap*, he moaned softly.

Through despairing eyes he watched Newton strike off westward. Stanger, too, kept his gaze on the departing man for a time, then turned, walked leisurely toward Danny. His jaw was set and his hand rested on the butt of the pistol hanging at his hip. Danny felt his throat tighten. He would have no chance against a killer such as Bill Stanger; all he could do was lie still, feign unconsciousness. Maybe something would turn up—a bit of good luck. . .

Luck!

The word caught in Danny Thorpe's mind, began to glow vividly. What was it old Pat McCoskey had said? *A man makes his own luck*. It was true, he realized. It was wrong to just sit back, take what fate threw at him—and not fight. When a man fought for his rights, he changed things, made them go his way. Maybe he failed in the trying, maybe he even died—but at least he'd had a hand in his own destiny.

A hard core of denial, of brittle resentment, began to build within Danny Thorpe. He still had his pistol. Bill Stanger and Newton held him in such low esteem they had not bothered to remove it. But it was under him and he could not reach it without moving. He dared not do that. Let Stanger think him still unconscious; against a killer like him it was necessary to lessen the odds in some way.

Stanger halted a step to his left, a tower of intimidation staring down at the small man. Danny could feel his cold eyes drilling into the back of his head. Stanger was considering his next move. Danny waited, utterly motionless. After an eternity Stanger turned, walked to where the open newspaper lay, something apparently capturing his attention.

Danny gathered his strength. He must act now or forever be lost. Ignoring the pain in his shoulder, he came to a crouching position, drew his weapon. Stanger was still reading, his back partly turned. A faint dizziness swept through Danny, and then a sudden wave of doubt. He brushed both away, sprang upright.

At the sound of crunching sand Stanger whirled. His mouth dropped open in surprise, then hardened. A broad, patronizing grin spread over his dark face.

"Now, Shorty, you know you're too little to go messing around with a gun," he said in a dry, sarcastic voice. "Better you drop it," he added, and reached for his own weapon.

Danny fired once. Stanger jolted as the bullet smashed into his chest. Again surprise blanked his features. He frowned and abruptly caved in, went full length onto the warming sand.

Danny wasted no time checking the effect of his single bullet. He spun, dropped to his knees beside the *mochila*. Scooping up the spilled mail, he crammed it into its pocket, snapped the flap into place. Rising, he ran to Stanger's horse, threw the leather blanket into position, and mounted. Spurring the long-legged bay roughly, he got him back to the road and struck out hard for the next relay station.

The bay should last that far, he reasoned, rubbing at his throbbing shoulder. Then, with a fresh horse he would have a good chance of overtaking Pete Newton. He had lost a good half hour, possibly more, so he could forget his hopes of making a record run. But he would get the mail through.

The bay began to tire after the first five miles of steady running. Danny slacked up on the reins. It would be folly to run the horse into the ground. He must nurse the brute along, keep him going even if it resolved into a slow trot. Anything would be faster than being on foot.

He wondered if Pete Newton's horse was in the same condition, guessed it likely was. A new thought entered his mind: Tobin had probably set up a relay of his own. Courtright had mentioned three strangers. Two of them would have been Stanger and Newton. The third was likely stationed somewhere further along the route—and if that was true then there would be others strung out all the way to San Francisco. Overtaking and halting Newton loomed more important to Danny Thorpe at that realization.

He reached the relay point with the bay near exhaustion. The hostler stared at him as he came off the saddle and leaped onto his remount.

"You're late!" the man shouted.

Danny shook his head, called back: "Lincoln won!" and raced on down the road.

He felt better now with a fresh horse under him. He wished there had been time enough to inquire about Newton, ask the hostler if he had noted a passing rider, but he could not afford the delay. Arriving so far behind schedule was going to be a mark against him, could even place his hopes for permanent assignment in jeopardy. It was best he recover all the time possible. He would see Pete Newton soon enough. The sorrel he now rode was covering the ground with amazing speed—or else it seemed so after the slow grind on Stanger's worn bay.

He caught a glimpse of Tobin's man a half hour later. Newton was topping out a rise a quarter mile distant. He heard the beat of the sorrel and Danny watched him twist about, could visualize the surprise that would cover his face.

Immediately Newton began to flog his horse, moving then at an easy gallop. Danny considered the man's frantic efforts to pull away, at least to maintain his lead. But his mount was no match for the fresh sorrel. The gap closed rapidly. When no more than a hundred yards separated them, Newton resorted to his pistol and began to shoot. Danny had hoped it would not come to gunplay; the shock of having killed Bill Stanger was still a heavy sickness within him. Yet he knew deep in his mind that it was useless to hope; men such as Newton and Stanger recognized no other solution when cornered.

He drew his own weapon, bided his time. The distance between them was still too great for a handgun. The sorrel thundered on. The spread decreased. Newton, reloading, opened up again. Danny heard the angry whirr of bullets. He was close enough. He leveled off on Newton, aiming for the man's shoulder, squeezed the trigger twice. Newton bucked on his saddle, heaved to one side. Immediately his horse slowed, began to veer away. Newton's gun fell to the ground, sending up a spurt of dry dust when it struck.

The horse stopped. Newton folded, clung to the saddle horn.

Danny, not slackening his speed, drew abreast. He threw a searching glance at the man, saw that he was only wounded. He sighed in relief, shouted: "I'll send somebody back for you!" and rushed on.

He was feeling better now. He had halted Tobin's makeshift relay, checked his scheme to fleece a lot of people—a scheme in which the Pony Express had been an innocent participant. And he had won over himself. He smiled grimly at that thought; yes, he had won the battle—but likely he had lost the war.

He swept into the next relay station, paused only long enough to shout instructions concerning Pete Newton, and then hurried on determined to make up as much lost time as possible. But a mile is a mile and a horse can do only so much. When he rode into Smith's Crossing late that night, he knew he was nearly an hour behind schedule.

Weary, dejected, expecting the worst, he entered the station. Explanations would mean nothing; they would sound like alibis. To be sure, he could produce the reason for his delay. He could have Newton brought in, but Newton, of course, would deny everything—as would Nate Tobin. And Stanger was dead. It would help little anyway. Other Pony Express riders had such problems, dealt with them, and still managed to maintain their schedules. It was a part of the job and expected of them.

"Running a mite hehind, ain't you, boy?"

Pat McCoskey's raspy voice cut him like a whip. He hauled up sharply, stared at the superintendent while his spirits sagged lower. McCoskey had ridden out to check on him, to see what sort of job he was doing. On that he would base his decision as to whether Danny Thorpe became a permanent employee or not.

"Afraid I am," Danny said miserably. "Sorry about it."

"Sorry!" McCoskey rumbled. "What're you being sorry for? Far as I'm concerned, you done fine. New men generally get all fired up trying to impress everybody about how good they are. Do their best to make the run faster'n it ever been done before. Glad to see you ain't that kind. Show's you'll make a good rider."

Danny's eyes filled with disbelief. A grin cracked his lips. Then he sobered. He had to be honest about it. "Yes, sir, but I was—" he began and then checked his words as Wylie Courtright frowned, shook his head meaningfully at him.

"Time average was real good," station agent said, stepping up to McCoskey's side. "Figures out a little more than sixteen and a half hours each way. And you had a heavy *mochila*. Can't ask for much better from a new man."

"And I ain't," McCoskey added, smiling, something he was seldom guilty of. "Hope you like it here with Wylie, son. It's going to be your regular station."

Danny could only bob his head happily. Something was blocking his throat, choking him, causing his heart to sing with a joy he had never known. He couldn't put it into words even to himself, but a wonderful thing had happened; Danny Thorpe had at last found himself and his place.

The Debt of Hardy Buckelew

by Elmer Kelton

I GUESS you'd call him crazy. We did, that spring of '78 when old man Hardy Buckelew set out to square his account against the Red River.

That was my third year to help graze the Box H steer herd from South Texas up the Western Trail toward Dodge. The first year I had just been the wrangler, bringing up the *remuda* to keep the riders in fresh mounts. A button job, was all. The second year they promoted me. Didn't matter that they put me back at the dusty tail end of the herd to push up the drags. It was a cowboy job, and I was drawing a man's wages, pretty near.

Old Hardy Buckelew had only one son—a big, rawboned, overgrown kid by the name of Jim, wilder than a Spanish pony. They used to say there was nothing Jim Buckelew couldn't whip, and if anything ever did show up, old man Hardy would whip it for him. That's the way the Buckelews were.

I never did see but one thing Jim couldn't whip, but we'll get to that directly.

Jim was only nineteen first time I saw him. That young, he wasn't supposed to be going in saloons and suchlike. He did anyway; he was so big for his age that nobody paid him much mind. Or, if they did notice him, maybe they knew they'd have to throw him out to get rid of him. That wouldn't have been much fun.

One time in San Antonio he fell into a card game with a pair of sharpers, and naturally they fleeced him. He raised a ruckus, so the two of them throwed together and lit into him. They never would have whipped him if the bartender in cahoots with them hadn't busted a bottle over Jim's head.

Now, a man who ever saw old Hardy Buckelew get mad would never forget it as long as he lived. He was one of those old-time Texas cowmen—the likes of which the later generations never saw. He stood six feet tall in his brush-scarred boots. He had a hide as tough as the mesquite land he rode in and a heart as stout as a black Mexican bull. When he hollered at a man, his voice would carry a way yonder, and you could bet the last dollar you owned that whoever he hollered at would come a-running, too.

Old Hardy got plenty mad that time, when Jim came limping in broke and bruised and bloody. The old man took him way off to one side for a private lecture, but we could hear Hardy Buckelew's bull voice as far as we could see him.

Next day he gathered up every man he could spare, me included, and we all rode a-horseback to San Antonio. We marched into the saloon where the fight had taken place and marched everybody else out—everybody but the bartender and the two gamblers. They were talking big, but their faces were white as clabber. Old Hardy busted a bottle over the bartender's head and laid him out colder than a wedge. Then he switched those fiery eyes of his to Jim Buckelew and jabbed his stubby thumb in the direction of the gamblers.

"Now this time," he said, "do the job right!"

Jim did. When we left there, three men lay sprawled in the wet sawdust. Jim Buckelew was grinning at us, showing a chipped front tooth like it was a medal from Jeff Davis himself. His knuckles were torn and red-smeared as he counted out the money he had taken back from the gamblers' pockets.

Old man Hardy's voice was rough, but you couldn't miss the edging of pride in it. "From now on, Jimbo, whether it's a man or a job, don't you ever take a whippin' and quit. No matter how many times it takes, a Buckelew keeps on comin' till he's won."

Now then, to the debt of Hardy Buckelew.

Late in the summer of '77 we finished a cow hunt and threw together a herd of Box H steers to take to Kansas and the railroad before winter set in. Hardy Buckelew never made the trip himself any more—too many years had stacked up on him. For a long time now, Will Peril had been his trail boss. Will was a man a cowboy liked to follow—a graying, medium-sized man with the years just commencing to put a slump in his shoulders. His voice was as soft as the hide of a baby calf, and he had a gentle way with horses and cattle. Where most of us might tear up enough ground to plant a potato patch, Will Peril could make livestock do what he wanted them to without ever raising the dust.

He handled men the same way.

This time, though, Hardy Buckelew slipped a joker in the deck.

"Will," Hardy said, "it's time Jimbo took on a man's responsibilities. He's twenty-one now, so I'm puttin' him in charge of this trail herd. I just want you to go along and kind of keep an eye on him. You know, give him his head, but keep one hand on the reins, just in case."

Will Peril frowned, twisting his mule-hide gloves and looking off to where the cook was loading the chuck wagon. "Some men take longer growin' up than others do, Hardy. You really think he's ready?"

"You want to teach a boy to swim, you throw him in where the water's deep. Sure, he'll make some mistakes, but the education he gets'll be worth the price."

So we pointed them north with a new trail boss in charge. Now, Jim was a good cowboy, make no mistake about that; he was just a shade wild, is all. He pushed too fast and didn't give the cattle time enough to graze along and put on weight as they walked. He was reckless, too, in the way he rode, in the way he tried to curb the stampedes we had before we got the cattle trail-broke. He swung in front of the bunch one night, spurring for all he was worth. His horse stepped in a hole and snapped its leg with a sound like a pistol shot. For a minute there, we thought Jim was a goner. But more often than not a running herd will split around a man on foot. They did this time. Jim just walked away laughing. He'd have spit in the devil's eye.

All in all, though, Jim did a better job than most of us hands thought he would. That is, till we got to the Red River.

It had been raining off an on for three days when we bunched the cattle on the south bank of the Red. The river was rolling strong, all foamy and so muddy you could almost walk on it. You could hear the roar a long time before you got there.

The trail had been used a lot that year, and the grass was grazed down short. Will Peril set out downriver to find feed enough that we could hold the cattle while we waited for the water to run down. He was barely out of sight when Jim Buckelew raised his hat and signaled for the point man to take cattle out into the river.

"You're crazy, Jim!" exclaimed the cook, a limping old Confederate veteran by the name of Few Lively. "A duck couldn't stay afloat in that water!"

But Jim might have had cotton in his ears for all the attention he paid. When the point man held back, Jim spurred his horse out into that roaring river with the same wild grin he had when he waded into those San Antonio gamblers. Him shaming us that way, there was nothing the rest of us could do but follow in behind him, pushing the cattle.

The steers didn't like that river. It was all we could do to force them into it. They bobbed up and down, their heads out of the water and their horns swaying back and forth like a thousand old-fashioned rocking chairs. The force of the current started pulling them downriver. Up at the point, Jim Buckelew was fighting along, keeping the leaders swimming, pushing them for the far bank.

For a while there it looked like we might make it. Then, better than halfway across, the lead steers began to tire out. They still had heart in them, but tired legs couldn't keep fighting that torrent. Jim

Buckelew had a coiled rope in his hand, slapping at the steers' heads, his angry voice lost in the roar of the flood. It was no use; the river had them.

And somehow Jim Buckelew lost his seat. We saw him splash into the muddy water, so far out yonder that no one could reach him. We saw his arms waving, saw him go under. Then we lost sight of him out there in all that foam, among those drowning cattle.

The heart went out of all us. The main part of the herd milled and swam back. It was all we could do to get ourselves and the cattle to the south bank. Not an animal made it to the far side.

It was all over by the time Will Peril returned. We spent the next day gathering cattle that had managed to climb out way yonder down the river. Along toward evening, as the Red dropped, we found Jim Buckelew's body where it had washed in with an uprooted tree. We wrapped him in his blankets and slicker and dug a grave for him. A gentle rain started again like a quiet benediction as Will Peril finished reading over him out of the chuck-box Bible.

The burial done, we stood there numb with shock and grief and chill. Will Peril stuck the Bible inside his shirt, beneath the slicker.

"We haven't got a man to spare," he said tightly, "but somebody's got to go back and tell Hardy."

His eyes fell on me.

It had been bad enough, watching Jim Buckelew die helpless in that boiling river. In a way it was even worse, I think, standing there on the gallery of the big house with my hat all wadded up in my hand, watching old Hardy Buckelew die inside.

He never swayed, never showed a sign of a tear in his gray eyes. But he seemed somehow to shrink up from his six feet. That square, leather face of his just seemed to come to pieces. His huge hands balled into fists, then loosened and began to tremble. He turned away from me, letting his gaze drift out across the sun-cured grass and the far-stretching tangle of thorny mesquite range that he had planned to pass down to Jim. When he turned back to me, he was an old man. An old, old man.

"The cattle," he whispered, "did Jim get them across?"

I shook my head. "No, sir, we lost a couple hundred head. The rest got back to the south bank."

"He never did quit, though, did he? Kept on tryin' all the way?"

"He never quit till he went under, Mister Buckelew."

That meant a lot of him, I could tell. He asked, "Think you could find Jimbo's grave for me?"

"Yes, sir, we marked it."

The old man's voice seemed a hundred miles away, and his mind, too. "Get some rest, then. We'll leave at daylight."

Using the buckboard, we followed the wide, tromped-out cattle trail all the way up to the Red River. We covered more ground in one day than the herd had moved in three or four. And one afternoon we stood beside Jim Buckelew's grave. The cowboys had put up a little brush fence around it to keep trail cattle from walking over it and knocking down the marker.

The old man stood there a long time with his hat in his hand as he looked at his son's resting place. Occasionally his eyes would lift to the river, three hundred yards away. The water had gone down now. The Red moved along sluggish and sleepy, innocent as could be. The dirty-water marks of silt and debris far up on the banks were all that showed for the violence we had seen there.

Then it was that I heard Hardy Buckelew speak in a voice that sent fingers of ice crawling up my spine. He wasn't talking to me.

"I'll be back, Jimbo. Nothin' has ever beat a Buckelew. We got a debt here, and it's goin' to be paid. You watch, Jimbo, I'll be back!"

I had never really been afraid of Hardy Buckelew before. But now I saw something in his face that made me afraid, a little bit.

He turned toward the buckboard. "Let's go home," he said.

All those days of traveling for that single hour beside the river. And now we were going home again.

The old man wasn't the same after that. He stayed to himself, getting grayer and thinner. When he rode out, he went alone and not with the boys. He spent a lot of his time just puttering around the big house or out at the barn, feeding and currying and petting a roan colt that had been Jim's favorite. He never came to the cook shack any more. The ranch cook sent his meals up to the big house, and most of it would come back uneaten.

When the trail crew finally returned from Dodge City, old Hardy didn't even come out. Will Peril had to take his report and the bank draft up to the big house.

Will was shaking his head when he came to the

cook shack for supper. There was worry in his eyes. "The thing's eatin' on him," he said, "turnin' him in on himself. I tell you, boys, if he don't get off of it, it'll drive him out of his mind."

Knowing how much Will loved that old cowman, I didn't feel like telling him what Hardy had said at the grave by the Red River. The way I saw it, Hardy Buckelew was pretty far gone already.

When winter came on, he just seemed to hole up in the big house. He didn't come out much, and when he did we wished we hadn't seen him. For a time there, we didn't expect him to live through the winter. But spring came and he was still with us. He began coming down to the cook shack sometimes, a living ghost who sat at the end of the long table, deaf and blind to what went on around him.

Time came for the spring cow hunt. Hardy delegated all of his responsibility to Will Peril, and the chuck wagon moved out.

"He won't live to see this roundup finished," Will said. You could see the tears start in his eyes. "One of these days we'll have to quit work to come in and bury him."

But Will was wrong. As the new grass rose, so did Hardy Buckelew. The life that stirred the prairies and brought green leaves to the mesquite brush seemed to touch the old man, too. You could see the change in him from one day to the next, almost. He strengthened up, the flesh coming back to his broad shoulders and his square face. He commenced visiting the wagon more and more often, until one day he brought out his bedroll and pitched it on the ground along with the rest of ours.

We thought then that we had him back—the same

old Hardy Buckelew. But he wasn't the same. No, sir, he was another man.

The deep lines of grief that had etched into his face were still there, and we knew they would never fade. Some new fire smoldered in his eyes like camp coals banked for the night. There was a hatred in that fire, yet we saw nothing for him to hate. What had happened was nobody's fault.

As the strength came back he worked harder than any man in the outfit. Seemed like he never slept. More often than not, he was the one who woke up the cook of a morning and got the coffeepot on to boil. He was always on the go, wearing out horses almost as fast as we could bring them them up for him.

"Tryin' to forget by drivin' himself into the grave," Will Peril said darkly. "I almost wish he was still mopin' around that ranchhouse."

So did some of the others. Hardy got so hard to follow that three of his cowboys quit. Two "reps" for other outfits left the Box H wagon and swore they wouldn't come back for anything less than his funeral. Hardy didn't even seem like he noticed.

We finished the regular spring works, and we had a sizable bunch of big steers thrown together for the trip up the trail to Dodge. For those of us who usually made the drive, it was a welcome time. We were tickled to death with the idea of getting away from Hardy Buckelew awhile. I think even Will Peril, much as he thought of the boss, was looking forward to a little breathing spell himself.

We spent several days getting the outfit ready. We put a fresh trail brand on the steers so that if they ever got mixed up with another bunch we could know them easy. We wouldn't have to stretch a bunch of them out with ropes and clip away the hair to find the brands.

You could tell the difference in the men as we got ready. There wasn't much cheer among those that were fixing to stay home, but the trail crew was walking around light as feathers. Trail driving being the hard, hot, dusty, sleepless and once-in-a-while dangerous work that it was, I don't know why anybody would look forward to it. But we did.

The night before we started, Hardy Buckelew dropped us the bad news. He was going, too.

Will Peril argued with him till he was blue in the face. "You know what it's like to go up that trail, Hardy—you've done it often enough. You're not in any condition to be makin' the trip."

Will Peril was the only man Hardy Buckelew ever let argue with him, and even Will didn't do it much.

"Who owns this outfit?" Hardy asked.

"You do," Will said.

"What part of this outfit is yours?"

"None of it," Will admitted.

"Then shut up about it. I'm goin', and if you don't like it you can stay home!"

Right about then I imagine Will was tempted to. But you could see the trouble in his eyes as he studied Hardy Buckelew. He wouldn't let the old man get off on that trail without being around someplace to watch out for him.

Hardy didn't bother anybody much the first few days. It was customary to drive the cattle hard the first week or so. Partly that was to get them off the range they were used to and reduce the temptation for them to stray back. Partly it was to keep them too tired to run at night till they were used to trail routine.

Hardy rode up at swing position, leaving everybody pretty much alone. Once in a while you would see him turn in the saddle and look back, but he didn't have anything to say. Seemed like everything suited him—at first.

But one morning after we had been on the trail a week he changed complexion. As we strung the cattle out off the bedgrounds Will Peril told the point man to slow it down. "We got them pretty well trail-broke," he said. "We'll let them start puttin' on a little weight now."

But Hardy Buckelew came riding up like a Mexican bull looking for a fight. "You don't do no such of a thing! We'll keep on pushin' them!"

Will couldn't have been more surprised if Hardy had set fire to the chuck wagon. "Hardy, we keep on like we started, they won't be nothin' but hide racks, time we get to Dodge."

Hardy Buckelew didn't bother to argue with him. He just straightened up and gave Will that "I'm the boss around here" look that not even Will would argue with. Hardy rode back to the drags and commenced pushing the slow ones.

From then on, Hardy took over the herd. The first couple of days Will Peril tried every way he could to slow things down. But Hardy would just run over him. Will finally gave up and took a place at swing, his shoulders slumped like he had been demoted to horse wrangler. In a way, I guess you might say he had.

Hardy Buckelew was as hard to get along with on

the trail as he had been on the cow hunt—harder, maybe. He was up of a morning before first light, routing everybody out of bed. "Catch up on your sleep next winter," he would growl. And he wouldn't let the drive stop till it was too dark to see. I remember the afternoon early in the drive when Few Lively found a nice little creek and started setting up camp on it. It was about six o'clock when the point came even with the place. If Will had been bossing the outfit, right there's where we would have bedded the herd. But Hardy Buckelew rode up to the wagon in a lope, looking like he was fixing to fight somebody.

"What're you doin' here? he demanded.

Few Lively swallowed about twice, wondering what he had done wrong. "I always camp here if we make it about this time of day. Good water, plenty of grass. Ain't nothin' ahead of us half as good."

Hardy's face was dark with anger. "There's two more hours of good daylight. Now you git that team hitched up and that camp moved a couple more miles up the trail."

As cook, and as one of the old men of the outfit, Few wasn't used to being talked to that way. "There's ain't no good water up there, Mister Buckelew."

"We'll drink what there is or do without. Now you git movin'!"

Hardy was like that, day in and day out. He would wear out four or five horses a day, just riding back and forth from drag up to the point and back again, stopping every little bit to cuss somebody out and tell him to push them harder. We rode from can-see to can't, Hardy's rough voice never very far away. Not able to fight Hardy Buckelew, and having to work it off someway, some of the boys took to fighting with one another. A couple of them just sneaked off one night while they were on night guard. Didn't ask for their time or anything. Didn't want to face Hardy Buckelew.

Time we got to the Red River, the whole outfit was about ready to bust up. I think if any one man had led off, the rest of us would have ridden out behind him, leaving Hardy Buckelew alone with all those steers. Oh, Will Peril probably would have stayed, but nobody else. That's the way it usually is, though. Everybody waits for somebody else to start, and nobody does.

Like the year before, it was raining when we got to the Red. The river was running a little bigger than usual when Will Peril rode up ahead to take a look at it. He came back and told the point man to keep on going till he reached the other side.

Hardy Buckelew had loped up right after Will Peril and took a long look at the river. He came back holding his hand up in the air, motioning the men to stop.

"We're goin' to camp right here."

Middle of the day, and Hardy Buckelew wanted to camp! We looked at each other like we couldn't believe it, and I think we all agreed on one thing. He'd finally gone crazy.

Will Peril said, "Hardy, that river's just right to cross now. Got just enough water runnin' to swim them and keep them out of the quicksand. Not enough current to give them a lot of trouble."

Hardy shrugged his shoulders as if he had already said all he wanted to about it. "We're goin' to camp—rest up these cattle."

Will was getting angry now, his face red and his fists clenched up. "Hardy, it's rainin'. If we don't get them across now, we're liable to have to wait for days."

Hardy just turned and gave him a look that would melt a bar of lead. "This is *my* herd, Will. I say we're goin' to rest these cattle."

And rest them we did, there on the south bank of the Red, with the rain falling and the river beginning to swell. Will Peril would go down by the river and pace awhile, then come back and try arguing again. He had just as well have sat down with the rest of us and kept dry under the big wagon sheet stretched out from the wagon. He couldn't have moved Hardy Buckelew with a team of horses.

We were camped close to Jim Buckelew's grave. Old Hardy rode off down there and spent awhile. He came back with his eyes aglow like they had been the fall before, when I had brought him here in the buckboard. He spent little time under the wagon sheet, in the dry. He would stand alone in the rain and stare at that mud-red river.

"He'll catch his death out there," Will Peril muttered, watching the old man like a mother hen watches a chick. But he didn't go out to get him.

The old man had never said a word to anybody about Jim. Still, we knew that was all he was thinking of. We could almost feel Jim right there in camp with us. It was an eerie thing, I'll tell you. I would be glad when we got out of that place.

The second day, after standing by the river a long time, Hardy walked in and spoke to Will Peril. "Is the river the way it was the day Jim drowned?"

Will's eyes were almost closed. "No, I'd say it was a little worse that day."

The old man went out in the rain and watched the river some more. It kept rising. He came back with the same question, and Will gave him the same answer. Now an alarm was starting in Will's face.

Finally the old man came back the third time. "Is it as big now as it was that day?"

Will Peril's cheekbones seemed to stand out as the skin drew tight in his whiskered face. "I reckon it is."

The look that came into the old man's gray eyes then was something I never saw before and have never seen again. He turned toward his horse. "All right, boys," he said evenly, "let's go now. We're puttin' them across!"

Talk about surprise, most of us stood there with our mouths open like we'd been hit in the head with the flat side of an ax. But not Will Peril. He must have sensed it coming on. He knew the old man better than anybody.

"You've waited too long, Hardy," he said. "Now it can't be done."

"We couldn't go across earlier," spoke Hardy. "We'd have been cheatin' Jimbo. No Buckelew ever started anything but what it got finished. We're goin' to finish this job for *him*." Hardy shoved his left foot in the stirrup and started to swing into the saddle.

Will Peril took three long strides toward him. "Listen to me, Hardy; I'm goin' to tell it to you straight. Jim rode off into somethin' too big for him and knew it. He was playin' the fool. You've got no call to take it up for him."

Hardy's eyes blazed. If he had had a gun. I think he would have shot Will.

"He was my boy, Will. He was a Buckelew," Hardy's eyes left Will and settled on the rest of us. "How about it, you-all comin'?"

We all just stood there.

Hardy looked us over, one by one. We couldn't meet his eyes. "Then stay here," he said bitterly, swinging into the saddle. "I'll do it alone!"

Will Peril was close to him now. Will reached out and grabbed the reins. "No, Hardy. If you won't stop, I'll stop you!"

"Let go, Will!"

"Get down, Hardy!"

They stared hard at each other, neither man giving any ground. All of a sudden the old man swung down and waded into Will.

Will wasn't young but he was younger than Hardy Buckelew. Most of us thought it would be over with in a hurry. It was, but not the way we expected. Hardy was like a wild man, something driving him as we had never seen him driven before. He took Will by storm. His fists pounded Will like mallets, the sound of them solid and hard, like the strike of an ax against a tree. Will tried, but he couldn't stand up under that. Hardy beat him back, and back, and finally down.

The old man stood over him, swaying as he tried for breath. His hands and face were bloody, his eyes afire. "How about it now?" he asked us again. "You comin'?" When we didn't, he just turned and went back to his horse.

You almost had to figure him crazy, the way he

worked those cattle, getting them started, forcing the first of them off into the water. We stood around like snake-charmed rabbits, watching. We'd picked Will Peril up and dragged him under the wagon sheet, out of the rain. He sat on the muddy ground, shaking his head, his gaze following Hardy Buckelew.

"You tried," I told Will. "You can't blame yourself for what he does now."

Will could see that Hardy was going to take at least a few of those cattle out into the water, with or without us. The trail boss stood up shakily.

"You boys can do what you want to. I'll not let him fight it alone!"

We looked at Will, catching up his horse, then we looked at each other. In a minute we were all on horseback, following.

It was the same as it had been the last time, the water running bankwide and strong. It was a hard fight, just to get those cattle out into the river. They were smarter than us, maybe—they didn't want to go. I don't really know how we did it, but we got it done. Old Hardy Buckelew took the point, and we strung them out.

Time or two there, I saw the leaders begin to drift and I thought it was over for Hardy the way it had been for Jim. But Hardy Buckelew was fighting hard, and Will Peril moved up there to help him.

I can't rightly say what the difference was that we made it this time, and we hadn't the time before. Maybe it was the rest the cattle and horses had before they started across. Maybe they were tougher, too, the way they had been driven. But mostly I think it was that determined old man up there ahead of us, hollering and swinging his rope and raising hell. He was crazy for going, and we were crazy for following him.

But we made it.

It was a cold and hungry bunch of water-soaked cowboys that threw the herd together on the north bank of the Red. We couldn't get the chuck wagon across—didn't even try—so we went without supper that night and slept without blankets.

But I don't think anybody really minded it much, once it was over. There was the knowledge that we had taken the Red's challenge and made it across. Then, too, there was the satisfaction we got out of seeing peace come into Hardy Buckelew's face. We could tell by looking at him that he was one of us again, for the first time in nearly a year.

Next morning we got the wagon across and had a chance to fill our bellies with beef and beans and hot coffee. At Few Lively's fire, Hardy Buckelew looked at Will Peril and said:

"From here on, Will, I'm turnin' it back over to you. Run it the way you want to. I'm goin' home."

Surprised, Will said, "Home? Why?"

Hardy Buckelew smiled calmly. "You were right, Will, I'm too old for this foolishness. But I owed Jimbo a debt. And I'd say that you and me—all the boys in the outfit—have paid it in full."

The Man We Called Jones

by T. V. Olsen

THE GUN? The .45 hanging over the mantel? Why, sure; look at it. Look at it, but don't handle the belt, son. It's old, over sixty years old. Leather's brittle, hasn't been worked. Like to fall apart.

Why do I keep it there? I can tell you a story about it if you want. Really a story about the man who owned it. The bravest and best man I ever knew. . . .

It was way back, the summer of 1890. This same valley. I was seventeen that year. You weren't yet a twinkle in your pappy's eye, so it'll take a sight of doing for you to see it as it was then. You made your way by team, by horseback, or walked. Roads were mud, mud, mud.

The valley was all big ranches, or rather most one big ranch. That'd be Kurt Gavin's Anchor. Gavin came into the country early after the last tide of gold-seekers was drifting out, drove his stakes deep and far, and being a little bigger and a little tougher than most others, he made it stick.

By '90 with the Cheyennes long pacified and the

territory opened to homesteading, Gavin was the biggest man in the valley, nigh the biggest in the territory. Even his swelling herds couldn't graze the whole of the open range he laid claim to. Least, that's what the homestead farmers figured. Or sodbusters, as the cattlemen called 'em—the *damned* sodbusters who came in with their plows and chewed up the good graze.

Which is what we did in Gavin's eyes to the range he called his, because Uncle Jace and me were among the first. We'd had strong ties back in Ohio, but my ma had been dead a good many years. Typhoid-pneumonia had taken Pa in '89. Uncle Jace and Pa had been mighty close brothers. They'd run the farm together for years, and the old home held too many memories for Uncle Jace. He hadn't any family or close kin left, 'cept for me, and nothing to hold him from pulling stakes for the West, which he'd always wanted.

A year after Pa's death saw me and Uncle Jace running a shoestring outfit on Gavin's east range. Gavin give word to his riders to hooraw us off, and I tell you the high-spirited lads made our lives some miserable what with cutting our barbed wire and riding shortcuts through our fields, or riding past the house of a midnight after a drunk in town, screeching, shooting at the sky.

You could call Uncle Jace a peaceable man, but he was that stubborn he wouldn't budge off what was his by law. And when Gavin's crew pulled down a whole section of fence by roping the posts and dragging it away with the ponies, Unc's temper busted. Him and me were out scouting boundary that morning when we found the fence down and some Anchor cows foraging in the young corn. They'd even left one rope on the fence to make their sign plain.

Unc was mad clean through, though not so's you could see it—'less you knew Unc. Me helping, he hazed the cows out cool as you please, and we got tools and repaired the fence, Uncle Jace giving brief, jerky orders in as few words as needed.

Afterward, grimy and soaked with sweat, he turned to me. "Get on your horse, Howie. I'm going to see Gavin."

We cut across the Anchor land on a beeline for the ranch headquarters, Uncle Jace riding ahead. He was a huge-framed man, though so leaned-down with hard work, the clothes hung on him like tattered cast-offs on a scarecrow. Even so, with the big back of him erect and high in his wrath, I could almost hear his rage crackle across the space between us.

Unc didn't pack a sidearm. He had his old Union issue Spencer .54 in the saddle boot under his leg, and I'd seen him drive nailheads with it, and I was some squirrelly, I tell you.

It must have been ten minutes later when we sighted the little knot of horsemen off to our left, and Unc quartered his bronc around so we were heading for them. I caught his thought then—that these were the jiggers who pulled the fence down and ran that Anchor beef through the break.

Coming near up, we saw all five of them were mounted but not moving, and then we saw why. They were grouped under one of the big old ironwoods you don't see anymore, and there was a rope tied to a spreading bough. The end of the rope was noosed around the neck of one of them, a little fella with his hands tied at his back. They were all of them motionless, waiting on our approach.

The little one I'd never seen, but the other four all were all Anchor crewmen I recognized—one of them Gavin's tough ramrod, Tod Carradine. He was a tall, pale-eyed Texan with ice in his smile, cocky, sure of himself. The others were ordinary punchers with the look of men ready for a dirty job they didn't relish, but held to be necessary.

"Howdy, Tod," Uncle Jace said in a voice easy-neutral without being friendly. "Hemp cravat for the man?"

"Why yes, Devereux," said Carradine in a voice amused, also without being friendly. "You ever see this little man before?"

Unc shook his head no without taking his eyes off Carradine. He wasn't worried about the others.

Carradine pointed lazily at the hip of the horse the little fella sat. It bore an Anchor brand. "We found him hypering off our range on this bronc." Carradine smiled, altogether pleasant. "Suit you, Devereux?" he then asked in a voice suggesting he didn't give a damn how Unc was suited.

It was open and shut, far as I could see. A stranger had been caught riding off Anchor range on an Anchor horse. The answer for that was one no Westerner would argue. That's why I was surprised when Uncle Jace's glance shuttled to the little fella.

"Friend," Unc said quietly, "speak out your say. It's your right. How'd it happen?"

The little man looked up slowly. His head had been bent and I hadn't seen his face full till now. It was shocking, pitiful, ravaged somehow in a way I couldn't explain. He gave a bare tilt of his head toward Carradine, murmured, "However he says," and looked down again.

Carradine smiled fully at Unc. He repeated: "Suit you, Devereux?"

"Not quite," Uncle Jace frowned, looking back at the Anchor foreman.

Carradine was still smiling, uncertainly. It had only come to him then what this was building to. He was the only Anchor man packing a gun, and I saw the instant impulse chase through his mind.

Uncle Jace didn't waste time. He never wasted time, or words either. Somehow the old Spencer cavalry carbine was ready to his hand, and he laid it light across the pommel. "Don't even think about it, Tod," Unc advised mildly. "Howie, cut the gent loose. Give him a hand down. Tod, take what's yours and keep your dogs off my fence-line. Or I'll larrup you out of this valley at the end of a horsewhip."

Carradine's hands hung loosely, his eyes hot and wild—wicked. He said, "I'll mind this, Devereux!"

"Do that. I'd kind of deplore having to remind you," Unc said mildly.

We silently watched the four Anchor men out of sight. I found my voice. "Unc, we going to see Gavin?"

"We won't have to. He'll hear about this."

Uncle Jace got off his horse, only now taking a close look at the raggedy drifter, and his eyes went quick with a pitying kindness as his hand went out. "I'm Jace Devereux. My nephew, Howie. We homestead over east."

The little horse-thief looked at Unc in a grave, considering way. He said in a bass deep, startling in such an undersize man, "My name is Jones. I'd admire to work for you. For nothin'."

Unc looked at the hand in his own, seeing it crossed with rope-scars. "Well, now, as a cowman, ain't you afraid of some farm stink wearing off on you?"

"I'd admire to work for you," Jones repeated, adding, "for nothin'."

I knew a kind of warm surge for this runty, spooky-looking gent with his sad and faded eyes looking up from the shadow of his Stetson at Unc's great height. And glancing at Uncle Jace, I saw he felt the same.

He said in his rich big voice, "Come along, and hang up your hat, Jones."

That was the way of it, and Jones settled into the workaday routine of the farm, as natural a part of it as the buildings themselves, already dry and gray and weatherbeaten. Jones was all of those, too. He was that colorless he might have been anywhere from thirty-five to fifty-five. He fitted to the new work like an old hand, so quiet you'd hardly know he was there but for the new-improving ways the farm began to shape up.

He stayed, and we called him Jones, just Jones. He never gave another name and we never asked. I reckoned Unc had been shamed into hiring him. Shamed by the little fella's offering his services for nothing, though the main reason he'd saved Jones was to retaliate on Anchor and show what he thought of all its power. Jones must have known that. How could life kick a man into such a corner he could be so beggar-grateful? It was as though no one'd done him even a half-intended kindness till now.

I saw him right off as a man a boy could tie to. He worked alongside Uncle Jace, who was twice his size and three times his power, and he let Unc set the pace. He'd be so tired he could barely stand, and never a whimper. Watching him hump alongside Uncle Jace in the fields, he cut a comical earnest figure that made you want to laugh and cry all at once. It might be that I'd laugh, and sometimes, if you laughed too hard, he had a way of looking at you that made you feel you'd need a ladder to reach a snake's belly.

But there was another special way he could look, a way that made you feel two feet taller, like the wry grin of him when I'd lick him in our nightly games in the kitchen. He was mighty proud of his checker game, was Jones. It was the one little vanity he had, yet he was the best loser ever I saw.

We got close, the two of us. Mind, I was just seventeen, a hard time of growing up. You get that age, you'll know what I mean. A lot of things are confusing to a fellow. In the one month he was with us, it was Jones helped me see my way to the end of more than one bad time. He had a way of looking at things, of talking them out so they'd seem a lot clearer. Fact, he was as much pa as I ever knew after my own pa died. He sort of took up that empty place in one boy's life that Uncle Jace, for all he was as big a man inside him as outside, couldn't quite fill.

Jones would go into the settlement of Ogallala now and then to get supplies, and Gavin's riders hoorawed him every time, and sent him packing out of town. They never hazed him if Unc or I was along, so I never seen it. Heard plenty, though. Neighbors saw to that. Folks would snicker behind their hands watching Jace Devereux's new man go out of his way to walk around trouble. Never carried a gun, either. Not even a rifle on his saddle.

Never spoke of his past, did Jones. But he had one behind the face he showed the world. Remember, he'd come to us a reprieved horse-thief. And strange how Uncle Jace in taking him on hadn't thought, being a middling cautious man, that he might be getting a pig in a poke. But seemed like it hadn't even occurred to Unc.

Uncle Jace was right that Gavin had heard his warning to leave us be. His riders hauled off their war of nerves, at least on Unc and me and our fences and crops, and rode herd on the homesteaders—and, of course, Jones. Gavin had soft-pedaled on us, but we only wondered what he had up his sleeve.

We found out about a month after Jones came to the farm. Gavin himself, sided by Tod Carradine, came riding into the yard one night after supper, as Uncle Jace and Jones and me was sitting on the front steps, breaking in some new cob pipes.

Gavin's hardness was a legend in the territory, and it was easy to see that age hadn't softened him. He was a blocky, well-fed man in the slightly dust-soiled dignity of a black suit, and his habit of authority sat him like a heavy fist. There was even a touch of arrogance to the way he bent the hand holding his cigar.

Uncle Jace got off the step, knocking out his pipe. "Light down a spell, Gavin. You too, Tod."

"I'll speak my piece from here," Gavin said. "Your tracks are big, Devereux. Big enough so I respect 'em.'' He paused, and Unc didn't speak, wondering, like me, where this was leading to.

Gavin said it then: ''I need men like you, Devereux. Sign on with me for double wages. The boy, too.''

Unc said, ''No,'' instantly, as I knew he would. We Devereuxs aren't that way we work for other people. And even if Unc was, it wouldn't be he'd work for the likes of Gavin.

The rancher didn't look mad, not even greatly concerned. He'd had his own way for too many years. There was only a faint irritation in his voice. ''You go, Devereux. You go this week—or next week you'll crawl out of this valley on your belly.'' He turned his horse in a violent way and rode out of the yard.

Carradine's soft drawling chuckle slid into the quiet like a gliding rattler. ''I always suspicioned you was a Sunday man, Devereux. Now we'll see.''

''A Sunday man?''

''A man who's a man one day—when he talks big. I don't think you'll back up what you said when you saved that horse-stealer.'' Carradine smiled with full insolence. ''I don't think you can.''

''You tell me that with Anchor behind you,'' Uncle Jace said, the snap of an icicle in his voice, ''which by my lights makes you a yellow dog, Tod.''

Carradine smiled, ever so gentle. ''I'll be in town tomorrow afternoon—in front of Red Mike's. You be there, and we'll see if you're man enough to call me that again. Or send your big bad hired man. . .''

So the issue was in the open now.

When the sound of Carradine riding off had died on the still evening air, I turned to Unc. ''He's a mean one, Uncle Jace. With a gun. There's stories followed him from Texas."

"And I offer there's something to 'em," Jones said softly, his voice startling us. He could kind of fade back so you forgot he was there. "It's why he needled you. I reckon you'd better not take him up, Jace."

"And I reckon I had," Unc said grimly.

Jones only nodded. "I figured so," he said, and walked around back. I wanted to say more to Uncle Jace, but a look in his face warned me, and in a minute I followed Jones around back where he was working with the ax on some stovewood. He had his shirt off against the heat, and the scrawny, knobbly upper body of him gleaming with sweat made him look like a plucked chicken.

Jones paused, leaned on the ax and mopped his face with his shirt. "Why has Gavin got his sights primed for your unc, Howie? There's other farmers squattin' on his land, and more comin'."

"Squatting" was the word a *cattleman* would use for a legal government homestead. It was Jones saying it, though, so I let it ride. You didn't get mad at Jones.

"The others got no heart to 'em," I said with contempt. "Unc's got more gall than a government mule, and the homesteaders know it as well as Gavin. If he can stampede Unc, the others'll follow suit."

"Hum," said Jones, and went back to his work. I got the other ax and helped. But a couple times I caught him leaning on his ax and looking off toward the hills with that air like a considerable thought was riling him.

I didn't sleep much that night, thinking about the next day, with Carradine waiting in front of Red

Mike's bar and Unc dead set on meeting him. Uncle Jace was no gunman. He knew it, I knew it. Even Jones knew it.

So I was near relieved when about noon of the next day Jones came into the kitchen where I was fixing some grub and quietly told me that Uncle Jace's leg had got broken. They'd been heisting the massive ridgepole timber of the barn Unc had finally got to building, raising it into place, and it fell. . .

Between the two of us we splinted up Unc's leg and got him into bed. His face was white and drawn, and his eyes near starting from his head with the pain.

Jones said in his gentle voice, "I reckon this is in the way of a lifesaver for you, Jace."

"But won't they say Unc ran away from it?" I asked.

"They'll say more," Uncle Jace said bitterly between set teeth. "They'll say I got stove up a-purpose to get out of meeting Tod. And it'll be a spell before I can call any of 'em a liar and back it. By that time the farmers will be out, and Gavin'll swallow up their homesteads."

Jones and I looked at each other. Unc was right; he was the backbone of the homesteaders. With him broken, they'd cut and run.

"That leg'll need a sawbones," Jones said, unruffled. "I'm going into town, and I'll send one."

There was a note in Jones's voice that left me curious, and after a while, when Uncle Jace was resting more easy, I followed Jones out to the harness shed where he'd rigged his bunk. I came to stand in the doorway as I saw him, and I almost fell over. Jones didn't see me. He was facing a shard of mirror he had nailed on the wall over an old packing crate which held his possibles—and there was a gun in his hand.

For thirty seconds I stood and watched as he drew and fixed a mock bead on his own reflection, the hammer falling on an empty chamber each time. I tell you, he made that fine-balanced gun do tricks.

The truth all rushed down on me at once. I'd had it figured how Jones's hell-born past was that of any rabbity little gent who couldn't hold up his head in a world of big men. But the man who could make a cutter do his will like this one—why, he was head and shoulders over the biggest man.

It was the gun—that was the hell in Jones's life. That's why he'd never packed it, why he walked soft and gave Gavin's loudmouths a wide berth. It wasn't them he was afraid of, it was himself. His own skill, his deadly skill. That was the real truth and tragedy of his backtrail. While the rest of us, rancher and homesteader, talked war and primed ourselves for it, Jones was already fighting his own private battle, a harder one than any of us would ever know.

Now he'd lost his war. Lost it in the way a real man would—by facing out the enemy of the only one who ever befriended him. . .

He'd loaded the gun while my thoughts raced. Like magic, that gun it was in the fine-tooled holster, and then he swung toward the door and saw me.

For a full five seconds he didn't speak. "I'm going to see Carradine, Howie. You won't try to stop me." There was the thinnest undercore of steel to his voice, and I wouldn't have tried even if I'd been of a mind to.

But I was going with him, and I said so. He didn't comment, and it was that way the whole ride.

Neither of us spoke a word till we'd nearly reached Ogallala.

"Jones," I said. He grunted. "Jones, I wouldn't be surprised you let that beam slip on purpose to keep Uncle Jace from going out."

"You talk too much," he said mildly, and that was all. I didn't care, I was that sure he'd saved Unc's life.

Ogallala was drowsing in the westering sun. One horse stood hipshot at the tierail in front of Red Mike's: Carradine's blazeface sorrel.

Jones hauled up across the street, stepping down and throwing his reins. His gaze fixed Red Mike's as he said to me, "You get in the store and stay there." I didn't, but I got back on the walk out of the way, and he didn't even look at me.

"Carradine!" That was Jones's silence-shattering voice. A big voice for a little man. Maybe as big as the real Jones.

After a little, the batwing doors parted and Tod Carradine stood tall in the shadow of the weather-beaten false-front. Stepping off the walk, bareheaded, the sun caught on his face, showing it red with heat and whiskey. He'd been drinking, but he wasn't drunk.

When he saw who it was hailed him, he looked ready to laugh. Almost. He peered sharp at Jones, and something seemed to shut it off in his throat before it started.

"Carradine," Jones said. "Carradine, you brag something fierce. Back it."

Carradine began to smile, understanding, his teeth showing very white. He cut a mighty handsome figure in the sun. "All right, bravo," he said. "All right, bravo."

But I watched Jones. And I watched it happen.

Carradine was fast. Mighty fast. But Jones was the man. The last of a dying breed. Not one of your patent-leather movie cowboys with their gun-fanning foolery and their two fast-blazing sixguns. The man Jones knew you couldn't hit a barn fanning. He got his gun out right fast, but then took his time as you had to when it was a heavy single-action Colt you were handling. Carradine got two fast shots off before Jones's one bullet buckled him in the middle and smashed him into the walk on his back. . .

He didn't touch Jones; the other fellow did. The one in the alley between the store and the feed-barn, at our back—stationed there in case this happened. I heard this dirty son's gun from the alley and I saw Jones's scrawny body flung forward off balance. Before the shot sound died, I saw Jones haul around, his gun blasting, and this bushwhacker, hard-hit, fling out away from the alley with his gun going off in the hot blue face of the sky. He went down and moved no more.

Jones was sinking to his knees, the light going from his eyes and a funny little smile on his face. It was the first and the last time I saw him smile with all a smile should mean.

When I reached him and caught him as he slipped down, he looked up, recognizing me, and said, "Tell your unc—you tell him to keep that peg dusted, Howie. My hat won't be on it. . ." The smile was gone as he lifted his head to stare at me with a fierce intensity. "Howie, mind what I say. If you forget everything else about me, never forget what I learned—the hard way. You can't run from what you made of yourself. You can't run that far. . ."

The voice trailed, and the eyes looked on, not at me . . . or at anything.

I eased down the meager body of the man we called Jones, and wanted to cover his face from the prying, question-rattling crowd. I remember I had to do that, and there was only my ragged pocket bandana. When I'd finished and looked up, there was someone standing over me I didn't at first recognize for the wet blurring in my eyes. But then I blinked and saw it was Gavin.

He was holding his cigar in his arrogant way, frowning around at his two dead hirelings and at Jones, and not believing it. I went up and after him with my fists doubled. Then a big man with a close-clipped Vandyke threw a beefy arm across my chest.

"Hold it, son. I have a word for Mr. Gavin."

Gavin fixed his cold stare on the newcomer. "Who the hell are you?"

"Baines, special agent for the U. S. Land Office. Washington has been getting notices about your terrorizing government homesteaders. And I've seen enough to validate it. You and I'll discuss that shortly." The big man turned back to me and nodded down to Jones. "He a friend of yours, son?"

I managed to find words. "Jones was the best."

"Jones?" Baines eyed me closely. "I reckon you didn't know him very well. Suggest you write to the sheriff at Cheyenne. He'll give you particulars. So can a lot of others."

That's about all. Within weeks, a new flood of homesteaders filled the valley. I saw Gavin a few times after, a broken old man. I don't know what Baines told him, but the hand of the government can be right heavy.

About Jones?

Yes, I could've written to Cheyenne and found out. But I didn't. I never wanted to find out.

All I can tell you is what he was to me—friend of the Devereuxs, the bravest and best man I ever knew. The man we called Jones.

Westward Rails

by Giles A. Lutz

CASS DALTON GLANCED wistfully at Neva Moran across the aisle of the emigrant train. He knew he was losing her. It had started a couple of months ago when she first saw Quincy Ridgeway. He wished to God he had never heard the name; he wished Neva hadn't, either. But if it hadn't been Ridgeway, it would have been somebody else. He knew what he had to offer a woman. He had made that analysis a long time ago, and it wasn't pleasant to him.

He shifted uncomfortably on the hard seat. The floor of the car was a huge sounding board, sending each jar and jolt of the uneven roadbed to numb passenger flesh.

An emigrant car was little more than a long, narrow box on wheels, sparsely furnished. Unupholstered benches lined each side of the car, a wood stove at one end, a water closet at the other. Feeble lamps suspended from the ceiling furnished inadequate lighting at night. The sleeping accommodations fit the rest of the car—a board cut out to fit the space between the facing benches with cotton bags leanly stuffed with straw that did little to soften the boards. A passenger furnished his own blankets, or he slept without.

The long string of cars creaked and groaned as the engine picked up speed on its plunge from the summit. The floor of the California desert rushed to meet the train, and each hundred feet of drop intensified the heat. Most of the four days and nights from Omaha to here had been spent in heat: at first the summer heat of the seared prairies, then the blistering reflection of the sun's rays from Utah's salt-encrusted, barren land, followed by the equal aridity of Nevada's high plains with their persistent, irritating alkali dust. The wind's constant stirring kept great clouds of dust in the air, clouds that enveloped a man until his skin itched from it. Each successive crossing of a state seemed to increase the heat, or else a man's weariness had weakened him to it. There had been a brief relief in crossing the crest of the moutains, but that had been short lived.

Usually one car was allotted to a family, because of the possessions they owned. This car had two families, three if he counted himself as a family. The rest of the car was crammed with household furniture, farm implements, horses, cows, dogs, and cats. Young fruit trees and seed for the first season's planting were jammed in every nook and cranny. The reek of unwashed human bodies was becoming overbearing, and when the smell of hot animal flesh and the rich, ripe aroma of manure rose, a man gagged on it.

His fretting grew with each passing mile. Impatience was a great fault of his, and he fought constantly to contain it. He could add another flaw, a more serious one. Since he had been twelve he had fought to curb his temper. Even now he couldn't say with certainty that the temper was whipped. The first time Cass knew his temper was a serious problem had occurred in a boyish fight with his brother. Jim was four years older and bigger at the time, and he had hurt Cass enough to make the hot tears of rage flow. Jim had made a serious mistake then; he had jeered at Cass, and Cass had lost all restraint. When his father had broken it up, Cass was astride Jim, holding him by the ears and banging his head on the hard ground.

"Are you trying to kill him?" his father had roared.

Cass had looked at the white, unconscious face of his brother. That was exactly what he had been trying to do. His father hadn't whipped him, but he had talked to him for long hours about it. "A temper like that is a frightening thing, Cass. You're going to be a huge man. A man that size can't afford the luxury of an insane temper. Do you want to kill somebody?"

Cass had never forgotten it, and he had backed away from potential fights until other men looked at him with speculating eyes. But he managed to keep the promise he had made to his father and to himself.

He shifted his position again and stared at his knuckles in gloomy meditation. The oversized hands fitted the rest of his body. He was a huge man, his arms and legs massive. Those hands could tend sick livestock, or give an ailing plant additional care. But they would never be able to do delicate, fine work.

His shifting gave him the briefest of relief. He changed to the other cheek. How did women stand this trip? He supposed their padding was deeper and better placed. He smiled sourly at the thought.

He looked across at Neva, and she was smiling. Maybe she guessed his thoughts. That smile could have been mocking or in sympathy, and he hoped it was the latter.

He crossed the car and sat down beside her. "Rough trip, Neva." He knew he would never be the master of light talk, either.

"Yes," she sighed. "I'll be glad when it's over."

He wouldn't be. As long as the trip lasted he would be thrown in close proximity to her. Her father didn't think much of him. Neal Moran had the same opinion of him that so many other men had. Despite his size, Cass was a timorous man.

He stole glances at her profile. She was graceful when she was still and graceful when she moved. She was six years younger, and he had always been dumbstruck in her presence. Her startling blue eyes had a fathomless mystery that he would have been willing to explore for the rest of his life. She was only eighteen, but already she was a woman in all ways. For a while he had imagined that she returned his interest, then he had realized that he was only fooling himself.

He knew a deep sorrow when he realized how clumsy and inept he must appear to her.

He wanted to catch her attention, and a brilliant thought occurred to him. "Neva, how do you manage to keep so fresh?"

She made a small grimace. "I'm not. It's the perfume you smell. Women have that advantage over men."

"Maybe we should use it, too," he said, and grinned.

She laughed, then broke it off, and her nose twitched. "There's that awful smell again."

For an instant, he was afraid it was him, then he identified it. That wasn't hard; he had smelled it before: Ben Andrews had tongue in this car again.

She started to rise. "I can't stand that any longer."

He caught her wrist. "I'll do something about it, Neva."

He stood, and the old promise picked at him again. But there was no reason for violence to spring out of this; not if he kept his temper.

He approached the Andrewses at the far end of the car. Ben and Bess Andrews were a fat couple. They had fat people's jovality and weren't too clean. A man kept a high wall between himself and the Andrewes, or they absorbed him.

This train was made up of people of the same ilk; the shiftless, the hard-luck ones, the beaten people. All of them were running from one piece of land to another, fooling themselves by believing they would find better luck at the end of this ride. It worried Cass to think that he was one of the same breed—but with one small difference. He wasn't leaving any land. When his father had died, the farm had gone to the older brother, and that was as it should be. Cass had received a small cash inheritance. He could have stayed in Ohio, but it would have been as his brother's hired hand. He didn't have enough money to buy another piece of land. He had jumped at the railroad's offer of land in California. There were many things he didn't like about it, but a man couldn't tailor-make everything that came his way. Deep down, he admitted the real reason. Neva's father had wanted California land, and Cass had come along to be as near to her as he could be; at least, until he had permanently lost her.

He stopped before the Andrews couple, balancing himself against the lurching of the car. He didn't want to do this, but a man's right shouldn't be big enough to forgive spoiled tongue. Tongue was either cheap, or Andrews' favorite food. This had happened in Nebraska and again in Nevada. Tongue turned bad in a few hours of heat, and its stink could be unbearable.

Bess Andrews fawned on him, and Cass gave her a pained smile. Andrews stared out the window, and Cass touched him on the shoulder. At the same time, he saw the food box under the bench.

"Have you got tongue in there again?"

"I told him to throw it out last night," Bess Andrews said.

Cass never liked this kind of woman. She would do anything, even turning against her husband, to get attention.

Cass stooped and dragged out the box.

Andrews grabbed Cass's wrist as he straightened. "Here now. That's my property. A man's got a right. . ."

The words faltered before Cass's eyes, and Andrews let go of his wrist. Cass took out the tongue, and this close to his nose the stench was nauseating. "Your right doesn't include spoiled tongue." He pitched it out of the window. "If you want to buy tongue, eat it. Don't try to store it up."

Andrews met Cass's stare. Which way this went depended upon the depth of Andrews' truculence, but then, he didn't know Cass's reputation.

Cass's size overawed him. "All right," he said sullenly.

Cass thought, he doesn't know if he pushes, I'd back up. He nodded to Bess Andrews and moved back to Neva. Could that be approval in her eyes?

"I guess he looked at you, Cass, and decided it was smart to let it go."

"Maybe," he said moodily. He tried never to intimidate another man with his size. "I didn't wave a fist in his face."

"You didn't have to. He was there, too, when the engine went off the track. He saw you help pry it back on."

Cass frowned. Maybe some of the passengers gave him most of the credit for that, but he denied it. "Damn it, Neva, there was twenty of us prying at that engine." The seventeen-ton engine had jumped the track in Nebraska. The derailment wasn't bad enough to warrant calling out the wrecker. A nearby fence had been stripped of posts which they used to lever the engine back onto the track. Cass wasn't waving his part in the incident around.

"What would you have done if he hadn't let you throw the tongue out the window?" Neva asked softly.

He gave her a pained smile. "I dunno, Neva." He wished he knew what thoughts were behind her eyes. Would it have made any difference if he had told her about the fight with Jim? Maybe she wouldn't even be able to understand the promise he had made his father.

He started to say something more to her, but her eyes were fastened on the far end of the car. He turned his head, and that numb sickness hit him again. It always did when he saw Quincy Ridgeway.

The man was tall and lean. He came down the car, balancing effortlessly against its lurching. He paused to exchange a word with the Andrewses, and Cass saw how eagerly they answered him. Oh, the man had charm, all right. Beside him, Cass looked like a huge, misshapen clod. Ridgeway's clothes were good, and he wore them with flair. His blond hair was thick and wavy, and he carried his head high. Either for people to see his hair, or to show off the clean cut of his chin, Cass thought sourly. How many times had he wanted to wipe off that smirk on Ridgeway's face! He had never given in to his wish, but it hadn't done him any good; he had lost Neva.

Ridgeway worked for the railroad, though Cass didn't exactly know what his job was. Maybe he was on this train to herd the passengers to California, or maybe he had taken it solely because of Neva.

Ridgeway stopped before them. "Neva, I had hoped to find you alone."

He hadn't spoken or even nodded to Cass, and it put a dull flush in Cass's face. If he could only break the promise he had made to his father, for only the few seconds it would take to cut Ridgeway down!

"Cass was just leaving," Neva said brightly.

Cass was sure that was contempt in her eyes. "Why yes, I was," he mumbled. He got up and didn't look back until he reached the end of the car. They were in animated conversation, and he had never seen her eyes sparkle more.

There it is, he thought dully, and stepped into the vestibule between the cars. He was a damned fool to have ever thought of coming to California. He had been a glutton for punishment, but he would correct that. He would catch the next train back.

The train was pulling to a stop, and Cass indifferently looked out. This was a sorry excuse for a town. A sad, small building that might be called a station and a water tank were beside the rails. Behind them was a dreary-looking house, stripped of paint by the sand-laden winds. The train had stopped to take on water, and Cass had seen these jerkwater towns before. Up ahead, the water spout was being put in place, then somebody would jerk on a rope, releasing the water. The train would be here only long enough to fill its boilers.

"Excuse me." There was impatience in the voice.

Cass had heard this man called Waverly. He had a furtive expression on his ferret face that only heightened the air of sharpness about him. Cass had seen him in several card games, and yesterday Neal Moran had been involved in one. He had wanted to warn Neva's father that Waverly was a professional gambler, but he had held it.

"Sure," he said and stepped aside. He wondered idly what Waverly wanted to get off here for. He watched Waverly until he disappeared into the depot, then moved on into the next car. He had no aim; he only wanted to put distance between him and the couple behind him.

By the time he had walked through the next two cars, the train was moving again. He saw Neal Moran in the next car. At first he thought that Moran was playing solitaire. He had a deck of cards before him on a makeshift table. Then he realized that Moran was waiting for somebody. Moran's frown increased as he looked beyond Cass to the door of the car.

Moran was a small man with a quick, explosive temper. It was odd to look at him and think that Neva was his daughter. Surely she had gotten her beauty from her mother, and Cass wished her mother hadn't died before he had known her. An old thought came back into his head. Would Neva's mother have accepted him with more approval than Moran showed?

He stopped before Moran and asked, "Are you waiting for somebody, Neal?"

Moran gave him a contemptuous flick of his eyes. "Any of your business?"

"Why, no," Cass said and swallowed hard. He knew Moran's opinion of him. Moran had seen Cass back away from incipient trouble. That wasn't Moran's way at all. He bragged he had never taken a backward step regardless of the size or odds he faced. How many times had Cass heard him say that if a man wouldn't fight, he wasn't worth his salt?

Cass had no desire to make things easier for Moran. "If you're looking for Waverly, he got off at the last stop."

The agitation in Moran's face puzzled him for a moment, then he put it all together. Moran was an inveterate gambler, and Neva was always scolding him for it. Oh damn, Cass thought. He'd gotten tied up with Waverly.

Moran's eyes turned wild. "You're crazy. He said he'd be back."

Cass knew distress for Neva; none for Moran. "He won't."

Moran read the truth in Cass's face. Profanity dripped from his lips, despite the fact that women were within earshot. He broke off and muttered, "He promised to come back and let me get even. My string of bad luck was beginning to wear out. Why would he want to get off?"

Cass didn't feel like sparing Moran. "How much are you behind?"

"Two hundred dollars," Moran said unwillingly.

"That's your answer as to why he got off. He'll wait for another train, going in either direction. He won't care. That's his business—riding these trains until he finds another pigeon like you."

Moran stared at him with rage-widened eyes. "I'll prove he's still on this train."

He jumped to his feet and rushed down the car, and Cass reluctantly followed him. He had to calm him down before Neva heard about this.

He followed Moran through two cars, and Moran's stubbornness was showing. He wouldn't believe Cass until he searched every car.

The conductor blocked his way in the next car. The brakeman was behind him, a burly man with a massive head set on a short neck. His face was red and coarse-featured, and his eyes held a hungry shine. The shine said he remembered the derailed engine and Cass's display of strength. Physical prowess meant everything to this man. He wouldn't be happy until he tested his own against Cass's.

The conductor scowled at Moran. "What are you storming through the cars for?"

"Where's Waverly?" Moran shouted.

"You won't find him." Both the conductor and the brakeman were enjoying Moran's rage. "He got off at the last stop."

It left Moran speechless, but Cass had something to say. "Did you give him protection while he worked the train? How much was your split?" The sharpening of the conductor's eyes told Cass how close he had hit to the truth.

The brakie's words confirmed it. "Mister, you've got a fat mouth."

The conductor flung out an arm. "Easy, Mike." His eyes never left Cass's face. "If you think you have a complaint, make it at the division office in Sacramento. You'll have enough time. We change engines there." He shoved brusquely past Cass. "Come on, Mike," he said over his shoulder.

Moran trembled with rage. "By God, I'll make that complaint," he shouted after him. "Don't think I won't." His face was pleading as he turned toward Cass. "Cass, do you think the railroad had a hand in this?"

This was the first time Moran had ever asked his opinion on anything. Cass nodded. "At least the conductor, and maybe the brakeman. But I'm accusing the railroad of a lot more than that."

Moran's eyes rounded. He was listening for the first time. "You think the railroad could be planning to cheat us out of our land?"

"There's something damned funny about it. We paid no money for that land. We're planning on moving onto it before patents are even issued. The railroad says its promise that the land is ours is all we need. It claims it'll fix a price later. What about the improvements we make on that land? Will our improvements jack up the price when we finally go to settle up? I wouldn't put it past them. Look how the railroad handles us; like animals. It takes our fares and gives us nothing in writing. Letting Waverly operate is only a small indication of what the railroad thinks of us."

Moran's eyes were dazed. He had never let Cass point out these things before, and they came too fast for him. "I can do something about Waverly. Cass, will you come with me when I make my complaint? You're a witness. You saw everything."

Cass wanted to refuse him, but this was Neva's father. "All right, Neal. But I wouldn't let Neva know anything of this."

"Lord, no," Moran said fervently.

Cass stayed by himself the remainder of the trip to Sacramento. He was an open man, and he was afraid his face would mirror his thoughts. Neva had a way of dragging the truth out of him. If it all came out, he would be caught in the middle between her and Neal.

Moran was the first off the train when it stopped before the wooden station at the foot of K Street. Cass's steps dragged as he followed him.

A ticket counter filled one end of the room. A potbellied stove was in the center of the room, and the walls were lined with hard, uninviting-looking benches. A stoop-shouldered man with a sour face was behind a counter. He wore a green eyeshade and black sleeve protectors. His face turned flinty as though he sensed trouble in Moran and Cass.

"Ask for somebody bigger than him," Cass said in a low voice.

Moran nodded, and his jaw jutted. "No damned clerk is going to block me."

Cass felt a premonition of trouble. He sighed. He guessed he had felt it ever since this started.

"I've got a complaint," Moran said to the clerk. "I want to see the head man."

The clerk sniffed. "Fill out this form."

Moran's eyes ran over the paper. "What happens to it after I fill it out?"

"That ain't your business, mister. Don't bother me any more."

He started to turn away, and Moran reached across the counter and grabbed him. He hauled him up against the counter, ripping the man's shirt in the process.

"Don't turn your back on me," Moran said hotly. "What did you intend to do with it? Throw it in a wastebasket? I told you to call the head man."

The clerk gulped. The big man was with Moran, and he appraised Cass's size. But suddenly his frightened look disappeared. "Take your hands off me."

The clerk had seen something to change his attitude, and Cass turned. The brakie, the conductor, and Ridgeway were coming through the doorway. The station was filled with passengers, and it wasn't the place Cass would have picked for a fight. He was only glad that Neva wasn't here.

He read the eagerness in Mike's eyes right. The man only wanted the smallest springboard to get into this.

Ridgeway's eyes swept over Moran and Cass, and he asked the clerk, "What's the trouble, Jason?"

"They came in looking for trouble, Mr. Ridgeway. They said something about a complaint, then refused to go through the ordinary channels. This one," he indicated Moran, "ripped my shirt. The other one was ready to back him up."

"There must be some misunderstanding, Neal," Ridgeway said easily. "Tell me about it."

"I will not," Moran said stubbornly. "I'm going to talk to somebody bigger than you."

Ridgeway's face flushed. "This is no place to start a row," he said curtly. "If you'll walk outside with me—"

"I will not," Moran said hotly.

Mike stepped forward, and his eyes had a burning eagerness. "I'll take him out for you, Mr. Ridgeway."

He grabbed Moran's arm and yanked on it.

Cass blew out a long breath. I'm sorry, Paw, he thought. "Let go of him," he said softly.

"Why you damned fool," Mike swore. He let go of Moran's arm and swung at Cass.

Cass ducked, and the fist grazed his ear. It must have torn some skin, for he felt a stinging there. He wrapped both arms around the man, and his power showed in the reddish purpling of Mike's face.

He started walking him toward the door, and Ridgeway's cheekbones sharpened under the honing of anger. "Take your hands off him. Jason, Wynn, help me with this."

Cass looked at him. "Keep them out of this," he warned.

Ridgeway swung a blow that Cass couldn't duck, for his hands were filled with the struggling brakie. It landed flush on the side of his face and filled his head with a roaring and watered his eyes.

"Let's take all of them, Cass," Moran said with delight.

It might be what Moran wanted, but it wasn't Cass's choosing. But no man hit him full in the face like that. I tried, Paw, he thought. He shoved Mike from him with enough force to send him spinning across the room. A bench hit him at the back of the knees, and he fell over it.

Cass looked around to locate Moran, and Moran wasn't going to be in this fight long. Jason clubbed him with something he picked off the counter, and Moran slowly sagged, a stupid look on his face.

Cass bellowed, picked up the clerk, and hurled him halfway across the room. Benches piled up under Jason, and his weight split and broke one of them.

A woman screamed, and people scurried toward the door, trying to get out of this madhouse.

Cass had momentarily forgotten about Mike, and the man was on his feet and took Cass from the rear. At the same time, Ridgeway hit him from the side.

That put renewed vigor in the pounding of the drums in Cass's head. The combined blows were enough to put him down, and Mike aimed a kick at his head. The boot sole scraped along Cass's cheek, tearing skin and drawing blood. He had not even the memory of a promise holding him now; he only wanted to hurt the men who had hurt him.

He clambered to his feet and dove into Mike, his shoulder hitting him in the stomach. The impact tore a great puff of air from Mike. Cass drove him to the floor and scrambled to a sitting position atop him. He took another blow from Ridgeway and paid no attention to it. He wouldn't until he took care of Mike. He slammed a fist into his face, then another. He started to hit him the third time and realized it wasn't necessary. Mike was unconscious.

Cass heaved himself to his feet, and Ridgeway hit him again before Cass made it. He felt something wet and sticky stealing down his face and supposed it was blood. He advanced toward Ridgeway and the conductor, his hands balled.

Ridgeway and the conductor retreated before him, and there was obvious alarm in Ridgeway's eyes. Evidently those two didn't think two-to-one odds were enough. Cass was sorry Neva had her eyes on Ridgeway, but Ridgeway had asked for what he had coming.

Three more men poured through the door, and by the authoritative way Ridgeway pointed at him, he would guess they were railroad men. That made it tougher, but even that couldn't stop him. Five men fanned out as they cautiously advanced on him. Cass picked up a bench and swung it like a flail. He should be allowed that to equalize the odds a little. One of his swings knocked down the stove, and it made a satisfying clatter.

He saw the consternation spread across their faces and said mockingly, "Come on. Isn't this what you wanted?"

He didn't see the man wearing a badge slip through the rear door. He didn't see the gun barrel rise and descend. He only felt a crashing weight against his head, and for an instant, he couldn't see against the blinding red wave. Then blackness swept quickly in behind the red, and his legs would no longer support him.

Justice moved swiftly in this town. The marshal came for Cass and Moran before Cass had fully gotten his normal head back.

Cass speculatively eyed him. "You the one who hit

me?" At the marshal's nod he said, "You don't take much chance, do you?"

"I never do with somebody your size," the marshal said dryly. "The judge wants to see you two."

Moran's head must have ached too, for a groan escaped him as he stood. "Neva will sure know about it," he said.

That couldn't be avoided. Cass had ought to be mad at him; Moran had dragged him into this. You weren't too hard to drag, he told himself. Maybe he had hoped to earn some credit in Moran's eyes that would be transferred to Neva. But none of it mattered now. He was going back just as soon as he could grab the next train east.

The courtroom was filled with curious spectators, and the lawyer for the railroad wouldn't let Cass talk. The judge listened to the lawyer, then put his angry eyes on Cass and Moran. "You people have to learn that you can't come out here and assault people and destroy property."

Cass took a slow breath. "You listen to only the railroad's side, Judge?"

The judge's face purpled. "That will cost you one hundred dollars fine and one hundred dollars for the damage."

Cass caught Moran's arm and checked his outburst. He imagined that his own had already cost them.

"We'll pay, Neal," he said.

It hurt to dig into his pockets for that sum. Moran breathed hard as he laid his money beside Cass's.

Cass turned toward the door, and Neva stood there. Moran had no more reason to worry about her knowing. She had heard it all.

"Oh, Jesus," Moran moaned. "What will I say to her?"

"Just what happened," Cass said.

He took her arm and pulled her outside. He thought she had the same weighing expression that the judge had, but he couldn't understand her eyes. If that was mirth in them, it didn't fit at all.

"Neva," he said awkwardly. He had advised Moran to tell her right out what had happened, but he found that hard to do.

"I'll tell her, Cass," Moran said. He looked at his daughter and gulped. "I got in with a card sharp on the train, and he fleeced me. Cass accused the conductor of being in cahoots with the gambler, and by the conductor's look Cass was right. The conductor brushed us off by telling me to fill out a complaint when we got to Sacramento. I tried to. . ." He made a helpless gesture and stopped.

"Yes," she said. There was no giving in the word, and Cass took it up.

"I was forced into. . ."

"Forced into what?"

Cass groaned inwardly. She was completely unforgiving. "The fight, I guess."

"I started it, Neva," Moran said quickly.

"And you dragged Cass into it."

"I guess I did," Moran muttered.

"He didn't," Cass protested. "Neal didn't have much chance against that many. I had to protect him, didn't I?"

Why was he trying to make her understand? He wasn't going to be around her much longer. "If it's any consolation to you," he said bitterly, "I didn't get much of a chance at your Ridgeway. He kept backing up."

Moran's eyes gleamed with a happy memory. "I didn't see it all. But I was told he was doing all right until that marshal clobbered him from behind."

"It looks as though both of you were wrong," Neva said acidly.

Cass stared at her in astonishment. Now he was the one who didn't understand at all.

"You were wrong, Father, when you said Cass wouldn't fight. You told me he wasn't the man to protect a woman, if she needed it."

Moran flushed. "I didn't know what I was talking about."

She whirled to face Cass. "And you were wrong, too. Quincy was never 'my man,' as you called him."

"But I thought. . . I—"

Neva nodded vigorously. "That's what I wanted you to think, Cass. Though I was beginning to believe that Father might be right. Quincy was a boring man. He thought he was doing me a favor to pay attention to me."

Hope dawned in Cass's eyes. "You mean. . . You. . ." He still couldn't get an entire sentence out.

She met his eyes squarely. "That depends on you. Though I'm not forgiving you for getting in that disgraceful brawl." She turned to her father: "Nor you, for gambling and starting it."

Cass held out his arms. "Neva," he said.

Her face turned a rosy red, but she came into his arms. "You've always been such a thick-headed man, Cass."

He held her close for a long moment, and some of

the assurance was flowing back. "You gave me every reason to think like that."

She pulled back enough so that she could see his face, and now he was sure there was laughter in her eyes. "If jealousy doesn't bring out what's in a man, nothing will. Do you still want to leave?"

"We can't let him go," Moran said, and his words were positive. "What if we run into more trouble? We need him around."

"He hasn't answered yet," Neva said, and the challenge was big in her eyes.

He pulled her back against him, and his laugh was joyous. "What do you think?"

Steel To The West

by Wayne D. Overholser

MY NAME IS JIM GLENN. I had come to Cheyenne months ago—when it was no more than a collection of tents and shacks—knowing the Union Pacific would soon reach it. I believed in the future of Cheyenne, so I invested everything I had in town lots and was building on one of them.

I had heard that steel would reach Cheyenne on November 13, 1867. After breakfast that morning I told my girl Cherry Owens and my preacher friend Frank Rush that it was a historic occasion and we'd better be down there somewhere along the grade and watch the spectacle. That was exactly what we did. Frank's wife Nancy came along.

Cherry was running a restaurant at the time and had all the business she could handle, so she was reluctant to leave, but I told her every man and his dog would be standing somewhere beside the grade watching the rails being laid and she might just as well enjoy the show. Besides, she wouldn't have any business if she stayed in her restaurant all day. When we arrived, we found that I was right. Every man and his dog was there, particularly the dogs.

We weren't disappointed. Laying the rails was the most interesting show I had ever seen, and the others agreed. The surveyors, bridge builders, and graders were all working miles west of Cheyenne. There had been some Indian trouble, even though soldiers out of Fort D.A. Russell near Cheyenne were constantly patrolling the route the railroad would take.

Most of the men employed by the Union Pacific were Civil War veterans who worked with their guns close at hand, but still we were constantly hearing of Indian trouble—particularly with the surveyors who had to work far out ahead of everyone else. They were the most likely to get killed, and many of them were.

The Casement brothers, General Jack and Dan, were responsible for laying the track, and much of the grading, too. Jack Casement had been a general during the War and had put together a well-organized, disciplined group of men. Most of them were Irish, a tough, brawling, hard-working bunch who would have been hard for anyone else to manage, but the Casements handled them well.

As we stood in the crowd and watched the rails being laid, I was amazed at the proficiency and speed with which the job was done. A light car pulled by one horse came up to the end of steel, the car loaded with rails. Two men grabbed the end of a rail. Other men took hold of the rail by twos, and when it was clear of the car, all of them went forward on the run.

At exactly the right second someone yelled a command to drop the rail. They did, being careful to put it into place right side up. Another gang of men was doing exactly the same thing on the other side of the track. I held my watch on them several times and noted that it took about thirty seconds per rail.

The instant the car was empty it was tipped to one side while the next loaded one moved up, then the empty car was driven back for another load, the horse galloping as if the devil was right on his tail. The gougers, spikers, and bolters kept close on the heels of the men dropping the rails.

Just a few minutes watching these men gave me an admiration for them I had never felt for a group of laborers before. I had not seen anything like it, and I never saw anything like it afterwards. It was cooperation to a T.

Then the thought came to me that I would make a fortune out of the lots I'd bought and the buildings I was putting up, and I owed it all to these men who were laying the rails and spiking them into place along with the graders and bridge builders and surveyors.

Of course, I really owed something to the Union Pacific company and General Dodge who headed the operation and the Casement brothers, but the men on top were making good money whereas the Irishmen who did the sweating and ran the danger of getting an Indian bullet in their briskets weren't getting rich.

There was a hell of a lot of banging as the end of the steel moved past us. I did some quick calculating as I watched: Three strokes to the spike. I counted ten spikes to the rail. Somewhere I had heard it took four hundred rails for a mile of track. About that time I quit calculating, but one thing was sure. Those sledges were going to swing a lot of times before the line was finished between Omaha and Sacramento.

We walked back to Cherry's restaurant in a kind of daze. The whole operation was incredible. Sherman Hill lay west of Cheyenne, then the desert that offered a different kind of resistance, with the Wasatch mountains on beyond the desert. Of course the Central Pacific with its Chinese labor had a worse kind of terrain to cover, with the Sierra an almost impenetrable wall.

Cherry invited us to dinner. Her hired woman, who had stayed behind, had the meal almost ready by the time we got there. We ate hurriedly, having heard the first train to Cheyenne would arrive that afternoon. The whole town would be down there beside the tracks to welcome it.

It was the day we had been waiting for, but still I had an uneasy feeling in the pit of my stomach every time I thought about an offer I'd turned down recently for my property. A thousand dollars was a lot! I'd paid a fraction of that, so it would have meant one hell of a big profit. I thought we hadn't reached the peak yet, so I'd said no, but I wasn't much of a gambler, and now I wasn't sure whether I'd made a mistake or not.

I'd heard plenty about Julesburg, the end-of-track town to the east of us. It had been on the boom for months. Early in the summer—or maybe it had been late in the spring—there had been only about fifty people in Julesburg. By the end of July it had exploded to about four thousand, with streets of mud or dust—depending on when it had rained last.

The prices the merchants had charged for their goods were outrageous. Apparently it was the grab for money that had made Julesburg the hell hole it had been, but it was the absence of law and order that worried me. I think all the businessmen of Cheyenne felt the way I did and had no intentions of letting the same thing happen here. Still there was the question of what we could do about it.

Julesburg had had more than its share of whore houses, dance halls, gambling places and saloons. The women, it was said, walked around town with derringers carried on their hips. They would rob a man by putting something in his drink, but he would not be allowed to take proper measures against them after he came to.

One reporter wrote that Julesburg had people who would kill a man for five dollars. I believed it. Dead men had been found in the alley every day, their pockets emptied of whatever they had been carrying. The part I could not understand was the obvious fact that the people living in Julesburg were indifferent to what was going on.

All of this ran through my mind as I ate. I didn't say much to Cherry, sitting beside me at the counter, but the thought began nagging me that neither Cherry nor Nancy Rush would be safe if we allowed Cheyenne to go the way Julesburg had.

In the long run it was the good women like Nancy and Cherry who built the towns and brought civilization to the frontier, not the whores who too often worked hand in glove with the sneak thieves and murderers who had made Julesburg a literal hell. Now that Cheyenne was the end of track, Julesburg would cease to exist as a town. I knew exactly what would happen. The riffraff from Julesburg would move to Cheyenne.

I knew what most of my friends thought: A vigilance committee was the only answer. As we hurried back to the track, I wondered if they were right. A few minutes later when the train pulled in with the cars banging and the bell ringing and the whistle shrieking, I decided I'd better think about it some more. Maybe they were.

A man on the train yelled, "Gentlemen, I give you Julesburg." That wasn't any news to me. While everyone else was whooping and hollering as the passengers left the train, I stood there as if paralyzed.

Frank nudged me in the ribs. "What's the matter with you, Jim?" he asked.

I shook my head and came out of it right away. I managed a weak holler, but my heart wasn't in it. I could see that the train was carrying the frame shacks and tents that had made up most of Julesburg, along with the barroom equipment and gambling devices that had given Julesburg the reputation of being the most notorious sin city in the West.

Along with the railroad men, mule skinners, and hunters who were on the train, there were the whores and the pimps and professional gamblers and con men. Within a matter of hours the Cheyenne of today would be a city of sin that would match the Julesburg of yesterday. It struck me that this historic occasion was not what I had expected it to be. Certainly I was having second thoughts about it.

Cheyenne had planned a big celebration, with a platform for speakers and big signs that read "The Magic City of the Plain greets the trans-continental rail way" and "Old Casement we welcome you" and "Honor to whom honor is due." I wanted no part of it, and I wondered if progress always meant that you had to swallow the bitter with the sweet.

I'd had more than enough. I said, "Cherry, let's get out of here."

She nodded. As we walked back along Ferguson

Street, she glanced at me and asked, "What's the matter, Jim?"

"It's funny how it is when you actually see something that you knew was coming," I said. "Cheyenne will be the hell on wheels that Julesburg has been. It scares me. Have you got a gun?"

"Yes," she said. "I knew this was coming and it scares me, too. I bought a pistol just the other day. I'll use it if I have to."

"Good," I said. "If you need any help, get word to me as fast as you can."

She laid a hand on my arm and squeezed it. "Thank you, Jim," she said.

I left her at the restaurant and went on home, more worried and upset than I wanted to admit. We had policemen, and we had a civilian auxiliary police force in which I had very little confidence. I knew damned well that our official law enforcers simply could not handle the number of toughs who had come in on that train. To make it worse, more would come. I had no doubt of that.

Frank Rush stopped in later and said it had been a festive day and wanted to know why I was so glum. I told him, adding, "If you're the kind of preacher who is looking for souls to save, a lot of them came in on the train today. I guess the people who have been in Cheyenne from the day the first settlers arrived aren't angels, but we've been pretty close compared to the riffraff that was on the train."

He frowned and scratched his chin thoughtfully, then he asked, "How do you know the train was carrying that kind?"

"I saw enough of them to know," I said. "All you had to do was to look at them to know what they were. Besides, we saw the stuff they were bringing in from Julesburg. I guess there isn't any way to keep the undesirables out, but we've got to control them once they get here."

He hadn't even thought of it, I guess. He was about like most of the Cheyenne people. He finally nodded and said as if only half convinced, "I guess you're right?"

"Has Nancy got a gun?" I asked. When he shook his head, I said sharply, "Damn it, Frank, get her one."

He nodded again and said, "I guess I will."

I didn't think he would. If one of those hardcases ever so much as touched his wife, I'd kill him if Frank didn't, but killing a man after it was too late wouldn't help Nancy.

I had another visitor that day after Frank left, a man who introduced himself as Jess Munro. He came after it was dark and for a moment I didn't know who he was. After he came inside and I saw him in the lamplight, I knew I had seen him around town, but I had never actually met him or talked to him.

He was about thirty, I judged, a dark-faced man with a black mustache and beard and black hair. His eyes were dark brown, his jaw square, the kind of jaw you'd expect to see on a forceful man. He was stocky in build with large hands and muscular shoulders. He'd be a hard man to whip, I told myself.

Munro carried himself with a straight-backed military stiffness that I associated with army men. I suspected he had been an officer during the war, probably on the Union side because his speech gave no hint that he was a Southerner. I had never seen him without a gun on his hip. He had one now, and I wondered about it because he claimed to be a real estate dealer and had an office on Ferguson Street.

He shook hands with me, his grip very strong. He pinned his gaze on my face as if making a judgement about me, then he said, "Some of your friends have told me you're a tough hand. I can believe it because I've seen how you handle yourself in fights. I think you'll do."

"Do for what?"

"You saw what the train brought in this afternoon," he said, ignoring my question. "Not that it had any surprises. The police can't do the job, even with the help of some of us who have been appointed law officers on a standby basis." Then he shrugged, and added, "I guess we would be of help in case of a riot, but that's about all."

I nodded as if I agreed, but I wasn't convinced the standby police would be of any help if the chips were down. Still, I had considered volunteering for police duty, in the hopes that something might be better than nothing.

When I told him I'd been thinking about volunteering, he said, "Good. Then you'll be willing to serve on the vigilance committee we're organizing. Several men, just four as a matter of fact, will serve as chiefs. That's why we want you. You'll have fifteen men under you to carry out any job that the central committee decides on. Will you do it?"

Here it was at last, laid out in the open. I had to make a decision now, one way or the other. I hesitated, looking straight at Jess Munro. I'd had doubts of the Vigilantes for years, but I'd been worrying about the situation here for a long time, too. Something had to be done if Cheyenne was to be saved.

Still I hesitated, saying, "I've always been leery of vigilante rule. They operate outside the law. It can become mob law very easily."

"That's right," he said grimly. "That's why we're seeking men like you to be leaders. We intend to take steps to safeguard against that very thing. I have appointed myself chairman of the committee for the simple reason that I've had some experience with vigilance committees and I know the dangers. Of course I will be subject to removal by a majority of the committee."

He paused, scratching his chin, then added, "Glenn, damn it, we just don't have much time. The toughs will be in control of the town before we know it if we don't do something. We've got to get on the job and do it quick. I'll be surprised if we don't have two or three murders before morning. We've got to organize and stay organized as long as Cheyenne is an end-of-track town."

I realized then I had no choice, doubts or not. I had as much responsibility as any man, maybe more than some because I was aware of what would happen if we let things go. I had to become involved because I knew damned well that the average Cheyenne resident wouldn't, any more than the good men in Julesburg had.

"Fine," he said. "We're meeting in the hall over Miller's store tomorrow night at eight o'clock. Don't mention this to anyone. Just be there."

We shook hands again and he left. I still wasn't sure I had done right, mostly because there was no certainty that Jess Munro wouldn't use the vigilance committee for his own purposes. But it was a chance I had to take. Maybe it would be wrong to participate in the Vigilante movement, but it would be more wrong to sit on my hind end and let Cheyenne go to hell.

We saved Cheyenne so that in time it really did become the Magic City of the Plains. You know, during all the years that followed, as I watched Cheyenne settle down from an end-of-track town to a solid city with schools and churches and women and children, I was never sorry about the decision I made that day when steel came to us from the East.

Caprock

by Nelson Nye

I'D JUST CROSSED THE last gully and was coming up out of the mesquites, thinking strong of grub and blankets but still with that daunsiness inside me, when I spied the gaunt shape of Rueburn's house—with a light in it.

Lights don't usually make me no never-mind but that one did. It stopped me short. In all the years I had worked for Lou Grimes this was the first time I could remember seeing a light in the place.

I was on my way to Bronco to pick up the Dubois horses and hadn't been figuring to work up no sweat. I didn't know what the hell ailed me. Been laying it to Hockmeat's baking soda biscuits, but was beginning to suspect punching Grimes's cattle for going on ten years might have more than a little to do with it. Man likes to get a little change out of life, and change was one thing Lou couldn't abide.

There was a heap of things that old buck didn't cotton to, but change topped them all. His Circle G spread covered forty miles of this west Texas country and he'd been scheming eight years how he could put another chunk to it, having in mind this Rueburn's twenty-odd sections laying empty now ever since that horse had drug Hank Rueburn to a better place. Lou'd been using the grass. Hank's wife and kids had gone back east and every year Lou'd write that Saint Louis bank, upping his offer by another reluctant hundred, scared to death some weedbender'd get his hooks into it, like the pool that had bought up them ten sections south of us.

I'd been taking it easy, not pushing Freckles none, having made up my mind I would camp the night here, water being scarce in this high plains country and no other chance to wrench our mouths between headquarters and the forty miles to town.

That light took me like a hoof in the gut.

Many times as I'd camped here I'd never been inside, never touched match to lampwick. Never know anyone else to. When Rueburn's folks had pulled their freight, they'd locked the place up fore and aft. And there wasn't no road come anywhere nearer than the east-west stage road twenty miles north. Even if they'd known of it, what cross-country stray would have come this far for shelter?

I told myself maybe I had better push on, it being none of my put-in no way. Then it come to me the outfit had probably been sold and, if it had, I knew Lou would sure want to know it. I guessed I'd better find out, and put Freckles up the slope.

There was a bitter wind blowing, bending the mesquite tops and crying through the stiff, dried grass and, what with the dust off that cleared land, was like to be full dark mighty quicklike. I was used to these caprock wind squalls, but that didn't mean I liked them any more than my horse did. I let him clatter up the slope without putting no brakes on. I caught a whiff of wood smoke with coffee smell stirred into it, and was less than three lengths from the front of the house when the light went out.

I didn't like it. I didn't like the way the look of Hank's place settled back into the feeling of forlorn abandonment I'd come to associate with its swaybacked roof and the gaunt, dreary lines of it. I pulled up, halfway wondering if I'd imagined that light, but I could still smell the coffee and wood smoke. I told myself the damn wind had probably blown the lamp out. I sat there a spell, but the back window where I'd seen the light stayed black.

Some uncomfortable thoughts got to churning through my head, but there's one thing about me: what I start, I generally finish.

I got out of the saddle and, pulling Freckles after me, bulled through the wind and dust till that black porch was square before me. Keeping hold of the reins I felt my way across the warped, dry-rotted planks of the flooring and got my hands on the latch. It was then I heard the well chain.

I felt better right away. The guy'd gone out for water—gone out the back door probably, which was what had blown the lamp out.

Stepping off the porch I called, "Hello! Hello!" but the wind tore my words away. The well was on my left, about forty strides straight out from the kitchen, and I was about to head that way when a second thought slowed and stopped me. *Better take this easy*, I told myself, *that feller might be a little nervous*. In the dark this way, in a strange place and all, he might be inclined to reach for his cutter.

No use being a fool, I thought; and went around the lee side of Hank's place, toward the kitchen, tying Freckles to a piece of fence rail, taking long enough to let the guy get back inside; waiting to see the lamp throw yellow shine against the windows.

I must of waited five minutes but the lamp didn't show.

Probably gone to bed, I thought; and tramped around to the back and put my fist to the door. "Hello inside there—anybody home?"

Only answer I got was the scream of the wind plowing through the mesquite brush, crying around the dark timbers, shaking groans from the eaves. Something clattered in the barn. A loose blind flapped somewhere off through the murk. With the wind and all this outside racket, the feller would be lucky if he could hear a train hoot. He'd probably gone off into one of the bedrooms.

I tried the back door. A gust ripped it out of my hand, slamming it against the wall with sound enough to wake the dead; but no one spoke.

It began to take hold of me. The feller was likely still pottering outside, maybe seeing to his horse, which reminded me of Freckles. I called out again anyway, not wanting any trouble.

"Jim Mawson here," I said. "Thought maybe you could put me up for the night. Wind's gettin' pretty wicked."

All's I heard was my words banging foolish through the blackness. Then I heard something else, a kind of shuddery something.

It sounded like a groan.

I didn't swallow for ten seconds, then I stepped in and shoved the door shut. The coffee smell was strong now. I could see the dim cherry gleam of the stove and I was thinking the guy might have stumbled over something. I said, "Where are you?"

"In here . . . oh, hurry . . . *hurry*!" a voice cried urgent from the depths beyond the black well of an archway. My legs near folded under me. The last thing I'd expected was to find a girl here!

I was too astonished to do any thinking. I plowed into the blackness beyond the arch, rummaging through my pockets to get hold of a match.

"Don't make any light. I'm in the big chair . . . over here by the window."

I couldn't make out the chair. In that thick musty gloom I couldn't even see the window, but I followed the pant of her voice to the right. Undressed, I thought, and reckoned it was snakebite.

I bumped knees with her and stopped. As I bent down, my outstretched left hand touched something firm that softly yielded, and I heard her insucked breath. She said choked-like, "Get my legs first . . ."

I could hear the rush of the gale outside and the groan of the timbers in this ramshackled house. The smell of dust was almost as strong as the coffee bubbling on the kitchen stove. Out of her head, I thought, and scratched my match.

I'd been wrong about one thing: She had clothes on, all right. A gay cotton print that right now looked like she had slept in it; and her hair had come loose. Gold, it was, like butter, curling down over shapely shoulders. But her eyes looked too big in that flickering light and her lips were drawn back like a wolf cub at bay. But she was a looker. And young—not over seventeen, I judged.

Her eyes turned frantic. "Put it out!" she cried, panicky.

That was when I saw the rope jerked tight and tied about her ankles.

The match flame skittered in a sudden draft. Before I could move, a man's voice said, "Light the lamp on the table."

I found the table. I rubbed the match across the lamp's wick and pushed the chimney down snug in its brackets and dropped the burnt stick in a dust-grayed saucer. And I stood there stiff and awkward as a kid caught stealing melons.

"Turn around," the man said, and I done so meek as Moses, being almighty careful to keep my paws where he could see them.

He wasn't no great shakes of a man, so far at least as size went. Matter of fact, he looked plumb puny, so thin he'd of had to stand twice to cast one shadow. But there wasn't nothing puny about the hogleg he had covering me. It was a Colt .45 with an eight-inch barrel. And his eyes was flat as fish scales.

"You got a lot of guts," he said, tight and thin, "waltzin' into my place without so much as a by-your-leave."

There was an answer to that, but I figured this likely wasn't the best time to give it.

"Make it a habit stickin' your nose into things don't concern you?"

"I called out and I knocked . . ." I let the rest of it go. I didn't like the way them fish scales was eyeing me. The skin was wrapped around the bones of his face like dried parfleche put on wet. A thin stubble of bristles stuck through the gray mask of it and he held that damn gun like for two cents he'd use it.

"It's a bad thing," he said, "to come between a man an' his woman. It can get a feller kilt. You ever thought about that?"

"Look," I said. "I called out a couple times and I knocked. The wind flung the door open and I called out again. I heard a groan and come in here—thought maybe someone was hurt."

"Then you scratched your match an' found out different. You ain't married, I take it." His eyes stayed on me but he spoke to the girl. "Ready to behave now, Kitten, if I turn you loose?"

She didn't say a word, but she must have nodded because the skinny man said, "No more of your tantrums?"

She said "no" so low I could just about hear it against the whooped-up howl of the wind outside. The man didn't move his glance by a fraction. He continued to watch me like I wasn't to be trusted no more than a skin-shedding sidewinder. He had his head cocked a little, almost like he was listening. Then he said abruptly, "You just driftin' through?"

"No," I said, "work for Old Man Grimes that ranches south and east of here—runs the Circle G."

"You picked a hell of a night to drop by for a call."

"I was heading for Bronco to pick up some horses. Figured to spend the night here . . ."

"You didn't know this place had been sold?"

"No. Nor Lou neither."

"You know it now," Skinny said, "an' you can tell him from me he better get his stock outa here." He twisted his lip in a smile that didn't get above his nose. "Bein's you're here you might as well take pot luck with us. Mostly I go by the name of Frank Jannings."

"Mine's Mawson," I nodded. "Jim Mawson."

"You can hang your cutter on the back of that chair," he said, lifting his chin toward the one against the far wall and sliding his own back in leather.

I went over and done so without much enthusiasm, feeling his eyes on my back the whole way. He was like a man with a cat by the tail, mean and edgy, with a pale fire burning back of the wicked watch he kept on me.

He had a right, I figured, to be looking uncomfortable, me finding his wife trussed up like a heifer. But there was more to it than that. He put me in mind of John Ringo. He had the same kind of eyes, the same turn of movement.

John Ringo was a killer.

"You can turn my wife loose now," he said and, stepping into the kitchen, dropped the bar in its slot.

"What's that for?" I said, and he showed that mean grin.

"Tired of hearin' that door rattle. Go ahead, help her outa them ropes. She'll be meek enough now. Nothin' like lettin' 'em know who's boss."

I went over to the girl and cut her free with my pocketknife. Brush had torn her stockings and put red scratches on the white of her legs and the rope had left purple marks round her ankles. She sat up and chafed her arms. She kept her mouth tight shut and never looked in my direction. I wasn't a heap surprised to see no gold around her finger.

"All right, go on. Get at it," Jannings said. "Get some grub on the table." He winked at me as she went out. "Set down," he grinned, "an' take the load off your feet."

I started to go sit in the chair I'd hung my gun on, but he said with a snort, "No sense us hollerin' across the room at each other. Take that chair she had."

He sat down by the table, straddling a chair and folding his arms across its back, still with his head cocked, listening and watching. You could tell there was something going around in his head. I reckoned to be careful, thinking how it would be with that girl left alone here.

I said through a welcome clatter of pans, "Would you be inclined to take a little profit on this place?"

"How little?"

"Well," I said, "there's a chance you might get shored up through bickering to maybe as high as fifteen hundred."

His eyes almost shut, Jannings laughed without sound.

That chair was too deep. I shifted my rump to the edge of it. Jannings didn't move, but the fish-scale look of his eyes flattened out and that mouth turned as thin as the edge of a knife.

The wind whined round the eaves like a lonesome dog that wants to be let in. There was a lull in the kitchen racket and his ears seemed to crouch along the sides of his head.

"Lou Grimes ain't exactly partial to neighbors."

"He's got one now," Jannings said; and I wondered how the hell I could ever have taken him for puny.

A fly buzzed round and finally lit to scrape his legs on the table. I watched him amble toward the base of the lamp and walk the rim of the dusty saucer. And all the while Jannings, still with his head cocked, straddled that chair without moving and watched me.

The girl came in with three plates and some hardware and, circling him widely, put them down on the table. Jannings hiked his chair back as though to give her more room, and cold air came in around the rattling windows and the fly buzzed off in her wake toward the kitchen.

Little shivers got to crawling up the back of my spine and the nerves in my legs got to aching intolerable. Something had to give, but nothing did. The room got colder. Jannings recrossed his arms. "Get much snow through here in the winter?"

"Not too much as a general thing. We got three feet the year before last."

"Drifts pretty bad, I guess."

"Piles up in the hollers."

I got to thinking how one winter me and Krantz had been snowed in at the Shale Cliff linecamp. Third year, that was, I had worked for old Lou. Drifts had piled up eaves-deep round that soddy. Lou, being the man with a eye to cut corners, had give us a few beans and eight hundred pounds of salt pork.

If you've ever punched cattle you know what salt pork is. Krantz beefed a yearling right after we got there, but we'd got down to the hocks by the time the snow struck. Ten days and eleven nights we'd been shut up in that place with not a damn thing to do but look at each other. We run out of wood and fed the fire with that hog meat.

It was a lark compared to this deal.

I wasn't fooling myself.

This skinny Jannings could've come without

cows. He could've come without punchers. But if he'd bought this place and come out here with his wife, even just to look it over, he'd have fetched along some truck. All he'd brought was the grub the girl was fixing.

I'd had a good look around after lighting that lamp. The dust in this place lay thicker than fleas on a mongrel's belly. This jasper hadn't been here half an hour longer than I had. If this Kitten was his wife, I was a kangaroo-rat's uncle.

She come back with three cups and some store bread and went out again. The fly circled back and bedded down on the bread and the wind kept howling like a damned spoiled brat.

I got out my knife and started fiddling with my nails. "If that thing slips," Jannings said, "you're like to lose a couple of fingers," but I kept on whittling. And he kept on watching.

I hadn't no need to look up at him to know. I could feel his eyes digging into me like dewclaws. I wondered what he expected to hear with his head still cocked to one side that way. Was he meeting someone here, or just thinking maybe I was?

Time dragged like a cow coming out of a mud hole. The girl come in with a pot and filled the cups up. The smell of that Arbuckle near made me puke. I put away the knife and watched the fly clean his wings on the top piece of bread.

The girl come back with a bowl of boiled beans and dish of jerked beef she had stewed with tinned milk. "Pull up your chair," Jannings said, hitching round.

"If you don't mind," I nodded, "I'll take one of them straight ones," but I knew better than to try for the one I'd hung my gun on.

Jannings motioned to the girl. "Go fetch yourself one outa the kitchen."

I saw her pause, saw color darken the grim-set look of pale cheeks. Her glance as she moved off slanched across to mine and Jannings, watching, gave me again that quick flash of teeth. As I pulled up my chair he drawled man-to-man fashion: "Women! God help us!" But he wasn't woollin' me any. Only thing I couldn't get straight in my head was why he hadn't stopped my clock when he come in. It seemed to me it must someway be tied to that damn listening.

When she got back we set down, all three of us. Jannings took the head of the table where he could watch the windows and that barred back door; I was on his right, direct across from the girl. He passed her the meat. "Have some of this, Mrs. Jannings. Mebbe it'll put some roses in them cheeks." The remark did, anyway. She took a small spoonful. I passed him the bread. He took the piece on the bottom. He took half the beans and what was left of the meat.

I scowled at my plate and kept my mouth shut. The girl lifted her cup and took a haul of her coffee. Jannings stuffed his mouth full. He looked like he was enjoying himself.

I had to think twice before it hooked its spurs in me. I looked again and he was watching me. The little bastard had made his mind up, had got my future all laid out in white linen. It was there plain and shining in the glint of his teeth.

I started up to fill my cup again. His hand waved me back. She'll git it fer you." I slumped down feeling ringy but knowing I wouldn't do that girl no good dead.

She filled my cup. She filled his too, and started the

pot toward the kitchen. "Put it on the floor an' git back in that seat!"

There was an edge to his tone. He wasn't drawling now; his words slammed into her mean and ugly. Her eyes got big and she got back in her chair. I got hold of it then—*the dim far sound of hurrying horses.*

He lurched onto his feet. There was a gun in his hand. He had it pointed at me and his eyes was like fish scales. "Git outa them clothes an' be goddamn quick."

The snout of that Colt looked as big as a cannon.

I got out of the brush jacket, commenced unbuttoning my shirt.

"Never mind that," he said, "git outa them pants," and backed off behind the Kitten. "You didn't have me fooled for one holy minute! Was gonna plug you quick's I seen you. Lot of guys would, but I'm a gent which has got a head on his shoulders."

He backed over to the wall, still talking, and put on my hat; broke my gun and shook the cartridges out. "You oughta had more sense, stickin' up that bank in broad daylight." The lips pulled away from his stumps of teeth. "Some guys never learn," he sneered. He pulled his shirttails out and sheafs of greenbacks slithered down his legs and raised little plops of dust off the floor. "You oughta worn a slicker, then they couldn't of told what you looked like. That's the trouble with you greeners—you don't have enough sense to pound sand down a rat hole."

He had his vest off now, and his wipe and his Levi's, had made a little pile of them and chucked his hat on top of it. "Grabbin' the Kitten for a hostage when you figgered they was gittin' too damn close was the dumbest thing of all you done. In this country, mister, they don't take kind of runnin' off women."

He gave me another of his bullypuss grins. Then his voice reached across like the crack of a whiplash. "Throw that brush jacket over here an' git' outa them pants!"

I threw him the brush jacket. I hiked my butt off the chair high enough to slide my pants down. I was hotter than a firecracker. No telling what I might of done if the girl hadn't been plumb in line with that pistol. I kicked the pants toward him underneath the table.

They got hung up on one of the legs of her chair. It looked for a minute like he would blast me right then. I could see his knuckles whiten round the grip of that gun. He said, tight and wicked, "Kick them over here, Kitten."

The girl's eyes was like green marbles in the stiffness of her scared white face. I could see what she was thinking. I shook my head at her. "Go ahead, ma'am. Never argue with a guy that's got a gun shoved at your brisket."

Her foot sent them skittering toward him. *If only she hadn't been in my way!*

Watching narrow, he picked them up. His boots was stuffed with greenbacks, too. He gathered up the rest of them, all but one pack which he left on the floor to make it look like I'd dropped it. He had my brush jacket on, buttoned clean to the throat. He got into my pants and felt pretty cocky. It was working out slick for him, just like he'd planned it while the girl was fixing supper.

He backed over to one of the windows at the side

I'd left my bronc on, with his left hand shoving the sash up. "You can step over an' put my duds on now . . . an' that gunbelt you been so lathered to git back to."

The wind had quit for a moment. The horse sounds wasn't more than a few rods off. I glared at the bastard, wild enough to defy him if there'd been any chance for me to beat that pistol. There wasn't, of course. The girl's green eyes pleaded with me.

Too mad to feel like a fool, I got up from the chair in my long-handled underwear and went over to the clothes he had left piled up so nice for me. He grinned at me, nastily, "Shake it up, shorthorn. Unless you want them fellers to find you with your pants off."

There was something about this that wasn't quite real. I looked at him bitterly. Maybe it was that daunsiness still working in me.

We was about of a size—except that I had more meat on my bones. It was while I was gloweringly getting into his things that I finally latched onto the flaw in his logic: In my clothes like he was he might get off on my horse but, quick as we told our stories to the posse, they'd be after him. My horse might not be so used up as his own nag, but after twenty miles of travel . . .

That was when I seen the full dimensions of his plan: *He'd not be leaving us in shape to tell no stories to that posse. He was going to gun us down before he ducked through that window.*

I picked up my gun-weighted shell belt. Jim Mawson, you damn fool, I told myself, you got this coming. That didn't let me off for the fate in store for this girl, though. I looked over and said to him, scowling, "They're going to wonder about this empty gun . . ."

"Not much." He shrugged. "You better take another look at it."

All the loops of the belt were empty but the rims of the shells made a pale thin gleaming from the cylinder of the gun he'd shoved back in my holster. "Empties," he grinned. "Now the both of you get over there under them winders lookin' into the yard."

"Ain't you going to put that lamp out?"

"Get over there, you numbskull, 'fore I put a slug through your guts!"

I could see the whole play now. The posse was pulling up out in the yard. They weren't rightly sure who was in here just yet. With us under the windows, he'd fire into that bunch to make sure they'd come smoking. Then he'd gun us down and fade out that back window. When them fellers got in here I'd be dead in his clothes with a empty pistol. The girl would be dead too, but they'd figure a slug had cut her down by mistake. That wouldn't help her—wouldn't help me, neither.

I was standing with the belt in my hands when she screamed. It was courage, not fright, that sent up that yell. It was a chance, and I took it. I let drive with the belt and dove for him after it.

Flame tore from his gun snout. He tried to duck, to bring the gun into line, but the holstered Colt took him square in the chest and the belt's heavy leather wrapped around his face. I had hold of him then. I like to beat his damn head off.

I didn't hear the door go down, nor the girl's excited talking. I kept slugging that jazzbo till they pulled me off him. A walrus-mustached old codger with a star on his coatfront grabbed my paw and pumped it like I'd named him in my will. Seems this Jannings was wanted for the bank—and forty other things. Wanted all the way from Eagle Pass to Tularosa.

I was looking at the girl and wasn't paying too much attention.

"Jim . . .you're hurt!" she cried, rushing over.

Sure enough. A darkish stain was leaking out of my left armpit. I didn't pay it much mind. I'd more important things to think of. I'd found out in them last moments what the hell it was that ailed me: it wasn't a doggone thing that yeller-haired girl couldn't cure in short order.

Dobbs Ferry

by Lewis B. Patten

JONATHAN DOBBS, sweating in the blazing New Mexico sun, turned his prideful eyes from his new ferry and out across the flooding, muddy Kiowa River to watch the slow approach of a wagon on the far bank. Even at this distance, he could tell from its cobbled-up appearance and rickety progress as well as from the half-starved condition of the oxen that this would be another ferry trip for which he would receive no pay.

Unless, as his wife Charity so often insisted that he do, he refused passage on the ferry until payment was made. He shook his head stubbornly. A man set up an obligation when he put a ferry here on the trail to California—an obligation to all travelers, not just to those who had enough money for the toll. Besides, to refuse passage would be to choose among his fellow men according to their ability to pay, and he knew that possession of worldly goods was no indication of character. He would tell Charity patiently, "I like to believe in people. Sometimes the ones least able to pay are the ones that need most to be ferried across."

A hundred yards downriver from the crossing he could see the wagon of Ute Weimer and his two companions. He wondered uneasily why they did not cross and move on. Their furtive watchfulness bothered him. He had the feeling they were counting up the tolls he collected. There in the high brush he could see a watching man's hat, the giant Kurt, he supposed, too tall to be completely concealed in the brush, too stupid to realize it.

He stepped onto the deck of the ferry barge, a tall, gaunt man of thirty, whose stern, clean-lined face sometimes reminded travelers of a New England deacon, and took up his long pole. Fifteen minutes later, he grounded on the opposite bank. The wagon was waiting, a frowzy woman sitting patiently on the high seat, a lanky boy of fifteen beside her. The boy was just a boy, towheaded, freckled, but too thin, his eyes too old. The other, younger, sprawled in the shade of the wagon, absently flipping a knife into the ground, taking it up, flipping it again.

Mumblety-peg, thought Jonathan absently. His eyes drifted toward the wagon of Ute Weimer, toward the still-watching Kurt. The woman got down and approached, her face telling Jonathan plainly with its hesitant expression that his earlier surmise had been correct. He called, "Drive on the ferry, ma'am. Have you across in fifteen minutes. You can't ford the doggone thing this time of year unless you go fifty miles north of here." The severity of his face was broken by the kindliness and understanding that looked out of his deepset eyes.

But the woman kept walking toward him and, when she was but a scant ten feet away, she said, her voice like the twang of a loose fiddlestring, "We can't pay, mister. I lost my man a couple of months ago. But my boys . . . maybe they can work it out."

Jonathan hated to look at her honest, pleading eyes. He didn't like to see anyone debased by having to ask for charity. He said again, more firmly now, "Drive on the ferry, ma'am. I reckon one trip for free ain't going to hurt a man."

For an instant her eyes gave him her gratitude, but then they slid away, refusing to meet his own gaze further. This momentarily upset Jonathan. He shrugged as the wagon creaked aboard. A quick glance toward Ute Weimer's camp told him he was no longer watched. He poled slowly, steadily, toward the other bank.

So many travelers along this trail were destitute nowadays, he thought. They started out full of hope for a new life in a new land, but the trail was too long and too hard for many of them. To the west of here the bones of their animals bleached beside the trail. Here and there a frail cross marked a solitary grave. Charity often said to Jonathan, "It would be a greater kindness if you'd refuse to take 'em across, Jonathan. Then maybe they'd go home and stay alive."

Yet even with all those Jonathan passed free, the ferry was paying handsomely. Maybe even enough to tempt Ute Weimer's sort, he reflected, and thought fleetingly about Charity's insistence that he carry a gun. She might be right in that. It was lonely out here, with no law save for what a man made himself.

The woman volunteered, "I'm Beulah Neely, mister. The oldest boy here is Jess an' the other's Mark. They're good workers. What would you like for 'em to do?"

Jonathan laughed. "Why ma'am, I don't reckon there's anything here that needs doin' very bad. Besides, there's a wagon train a couple of hours ahead of you. If you was to hurry, you could catch 'em yet tonight. Then you wouldn't have to travel all alone."

As he neared the western bank, he could see the curtains in their sod house pulled aside and a hint of Charity's sharp face in the window. He was a little disturbed sometimes by Charity's hardness and lack of generosity. He thought now, "She ain't naturally that way at all. It's just a quirk in her that makes her figure if she don't look out for herself, nobody else will." He grinned ruefully to himself, thinking, "Ute Weimer watches me on one bank and Charity on the other. Reckon I ain't got much chance for wrong-doin', even if I was inclined that way."

He watched the Neelys drive off the ferry and away and waved to them, embarrassed by their thanks, which had somehow seemed a little forced and not as straightforward as they might have been. But their friendship made him feel warm. No traveler, paying or otherwise, ever continued west without feeling friendship for Jonathan. He was that kind of man. There was a bigness of heart to him that attracted men and women, young and old alike. He sometimes told Charity, "A kindness is like a coin, because it seems like a body gettin' it can't wait to turn around and spend it on someone else."

He watched the wagon creaking laboriously westward for a moment, then braced himself and went inside, as ready now as he would ever be for Charity's sharp upbraiding, her scolding tongue.

She did not disappoint him. As he entered the dim shanty, she said sharply, "You crossed 'em for free, didn't you? I can tell by the looks of you whether you get paid or not. When you goin' to learn . . .?"

He wished he could change her in this, could make her see. She was so generous underneath, if only she'd let it come out and not be so afraid. A hail from across the river halted her tirade and as Jonathan turned to go outside, she scolded, "Now you see you get paid for this one, you hear? A body gets tired of seeing you pass 'em without paying, and us needing things here for the house and all." He didn't answer and she shrilled, "You hear me, Jonathan? You see you get paid for this one!"

He felt the stirring of mutiny in him, felt his anger rise. He growled impatiently, "All right, all right! I'll get paid for this one. I promise you!"

He went down to the riverbank. He could see the wagon of Ute Weimer waiting on the other side. He'd soon know their intentions, he thought. Nervousness built up in his body. He thought of going back to the house for his gun, then put the impulse aside. At least he could make good his promise to Charity without working a hardship on anyone.

He poled the barge across, letting his eyes wander out across the limitless expanse of rolling grassland, dotted with cedars and sagebrush, along the river, lined with willows and cottonwoods. It gave him a feeling of insignificance. The sun hung low in the west, like a ball of molten gold.

Nearing the other bank, he saw Ute Weimer and the man they called Slasher waiting on the ground. The giant Kurt sat on the wagon seat. It had seemed strange to Jonathan four days ago to see their kind riding in a wagon. They seemed more the type to travel horseback. He had done some speculating about this, but eventually had shrugged off his thoughts as foolishness.

Ute had a face like a hawk, a hooked sharp nose and beady bright eyes above. His skin was like old harness leather, gray with age and dust, cracked and wrinkled from exposure to the weather.

Slasher was a slim young man who carried a broad-bladed knife in a scabbard at the back of his belt and no other weapon. Kurt was a monstrous man, powerfully muscled and obviously very strong. Yet Kurt's face was singularly blank of expression and his eyes were vacant and dumb. It was Kurt who did all the heavy work around the camp, obeying the orders of Ute and Slasher dumbly and unquestioningly.

The barge grounded. Kurt whipped up the horses and the wagon rolled onto the ferry barge. Ute and Slasher walked aboard and Ute grinned at Jonathan as he said, "Busy here, ain't you? Take in a sizable piece of money every day. We been watchin' you."

Jonathan's feeling of uneasiness came back, as if he could read in the thoughts of these men that they meant him harm. He wished suddenly that he hadn't scoffed at Charity's suggestion that he carry a gun. But he forced his nervousness away, thinking, "A man makes up troubles in his mind. That's all it is."

He nodded at Ute. "Yep. Been runnin' a little over a month now and I can't complain. Freighted the ferry here from St. Louis. Been pretty near six months putting her together and getting her afloat."

Ute and Slasher went over to the far side of the barge behind the bulk of the wagon. He could hear the murmur of their whispered talk over the rushing small sound of water slapping against the barge's side. Out of all of it, though, he only made out one sentence, spoken to the giant on the wagon seat, "Kurt, you watch the team."

He poled stolidly, steadily. He kept telling himself that this was only another crossing, like a hundred others before, that as soon as they reached the far bank, Ute Weimer and the others would drive on. But Charity's worried voice kept coming back to him, "I don't like the looks of that bunch, Jonathan. They're trashy and no good. You take your gun and carry it. Show 'em you ain't helpless, and maybe they'll move on."

That had been two nights ago, when Charity had ridden across on the ferry with him, "just to get out of that stuffy house for a while."

She had asked, "Why do they keep watchin' us all the time?" when she had seen Kurt half hidden in the brush. The surveillance had bothered Jonathan, too, but he hoped it was over now. He hoped Ute and his friends would drive on west tonight and there would be nothing more to worry about. The ferry grounded and Kurt drove the wagon off. He stopped and Jonathan said, "That'll be three dollars, one for each of you."

Ute and Slasher came forward as Jonathan was tying up the barge. "Reckon we could borrow a bit of salt from you?"

Jonathan nodded shortly and led the way to the shanty. He opened the door. Charity's shrill cry was the first inkling he had that all was not well behind him. Ute Weimer had a gun in his hand and Slasher's knife was out, naked and gleaming in the last rays of the sun. Ute growled, "Don't make no sudden moves. We've just decided to take over the ferry."

He shoved Jonathan aside and went into the shanty, pushing Charity roughly back. She stumbled and nearly fell.

Jonathan forgot their weapons in his sudden rage at this. He lunged at Ute, knocking the man to the floor with a single blow of his bony fist. The gun went sliding across the packed, clean-swept earth floor. Charity screamed, "Jonathan! The knife!"

Turning, Jonathan arched his body. Slasher drove past him, falling, and the knife buried itself in the floor to the hilt.

Jonathan kicked viciously. His booted foot made a crushing sound as it connected with Slasher's jaw. Blood welled out, the man lay still. Ute was up and had recovered the gun. He raised it, his sharp face cold and deadly. Jonathan, ten feet away, watched the gaping muzzle, the tightening trigger finger with fascination.

Then something flashed between him and Ute—something bright. It was Charity in her gingham dress. Jonathan leaped forward, crashed into her and knocked her sprawling to the floor. The gun cracked, but both Jonathan and his wife were down now and he covered her with his body, waiting, waiting for the pistol's second report.

The shot never came. Kurt came stooping through the door and Ute holstered the gun, still cursing softly. He growled, "He might look like a damn church deacon but, by God, he can scrap." He seemed to hold no animosity for the blow Jonathan had struck him or for Slasher's broken jaw.

Slasher was not so generous. He raised up, jaw hanging loose, face contorted with pain. He recovered the knife and stood wiping the blade on his pants, watching Jonathan steadily in much the same way a hungry cougar might watch a frightened colt.

Ute spoke to Charity. "Stir up some grub."

Jonathan could see nothing but death ahead for the two of them. Ute couldn't release them; he couldn't let them go. He'd have to kill them if he intended to take over the ferry. And that was what he'd said he meant to do.

He helped Charity to her feet. Ute made him hold his hands out in front of him and then tied them with a length of rope. Jonathan supposed Ute had tied his hands in front so that he wouldn't have to untie them for him to eat. Ute pushed him toward the bed and he sat on the edge of it while Charity prepared supper. Slasher sat down on the one chair facing him, knife out hopefully.

Charity dropped a pot of stew in her nervousness and Ute cursed her. Jonathan scowled up at him, wanting to close Ute's mouth with his fist, knowing if he tried Slasher would open him up like a sack of grain. He'd be no help to Charity if Slasher took to him with that knife.

Soft dusk lay outside the shanty by the time Charity laid out the meal on the rude table. Ute and Kurt lined up alongside it and sat on the bench. Slasher stayed where he was, occasionally looking over his shoulder at the food, licking his lips, his face gray with pain. Jonathan felt no hunger, only hopelessness. There was no help for them now. Nobody would be coming to cross the river at night and by tomorrow . . .

Pleading now, the fight gone from his voice, he said, "I reckon I know what you figure to do with us, an' I guess it'll have to be all right for me. But for the love of God, let Charity go!"

Slasher chuckled, then stopped as his jaw pained from the movement of his laugh.

Jonathan held his temper. Furtively, his eyes swept the cabin. If a man was going to die, he'd feel better about it if he died trying, fighting, doing something. If he only had something to hold in his two bound hands. But nothing was within his reach.

It kind of made a man wonder, after all his talking about how decent people were and how it paid to do folks little kindnesses, to face dying like this. He guessed that now he could understand Charity better, her philosophy of "Devil take the hindmost. If you don't look out for yourself, it's sure nobody else will." Maybe there was some logic in her ideas.

With sudden surprise he thought, "Maybe this is the kind of folks Charity's seen the most of. With me, it's the other way around. I ain't seen many like these three. Maybe that's why Charity and me don't see eye-to-eye."

Speaking carefully because of his jaw and sounding as though he had a mouthful of mush, Slasher said, "Ute, what the hell you waitin' for? Lemme take this jigger out an'. . ."

Charity screamed, "You let Jonathan alone! You. . .!"

Her scream covered what Jonathan thought was a slight sound outside the open door. Hope boiled up in him, but the sound was not repeated and he decided he had imagined it. Then he heard a small, weak thud, and this sound was inside the cabin and unmistakable. Ute, sitting at the table wolfing the food Charity had intended for Jonathan's supper tonight, grunted explosively. Jonathan stared at him in surprise. Something whizzed through the air in front of his eyes and Ute yelled, getting up and falling backward over the bench.

Jonathan continued to stare at him, unbelieving. The handles of two boys' pocketknives protruded from Ute's back. Ute rolled on the floor, choking and gasping. Kurt still sat at the table, looking stupidly and uncomprehendingly at the man thrashing around on the floor. Jonathan thought silently, "Mumblety-peg."

Surprised at his own quick thinking, he flung himself backward on the bed, bringing his feet up, doubling his knees against his belly. He roared, "Ouch! Oh, Lordy, somethin' hit me in the belly!"

Slasher looked at him murderously, sure that somehow Jonathan was responsible for the pain Ute was in. He got up and moved toward Jonathan, knife held ready in his hand. When he was close enough, Jonathan straightened his legs, kicking with both feet. He caught Slasher in the chest. The breath went out of the man with an explosive grunt. The knife flew into the air and Jonathan caught it coming down, but by the blade.

He felt its sharpness cut his hand to the bone, but he flipped it back into the air and this time caught it by the handle as it came down. He flung it at Kurt, who was dumbly trying to bring his gun to bear. The gun went off but the bullet caught Slasher, just rising in front of Jonathan, in the back of the head.

The heavy-bladed knife hit Kurt in the face, not cutting him but making him throw up his hands protectively. Jonathan hurdled the falling body of Slasher, and his hands, still bound and bleeding profusely from the knife, caught at the gun and wrenched it from Kurt's momentarily light grasp. Jumping back, Jonathan bawled, "Get back! Get back or I'll shoot!"

Kurt, great, stupid hulk that he was, knowing his two masters were dead, kept coming, his lips drawn away from his teeth. He was a big, grizzly bear of a man who would not stop now until he had torn Jonathan to pieces or until he was dead. He pawed at Jonathan, cuffing at him the way a grizzly might, but Jonathan kept backing until at last the wall was at his back. Then he fired, reluctantly, again and again, ducking sideways at the last minute to avoid the great hands trying to come to grips with him. Kurt went down, dying slowly and reluctantly.

Through all of this, an accompaniment to his action, Jonathan had heard the steady screaming of Charity and he had kept hoping with some part of his mind that she would not mix in, that she would stay out of it. When he was able to look for her, he saw that she stood holding a rifle, swinging the muzzle back and forth wildly, her eyes terrified, wanting to shoot but afraid of hitting Jonathan. He said, "Put it down, Charity. It's over now."

Kurt lay still on the floor and the land outside the door lay gray and bleak and empty. Jonathan yelled, "All right, boys! You can come in now!"

Jess Neely appeared in the doorway and behind him, Mark. Both were pale and trembling. Jess quavered worriedly, "Did we do right?"

"Well now, I'll say you did. Nobody could have done better, that's for sure."

Charity began, "What . . .?" and Jonathan answered her. "Mumblety-peg. It's a game kids play where they throw a knife and stick it in the ground.

Only tonight these kids stuck their knifes in Ute's back instead of the ground."

Charity cut the ropes on his wrists and bound up his cut hand. Then, with the assistance of the boys, he dragged out the bodies of the outlaws and laid them side by side ready for burial tomorrow.

Back inside, he asked young Jess, "What in tarnation made you come back?"

The older boy put a grubby hand deep into the pocket of his ragged pants. It came out clutching three silver dollars. He said haltingly, "Ma . . . well, Ma wasn't quite tellin' the truth when she said we couldn't pay. I reckon she meant to say that we couldn't hardly pay. She wanted Mark and me to work for you and save this for maybe later when we'd need it bad."

Jonathan felt a surge of renewed faith and asked, "But how'd you happen to come back?"

"Well, Ma kept feelin' meaner an' meaner about not payin' you. Purty soon she just couldn't stand it no more. She stopped the wagon an' told us to get on back here an' give you the money. We sneaked up . . ." the boy's face colored with embarrassment but he went gamely on . . . "playin' Injuns, an' when we seen somethin' was wrong, why, we listened, that's all. Soon's we knew what was wrong . . . well, we just tried to help."

Jonathan grinned at Charity. He stuck out his hand. The boy put the three dollars into it. Charity gasped, "No, Jonathan!"

Jonathan's grin widened wickedly. "Yep. We got to get paid. You said so yourself."

Charity looked at him as though he were a stranger. Jonathan said, "We owe you fellers somethin' too, though. After all, you kind of saved our necks." He scratched his head, trying to keep his face solemn and straight. "I got it," he said at last. "That wagon and them horses of Ute's. Those fellers ain't got use for 'em no more. You boys take the wagon and go catch up with your ma."

He had an arm around his wife's slim waist as they watched the wagon fade into the darkness. The starlight showed a softness in Charity's face Jonathan had never seen in it before. Did a woman good to be fought for, he thought. Did a woman good to know other folks cared enough to help her, too. He said, "Doggone it, you told me to be sure an' get paid for bringing Ute and them other two across. And I let that wagon go . . ."

No sharpness, only a shy sort of shame was in her voice as she answered him. "You can quit scolding me, Jonathan. Those boys showed me how wrong I've been."

Jonathan felt warm inside as he walked her back to the shanty. He tightened his arm around her waist and suddenly she giggled, snuggling closer like a girl.

One More River to Cross

by William R. Cox

THE CROWD jeered as the tall, erect old man lifted his strong chin and climbed into the carriage. His friend looked at the glowering crowd, began to speak, then shrugged and clucked to the bay horse, picking up the lines, heading toward the Houston Manse.

"A terrible decision," said Sam Houston. "Texas is lost."

Henry Lee Morgan gently checked the restive bay. "Always a Rubicon since Caesar wrote his memoirs. It turns a man's mind backwards."

"I can only think of the future, of the Texans who will die, of the women who will suffer, of the children who will have to pay."

Morgan was silent for a moment. His friend was seventy, he had made his stand against Secession and lost, sadness draped the huge frame so that once out of sight of the multitude the wide shoulders sagged.

Morgan said deliberately, "There is always a time of decision. Do you know why I am here, amigo?"

"To stand by me, as always, since San Jacinto."

"But how did I come to San Jacinto? You never heard the story. Do you mind Rab Rock?"

The thundering brow furrowed, then cleared, and a small smile hovered on the mobile lips. "Ah, the wild man."

"Wild as a desert stallion. Ignorant as a Mexican goat. Brave as a cougar. I met him in Nacogdoches. That was in eighteen and thirty-six and I was new come from Georgia."

The old soldier-statesman relaxed, listening. He needed respite, and Henry Lee Morgan was a noted teller of Texas tales.

Nacogdoches, you remember it, a filthy town filled with spies, couriers, rascals, murderers, all bearing their own rumors of war and devastation, almost none believing that Santa Ana could be defeated, that Cos would not follow to lay waste the land of the settlers. I met Bowie there, in the days when he had stopped drinking whiskey and was about to join the command at San Antonio de Bexar. He was a dour creature, unsure, defeated by the loss of his beloved wife and children, torn by the fact of his sworn oath of allegiance to Mexico, yet determined to be in the fight.

Irritated by his talk, I went looking for a certain young lady named Janet Drew. She was from Philadelphia and her aged, drunken father had taken up land southward, below the Llano. They were traveling in a coach, mind you, with only a small driver named Saunders, intending to make their way through that country without escort. She was a sweet, brave girl.

I knew little more than did she, but even the greenest pea had heard that Big Nose was out with a band of cutthroat Comanches. The stories they told about this renegade were blood-curdling but true. Women were his special pleasure, the Comanches being full-blooded men, unlike many of the other tribes.

I told myself this was none of my business, but there had been something about Janet Drew, something a young man from Savannah could cling to, a frankness, an honesty lacking in the lady from whom he had run away. The way between Texas and Mexico meant little to me, it was there, I could join it any time. I fretted about the girl and her footless father who had been an army man and thought he was competent to make his way anyplace under the sun. Colonel Drew had long since given in to John Barleycorn, but like so many, he was not aware of this. He confused his dreams with reality.

I could not find the girl. In my search, I came to a cantina run by one Pancho Arregiera, a man of no conscience and no loyalty. It was a low-ceilinged dive, full of smoke and bad odors, but I was weary. I sat against the wall at a table and a bold slattern brought me whiskey, taking another bottle to a nearby table. It was then I first beheld Rab Rock.

He had an enormous, shaggy head, you remember. His eyes were wide-spaced and his mouth was bold and gentle at once. He was six feet four in his buckskin and carried only the knife he had been given by Bowie, eschewing a pistol, in which he did not believe. Two of his men were with him, Hacker and Sancho.

Hacker was small and bony, a product of New

York slums, a ferrety man with quick hands. Sancho was part Yaqui, with the smoothest olive skin and the largest of brown doe eyes. They were drinking heavily, all three of them, as two empty bottles testified. Rab reached out as the girl served the whiskey and slapped her hard enough to hurt, but the girl laughed on a shrill note and waited for more. He was that way with women, they fell flat for him.

After a few moments four men came into the cantina. They wore serapes but it was evident they were heavily armed. By happenstance they were in my line of vision but behind Rab and his companions. The leader had a scar which split his right cheek, the others were mongrels. They sat down without removing floppy woolen hats which partially concealed their faces.

Rab Rock was saying in his loud voice, "Fella got in trouble here t'other day. His lawyer told him to get out, he didn't have no chance. Fella says, 'Where'll I go? I'm in Texas now.' "

His companions roared approval. Hacker was wanted for murder in New York, Sancho was an escapee from a Mexican jail. Rab—well, Rab had broken every law in a dozen states with his violence and original ideas of justice. They had lived off the country for several years at this time, they and the mulatto, French.

"Country full o' rascals," Hacker said in his flat accent. "War and damnation. Big Nose and Santa Ana. It's a grand place, Texas."

"Here's to Sam'l Houston," Rab cried, tilting his mug. "Here's to us'ns."

It was then the scar-faced man dropped his serape and leaped at Rab's back. He had a long knife in one hand and a pistol in the other. The pistol misfired.

I was wearing a cap and ball weapon which I had primed at Bowie's suggestion before going about this town. Scar-faced was directly in front of me. Without conscious thought, I shot him through the head.

The other three assassins were already in action. They were men who knew their business, coming in low with their sharp blades, slashing upward, hoping to cripple their victims, then finish the job at will. But Rab Rock was out of his chair, facing them.

Those awful hands of Rab's reached out and took two of the attackers by the napes of their necks. He brought them together like cymbals. He shook them and turned them around and banged them again. Then his Bowie was flashing and blood ran.

The other man found himself between Hacker and Sancho. He lost his nerve and tried to run. Hacker merely laughed as Sancho threw his knife so that it stuck neatly between the shoulder blades.

Rab turned the leader over with his toe and said, "I swan, it's old Diablo. He never did get over that business on the Llano."

"He's over it now," said Hacker.

They were all looking at me. My hands were shaking—I had never killed before. I sat there, staring back at them, a skinny young fellow from Savannah.

Rab said, "Now look at him, will you? Saved my life, he did."

"Señor, gracias," Sancho said, bowing, showing even white teeth, his eyes mocking. "It would have been but a shame to waste this newly opened bottle."

They brought the whiskey to my table. They did not so much as glance at those who came to lug away the corpses. They were merry and they were curious and they were cool, as though they had merely swatted three house flies, and I the fourth.

It is a time like this when whiskey is welcome. In an hour I was no longer shaking in my boots. I was drunk, but I had no qualms, no fear. I remember telling them of my search for Janet Drew, and I fear it must have been a dramatic story. Possibly I shed some tears. At any rate, Rab got it into his head that I had lost my lady love and was therefore devastated.

And since one good turn deserved another, always, in Rab's lexicon, I found myself with allies. They were not exactly the men I would have chosen. In fact, the next morning I was again scared stiff when I found myself in a lice-infested room with the three of them and French.

But you must know about French. He was bigger than Rab and handsomer. He was one half Creole and one half Negro, and he was sleeping beside me when I awakened.

And I was lately from Georgia.

While I was watching him, gap-mouthed, he opened his eyes. They were brown-green, slanting, almost oriental. He recognized the situation at once. He smiled reassuringly, the most wonderful and natural smile in the world.

He said, "You saved Rab's life. Since Rab long ago rescued me from worse than death, there is a bond between us." He extended his hand.

Do you remember French's hands? They should have been modeled by a great sculptor. They were long and lean and the fingers tapered. He had been educated as a doctor in order to save time and money on the plantation of his father. I have often wondered about that man, who had produced this magnificent creature and then had used him, beaten him, almost broken him before Rab came into the bayous on one of his crazy expeditions to provide the means of escape. A medical man, purportedly a gentleman, a wealthy man with every advantage—how could he do it? What manner of beast was in him? What were his nightmares?

I shook French's hand and was better for it. No one who ever knew him could forget him. Brief as was our acquaintance, he stands out even above Rab Rock in my recollections of that time. He was able to put me, a prejudiced Southron, at my ease.

We managed to wash up that morning in dirty water, we managed to eat, we managed to gather on the street opposite the livery stable. Nacogdoches was a beehive of seething disorder, but we seemed to be waiting for someone or something. There had been pick-me-ups, you understand, a sort of hard cider in which they poured a bit of liquor. Nothing was clear excepting that Rab Rock had a huge hatred for Big Nose and was determined to carry me southward on the trail of the coach and Janet Drew in hopes he might encounter the redskin chieftain. At the moment this seemed quite normal and correct. My horse was saddled, my warbag packed, I had an extra supply of ammunition to fit both dueling pistols and the hunting rifle from home.

It was then Bowie found us and took me apart. "Do you know who you are associating with?" he demanded. "Do you know these are the most dangerous outlaws in Texas?"

"I don't see that the law is attempting to take them

into custody," I responded. I did not care for the Bowie of Nacogdoches, a cantankerous, bitter man.

"Only because we are at war. They are guerrillas, Morgan. They prey on pack trains, they raid towns, they kill and rape and pillage whenever the mood is upon them. Rab Rock refuses to join our army. They are out for themselves—first, last and all the time."

I answered, "And so, my dear Bowie, is everyone I have ever met this side of Savannah. And about ninety per cent of the people back there in Georgia."

"Then you are not for us?"

"For whom?"

"For Texas."

"And who is Texas?"

He looked at me in that canny way he had. He said, "You are newly arrived, of course. Well, go your way. But remember I have warned you about Rab Rock and his men."

Yet when I rejoined the group, Rab waved to Bowie and yelled, "See you later, Jim."

And Bowie made a gesture and said, "San Antonio, if you change your mind."

And then Peter Decker arrived. He was deaf mute, it developed, a lank man with blond hair worn long on his shoulders. He seemed uneasy in even such a small town as this one, and I learned he had been a man of the mountains since early in the century, until he made some mistake with the Indians and they turned against him and drove him out.

Rab and he exchanged signs, then Rab said, "Your lady is gone down the Llano. Big Nose is in that part of the country. We better get goin'."

We all mounted. Their horse flesh was superb—they'd stolen nothing but the best. My own gray was weathered and had bottom, as I had found on my journey into Texas. We headed out of town, going south on that trail, which is now gone and forgotten as the Llano has altered its course and its shape in the years since. But you mind the road; it was along the river on the eastern bank and the settlers broadened it with their wagons and their cattle and sheep and the bare feet of their children when that part of East Texas was settled.

We rode two abreast, with Rab and Hacker in front, French and me behind them. Sancho was the rear guard. Peter went ahead and we did not see him. He was roving, swift as a ghost, searching out the countryside, even fording the river, which was swollen out of season. The Llano was blue and not very wide, but deep except at certain places which Peter well knew. It had a way of twisting through the land between its low, wooded banks. There was a murmurous sound to it in those days when it was wild and untamed. It was a small river, but a good one. It was a river which fed the countryside, and the land was productive, all that land in that country in that time.

We were a weird-looking crew, armed to the teeth, each of us from a different background and, in truth, a cross section of Texas in '36. French wanted to talk.

"If you'll excuse me, Mr. Morgan, I don't get to talk to gentry very often. Truth is, I try not to engage them in conversation. It is better not to."

"I have had my fill of the gentry," I told him.

"Yes. I can guess." His handsome features were heavy with thought. "It is about Rab."

"A remarkable man."

"Indeed. Remarkable. The things we have done, sir, would seem impossible. Just the few of us. We have slain more Indians than I can remember. We have taken what we wanted in this wild country. We lost a few men, from time to time, but the five of us have survived and prospered. Rab carries enough gold in his saddlebag to buy half the blustering politicians in Nacogdoches."

"In the jungle the strong survive."

"We have done as we wish. However, sir, we are all young. What of tomorrow?"

"There will be laws. Mexican laws or Texas laws. There will be men to enforce them."

"Precisely. And Rab should be a leader. He is a giant. His heart is pure." French's eyes flashed, he came alive when he spoke of his hero. "Do you know that Hacker was tubercular, dying, when we picked him up? Sancho was captive of the Comanches, we rescued him. Peter was a broken man, the torture he had endured nigh finished him, he was afraid of his own shadow. Rab restored them."

"With the aid of your medical knowledge."

French pushed away his contribution with a wave of his hand. "Where would I have been had not Rab come to the bayous? No, sir, you must believe me, Rab is worth saving. Rab could make you a country here, in this wilderness. Rab could dam this river and create a kingdom of his own."

"But he will not," I suggested. "It is not in him to do such a thing."

"You could talk to him. He likes you. We could join Bowie, fight the Mexicans. Bowie would use us as scouts, he has agreed. When the war is over, we would be respected men, not feared outlaws." Tears of earnestness were in French's eyes.

I could not help saying, "In a slave state."

French smiled. "Slavery will exist only so long as sensible men do not examine it. Are you, for instance, in favor of slavery?"

"No," I admitted. "But what about you, your future?"

"Can you believe Rab would let anyone attempt to harm me?" French laughed freely, then sobered. "No, it is Rab who must be considered. If he volunteers, if he joins the Texas army, he will become a legend in the land. If we continue in our present way, we will be killed, one by one, and our names will be anathema."

It was curious to hear this ex-slave speak in such terms, but he had, you see, been educated, and in learning to read, he had assembled his own philosophy. His analysis was perfectly correct, although at the time I was too young to thoroughly appreciate it.

I said, "French, I'm sorry, but I know nothing of the politics of this war. It seems very uneven. Houston has no army, not a real army. There will be thousands upon thousands of Mexican soldiery in Texas within the month. I should be careful about advising anyone."

"Mexican soldiers are indentured," said French. "That means they are slaves. Do you believe a slave will fight well for his masters?"

"I just don't know," I said. "I'll think about it."

"Speak to him when he is not with the drink," French urged. "You will find him a true man."

"I will talk to him," I promised.

We made camp early, before dark. I was puzzled at this and somewhat anxious about the girl. Peter had been tracking but was not in view. Sancho came up to report that no one followed, ate cheese and bread, drank from a goatskin of wine and vanished. Rab only sipped at the harsh native liquid, sitting cross-legged, towering, straight-backed, wiping his lips, then smiling at me. French slid apart and Hacker slept, his hatchet face on a curved, thin arm as the sun sank behind the blue, shimmering river.

Rab said, "It's a fine land, now ain't it? Tennessee's hills were never like this."

"I didn't know you were a southerner," I said.

"Am I?" He laughed then. "The way you say it, like it was a proud thing, I sure ain't. What I was, I was a bound boy to a man named Fisher, a German fella. He whupped me every night. There was a sturdy kitchen chair. One night I hit him and then I hit him again. And again." He was happy at the memory. "All the starvin' and the beatings went up in smoke. There he lay, his neck broke. He looked beautiful to me."

"And you came to Texas."

"In time, I came to Texas." He was sober and his aspect altered in a strange way. "You are an educated man. I reckon you agree with French."

"In what way?"

"French says I have no pattern. Must a man have a way planned? Must he live by rote?"

I was uncomfortable, being all of twenty-four years of age. "I can't say. For myself, I had none, until I met the girl, Janet Drew." I was amazed at myself for speaking so. "When we met in St. Louis, something seemed to be born, then to grow a little. It is a strange development. I was running from a woman, from family, from some dead, dull past which bore in upon me. It occurs to me that all of us here are somewhat alike, Rab Rock."

"All running." He nodded. This seemed to please him. "Yet come together strong and ready. Texas is good, a good place."

"But you won't fight for Texas," I said, remembering French's plea.

"No. We're not men for that. We may kill more Mexicans than Bowie's entire company. But we'll not join an army. We ain't the kind for it."

"But I understand Bowie would make scouts of you . . ." I broke off, embarrassed, but he only smiled again, looking off toward French, nodding.

He said, "You don't ken William Barrett Travis. Bowie goes to join him at San Antonio. 'Colonel' Travis, if you please, and on the ground first. And Sam Houston didn't make Bowie a general, only a colonel like Travis. Oh, no, sir. Not for Rab Rock. Nothing the like of that for me and my boys."

"But what do you want?"

He considered with care, spoke slowly. "I want a place where me and my boys can have a house. A big house, with women in it. And good horses in the stable and dogs for huntin'. I want all to share and share alike." He paused, then went on artlessly, " 'Course I got to be boss, because they will start argifyin' among themselves and Hacker gets notions and Sancho . . . Well, they need a boss. But I want us all to be even. 'Specially French. That's the way it's got to be."

"How are you going to attain all this?"

"Take it. When we find it, we'll just take it. Then we'll hold it and damn anybody tries to get it away from us."

"What about the government? There has to be

government in a country.''

''We'll be part of the government,'' Rab promised. ''You got enough land, enough money, you can be in any government. You oughta know that.''

And I did, I knew that. This man was illiterate but he had a grasp on things as they were and are and always will be. French was looking at me, shaking his head, but there was no more to say on that subject.

Rab went on, ''You take French, now. I got to look out for him. Why, he's saved more lives than we've taken.''

It was remarkable the way he dealt with life and death, impartially, since the two are inseparable. His respect and love for French went into it; I suppose, they had been closer than brothers for years.

''He'll be the doctor for the people around us,'' Rab said, dreaming his dream aloud now, unashamed. ''We'll start a whole new way down here, wherever we settle. Texas? It's been good to us, but only because we was able to grab and hold on. So long as we got French, we'll be all right.''

There was no mistaking the ring of those last words. The man meant every syllable. Whatever his wild, improbable goal, it was wrapped up in the person of the remarkable mulatto with the physician's hands. I knew better than to pursue the matter further.

''Tell me about Big Nose,'' I said.

''No good for his own people, no good for anybody. I been after him a long time, now. One of the things we got to do is kill him.''

Peter came suddenly into the twilight, standing, leaning a little toward Rab, gesticulating with nimble hands. French came closer and watched, then exhaled sharply, which seemed to awaken Hacker.

Rab stood up and put his fingers to his lips and whistled. Then he turned to me, his face kindly. "We're a little late. Big Nose hit the coach."

My blood turned gelid, I sat staring at him, unable to ask the question for fear of the answer.

Rab said, "Killed the coachman. The old father won't last long, they got him alive after he shot a couple of 'em. We got to go and get the girl."

"Get her away from them? Can we do it?" My heart began to beat again.

"There's twenty of 'em," Rab said. "We better be on the way."

I had heard plenty about the Comanches. The thought of the girl in their hands was pure horror. I was twenty-four and even then little more than a boy. I do not remember getting to horse, I only remember Rab ordering me to ride with him. The others all knew what to do; I was a neophyte, half scared, half murderous, riding like the wind down that grassy trail alongside the Llano.

Soon enough Peter stopped us with a sign. We had come up to the coach, which was on its side. The horses had been slain first, and then the driver, who was skewered to the ground by a long spear and otherwise resembled a gory pincushion. Rab yanked out one of the arrows and examined it by the light of a tiny flame provided by Hacker's flint and steel.

"Big Nose, all right. His marking."

Peter was already showing the way the Indians had gone, toward the south, along the river. Rab looked concerned and Sancho came in and shrugged, speaking rapid Spanish which I did not then understand. French sucked in his breath and they all looked dubiously at me, excepting Rab, who spoke in level accents.

"This here Big Nose, he's a canny savage. They is only one high point of land in this here country. It's a bluff over the river, with rocks down below, where the water runs swift and deep. They call it Lopez Leap. That's where the Injuns went to make their camp."

Hacker said, "They'll have scouts down the side of the hill. There ain't no use tryin' to get up there."

Sancho lifted one shoulder and said, "The girl, she is gone goose, no? We will lose our hair for nothing, I think."

But Rab still looked at me in the darkness; I could feel his glance, and French did not stir. "The river, what about the river?"

"I was raised on the Savannah. We might float a raft," I told him. "I can't ask you to do it, you know."

French said quickly, "I know about rafts."

Hacker and Sancho waited until Rab spoke. I think they already knew his decision; they merely stated their own positions, then let him tell them the way it had to be.

Rab said, "Wasn't no river in the hills. I can't swim."

"Me neither," said Hacker.

French said, "You can go by land, with Peter. We'll scale the bluff and create a surprise diversion. Perhaps you could come in, that is, if Peter can account for the scouts."

"Sancho and Peter can snake in better than me," said Rab. "That puts three on the land side and three on the river. I like it better that way."

"But if you can't swim," I began, then stopped, realizing that no one went against Rab's decision. I added lamely, I fear, "I wouldn't want to endanger you in the river."

"Reckon I can take care of myself if I have to," he said. "Now, about that there raft."

There was a tall cypress which had fallen in a storm. The long knife of Mr. Bowie had many uses, and now it became a machete, cutting branches away. Sancho came with long grasses of amazing toughness, and we had ropes with which to entwine the limbs we so hastily hacked to proper length. There is a trick to this, which at that time I knew very well, but it was arduous labor. We were sweating and the moon was high, if faint behind clouds, when we were finished and the raft on the riverside, ready to be launched. Hacker threw himself down and snorted.

"I don't like it, Rab. It's kinky."

"Sure, it is," agreed the leader cheerfully. "Ain't it always been? You just go ahead with the boys."

Hacker looked at me. "You come along and he goes all the way. Too bad you don't know what it means, Mister." He turned and followed Peter and Sancho, who merely waved as they melted into the shadows.

"I do know," I told Rab. "There's no reason for you to do it."

"No reason? I been after Big Nose for two long years," he said. "He's got an old man to torture and a girl; it's a time to tackle him."

"But the odds are against us. He has high gun on us. There are twenty to our six. And won't they kill the captives as soon as we attack?"

"They might try to kill 'em. They may not get the chance. If we don't get on with it, howsomever, them people won't have any show, now, will they?"

He turned toward the raft, a shaky vessel in the current which was running. He hesitated just a fraction of a second then, but French steadied the clumsy craft while we scrambled aboard with our rifles and pistols and knives very much in the way, and clung to the cross-ties which held the logs together. French slipped alongside us like a huge eel, and we were off.

It was a rough voyage. French and I had skinned poles with which we fended us off floating timber and several large rocks. The moon continued to play tricks in the most fickle manner, now revealing danger, now shrouding us in blackness by hiding behind heavy, scudding clouds. A young man has few fears for his own safety, particularly in crises of physical danger, but I was terribly afraid for Janet. Possibly this fright gave me strength, for we were able to accommodate ourselves to the turbulent river to the place where we could see the bluff rising above us, harsh against the lowering sky.

There were no words between us as we hauled and pulled, now deliberately aiming for the jagged rocks, not knowing any other means of going ashore. Rab lay at full length, his jaw set. The Llano began to rage beneath us as French and I poked with the poles until our arms nearly fell out of their sockets.

Then, an accident of fate, there was a protruding branch, growing from an underwater brush, heavy and strong. Rab seized it. We ran to help him, dropping our poles. The moon threw us a glimmer of light and we threshed and strove—and were out of the current and floating in a pool of still water.

In a moment we were ashore and checking our powder. Rab inhaled deeply and showed us a wide, carefree grin.

"Never been so scared in my life. We got lucky, didn't we? It'll be all right now. Luck's with us."

French shook his head. "Could be we used up our good luck. Could be there's bad ahead. Let's go cautious, Rab, real cautious."

"Cautious never wins," said Rab. He looked up at the cliff towering above us. "Betcha there's a way up yonder if we look right sharp."

We were a hundred paces from the river when he found it. Now we were speaking in whispers, already in the mood of skulking attack. Rab did not speak, he merely indicated with a fierce gesture that there was a path leading upward. It wound into what now became darkness as the moon went under, irregular footholds in the steep sides of the bluff, certainly not designed by man, a freak of nature. It might end halfway, but Rab believed in his luck and we began the ascent, he first, then myself, the greenhorn, then French.

If they thought of the danger of a dislodged rock rattling down to give our presence away, I never knew it. The night had turned quite cold, but I was sweating. And then, after we had climbed interminably, the moon again came swishing from behind the woolly clouds.

We hung there like three ants upon a stalk of grass, helpless. But Rab looked up, still grinning, and saw the way. His hand touched my shoulder and we turned our stares skyward. The next bank of puffy, gray, billowing vapor swam slowly toward the leering moon.

It was then that everything went wrong. There were shots above us and wild yells. Without hesitation, despite the moonlight, Rab began climbing, reckless now of any consequence. Behind me French pushed, so that I must needs follow the leader. My hands were torn on the sharp edges of stone, but we kept going, unthinking of anything but possible disaster.

The shots continued and the sound of howling savage grew with it. We had reached the last yards of the ascent and had come over the top when portentous silence fell. We lay prone, our eyes fixed upon the scene.

The Indian fires were high. Stakes had been driven into the earth. The old man, Colonel Gray, was tied to one, hanging in his bonds, bleeding, his beard upon his chest. The other, nearer one, Janet was attached to by leather thongs, held upright by them, her head fixed so that she must see everything that went on.

You know the Comanches, like the Kiowas, their cruelty is their amusement, their only reason for mirth. They had been torturing the Colonel, of course, when the trouble began with Peter and Sancho and Hacker. They had almost been caught between us. We did not know then nor ever what went wrong. We only know that somehow the ambuscade from the other side had failed and that our men were discovered too soon.

Hacker was down on his knees. A huge Indian had sunk a tomahawk into his skull. Sancho was struggling with two captors. Peter was prone, his head in the farthest corner of the fire, unmoving. A brave was hauling him out, brandishing a small scalping knife.

There were four or five dead redskins lying about. We three lay there a moment, estimating the chances. French breathed, "No good. The luck ran out."

"They'll be slaves," Rab warned. "The girl and Sancho. You know what will happen to them."

French breathed the word again, "Slaves," and was silent. He knew too well the import.

Rab said, "The guns first. Ready?"

We remained in our prone positions, drawing beads as Rab muttered, "You take the right. I've got Big Nose. French—the left."

It was like a scene from Dante's Inferno. Even as I triggered my overloaded fowling piece, I had no sense of killing people. These were not people, they were figures in an awful pageant.

We had little enough against them. Three shots from long guns, three pistols. It was point-blank, however, and we did have the element of surprise, as Rab well recognized. We drew our long knives and screamed, rushing toward them.

By the grace of God, our shots took some effect. Rab missed Big Nose, but his bullet caught the Indian who was scalping Peter. We also had the advantage of temperament. Indians will fight at their choice, but were always inclined to flinch upon continued pressure. We struck them.

My own part was small. I hacked at a brave reeking of sweat and fear and he went down. I saw a squaw making for Janet with blade in hand, and without conscious volition I cut her throat. I slashed Janet loose with the razor edge of the Bowie and yelled to her to get away, to hide.

From that angle I could see Rab and French. It was an awesome sight.

Rab had found Big Nose. The Indian was huge, an animal of a man. Rab was holding his left wrist as he cut him with the point of the knife. French was killing with the unbelievable agility and strength of a born warrior. The Indians, recovering, seized lances, anything that came to hand. There was a ring around the two of them, pushing and mauling. I came laterally upon it, dancing around, hitting at naked red spines.

Then a shot rang out. I heard Rab's wild yell and out of the corner of my eye saw an Indian with an old musket. I took after him, but he ran into the darkness toward the river.

I turned back and Rab sent two Comanches reeling, their bodies scarlet with blood. I tried to get to him and fell ignominiously over a dead body.

When I sat up, it was all over. There wasn't an Indian in sight, except those who were unable to run. Big Nose lay dead at Rab's feet.

But Rab was the only one of us standing. His face was wet with sweat, his great arms, blood-stained, hung loose at his sides. His strange eyes were sunken in his head.

French lay at full length. I rushed to him, but the bullet from the musket had gone through his heart. Rab did not even bend his head toward his dead friend.

"He was right," he rumbled in his throat. "The luck ran out."

Sancho was alive. He stumbled toward us, holding his right arm in his left hand. The others were dead. Janet came from the rocks, creeping, weeping. I held her and she was shivering as though with ague.

I said, "I'm sorry, Rab," words as futile as the

babbling of the Llano, which now could be heard below us.

"It was the luck, the damnable luck." He turned to Sancho to ask what had happened, what went wrong.

Sancho pitched forward. There was a horrible hole in his back. He was dead when he hit earth.

"All gone," said Rab. "All the boys."

An Indian dying well, as they sometimes did, keened on a high note and thrust from the ground with a spear. Rab took hold of the shaft, reversed it, and without changing his bemused expression, skewered the attacker to the ground. He moved slowly, among them, then, head bowed, preoccupied, making sure all were dead.

It was then I realized why we had so quickly prevailed. Peter's count had been correct; there were twenty Comanches. But possibly half of them were squaws. They all held weapons, or there was a knife or a hatchet nearby their bodies, yet they were females and not fit to cope with such as Rab or French. A baby squawled from afar and Rab went to it with as much abstraction as though it were an infant wolf, and I took Janet away from the scene. She could endure no more.

We made a rude camp and then Rab and I built up the fires, for there was no time nor energy for burial here. I tried to say something for the fallen men of our party, but knew Rab was not listening as the flames leaped higher and higher and we had to turn away. He sat with us through that night while we slept.

In the morning he had drawn a map upon a piece of bark. With infinite detail he showed us how to follow the river, how to branch off and come safely to the property which was now in Janet's name. He went over it several times to make sure we innocents understood.

Janet said a last, "But surely you'll come with us? You could share it with us. We want you to have half of everything. We have funds to build and stock the ranch and hire workers. You would be our partner. You won't refuse us?"

I interjected, "We need you, Rab."

He almost smiled. "It's right good of you all."

"Without your men this life is ended for you," I insisted. "Why not make a new one, with us?"

"Aye, ended," he agreed. "French is dead." He looked at the morning sun, squinted, shook his head. "One favor is all I ask of you. When the story is told, make it plain that my boys were not seeking booty. We raided, we stole. We killed. But this last hooraw, it wasn't for loot."

"It was for me," cried Janet. "I'll always know it."

"Mebbe. Mebbe not. We was after Big Nose. We was after a fight. We was always like that." He pondered. "Thank ye kindly, but just say it wasn't for loot."

He got up, shook himself and stared down at the river. He said, "I'm goin' across."

"But, Rab, we do need you," I said. "Can't you see us down there, then make up your minds?"

"Ain't got much of a mind to make up. I been fightin' and brawlin' for me. Me and mine. Now I reckon it's got to be played out another way."

"What do you mean?"

"Texas," he said, grinning without mirth. "Across

that river to the west is San Antone. Bowie's there. I figure to join him."

He made a polite, awkward little bow and started for the place where we had come up to the bluff. His shoulders had been bowed, but now he straightened and was jaunty, turning, bowing, waving. "Adios, amigos. Go make a place for me, just in case. Mebbe I'll come see you all one day."

Then he was gone out of sight, down the rocky side of the bluff, toward the river, the way we had come. I often wondered how he got across and where, since he couldn't swim.

The carriage turned into the path leading to the Houston manse. The two ladies on the veranda arose and started forward.

Sam Houston said, "We know he crossed, all right."

"That we know."

"And you did not cross, but later came to battle." Sam Houston's wide mouth relapsed into a smile. "What you are telling me is, we never know what lies the other side of the Rubicon. Each crossing brings its own answer, eventually."

"I think you are right about Texas in 1861," said Morgan. "But somehow, Texas will survive."

Houston nodded. He clambered down with his head high.

Morgan went to greet the small woman with large eyes, holding her close.

"Janet," he said. "It's going to be all right. Sam forded his river."

Peaceful John

by Kenneth Fowler

JOHN REMSBERG reined up the dun in front of the ranch house's weed-fringed doorstep, halting the buckboard. The low-roofed weathered adobe stood commandingly on a ridge overlooking a coffee-colored creek which lost itself in sinuous wandering a half mile distant, in a motte of cottonwoods.

Hunched forward on the buckboard seat, Remsberg sat motionless for a long moment and with an air of introspection gazed out upon the biggest, the wildest, the loneliest stretch of country he had ever seen. The sand and rock and tough, spiny vegtation molded into rolling hills that ran as far as the eye could reach. The sky above them was an immaculate blue dome, anchored against remote peaks. The air of a fine September day fairly sparkled.

Savoringly, Remsberg drew its tang into his lungs. The view from what was now his own dooryard made him feel little—and big. Little because of its immensity. Big because it strangely gave him a sense of liberation and power. Because this land was so virginal and big, it built bigness in a man's thoughts.

His right foot dangled over the edge of the buckboard. He swung it idly, enjoying the warmth of the sun soaking through his frayed cotton shirt and into his solidly thewed shoulders. He wore homespun breeches, and a campaign hat of the Union Army, stripped of its identifying insignia, lay cocked back on his broad head, exposing a swatch of straw-colored hair, flagrantly awry. His eyes, of a faded blue-denim hue, scanned the horizon with a fixed look of abstraction.

Ja. He nodded solemnly to himself, reflecting. *A land like this puts a fever in a man. It works into his blood and bones, like the feeling he can get from one special woman.* And suddenly he wondered. Was it the land stirring this peculiar restlessness in him, or the still vivid image of the girl he had met at Ellsworth's Mercantile this morning, when he had bought his supplies?

Of her he must not think. An aristocrat. He had heard of the Ellsworths, one of the oldest families in the region. Their house on the outskirts of town was the biggest in the neighborhood, and Abby Ellsworth had been raised as a lady of quality. Undoubtedly she worked in her father's prosperous business establishment only now and then, for something to do. And what was he? Ten years ago he had landed on the shores of this country, in New York, from the deck of a cattle boat.

Dream then, John Remsberg. But do not be a fool!

There had been a way about her, though—a frank and open manner almost blunt, yet inoffensive.

She had called him at once by his name, as if knowing all about him, and when he had shown surprise at this, her eyes, a soft and smoky gray, had twinkled. "This is the town's gossip forum, Mr. Remsberg," she had told him, smiling. "You are the man they call 'Peaceful John,' aren't you—the one who is taking over the old August Remsberg place?"

It was more a statement than a question and he merely nodded, seeming really to see her then for the first time—a slender, vital girl wearing a dress of some woolly dark green material and with black hair that shone like ice where it was plaited at the nape of her neck into a graceful chignon.

"Why do they call you 'Peaceful,' Mr. Remsberg?"

He looked down at her searchingly. "It is funny—that name?"

"Yes and no. It is, applied to you, I guess," and her eyes frankly measured his stalwart frame.

She made him think of an impudent puppy, teasing for attention. He said: "It is not funny in the north, not to carry a gun," and pondered solemnly. "Here it is a big joke, if a man does not?"

"It's unusual. Times are unsettled. Most ranchers wear them—for self-protection."

He held up his big fists before her. "These are my protection. I fought in the war for the Union. I have seen enough of guns. Now we are all neighbors again."

"Even neighbors quarrel, Mr. Remsberg. Down here you are less apt to meet trouble with a gun than without one."

"I mind my own business. I have no trouble." And he handed her the scrap of paper on which he had methodically written down the list of staples he required.

She apparently noticed his cautious pricing of each item as she laid it upon the counter, for when the order was completed, her mention of credit had an overdrawn casualness.

"Your uncle always ran an account here," she told him. "Pay us when you are able."

Color sprang in his cheeks as he spread the coins from a worn money pouch before her.

"I am able to pay for what I buy."

"Do you know what I suspect, Mr. Remsberg? I suspect that you are being foolishly proud! I could see only a few coins left in your purse."

Her outspokenness faintly shocked him. He stared at her and was surprised at the briefness of his discomfiture. Her words were blunt, but without sting. Popcorn cracked, but then you saw the golden kernel. And caught the savor. Her straight way of looking at him was not bold, but had simply an unaffected human curiosity—a kind of warmth. Then he noticed her hands, and had a sinking awareness of the gap between them. They were slim and unroughened, with fingers meant for delicately holding a wineglass or skimming gracefully over the keys of a piano. The hands of a lady.

Without visible effort he hoisted the heavy gunny sack of provisions and heaved it across his shoulder. Then he picked up the pouch.

"This pouch will not remain empty," he said stiffly.

"Of course it won't! You should do very well if you go after mavericks. I have heard of some fine herds being built up that way."

The warm animation in her voice made him instantly ashamed.

"Yes," he agreed, "I would like to build up a herd," and for an instant felt an awkward interrogation in their crossed glances.

"You must visit us again when you are in town."

"These stores will last me a long time."

"You will not want your nose at the grindstone all the time." She smiled. "Unless you intend to become a hermit."

Now, sitting hipshot on the buckboard's straw-cushioned seat, John Remsberg tried to shut her from his thoughts as he stared out over the ranch's run-down outbuildings. He had his supplies. Now he must get to work. There was brush to be cleared, sheds to be repaired, and somewhere out there in the brasada he must build a holding pen for the mavericks he hoped to rope and brand. A man could not let himself be distracted and still do the job he had to do here.

She had worn paper sleeve guards over the lacy cuffs of her blouse, so as not to soil them. And so tiny she had looked, standing beside him. Just one of his hands would have gone around her waist.

But the cattle. They must come first. Cattle that had multiplied extravagantly during the war years, and now could be legally claimed by the first man to go out and dab his loop on them.

Ach, but those dainty hands of hers! Wives of ranchers, seen waiting for their husbands in buckboards and spring wagons in town, had not had such hands.

Ja. The cattle first. And up north, in centers like Abilene, Ellsworth, Dodge City, were the buyers, ready and waiting, and already great dusty herds were thundering northward across the plains, and opportunity was for the foremost.

The hands of the ranchers' wives had been reddened and ugly—work hands. But was that all a man wanted of his woman—work?

Squinted against the brassy sunlight, John Remsberg's eyes built their dream as he stared out over the craggy, tawny hills. He shook his head, slowly, thoughtfully. No, he must not let himself be sidetracked. Besides, there was the talk about him in town—and what woman would want a man who disregarded the country's frontier code of law by the gun, and thus held himself up to scorn and ridicule?

Damnyankee carpetbagger! Won't last here six months. All those backhanded whisperings and slyly amused glances he encountered now, whenever he was seen in town.

Peaceful John . . .

He broke with a start from his introspection. Two riders had come up to the edge of the ranch yard and now sat saddle there, blowing their lathered horses as they talked briefly together, staring down at him. Then, suddenly, they swung their mounts into the yard, and reining in alongside the buckboard, dismounted.

One of the men was broad and stocky, with heavily jowled jaws and chilly eyes that lay on Remsberg with a studying fixity. His companion was small, almost runty. He sucked on the stub of a brown-paper cigarette, his amber-toned eyes narrowed against a twirl of smoke.

The bigger man stepped up beside the buckboard. "Name of Dan Shiffley," he said, and stretched out his hand. With faint surprise, Remsberg met it. Shiffley nodded across his shoulder. "My partner, Maxie Fass."

Fass's head jerked slightly.

"I am pleased to meet neighbors," Remsberg said.

Shiffley grunted. "Heard in town you were takin' over here. Waste your time on a cocklebur outfit like this."

"Is so?" Remsberg asked mildly, but Shiffley ignored the remark.

"Come to offer you a job," he said. "Pay you fifty cents a head on every cow you can put in my Dollar S iron. Get the hang of it, you could do six a day, easy."

"Three dollars a day," Fass said. "Good pickin's for a greener."

Remsberg's mouth made a closed smile.

"Then I pick for myself—no?"

Shiffley looked at Fass. "Didn't I tell you, Maxie?" His glance swung to the sack of provisions canted against the back of the buckboard seat. "All set to lay in his store-boughts—see? Too almighty proud to hire out and turn a quick dollar."

Remsberg flushed. "I did not say it that way! I—"

"Only we got no hard feelin's, have we, Maxie?" Shiffley broke in. "Let's give Peaceful John here a hand with that sack."

Remsberg was not quick enough, leaping out of the buckboard. Shiffley was already at the back of the rig, tugging on the loaded gunny sack. As Remsberg lunged to seize it from him, the top fell open and its contents spewed out.

"Doggone!" Shiffley looked dumbly surprised as his boot tramped heavily on a paper sack of sugar, splitting it open, and then Remsberg was roughly fending him aside.

"Leave it! I will take care of this." Remsberg was stooped over and reaching out as Shiffley straightened suddenly and kicked him idly in the right temple.

Momentarily stunned, he saw Max Fass's spindly figure poised above him as he tried to raise himself. The gun in Fass's fist swished down at him in a glittering arc. He groaned and collapsed across the empty gunny sack. Everything went black.

Abby Ellsworth was putting on her hat, primping before a mirror in back of the counter, when John Remsberg walked into Ellsworth's Mercantile for the second time in one day. An austere-looking man in his middle years stood behind the counter near her, and from just a passing glance Remsberg knew this must be her father. Clayton Ellsworth had the same fine, delicately boned features, the same smoky swirls in his granite-cool eyes.

Abby caught his reflection in the mirror as he shuffled hesitantly up to the counter, and as she spun around and their eyes met, color surged into their faces at the same instant.

"Why—Mr. Remsberg! This—this visit is sooner than I had expected."

Embarrassment at her mistake sank deeper color into his high cheekbones. "I . . . I do not make a visit," he blurted awkwardly. "I have come to buy more things."

"Oh! I see." Her voice chilled faintly before she caught herself and hastily erased the note of pique from it. "You forgot some items. And I judged you for the kind who never forgets anything."

"I did not forget the items."

"But you just said—"

He interrupted humbly: "Forgive me that I do not make it clear. There was out at my place a little . . . fuss. You could perhaps credit me for the same order again—no?"

A startled look crossed her face, then shock spread fully over it as she noticed the bruised swelling at his right temple, where Dan Shiffley's spur had raked it open.

"You were hurt!" she exclaimed.

"It is nothing."

"Who did this, John?" His given name burst from her before she was aware of it. She covered her confusion by angrily shaking her head. "If you had taken my advice and worn a gun, this would not have happened."

"A gun?" He looked at her doggedly. "A gun I would forget I had."

"Who did this? Who did it?" she demanded tensely.

He told her about Shiffley and Fass, ending it lamely: "Next time I will be prepared for such monkey business. I would have invited them in for a *Klatsch*. A neighborly call, I am thinking, when I see them come into my dooryard."

"A neighborly call! And they beat you up and destroyed your supplies!" Abby Ellsworth bristled. "I've heard of those sneaking carpetbaggers! Cheap Northern trash! I—" She stopped suddenly, a furious blush mantling her cheeks. "I'm sorry," she said. "I didn't mean to—"

"It is all right. We are all under the same flag now."

She swung abruptly, her glance going to where Clayton Ellsworth stood, his eyes narrowed and dour, shuttling between them.

"Father, this is John Remsberg. You knew that he was taking over the old Remsberg place."

"I knew that, yes. I have also heard talk in town about Mr. Remsberg that has not been favorable."

"You have heard nothing but a sly whispering campaign spawned in some dirty saloon! That has nothing to do with this. Credit for a few staples."

"I also overheard your conversation with him just now," replied Clayton Ellsworth coldly. "What happened out there today at his ranch can happen again. A storekeeper cannot afford to pour molasses into a leaky barrel."

"But, Father! This is not a leaky barrel. Mr. Remsberg owns a ranch. He is not a . . . a saddle tramp!"

"I did not say that he was. But if slander has been spoken against him, he cannot honorably ignore it."

"Is 'Peaceful' a slanderous word, Father?"

"It is, when spoken with intent to defame."

"It is not when spoken by a vicious little clique of drunkards and town riffraff who have not the courage to come out and speak it to his face! Mr. Remsberg may not have fought on our side in the war, but he was a soldier. He is not a coward! He—"

John Remsberg's voice trembled out across her words. "It is no matter. Thank you. I will try at the Eagle Mercantile." And he turned to go.

A slow comprehension broke in Clayton Ellsworth's eyes as Abby spun around, facing him.

"Father," she demanded fiercely, "have you ever lost a single dollar from credit I have written for this store?"

"Why—why no, Abby. I don't guess I have. But—"

"You have not and you will not! Anyway, it is not the money you are concerned about—or need to be!"

Abby's voice shook. Clayton Ellsworth stared with a numbed look at her flashing eyes, at the sudden pallor skirting the frail line of her mouth. She swished around, and the impelling vehemence of her voice halted John Remsberg just as he reached the door.

"Mr. Remsberg! Wait!"

Regularly, after that, two nights each week, John Remsberg drove in to Bandera to see Abby Ellsworth. The fact was accepted in town now. Abby Ellsworth and the carpetbagger who had inherited Gus Remsberg's old siwash outfit were goin' steady. Clayton Ellsworth's daughter—the younger, sassy one. Clayton's only boy had died of a Federal bullet at Bull Run. One of the first to volunteer. And now Miss Abby, apple of the old man's eyes, tarry-hootin' around with a damn blue-belly. Be a scandal, surer than hellfire, if a match come of it.

The town gossip. The sly winks and covert whisperings. They ignored it all. They were too busy with each other, moving alone and uncaring in a world apart, and content just to hold their dream.

After a long day's work out in the brasada John Remsberg was usually exhausted, yet the satisfaction he derived in making the ten-mile drive into town and reporting his progress to Abby more than compensated him for the hardship the trip entailed. He had better than threescore of cows put in his iron now, and penned up in a boxed canyon, a mile from the house. Sentimentally he had chosen 7T6 as his brand—the year in which he would take Abby for his bride and start his new life in this new and wonderful land.

With the last of his savings, money he had kept cached under a loose board in his kitchen floor, he had bought a good rope horse and a pair of home-tanned *armitas*, and while he had not yet become a skilled rider he had quickly caught on to the knack of throwing a rope, and the muscles in his corded arms and anvil-thick shoulders were strong as a bull's.

He had never been to her home. Their meeting place was the dingy lobby of the hotel, and from there they took long walks together, sometimes strolling far out of town, often filled with chatter and as often not, and as content when they were silent as when they talked. Then one night she stopped and look straight at him. "You have not met my older sister. Saturday I want you to call on me at home."

To pay his call, he put on the only store-bought suit he had. And in the Ellsworths' fine front parlor he sat stiff and awkward on the horsehair sofa beside her, unused to such elegance and feeling confused and uneasy in spite of her efforts to put him at ease.

Abby's older sister, Tilda, who had babied her from the time she was ten, when their mother had died, finally came in to be introduced, a prim, severe-looking young woman with a tight-drawn mouth and eyes that seemed to skim over John Remsberg in unspoken derogation. With grudging clemency she went through the formality of sipping a cup of tea with them, then quickly excused herself. Clayton Ellsworth did not make even this pretense of hospitality. Coat and hat across his arm, he accorded John Remsberg a brusque nod as he passed through the room, saying, "Good evening, sir," and then marched on stiffly to the door.

Watching Abby sitting erectly beside him, in hurt dignity, John Remsberg felt her misery more than he did his own. He stood abruptly.

"I told you it would not work out. They do not want me in this house, Abby."

With an angry gesture, Abby shook out her skirt and rose. "Then they do not want me here, either."

John Remsberg's big hand motioned over the richly appointed room. "I cannot give you fine things like this, Abby."

Her vehemence startled him. "John Remsberg, you are a fool!"

"I am not welcome here, Abby. I will not come again."

"You will not have to."

"It is not much I can offer you."

"It is enough that I will have you, John."

A week later they were quietly married in the little Baptist parsonage on lower Main Street. The Reverend Adam Doan and his wife were the only witnesses.

He improved his holding pen and learned to throw a hoolihan, and time like a great wheel slowly ground its grist of days, and his herd increased, and Abby was going to have a baby. It was so. Not for months yet, but the doctor in Bandera had assured them. He prayed it would be a boy. A son and heir for the greatness of what he would someday build here. His dream stretched in bigness. An empire of golden hides and ivory horns. Great herds with his 7T6 branded on each brute's flank, and streaming northward in a never-ending tide. In this vast land the imagination spilled over, for there was no bottom to its wellsprings.

He grew lean and saddle-hammered from his work in the brasada, and there were upwards of a hundred and fifty cows in his pen now. He could get two, maybe three dollars a head for these, in Bandera. He would take it. He would drive to town soon, with Abby, and make the necessary arrangements. With three hundred dollars in his pocket—*ja*, maybe more!—he would buy her a fine present. And build another room on the house. *Ja, ja*. Time did not stand still. Soon they would be needing it.

But he was not always happy coming in at dusk, exhausted from a hard day working the brush, even though Abby usually was at the door to meet him, her arms often flour-powdered from baking, and her greeting kiss was something he looked forward to the whole day through. He noticed that she had seemed strangely quiet and preoccupied of late, and this worried him. Women in a delicate condition were prone to the vapors, he knew. It could be that. Or it could be that she was pining for the softer, easier life that she had left behind her, in Bandera.

With a few of the personal belongings that she brought here from her home, she had titivated up their bedroom until it seemed almost as pretentious as a room in Clayton Ellsworth's big house in town. There was an old walnut highboy, with curved brass handles which she assiduously polished every day; a huge mirror framed in cherry wood, and a dainty cherry-wood chair, with legs so thin and fine that he had never dared sit in it; and a great walnut four-poster bed, so wide that it left only a narrow space on one side of the small room, to come in to it.

By comparison, the rough-hewn furniture that August Remsberg had made for the living room looked poor and shabby. When the bedroom door was open the mirror reflected the living room's drabness, and John Remsberg took an aversion to it, since it seemed to rebuke him for the littleness of what he had been able to give her, in contrast to the bigness of his dreams.

Then one night when they were in the kitchen, finishing supper, he learned what was troubling her—not her condition, nor a yearning for geegaws and fripperies beyond their present means, but simply concern over him.

"John," she said out of a clear sky while he sat packing his pipe and watching the lamplight play over the frail planes of her face, "it is too quiet. I have been expecting something to happen, and it has not."

"Something to happen?" He knew immediately what she was driving at. He did not want her to know that he knew. "*Ja*. It has been quiet. And peaceful." He held a match poised, looking at her. "But you do not call it something happening when we have one hundred and fifty cows in our holding pen?"

"You know what I am talking about, John Remsberg!"

He scratched the match alight and applied it to the charred bowl of his meerschaum, puffing a moment before answering: "*Ja*. You are talking of Dan Shiffley. That is finished. There is no more trouble."

"I know that shirt-tail Shiffley clan! And I think you should carry a gun."

He sighed, relaxing in his chair. "You are very beautiful when you look so serious, *Liebchen*."

"Do not put me off with sweet talk!"

"There is a rifle in the house."

"A blunderbuss, you mean! You should wear a side arm. It won't mean you are looking for trouble. Just that you'll be ready, if it should come."

"Fiddle-faddle."

"Don't you fiddle-faddle me! You cannot let yourself be run over, John. Or let anyone think you can be."

"No one is going to run over me, *Liebchen*."

"We are just out of coffee." Abruptly, Abby rose and began clearing the table. "Tomorrow you can drive me to town in the buckboard. And if you will not buy a gun, I will buy one for you."

"Tomorrow is fine. Tomorrow while you buy your coffee and guns, I will see the cattle buyer. Estes Trenholm. Three hundred dollars we will have, Abby. We will shoot up the town together—*nein*?"

She did not answer him. It was their first quarrel.

All during their drive to town the next morning Abby sat beside him withdrawn and silent, and their quarrel was still unresolved when they arrived finally at the Eagle Mercantile, where, since Abby's estrangement from her family, they had done what little trading had been necessary for them. But the real blow had not fallen until half an hour later, after he had talked with Estes Trenholm in the lobby of

Huffmeyer's Hotel and afterward had rushed across the street to the Bandera county clerk's office, spurred by a wild hope that the cattle buyer might have been mistaken in what he had told him. Trenholm had not been mistaken.

In the county clerk's office he could feel his heart's dull, panicked hacking against his ribs as he stared at the clerks's smugly calm face.

"You . . .you are sure of this?" he blurted out tensely. "There is . . . no chance of mistake?"

"We don't make that kind of mistake here, mister. There it is—right in the book." The clerk jabbed his pencil at an inked notation in the ledger opened before him. "Brand 7T6—registered in the name of one Max Fass." He thumped the ledger shut. "Looks like you ain't got no cattle, mister—till you ketch you some more. Even a greener should savvy you can't legally claim a brand in this county till it's recorded."

John Remsberg wheeled slowly and stumbled out of the office. Outside he stood tracked for a long moment on the boardwalk, staring around him with the vacantly disconcerted look of a man suddenly realizing that he has become lost. Finally, lurching around, he broke distractedly into a long-gaited stride, heading downstreet.

His brain whirled. He had been played upon for a fool, and a fool he was. A *Dummkopf*, unworthy to possess a ranch, or a wife like Abby. Had not she warned him, again and again? But even Abby had taken it for granted he must be aware of this simple, commonly known rule about registering brands. Who but a dolt like himself would not have known about it? And last night, when she had again warned him against Shiffley, what had he done but strut before her like a stupid jackass and make a joke of her advice!

Ja, it was his own stupid pride and conceit that had brought him to this. And because he was such a simpleton this herd he had toiled so hard to collect now belonged legally to Max Fass. Or to Fass and Shiffley, since they were undoubtedly in on this deal together. No doubt they had already driven the gather to their own pens. And there was not a thing he could do about it. With a sinking despair, he remembered the clerk's words. *Looks like you ain't got no cattle, mister—till you ketch you some more.* How would he ever be able to face Abby—now?

I cannot, he thought miserably. *I cannot do it.* He lost all awareness of time and was far out of town when he awoke suddenly to the fact that he had been walking steadily for almost an hour. He turned and started back.

There was no prelude to it. He was on lower Main Street and passing the Steamboat Saloon when the batwings swung open and there was Dan Shiffley. Without a word he walked up to Shiffley and struck him across the face. Shiffley's eyes stretched in startled recognition as he made a bull-like rush at him, but the fight did not last long. His pent-up fury had needed this outlet and his final cudgeling blow belted Shiffley up off his feet.

There was a nebulousness and unreality to the rest of it. The blurred sea of faces circled around him. Shiffley blundering to his feet, and the bloody pincers of his mouth opening to gust the savage, wheezed-out words.

"All right, damn you, all right! Now you get a gun or be out of town by noon."

The sea of faces becoming a wall, a wall of prejudice and hostility shutting off the sun and sky and the dream he had brought to this harsh raw land. John Remsberg rammed his knotted shoulders against the wall and it broke. He began walking away from it. He knew it was still there, re-forming, behind him. He knew there was one way to break it, permanently. Only one.

The owner of the hardward store had let in the first ray of light. As he had stood at the counter, buckling on the new, shiny Walker pistol, the storekeeper told him: "Punch it at him fast, mister. Dan Shiffley's bad medicine. He's quick on the pull."

The first ray . . . Was it the beginning of full, clear light? The first breach in the wall? Outside the store, under its wooden awning, Remsberg heaved a sigh. Until he had asked to look at guns, the storekeeper had been as aloof and withdrawn toward him as those others had been earlier, in front of the Steamboat. With his intentions made clear, a constrained, grudging kind of friendliness had come over the man. It was wrong. Ironically, stupidly wrong that his mere strapping on of a gun belt should have made this difference.

Absently Remsberg's hand stoked down against the unfamiliar weight of the holster sagging from his hip. But wasn't there, perhaps, a degree of rightness in it, too? No one could deny the wrongness of the method. But did not the method stem from necessity?

And Remsberg felt, now, that he had found his answer to that. *Progress is slow*, he thought, *and where the law is weak, men must be strong. Custom is not changed by a few, or in a day.*

He moved out from the shelter of the awning, sensitive to a sudden preternatural quiet that seemed to have descended upon the town. The boardwalks were deserted, buckboards and spring wagons stood unattended at the hitch rails. And this was Saturday. Something portentous and unnatural about it pulled at Remsberg's taut nerves.

The word has gone out, he thought somberly. And suddenly it hit him. The stillness was not complete. Behind it lay a muted overtone, a vague humming sound, like the drone of voices in a theater before the curtain rises and the play begins. And then he noticed the pulled-back window curtains, the eyes peering at him from shadowy doorways. Oddly, though, the eyes seemed neither friendly nor unfriendly but only stiffly, curiously expectant.

Unconsciously his pace had adjusted to the slow, stalking gait of a hunter's, and at this moment he remembered the hardware merchant's words, and an odd feeling of stimulation rose in him. *Punch it at him fast, mister*. There had been a ring of sincerity in the man's voice; maybe there were others who felt as he did. Maybe, today, he did not walk alone. . . .

He caught a sharp ammonia reek as he was passing Neubauer's Livery and he was just beyond it when the voice floated after him from the wide stable doorway.

"He's still down at the Steamboat. Walk up on him easy, Yank."

He did not look back, but a sudden warm tightness tingled in his throat as he paced on, swallowing vainly against it. And then his belly plunged coldly. Forward a block, sharp noon sunlight glinted on the brass ship's bell hanging above the doorway of the Steamboat Saloon. And two doors below, on the opposite side of the street, the white-painted false front of Ellsworth's Mercantile canted its low wooden awning out over the boardwalk.

Abby, thought Remsberg. *Is she there—in the store?* And then he remembered, and relief was like a strong, warming drink in his belly. Abby had not been to the store or seen her father since the day of their marriage.

His pace slowed. He was less than a hundred yards from the Steamboat now. Abby. His *Süssliebchen.* So little he had been able to do for her. And now—a few months only—and the baby would come. Of that he must not think. A boy. A boy it must be. He had prayed for that. He had talked solemnly, with God. So that if anything happened to him, now . . .

Now! Now it would be, or it would not be. Like walking out of a dark cave against a tearing wind. It grabs your breath. Your lungs suddenly are dry and empty.

The Steamboat's batwings swung open and flapped shut behind Dan Shiffley. His chilly eyes accosted Remsberg's. He was smoothing a finished cigarette between his fingers and as Remsberg halted he did a disdainful thing. He scratched a match against his black whipcord breeches and idly touched its flame to the tip of the cigarette.

Remsberg sensed a wrongness in the picture. Shiffley was bluffing. He could not feel that sure. The range. That must be it. The range was not right yet. Shiffley was trying to panic him into a fast draw, into making a wild first shot. Then . . .

A cramping numbness was in Remsberg's legs as

he started moving them again. He remembered that feeling. At Sharpsburg. The bridge over Antietam Creek. Elements of General Toombs's 2nd and 20th Georgia Regiments had held it. Warren's Brigade was ordered to cross. And under deadly enfilading fire to those Rebel sharpshooters they had crossed. And on legs that had felt like brittle sticks, he, John Remsberg, had crossed. . . .

"Don't slow down, Dutch!" Shiffley's voice carried a jeering vehemence, reaching him. "You got sand enough in your craw, keep a-comin'."

It was a trick. Shiffley was egging him on. Trying deliberately to provoke him into a blunder. But how much longer could Shiffley wait?

Remsberg moved on, doling each step, feeling the pressure within him now, like a slowly tightening spring. He estimated sixty feet, fifty. Then forty.

Shiffley spat the cigarette from his mouth. He still did not move.

Suddenly the odd prescient feeling in Remsberg sharpened. Something about Shiffley's studied unconcern struck a false note. Remsberg halted.

And at that moment the shot blared. *Not from Shiffley's gun.* The realization rang a warning in Remsberg. *Don't turn. Don't turn!* The vital split-second advantage that should have been Shiffley's tipped in Remsberg's favor. Shiffley's eyes were stretched in a look of shocked disbelief staring past Remsberg and as he recovered to start his draw Remsberg cleared leather first and fired.

The mighty, walloping report bounced between the street's false fronts and skirled away in a fading rataplan of echoes. Shiffley had the appearance of a man vaguely preoccupied by a need to sit down suddenly. He took a squatting position as his knees buckled, holding on to his belly. And as he rocked backward and down, he gave the grotesque impression of a person who has had a chair abruptly drawn from under him.

Remsberg turned. All along Main doors were opening and people were pouring into the street. Already a sizable crowd had gathered in front of Ellsworth's Mercantile, and Remsberg stared vacantly at it for a long moment before suddenly recognizing Clayton Ellsworth's tall, spare figure standing at its forefront. Shock froze his eyes then. A big Walker pistol hung slackly in Ellsworth's right hand, and as Remsberg swung his head, following the storekeeper's fixed forward gaze, he abruptly went rigid.

The body lay sprawled on the boardwalk in front of Buckley's saddle shop, twenty feet from the Mercantile. Max Fass's head dangled over the walk's high edge, his skinny arms outthrust like those of a swimmer arrested in the midst of a breast stroke. The gun he had never come to fire lay in the gutter beneath his right hand, glittering diamondlike in the bright sunlight.

Fass! Clayton Ellsworth had shot *Fass*! Light burst through the fogginess in Remsberg's brain as he stared at the crumpled body. Now, like the final piece of a picture puzzle falling into place, it was all complete for him. While Shiffley had been baiting him on, from in front of the Steamboat, Fass had been moving stealthily out of that alley between the stores, intending to ambush him. And Ellsworth had seen him. That one shot he had heard. The shot that had brought the look of panic in Dan Shiffley's eyes.

Shiffley had been faced toward Fass. He had seen it happen. And the shock had slowed his draw.

Remsberg's breath caught. He saw a jostling movement in the crowd. Then Abby had fought her way through it and was running toward him. When she was in his arms, his throat was too tight for words as she hugged him fiercely to her. He stroked her tumbled hair and at last got through the tightness to murmur, "*Liebchen*," feeling a giddy whirling in his head as she kept sobbing his name and punched her cheek deeper into the pit of his shoulder.

He had, at first, only a remote awareness of the other voices.

". . .like to have sprained my wrist, gettin' the gun away from her. Ellsworth women always were a notional lot. Don't guess there's any way to cure 'em, either, except switch their bottoms when there's a needin' to."

Dazedly, Remsberg looked up and saw Clayton Ellsworth.

"What . . . what was that? I am sorry. I did not hear—"

The storekeeper's thin, pinched mouth relaxed slowly in a grin.

"You better never mind that part of it." The grin widened as John Remsberg stared down at the knotty fingers splayed out in front of him. "Shake hands, son," Clayton Ellsworth said. "And welcome to Texas."

Danger Hole

by Luke Short

THE FIRST TIME I saw the Diver, I only saw his shoes. Among all the pairs of miners' boots, claystained and muddy, that lined the bar of the O'Hanlon's Saloon, those shoes stood out as startlingly as a seal in a patch of cockleburs—black, shiny, and Eastern. From where I sold my papers in front of the half-doors of the saloon, I could see the shoes but not the man, yet I knew.

It was close to six of a pleasant summer evening and I had four papers left. I weighed their value against the prestige of announcing the Diver, but it wasn't much of a struggle. I cut across the street, outrunning the team on Mayhew's dray, turned the corner past the Apex Drug Co. and burst into the offices of the Enricher mine.

Behind his glassed-in cashier's cage, Mr. Philips didn't even look up until the door crashed shut, and by that time I was through the gate beside Miss Carney's desk. The door ahead of me was usually forbidden ground, but not tonight.

I threw open the door and called, "Pop! Pop! The Diver's here."

Miss Carney was standing beside Father, leaning over his shoulder and looking at the sheet of paper he was reading. At my announcement, they both looked up, my father rather sternly, and then he resumed where I had interrupted him. "Be sure to say that this is the last notice of assessments due. The deadline for acceptance of proxies will be midnight of the first."

Miss Carney said, "Do you want them tonight, Mr. Banning?"

"Don't be absurd," father said drily. "You have a half day's work there."

Miss Carney straightened with the papers in her hand, looking as if she were deeply injured. On her way out, she smiled sadly at me, and closed the door in a gentle, resigned way.

Father tilted back in his chair and looked at me. "How do you know? Was he wearing his diving suit?"

"I just know. Everybody in the barroom was crowded around him, and he had shoes on."

"I wear them," Father said.

"But you don't drink at O'Hanlon's Saloon," I cried. "Everybody with shoes drinks at the Mansler House."

Father smiled faintly, lifting the corners of his full chestnut mustaches. "Well, Tim, that's one way of putting it." He looked absently at the big glass case of ore samples across the room, and then returned his glance to me. "I met him. They were in this afternoon."

"Who's they?" I asked, already disappointed.

"He and his boss, Mr. Dickson," Father smiled again, as if with some inner amusement, and then said, "they're coming for supper tonight. Now you run along with your papers."

"Did you ask him about sunken gold?" I asked. "Is he big?"

Father said, "You'll see him tonight. Stay out of the saloons, now, and don't be late for supper."

"Yes sir."

I ran out, my mind in a tumult of excitement. When I thought of supper, it was with an unbearable impatience. A real diver was going to eat at our house. For months now, ever since Father had announced the strange negotiations with the salvage company, I had been in an agony of uncertainty. As General Manager of the Enricher mine, Father had opened the long correspondence that discussed the probabilities of success, the price, and the guarantees; his progress, which he told us, had me alternately in grey despair or delirious expectancy. At one time I was sure I'd never get to meet the Diver and talk to him. To understand my excitement was to understand that Apex was a mining town almost lost in the high Colorado mountains, and that only a half dozen persons in our town had ever seen the ocean. To understand the town's interest was to understand that its prosperity was linked with the Diver. As for divers in general, those men who risked their lives to retrieve pirates' gold, they were as remote from us as Solomon Islanders, and twice as romantic.

I decided to take the loss on my papers rather than risk being late for our company, and I ran the four blocks home. Approaching our house, which was of brick and big like all the others houses in our end of town, I wondered what the Diver would think of it. He was rich, no doubt, and from New York, where everyone was rich. And our house, while it wasn't old and had electricity and a telephone, was even plainer than the houses in Denver, so Mother said.

I vaulted the iron fence by the lilac bushes, hid my four papers there, and went in the back door. Sophie was at the stove and Mother, an apron over her best dress, was unwrapping our good silverware.

I wasn't going to be trapped twice, so I said cautiously, "Hello, Mom. I suppose you know we're having company for supper."

"I do know," Mother said, and she glanced knowingly at me and smiled. "I think you'd better clean up for them, don't you?"

Just then Cornelia come in from the pantry. She bumped into me and said, "Out of the way, brat."

Mother put the silver down and said quietly, "Cornelia, you know where the dictionary is. Go in the library and look up that word 'brat'."

Cornelia said, "I know what it means, Mother."

"You," mother said, "were our first child. If I wasn't married to your father when Timothy was born, I wasn't married to him when you were born. What does that make you?"

"Illegitimate," Cornelia said. "There's another word too. You want me to say it?"

"Cornelia!" Mother cried.

"Well, you asked me," Cornelia said defiantly.

She and Mother looked at each other for about three seconds, and then Mother burst out laughing and Cornelia did too. Cornelia was nineteen, and she looked exactly like Mother, which always vaguely affronted me. Her hair was dark where Mother's was light, though it curled off the temples in the same way, and she had Mother's short nose and blue eyes, but not her height by a head.

"I don't see anything funny about that," I said.

"I *hope* not," Cornelia said, and she laughed again, and so did Mother, with Sophie joining in this time.

Mother said then, "Run along, Timmy, and hurry."

I went upstairs and began to clean up, and I heard Father come in. I listened, but he was alone. I kept my old stockings on until I'd changed into my good shoes, and then I shined them by rubbing each shoe on the back of the stocking on the opposite leg. Afterwards, I changed stockings, and then I had to go into Mother's room and borrow her button-hook. By this time I was in a hurry, fearful I'd miss the company.

When I got downstairs, Father was in the living room, standing under the chandelier. He looked at me and said, "Confound it, with a newsboy in the family, we can't even get an evening paper. Where is it?"

In my haste to get home, I'd hidden our paper with the others in the lilac bush. I said, "I'll get it," and ran out through the kitchen to the back door.

When I returned with the paper, I knew immediately I'd missed them. They'd come in while I was gone: I could hear strange voices, one of them a harsh, nasal voice that overrode Cornelia's giggle. I said to Sophie, in genuine anguish, "Oh, Lord, they won't even give me a chance to talk to him."

"You'll get your chance, but not before supper," Sophie said. "They're late, and supper's almost ready."

I tucked the paper under my arm and went through the hall into the living room. There were two men there, one of them very tall, but his back was to me and I could see he was bald. I know I stopped in surprise, and Mother seeing me, held out her hand, saying, "And this is our son, Tim. Come in, Tim."

The tall man turned; he had a cadaverous, unsmiling face topped with great fierce black eyebrows and crow-wing mustaches, and I thought miserably, *Why he's an old man*. It was only when he stepped aside that I saw the other man facing me. He wasn't awfully tall, but he was one of the widest men across the shoulders I had ever seen. His curly hair was cut short, and the smoothshaven dark skin of his face was burned a brown darker than his hair. He had black merry eyes, a very full jaw and a straight mouth; he seemed to be about twenty-five, although his black suit made him look older. He was the first to speak, and it was not his voice that I had heard in the kitchen; his was deep and mellow, oddly cheerful as he put out his hand and said, "Hello, Tim."

"This is Mr. Devoe, your diver," Father said.

I took his hand, big and warm, and said, "Good evening, sir." And then, because he was what he was, I said, "Would you like the evening paper?"

Cornelia started to say something to me, but Mr. Devoe only nodded gravely. "Why, yes. I haven't seen it."

He took it and I glanced at Father, who nodded to the other man and said, "And this is Mr. Dickson, Tim."

I shook hands with the tall man. I was greeted by a nasal "Hello, sonny."

We sat down, Mr. Devoe with my paper folded in his lap, and Mother asked the usual questions about their trip. Mr. Dickson was polite, but seemed faintly amused that anyone should wonder at a two thousand mile journey, and he contrived to make us seem childish and provincial before he engaged Father in a discussion of the state of business. But Mr. Devoe was different, and I do not think by calculation. He asked Mother and Cornelia questions about our town, saying that he had seen many mining towns in Pennsylvania and, because of their drabness, had dreaded this visit to ours. But the vaulting mountains, which began at the very ends of our streets here, were as clean and unmarred as the highest Alps in pictures, and what were their names, and could a man climb them without losing himself, and where was the smoke and grime he had expected?

Sophie announced supper, and Mother seated me next to Mr. Dickson, with Mr. Devoe and Cornelia across the table. The talk never let up once, but when we were passing Father our plates for a second helping, there came the pause that I had been waiting for, and I got the wedge in.

"Mr. Devoe, did you ever find any pirate's gold?" I asked. Mr. Dickson chuckled and looked down at me, but Mr. Devoe's brown face was unsmiling. "Why, no, Tim, I've never worked in those waters."

"You could, though, if you knew where any was?" I asked quickly, and he nodded.

"Did you ever have a fight with an octopus?"

"They're a warm water fish, Tim. No."

"Sharks?"

"I've seen small ones when I was diving. They were usually more afraid of me than I was of them."

"Were you afraid any?"

"Tim," Cornelia said, in a voice of mock outrage.

Mr. Devoe looked quickly at her and said, "That's

a fair question, Miss Banning,'' Then he returned his glance to me, and smiled. ''A little. But I'm more afraid of fouling my air line, Tim.''

Sophie had been filling our water glasses. Now she said, ''Elbows off the table, young man,'' and spoiled it. Cornelia was talking now, but as Mr. Devoe turned his head to listen to her, his glance lingered on me and he smiled, and I knew as soon as we could get alone he'd tell me everything I wanted to know.

When we had finished dessert and rose from the table, Mother said, ''I expect you men will want to talk, Charles. Why don't you go into the library where you'll be alone?''

Father said that was a good idea, and Mr. Devoe turned to Cornelia and Mother and said, ''Will you excuse us?''

I wanted to remember that, because Mother smiled charmingly and nodded, leaving it to Cornelia to say, ''Of course.''

The library opened off the dining room, and I edged around the table, following Mr. Dickson. Father stood aside to let them pass, and then, seeing me trailing Mr. Dickson, a look of surprise and negation rose in his eyes.

''Please, Pop!'' I begged. ''I won't open my mouth. Honest I won't.''

I think Father was startled at the urgency in my voice; he looked across the room at Mother, who said, ''Try him, Charles.''

''But this is not a child's business,'' Father protested.

''You know he'll watch it anyway when they get to work. Let him see how they plan it.''

I saw Father was relenting, and I dodged past him into the library. I dragged a footstool off to the farthest corner and sat down, folding my arms. Mr. Devoe had been looking at the books that lined the far wall; he shook his head now, and hearing me move the stool, looked in my direction. "Your father is an engineer?"

"Yes sir. Cornell, class of '78."

Father, stepping into the room and closing the door, heard me. He glanced at Mr. Dickson, who was seated in the black leather tufted armchair beside Father's desk, and said with a snort, "A divinity student. Everyone was in those days. I wonder why? That cursed Beecher, I suppose."

Mr. Devoe said, "Did it ever hurt you?"

Father looked at him sharply, was about to answer, and then hesitated. "Why, no, come to think of it," he said mildly. He looked searchingly again at Mr. Devoe and then looked away and asked, "Like to take your coats off, gentlemen?"

While they eased out of their coats and lighted the cigars Father offered them, Father got out the blueprints. He talked as he unrolled them, laying them on the desk and weighting them with the inkstand and pen tray.

"I don't suppose it'll interest you gentlemen much to know how we got ourselves in this trouble. As a matter of fact," he said, looking at Mr. Devoe, "I don't suppose you know anything about silver mining."

"Nothing except that I like what comes out of them," Mr. Devoe said soberly.

"You'd have liked the Enricher back in ninety-three, then," Father said. "Before the British quit buying silver for the India mints that year, the Enricher was putting out three million dollars a month."

He was silent, as if contemplating those wonderful days, before he went on, "When we fell off the dollar twenty-nine an ounce, it left a good many of our mines here as marginal operations. They had a hard time staying in operation. When they weren't dodging the sheriff, they were fighting stockholders' injunctions and bill collectors. You've guessed of course, that we were all wet mines here, and that each mine was required to do its share of pumping to keep our lower levels from flooding."

Mr. Devoe nodded.

"Well, things got so bad finally that the power company, with months of uncollected bills from these mines, threatened to cut off their power. That was the first warning of trouble the Enricher had, and we hustled in auxiliary pumps. But before we could get them set, the power was shut off, and a half dozen mines pulled their pumps, throwing all the water onto us, the deepest mine."

"How deep?" Mr. Dickson asked.

"Twelve hundred feet."

Mr. Dickson's fierce black eyebrows raised in silent exclamation.

Father went on, "Being the oldest mine in the field, our big pump was a steam pump. It's a big Janesville compound Monarch—the Emma, we call it. She was on the twelfth level—the bottom—and she could lift twenty-six hundred gallons of water a minute fifteen hundred feet. She had been doing it only twenty minutes a day for eight years, and keeping us dry. But once the other mines pulled their pumps, she was on twenty-four hour duty and losing the battle. Being a steam pump, she couldn't be drowned, and she was working under thirty feet of water when she got tired and quit. Within twelve hours, all the auxiliary electrics in the shaft were drowned too, and the Emma was under two hundred feet of water. She's been there for three years."

"But you're in operation now," Mr. Dickson said. "We looked you up."

"Marginally, and only on four levels," Father agreed. "The big body of ore is under seventy feet of water, below the Emma."

"You said two hundred feet," Mr. Devoe said.

Father looked sharply at him. "We've got three Starret electrics with windjammers working the clock around, but they can't get the water below the eleventh level," Father added drily, "It's as we wrote you. You'll dive seventy feet to the Emma. And it'll take the Emma to unwater us."

Mr. Devoe shifted faintly against the books, and glanced at Mr. Dickson before he said to Father, "You weren't in any hurry, were you? You've waited three years to make up your minds."

"I don't see what difference that can make to you," Father said bluntly.

"Rust," Mr. Devoe said.

Father tapped his cigar ash into the tray with an angry gesture and said wryly, "Mr. Devoe, have you ever worked for millionaires?"

Mr. Devoe looked at Mr. Dickson and said slyly, "How do you stand, Jack?"

"Short," Mr. Dickson said.

Father almost smiled. "You're lucky. I work for four. They vetoed every assessment, experimented with every type of pump, quarreled, pinched pennies here, spent drunkenly there, fired good men and even shut down the mine before they arrived at this. A little rust doesn't seem of much consequence at the moment."

"Except you're paying us by the day," Mr. Devoe said.

"And rust means more days for you, I take it."

Mr. Devoe said soberly, "That's true, so now you won't think I'm sitting down there counting my toes while I'm really chipping rust."

He and Father regarded each other with not much liking, and now Mr. Devoe pushed away from the bookshelves, saying, "What do you think is wrong with the pump?"

"Just what we wrote you—we don't know."

Mr. Devoe took a deep breath, as if renewing his patience. "Mr. Banning, you're an engineer. You must have a guess. Aside from the fact you're paying us a hundred dollars a day, I'll be in the bottom of a hole with seventy feet of water over me. I'd like to spend as little time there as you'll let me."

Father shook his head stubbornly. "A lot of things can wind up in the bottom of a shaft in three years—ore cars, timbers, rocks. The Noonham found an elk in theirs one morning. Any of those could damage a pump. Then there are many moving parts in a pump that could fail. The base bolts could sheer or the casting crack. As for the water over you, I don't recollect writing you that there wouldn't be any."

Mr. Devoe looked at me then and grinned. "No, you didn't."

Father used his cigar as a pointer toward the desk, saying, "There are the blueprints of the pump."

Mr. Dickson rose and spread his big hands on the

desk and looked at the prints. Mr. Devoe came up behind and looked over his shoulder. Father watched them closely; he had forgotten me. Presently, Father said, "Well, gentlemen, do we go to work tomorrow?"

"We do not," Mr. Devoe said flatly.

Mr. Dickson said, "Our equipment isn't due until tomorrow morning."

"Tomorrow afternoon, then."

"No sir," Mr. Devoe said.

He and Father regarded each other in silence. "I'll tell you when I'm ready, Mr. Banning," Mr. Devoe said.

"And when might that be?" Father asked drily.

"When I can make a freehand drawing of that pump from memory."

When Father looked surprised Mr. Devoe asked, "Have you ever been under water, Mr. Banning?"

"Only swimming, and then no longer than I could help."

"There's very little light in seventy feet of open water even with the sun on it," Mr. Devoe said. "In a closed mine shaft twelve hundred feet down with seventy feet of water over me, there won't be any—at least, not enough to read a blueprint by."

Father's face flushed, and he shrugged. "Well, you know your business."

"I do," Mr. Devoe said quietly. "You've waited three years for us; you can wait three more days."

Mr. Dickson came upright, and Mr. Devoe rolled up the blueprints, and that was all there was to it. Mr. Dickson and Mr. Devoe put on their coats and Father showed them out.

Mother and Cornelia were in the living room, and Mother asked them to sit down.

"Thank you, Mrs. Banning," Mr. Dickson said, inclining his head, "but I swear I'll be asleep in ten minutes, wherever I am. I'd best get to my room for that purpose."

"It's this altitude," Mother said. "It makes everyone sleepy at first."

While they were talking I saw Mr. Devoe quietly regarding Cornelia. Mr. Dickson thanked Mother for the dinner and shook hands all around, and then Mr. Devoe thanked Mother too, adding, "Mrs. Banning, if I came around in a rig tomorrow, do you suppose you'd let Cornelia show me some of this country?"

"I'll show you," I said quickly. "I've only got the lawn to mow tomorrow. I'll hurry."

Everyone laughed at that except Mr. Devoe, whom I was watching. He nodded and said soberly, "As soon as I get my bearings, Tim, you'll take me fishing, won't you?"

"Sure. When?"

"Timmy," Mother said reprovingly. Then she looked at Cornelia. "I think Cornelia might enjoy it. Wouldn't you, Cornelia?"

Cornelia was blushing, but her chin was high and there was a small pleasure in her eyes. "I'm all right as a guide if I stick to picnic grounds."

Mr. Devoe smiled. "Then let's try one tomorrow."

I saw Father scowl, but it vanished as he shook hands with Mr. Devoe and started for the door. Father saw them out.

When he came back, looking at his watch, he said to me, "Bed for you, young man."

"Pop," I asked, "were you mad in there?"

He looked sternly at me and said, "Of course not."

"Don't you like Mr. Devoe?"

"Why—I neither like him nor dislike him. This is purely a business deal. I think he's unnecessarily independent and maybe too cautious."

"Cautious?" Mother asked slyly. "If he is, he can turn it off at the sight of a pretty girl."

Father snorted and said, "You go to bed, Tim."

I went up to my room and undressed and got in bed, and I lay there thinking of Mr. Devoe; of the conversation between Father and the two of them that sounded more like a fight than a conversation; of Mr. Devoe coming clear from New York to dive in the shaft of the Enricher and fix the Emma; and, of course, of Mr. Devoe's demanding time to memorize the blueprints. That was what Father was always trying to tell me, to look before I leapt, yet he had been almost angry with Mr. Devoe for being so cautious.

I heard the rumble of Mother and Father talking below, and then the noise swelled and I looked at the door and saw it open. It was Cornelia, in her night dress and barefoot. She came over to my bed and whispered, "Are you awake?"

I snored, and she giggled and I did, too; and then she sat down on the edge of the bed. "What did you talk about in there?" she asked in a whisper.

"Business," I whispered back. I told her everything that had happened, just as it did happen, and when I was finished she was silent a moment.

Finally she said, "Do you like Mr. Devoe?"

"Golly, yes."

"Why?"

I thought a moment, and then I said, "Well, he's a diver, and that's dangerous." And then, "Besides, he's just like Pop. He doesn't laugh at me." I thought a moment longer. "I wish they liked each other, don't you?"

Cornelia didn't answer for a long moment, and then she said, "Yes, I do." She mussed my hair and went out.

That was the beginning of a summer I will never forget. It began being good the next day and it never let up. Father had never allowed me to hang around the Enricher, even if he was its manager, but now, with Mr. Devoe as my friend, I went everywhere.

The Enricher was across the Raft River that half circled the town before it boiled off down the broad valley. It was a big mine, the ghost of a giant. Its gallows frame over the shaft house was ninety feet high, and built of massive timbers that held the shivs. Its mill was enormous, its ore house huge; and even against the bulk of Black Mountain, on whose slopes it lay, it made an impression. All it lacked to come wholly alive was the swarm of men who had once worked it, and as long as the water lay in its shaft they would never come. It had always seemed a miracle to me that, before the twelfth level was flooded, a man could cross over to the Sally Garfield, thence into Morgan's Gate, and from its extreme edge pick up a drift that led him into a stope of the Noonham whose shaft rose to the surface four miles on the other side of town beyond Apex Mountain and Christopher

Park. These were the mines whose ore had built our brick houses, paved our streets with brick, built our stone opera house, our three storey brick hotel and brought in our railroad, but they were all dead or crippled now—all save the Enricher.

I was waiting for Mr. Devoe in the Mansler House lobby when he came out from breakfast that first morning. He wore an oddly matched duck jacket and trousers, and his shirt, though clean, was collarless, and he wore no hat. He looked like any workman in his Monday-clean clothes, and if the well dressed patrons of the Mansler House stared at him curiously, he seemed not to notice it. He smiled when he saw me and said, "Going to show me the mine, Tim? How's your fine family this morning?"

We walked out together and turned toward the river, and then I asked him some important questions about his business. He answered my every question, explaining in detail all the things I'd wanted to know about diving. In ten minutes, I felt as if I'd always known him. He had a curious, restless habit of snapping his fingers softly at each step and of whistling noiselessly when a silence fell between us. He spoke to everyone he met as if he'd seen them yesterday and, strangely enough, they replied in the same manner.

But at the time, he was something different again. Mr. Rinker, the superintendent, was expecting him. Mr. Rinker had called Bill Wehr, the Master Mechanic, and John Fox, the Head Pumpman, into his office. Mr. Devoe shook hands with them and then started asking questions; and they were slow and considered ones, probing and endless. He looked over the boiler house and then asked to see the shaft. In the shafthouse, we all got candles and stepped into the cage.

The Enricher had a three-compartment shaft—two hoist ways, and a manway housing the water and steam columns. We descended swiftly to the eleventh level, past the Starrett pumps and the windjammers laboring to keep the water down. Below that, our descent was slower until we stopped flush with the station our miners had just finished drilling for the diving equipment.

Below us a few short feet lay the black water stirring slowly around the pump intakes. It reflected the light from our candles in little splinters of orange color, and it looked a thousand feet deep. The faint smell of giant powder and raw rock still lingered in the air as we stepped into the station. Across the shaft ran the steam and water columns for the drowned Emma, and I saw Mr. Devoe regard them scowlingly. It seemed so simple that steam should go down one column and move a simple piston that pushed water up the other column but somewhere down there the magic chain was interrupted; it was just pipe, his face seemed to indicate, but how to bring it to life? There were more questions then, and then finally, the oddest one of all.

"Who set this pump, Mr. Wehr?"

Wehr looked at Fox and Fox scratched his head.

"Con Drury?" Fox volunteered.

Wehr said suddenly, "No, by George, it was old Frank Moore."

"Is he still around?" Mr. Devoe asked.

Wehr nodded. "He's got a machine shop in town—Moore's machine shop."

"I'd like to see him," Mr. Devoe said.

Presently, we went up again. Mr. Devoe thanked them all, then looked around for me and started out toward town.

At Moore's big machine shop, down near the tracks, we found old Mr. Moore in his cubbyhole office. He was white-haired, slow-talking, the man to whom half the machinists in town had once been apprenticed and to whom every miner paid obeisance. He was the gentlest of souls married to a harridan of whom Father once remarked that she alone justified the revival of the Salem ducking stool.

And there were more questions here from Mr. Devoe. He wanted to know the character of the rock on which the Emma was set, bolt sizes, dimensions of the station, its accessibility, diameter of the bore, and a thousand other questions. It was then I discovered that Mr. Devoe, since last night when he left us at ten o'clock, had memorized enough of the blueprint to challenge Mr. Moore time and again.

This was the way I spent most of three days, and all Mr. Devoe asked of me was to keep out of the way, which I did, and show up at home for mealtimes, which I tried to do.

I remember coming home the third day late for dinner, and not for the first time. But I was full of news that noon. The diving equipment, delayed en-route from Brooklyn, had come in on the morning train, and I described it at length. When I finished, Father said, almost grimly, "Well, I'm glad we have an agent in the camp of the enemy, so we know what's going on."

"What does that mean?" I asked.

"It means that pair never let a man know what either their right or left hands are doing," Father said. "I'm general manager of the mine that's employing them. Quite a bit of the town's prosperity depends on their success. You'd think they'd let me know their progress, at least."

Mother asked, "Jealous?"

Father stopped eating and put both fists on the edge of the table, his knife sticking from one, his fork from the other. He leaned forward a bit, looked carefully at Mother and then said, "For three days, now, he's kept my son out all day and my daughter out all night. Why aren't *you* jealous?"

Mother looked startled. "Why, he seems a nice man, Charles. Isn't it all right?"

"What do you know about him?" Father challenged.

"What do you?" Cornelia asked sharply.

"Nothing. That's the trouble."

"Is it because Andy's a working man?" Cornelia demanded angrily. "Because he has grease under his fingernails?"

"My child, I am not a snob," Father answered carefully. "For more years than I like to remember, I had grease under my own fingernails."

"Then what is it?" Cornelia demanded.

"I told you. I don't know the man. He may be some guttersnipe with a talent for machinery and the nerve of the devil, or he may be some Senator's little brother."

"What do you want to know about him, Pop?" I asked.

Father looked at me and said grimly, "More than that his name is Andy, which your sister already knows."

"He was a sailor for two years," I said. "He worked

in the engine room of the *Istria*. That's a big steamer. He went to sea when he got out of high school because the parish where his father was a preacher didn't pay him—his father, I mean. They didn't pay him enough to feed them all. That was in Canandaigua. Where's that, Pop?"

"York State."

"Well, he got a shore job in a machine shop of this Brooklyn Salvage company because he'd saved up enough to be a machinist. One day two boats rammed in the fog and one sunk in shallow water, and they gave him a diving suit and told him to go down and see if the engines were hurt. That was how he started and pretty soon he was a real diver. He's almost twenty-five years old, and he doesn't trust anyone on a tough job but himself. And he wants to be a farmer."

I stopped talking. Father looked at Mother, and then he looked back at me; there was a sort of twinkle in his eyes, but his face was serious. "What's his middle name?"

"Brian."

Again Father looked at Mother. Cornelia said, "How do you know he wants to be a farmer, Tim?"

"Why, he told me."

Father said, "Any more of this pudding, Margaret?"

"Yes. Lots."

Father rose. "Give Tim another helping, then." He went into the living room, got his hat, came back and kissed Mother and went out.

When the screen door shut, Cornelia said to Mother, "What do you make of that, Mrs. Banning?"

"I know what I'd make of it in your place," Mother replied. "I'd skip a night now and then with your Mr. Devoe."

"I didn't mean that," Cornelia said slowly, watching me. "You didn't make that up about the farming, did you, Tim?"

"That's what he told me," I protested.

I had my second helping of pudding and then started out for the hotel and Mr. Devoe. Father's feelings about Mr. Devoe made me uneasy. I knew it was true about the town depending on Mr. Devoe. It hadn't occurred to me before, but it was so. Before silver went off, the Enricher was one of the biggest mines in the West. It had made millionaires of Mr. Calpher, Mr. Oliver, and the two Good brothers, T.W. and J.B.; it had allowed them to scatter from Vienna to San Francisco while their appointed manager, Father, stayed here and kept their mine running, arbitrated their fights, begged for money, fended off the smaller stockholders and, with dogged optimism, looked forward to the day when the Enricher was unwatered and in full operation again. The Enricher, with full shifts, couldn't carry the town on its back, but it could help.

No wonder Father was sensitive—and his touchiness might affect me. For there had been in the back of my mind for days now a doubt that gnawed at the pleasure of my waking hours. Would I be allowed to watch the diving? I had no business there; it was dangerous, and no place for a boy. But I wanted to watch it more than anything in the world. If I could get Mr. Devoe's consent, I might persuade Father—but not if their dislike of each other was aggravated any further.

Mr. Devoe was not in the hotel dining room, but I saw Mr. Dickson finishing lunch with Mr. Rinker. When he came out, a toothpick jutting out from beneath his crow-wing mustaches, I was waiting in the lobby.

"Has Mr. Devoe gone over to the mine?" I asked.

"I left him at the depot," Mr. Dickson said.

I ran down to the station, thinking that perhaps there was more equipment to unload. Approaching it, I could see that the train which came in around eleven o'clock each day had pulled out on its return trip down the valley. The freight door of the depot was open, but there was no dray waiting for a load. I found Mr. Embree, the agent, wrestling freight inside the big dark room, and I asked him where Mr. Devoe was.

"He took the train, son," Mr. Embree said.

I just stood there, not understanding, and finally I asked, "He's gone? He's left town?"

"Oh, no. He just took a ride down the valley with O'Manachan, the engineer. Said he wanted to look the country over."

I turned away, disappointed. I suppose, too, I was a little hurt that he hadn't included me in his excursion or even mentioned that he planned this trip.

When I got back to the house Mother and Cornelia were ironing out on the back porch. At my entrance, Mother looked up and said, "Now what? Is your Mr. Devoe sleeping?"

"Oh, he took a ride on the engine down the valley," I said.

"He what?" Cornelia had been sprinkling clothes; now she turned to look at me. I repeated myself, and she said, "Well, what for?"

I told her I supposed he wanted to see the valley. I saw Mother had ceased ironing, and was regarding Cornelia with a curiously attentive air. Cornelia was just staring past me at the big spruce out by the blackberry bushes in the backyard. Nobody said any more.

That evening Mother and Dad went to the church social. I had permission to go, too, stay until the ice cream was served, and then I was to come home to bed. We left Cornelia dressing; she and Mr. Devoe were coming later.

There was a big crowd at the social, which was held on the church lawn, Davy Myers was there and, between us, we didn't pay much attention to who else was. After the ice cream, we left, and I dropped Davy at his house and went on home.

When I went in the house, I looked in the living room and saw Cornelia, dressed for the social, reading a book.

"What color ice cream?" she asked.

"Three kinds. Why'd you come home so early?"

"I've never been," she answered.

"Where's Mr. Devoe?"

"Still riding with the engineer, I suppose."

"There's no use going now," I said. "The ice cream'll be gone."

"I know," she said. "Still, I'll stay up till the votes are counted."

"What votes?"

"Nothing. Go to bed." She returned to her book, and I went upstairs to get ready for bed. I was undressed and was shrugging into my nightgown when I heard footsteps on the porch. Through the open door, the sound of that soft snap of the fingers, the noiseless whistle came to me before the bell rang. I remembered what I was going to ask him and I headed for the top of the stairs as Cornelia went to the door.

"Do come in, Andy," Cornelia said, and then, "You're early, but I suppose we can take our time getting there. And there was no use your getting *that* dressed up for just a church social." At the tone of Cornelia's voice, I stopped, listening.

"I just got back to town, Cornelia. I got a lift in a wagon part way, but I didn't know I'd gone so far." Mr. Devoe's voice wasn't apologetic or sheepish. He added, then, "I came straight here. I didn't even change clothes."

"I'd never have guessed it," Cornelia said drily. "Did you find any nice farms?"

A pause, then Mr. Devoe asked, "Who said I was looking at farms?"

"You've been looking at them since the day you got here. When you said you wanted to see the country, I thought you meant the canyons and the mountains, but I've noticed our drives always wind up down the valley."

"All right, I did find some nice ones. Three."

"After you buy them, what'll you do about the diving business?" Cornelia asked sweetly—too sweetly.

"If I owned a farm, I'd be a farmer," Mr. Devoe replied immediately.

"I wouldn't," Cornellia said, just as promptly. "I'd sell it so fast you could almost say I'd never owned it."

There was a long silence, and then Mr. Devoe said

quietly, "You're your own man with a farm, Cornelia."

"Not if you're a woman," Cornelia countered. "You belong to everything—the cows, the chickens, the frozen pump, the blizzards, the washtub, the crops, the mud and the solitude."

"And to your man. You forgot that."

"He wouldn't want you—not with your stringy hair and knobby knuckles and your flour-sack dress and his cast-off shoes."

There was another silence and then Mr. Devoe said with a gentle chiding in his voice, "It's odd but anybody would think it was you who was the New Yorker, not me."

"Oh no they wouldn't," Cornelia said swiftly. "You wouldn't fool anybody. You're just one of the city sports who rents a team on Sundays for a drive in the country. Back of a six-inch cigar and with a couple of bottles of beer in you, it all looks lovely—from a buggy."

Mr. Devoe didn't say anything for a moment, but when he spoke, it was with mildness. "I guess we've picked the wrong night to talk about it."

"Pick any night, and see if I change my mind."

"All right," Mr. Devoe said calmly. "I'll pick tomorrow night."

Cornelia didn't think that worth an answer. I heard her good night and then she swung into my sight, running up the stairway. Then, remembering her dignity, she settled into a walk.

I knew this was wrong time to put my question, but I had to do it. I ran down the stairs past Cornelia, calling "Mr. Devoe! Mr. Devoe!"

When I came in sight of him, I stopped on the stairs. He was in the hall, watching Cornelia's ascent, an expression of puzzlement on his dark face. At sight of me, the expression altered slowly; he smiled and said, "I missed you today."

"Are you going to dive tomorrow?" I blurted my question heedlessly.

He nodded. "Yes, why?"

"Can I watch you?"

A frown creased his forehead, and I read in it a premonition of refusal. I wanted to beg, as I would have with Father, but I was ashamed to. I held my tongue waiting.

"Why, of course. I'd counted on it."

I just grinned, too surprised to say anything. He smiled and said good night, and he was down the steps before I found my tongue to call good night. The fingers were snapping softly; I couldn't hear the whistle.

I didn't get to sleep soon; I was torn between staying awake to get Father's permission to watch the dive and the knowledge that such a move wouldn't be wise. And then, too, the conversation between Cornelia and Mr. Devoe depressed me. The thought of him exchanging the life of a diver for the life of a farmer was as incredible to me as it was to Cornelia. That was treason to the good life, and in some obscure way it made me sad to think about it.

Next morning, wearing Father's permission like a flag, I was at the hotel early. Mr. Dickson and Mr. Devoe and myself were picked up by the mine rig and taken across the river to the Enricher.

The center of activities, of course, was the shaft-house, and it was here, while Mr. Devoe was over at the boiler house, that I watched the work began.

The pump which would feed the air to Mr. Devoe was housed in a big oblong box, and had a heavy iron wheel, with crank handle to turn it, at each end. It was this pump, whose myriad gauges meant nothing to me, that Mr. Dickson would run, feeding air through the hose into Mr. Devoe's helmet at a constant pressure. The pump was loaded on to the hoist, along with the great coil of airline, the greenish white rubber suit and the almost round helmet; Mr. Dickson, Mr. Wehr and a couple of helpers went down to set it in the station.

When Mr. Devoe returned, he had a last talk with the hoistman on signals, and it was during this conference that Father came into the hoist shack. He looked oddly out of place with his dark suit, high collar, and black derby, but the few men there, mostly mechanics and men from the blacksmith shop, spoke to him with the odd tinge of comradeship which a miner extends only to another miner.

Father came over to me and said, "I thought you were superintending this job."

"I'm waiting for Mr. Devoe," I said.

Presently, Mr. Devoe broke away from the hoistman and came over to me. Greeting Father politely, he said, "Ready, Tim?"

I looked at Father, who asked drily, "Am I permitted to watch this?"

"It's your mine, Mr. Banning," Mr. Devoe replied.

"I wondered when somebody would think of that," Father observed mildly.

We all got our candles and candlesticks and moved into the north hoist which was waiting for us by now and which was exclusively ours for the day.

Father didn't speak as we began the descent, and neither did Mr. Devoe. The south hoist loaded with cars from No. 9 level, passed us with a whooshing clatter. When it was above us, Father glanced at Mr. Devoe and said, "Mr. Devoe, I'm curious. Did you ever get around to drawing the pump from memory?"

"I did," Mr. Devoe said. "Last night."

Father said nothing, and presently the hoist stopped at the station. We stuck our candlesticks in the timbers, and Father discussed mine business with Mr. Wehr and Mr. Rinker while Mr. Devoe climbed into his suit. It was quiet down here, almost ominously quiet and dimly lit, as if we were far below the life of the mine. The working hoist made a dim clatter on its rails above us; we might have been forgotten.

Mr. Devoe, in diving suit, looked thick enough for two men, his feet with the leaded shoes enormous. While one of the helpers slung a heavy canvas sack of tools on the hoist platform, Mr. Devoe and Mr. Dickson had a last conference on signals. Then, while a helper manned the pump, Mr. Dickson set the helmet, locked it, and stepped back to check the gauges.

Mr. Devoe gave the hand signal that all was well, and moved slowly onto the hoist. I could see the upper part of his face through the glass frontpiece of the helmet; its expression was utterly calm, in comparison to the one of wildest excitement that must have been on mine. He checked the signal line tied around his waist and raised a hand; Mr. Dickson relayed the signal to the hoistman and the hoist began to sink slowly into the black water. As the water crept slowly past his waist and then his shoulders and then drowned his helmet, we all held our breaths. Mr. Dickson slowly turning the pump handle was the only calm man there.

When the hoist frame disappeared, a small stirring of escape bubbles clustered around the hoist cables. The descent was agonizingly slow with many halts, as he had told me it would be. None of us spoke during that time; I think we were all picking out marks on the hoist cable and watching them disappear under the water, calculating in our minds the depth Mr. Devoe had reached, trying to imagine the weight and the pressure of water, the opaque darkness and the fear.

After an interminable time, the hoist cable halted and stayed halted, and we knew he was on the twelfth level seventy feet down. A signal on the line indicated all was well. I imagined him dragging the heavy sack of tools off the hoist into the drift, and laboring back the twenty feet to the station of the big Emma compound. Then recalling the blueprint, he would feel in the inky blackness until he touched the pump, and he would spend some time identifying the parts. Once he had his bearings, he would check them carefully, and then signal.

When eventually he did, Mr. Dickson relayed the signal, and in a moment we heard the rumble in the steam column. Now, I knew, Mr. Devoe would be clear of the great piston, alert, as steam was fed to the Emma waiting for any movement of the monster that was as big as a room. Suddenly, then, great bubbles burst on the surface of the water, and fear twisted in me. Was something wrong? Had his suit burst?

Father said, "There's steam escaping still. Will you bet it's a broken column, Ray?"

"I've quit betting on that brute," Mr. Rinker said.

My fear died slowly as the great bubbles continued to rise and break. There were no signals now, and I imagined Mr. Devoe was going over the great pump, feeling blindly, trying to read the vibrations of such a great pressure escaping. Could he hear it? No, I supposed not, and certainly he couldn't see it. It would have to be done by touch, by feel.

At long last, Mr. Dickson, still at the pump, looked at his watch, and gave a signal on the line. It was answered and Mr. Dickson waited. When another signal came, he answered, and then signaled above. The hoist cable began to move, and I knew that Mr. Devoe was using up the last of the forty minutes he could stay down safely.

Only when, minutes later, his helmet broke the surface of the water, did I realize that my heart was beating fit to burst my chest, and had been all this time.

He strode dripping off the hoist, and Mr. Dickson, turning over the pump to the helper, unlocked and lifted off the helmet. Mr. Devoe's face was ruddy, dripping with sweat, and his hair was matted wetly against his head.

"That water's just a shade off the boil," he announced.

"Locate it?" Mr. Rinker asked.

Mr. Devoe shook his head in negation. "It's not the head. I know that. Next trip, I'll cover the whole thing."

After a few minutes rest, he put on the helmet again, and was again slowly lowered. I can't account for the return of my excitement, but it came again, and added to it was the knowledge that we were on the verge of learning at last what was wrong with the Monarch.

Again the steam column rumbled, and the water boiled with the big bubbles. This time, however, Mr. Dickson got the signal to raise long before the forty minutes was up. I saw Father look at Mr. Rinker, a question, a hope in his eye, and Mr. Rinker shrugged. Father asked then, "All right to smoke, Mr. Dickson?"

"No," Mr. Dickson said, not taking his glance from the gauges.

And this time, when Mr. Dickson lifted off the helmet, Mr. Devoe was smiling, and he looked first at Father.

"Your pump's all right, Mr. Banning," he said. "The packing's gone out of the gland. There's no suction."

Father eyed him steadily a full ten seconds. "Is that all?"

"I believe so."

A slow smile broke on Father's face, and then he laughed. It was a short laugh, one that held both scorn and triumph, and I think all of us there understood it. It was a laugh compounded of anger at the malice of an unsuspected, trivial thing, appreciation of the fact that a part worth a few cents could hold up an operation worth millions, and delight in the fact of its discovery.

"Not much of a job," Father observed.

Mr. Devoe smiled faintly, a touch of malice was in his dark eyes. "It wouldn't be—except for the rust."

But it turned out to be very much of a job—one whose every minute I watched except when I was eating, sleeping or selling my papers during four solid days. It was a job of breaking through rust to get at the gland, and breaking loose the gland—all under the crushing burden of seventy feet of lightless water, where a fouled airline or a ripped suit meant a lonely, terrible death.

But if he thought of that, Mr. Devoe never showed it to any of us. Each night he would call on Cornelia, and I got so I listened for the cheerful soft snap of his fingers keeping time with his footsteps as he came up the walk, always with the almost noiseless whistle on his lips. Both ended with the ringing of the doorbell, and he always greeted me as if I hadn't watched him all day, as if he were glad to see me, as if there weren't a thousand new things to talk about that Cornelia always interrupted. No hero of a book was half so fine; none half so bravely oblivious to peril.

On the fourth morning, I wakened thinking this was the day the job would be finished. Cornelia beat me to the bathroom, so I was the last down for breakfast. It was a wonderful summer morning, cool and bright, and I felt that my good morning should be cheerful. It brought a subdued, or perhaps indifferent, response.

I looked at Mother as I sat down, and she smiled at me; Father, though, was frowning, and when I glanced at Cornelia I knew something was wrong, I'd watched her long enough to be able to tell when she'd been reprimanded; she was pale, her jaw had a faint belligerence in its set; and she kept turning over the food on her plate with her fork as if she were determined to dislike it out of spite.

I asked the question that I had asked for the last four mornings. "Can I watch today, Pop?"

Father groaned softly, and put down his fork, and

Mother said just as softly, "Charles."

"All *right*!" Father said flatly, looking at Mother. "Don't I get any relief from him? Doesn't *he* get sick of my family? Cornelia out with him until two, and now Tim is starting the day shift at six-thirty. Why don't we fix a room for him and ask him here? Then I could move to the hotel and get a little peace."

"I won't be working the night shift any more," Cornelia said quietly.

Father snorted. "Until you catch up on your sleep you mean?"

"I mean never. He's all Timmy's—and welcome."

Father regarded her carefully, and then glanced briefly at Mother before he returned his gaze to Cornelia. "You mean you are through seeing him? Why?"

"He wants me to marry him, and I won't."

We all stopped eating and looked at her, and she eyed each of us individually with individual defiance.

"Marry you?" Father asked finally, and his voice held a bottomless incredulity.

"Yes," Cornelia said sharply. "I'm not a freak, am I?"

Father looked at Mother again, this time for long seconds, as if asking help. Suddenly he brought his fist down on the table with a crash that made the dishes dance.

"My God, are you insane? You've know him a week!"

"I told him I *wouldn't* marry him!" Cornelia said angrily.

"But the damned gall of the man!" Father shouted. "Asking you a question like that! Did he ask me! Did he even consider your mother and father?"

"But he had to ask me first, to see if I said yes, didn't he?" Cornelia demanded.

"You're defending him!" Father accused her. He groaned again and said bitterly, "That blackguard. That—that whiskey-drummer in overalls!"

"He's nothing of the kind!"

"Would a gentleman do that?" Father countered.

"Then how *do* people get married?"

Mother put in quickly, "How did we, Charles?"

"I waited a civilized length of time! I asked—"

"You waited nineteen years, simply because you'd known me since I was three," Mother said.

"That's got nothing to do with it!" Father said sternly. "The fact remains, he barely knows Cornelia. It's indecent and—"

"Maybe he knows a good thing when he sees it," Mother said tartly. "Even fools do, sometimes."

Father leaned back in his chair, looking sharply at Mother. There was a long bleak silence.

I said, then, "Gee, why don't you marry him?"

"Be quiet, Tim," Father said sternly.

Cornelia was looking at me, and when she answered it was to all of us she spoke. "Because I won't be a farmer's wife, that's why."

Father leaned forward now. "Is that the only reason?"

Cornelia looked squarely at him. "If you really want to know—yes, that's the only reason."

"You'd marry him if he remained a diver?"

"Yes."

"If he took you away to New York."

"Yes."

"Even if it meant leaving your mother and me and Tim?"

Mother said tartly, "I don't see my mother and brothers here, Charles. Of course she'd leave us if she loved him."

Father looked both hurt and baffled. He glanced at his plate and a fleeting distaste crossed his face and he shoved the plate from him. He tilted his coffee cup, saw it was empty, put his napkin on the table, rose, and said with a strange bitterness, "A salvage diver for a son-in-law."

"It's better than having a farmer for one," Cornelia said calmly.

Father looked down at her. "Why does he want to be a farmer?"

"He's tired of working for other people. He wants to work for the weather," Cornelia said tartly.

Father said, "Thank God for that," and walked into the living room. Mother and Cornelia did not look at each other. I wolfed down the rest of my breakfast, drank my milk, and, after Father had kissed Mother, joined him in the walk downtown.

Father wasn't talkative this morning. Usually, when I walked to work with him, we played a kind of game. We would try to recite every pool, every riffle, every twist of the channel on one of our favorite trout streams. I would take it until I made a mistake, and it was proven. Then Father would take it, recalling the fish he had taken out, and sometimes, though not often, he would make a mistake, too. But when I suggested fishing Hunter Creek this morning, he said, "Oh, not this morning, Tim." Down the street we saw Mr. O'Hanlon come out of his gate and head downtown for work. The sunlight dappled the streets with early shade, and the air smelled of dew and woodsmoke from breakfast fires.

Father said suddenly, "Tim, I don't want you to say anything about what happened at home this morning."

"About Mr. Devoe's wanting to marry Cornelia?"

"Yes. That's her business and his, nobody else's."

"Yes sir," I said.

"Not even to him."

"Yes, sir," I said, and then I asked the question that had been troubling me. "What's the matter with being a diver, Pop? Aren't they all right?"

Father glanced down at me and then looked ahead. "Nothing, I guess, only, it's a little like being a steeplejack. It's a good and necessary business, but you have to be a little crazy to consider it." He was silent a moment, then observed drily, "I'd sooner taste food for the Russian Czar."

Before Father reached the office, I had his permission to watch the repair job, and I headed for the Enricher. Looking back on that day, I remember it as exquisite torment. And, in late afternoon, it got to be agony. Mr. Devoe was going down for what he thought was the last time to finish the packing of the gland. I wanted desperately to see the steam turned in the column and see the first water flow out at the surface. But my papers were waiting, and I knew that serious illness was the only excuse Father would tolerate for my not being on the job. It was his ironclad way of impressing on me that I must learn responsibility. At last, when Mr. Dickson told me the time, I asked if I could take the hoist up, explaining to Mr. Devoe why I had to.

He nodded. "It's nothing to see. It'll come out with a rush and that's all."

When I came out of the hoist shack, I saw a group

of men gathered around the Monarch's outlet, and I knew the word had got around. An hour later, in town, I was coming out of Shott's Billiard Academy when Will Steffy, an apprentice mechanic, burst into the room, yelling, "The Enricher's pumping!"

A crowd of men gathered round him, questioning him, and I hung on the fringe of the group, listening. Yes, it was good as ever, Casey Miles, the helper said. (Why shouldn't it be, with Mr. Devoe working on it?) It was shooting a stream that looked as if it would wash the dump away. (Exaggeration, and he knew it.) Yes, they were through, the job done. (Mr. Devoe fixed it, didn't he?) Already, the water level in the shaft was falling. (Wrong, because he didn't wait to find out.)

I went out, accepting this swindle of fate with a surprising philosophy. I'd watched it all; only four men could say the same. Mr. Cutler flagged me down at the bankcorner and bought a paper, saying, "Well, this is your dad's lucky day, isn't it? It's a lucky day for all of us. Congratulate him on his stubbornness for me, son."

Father wasn't home when I got there, but he had telephoned Mother and Cornelia the news. We ate supper without Father, and in the middle of the evening he came in, smelling of whiskey, his eyes bright, his cheeks flushed, and a lingering excitement still in him.

While Mother laid out his supper on the kitchen table, he told us the finale. In late afternoon, Mr. Devoe had passed word up that the job would be finished in an hour. The miners, instead of going home, hung around the dump, watching the pipe that emptied on its slope. A betting pool was formed and bets were placed on the time the first water would clear the pipe. When it finally came, the miners and the townsmen who had heard the news and come over, cheered wildly. Then they adjourned to the saloons to celebrate.

"You with them, it looks like," Mother said tolerantly.

Father grinned. "Everybody wanted to stand me a drink."

Mother regarded him a moment, then wiped her hands on her apron, came over to him, reached up and pulled his head down and kissed him. "They didn't stand you half as many as you deserve," she said.

"What's that for?" Cornelia asked.

"Oh, for fun," Mother said, and she was smiling as she went back to the sink.

"And that pair of Brooklyn fellows," Father said. "Give the devil his due, they know their business."

Cornelia asked, "They're finished?"

"They're moving up their equipment now. They'll be out on tomorrow's train." He started to say something then checked himself and looked at Cornelia. "So far as I know, there were no farms sold today." He smiled. "Still, there are other farms other places."

"Other girls, too," Cornelia said lightly.

Mother said quickly, "Charles, when will the shaft be unwatered? Now sit down and eat."

We all listened to Father talk as he ate, and I am sure that was the longest supper he ever sat down to. The telephone rang constantly; the doorbell was never quiet. People whom he'd never seen before—miners, townsmen, even farmers—called or stopped by to congratulate him. In between these interruptions, he told us of his plans for the future. The Emma would unwater the shaft in a week; as the water fell, new pumps would be placed immediately, and by the time the water was out of the sump, a battery of auxiliaries would be set alongside the Emma. The Enricher would be unwatered, a rich and busy mine again.

Perhaps because I had gotten used to it, there was one thing I missed that evening. It was Mr. Devoe's visit. But he never came around, and if Cornelia missed him, she did not show it.

Next morning, I was at the mine early, and my spirits were at rock bottom. This had been the most exciting week of my life, and now the donor of it, the cause of it, was leaving today. Being young, I had put off the realization of it until the last moment, but this morning it was overwhelming. Mr. Devoe was the finest, bravest man I had ever known, save for my father. I had accepted him completely and been accepted completely, and I knew bitterly that after he left there would be a hole in my life. His quarrel with Cornelia had made little impression on me, but now it seemed only another dismal part of a dismal day.

Mr. Devoe and Mr. Dickson were crating the pump at the carpenter shop when I got there. Mr. Devoe finished nailing a slat, tested it, and then turned to me.

"How are all the Bannings this morning—happy?"

"Sure," I said, and he grinned.

"Want to run up to Mayhew's and tell him this stuff will be ready for him by ten?"

I ran my errand, and when I came back, the

equipment was crated and waiting on the loading platform. Mr. Devoe looked at his hands, wiped them on his pants, and said, "Come up to my room with me, Tim. I've got to clean up." We had started down the platform, when Mr. Devoe halted, wheeled, and went back to his canvas sack of tools. He opened the drawstring, fished around inside, brought something out and put it in his pocket and then reaching in again took out a spinch bar which he tucked under his arm.

He was quiet on the walk to the hotel; his fingers snapped only occasionally, and the whistle was forgotten. Everyone we met spoke to him, and he greeted them courteously. Some of them stopped him and shook his hand, bidding him goodbye. Apparently, the whole town knew the Diver was leaving.

Up in his room at the Mansler House which he shared with Mr. Dickson, he peeled off his shirt, washed his upper body, then laid out his good black suit on one of the beds and began to climb out of his work clothes. As he stood there shirtless, he reached in the pocket of his work pants and brought out a big case knife. Looking at it for a moment, he handed it to me, saying, "That's for you, Tim, a present." I accepted the knife and handled it with the reverence due it, and he watched me soberly.

Then he picked up the spinch bar which he had placed alongside the bed and handed it to me, also. "Here's a souvenir. You can tell everybody that's the tool that got the Enricher pump working."

"Is it really? Did you fix the pump with this?"

"That's the tool I used for packing. That's the tool that fixed it."

I stammered my thanks and held the knife in my hand, feeling the heft of it, the warmness that still lingered from his pocket, and I knew no other gift could be half so magnificent. And the spinch bar was a wonderful keepsake of the whole adventure.

Mr. Devoe began to dress then. He put on the big black shoes which I saw the first day; their polish was deep and beautiful. Sitting on the bed, he toed a chair over and put his foot on it and began to lace the shoes.

He asked, then, very quietly and matter-of-factly, "Do you know what's been going on, Tim, between me and Cornelia?"

I hesitated, and then said, "I'm not supposed to talk about it, even to you, Father said."

He nodded. "Not unless I ask you, he meant, and I have. What do you think of it?"

I was silent a moment, and then I voiced what seemed to me the important question on which everything hinged. "Have you *got* to be a farmer?"

"How else can a man with just a little money be independent?" he asked, and he straightened up and regarded me seriously. "If I don't farm, I'll work for wages till I die."

"There are other things to do, businesses, aren't there?"

"And they all take money I haven't got."

"Doesn't farming take money?"

"Not so much—and you're independent. You've got your own land, and you build what you need when you need it. And all the time, you're your own man. You live in the sunshine where you belong, and you look at trees and grass and water—at water from the top, not the bottom. You watch things grow, and grow with them. Why," he added, as if mildly surprised at the thought, "nothing can stop things growing. It's been going on since time. How can a man fail?"

I didn't have an answer for that; at the moment, it all sounded true and sensible, and I wondered why it hadn't to Cornelia. He looked out the window and shook his head in bafflement. "Because a woman can't be independent, she won't have a man independent. Is that fair?"

I couldn't answer, and he resumed his dressing, putting on a white shirt and then fitting his tie into his high collar before he put it on.

As he walked over to the mirror I said, "Are you ever coming back?"

He began to knot his tie, and he didn't answer immediately. Then he said, "No, Tim. She won't change and I won't either."

He put in his stickpin, shrugged into his coat, brushed off his derby with the sleeve of his coat, and put it on.

"Do you suppose you could watch those draymen for me when they load? Just keep an eye on them and see they treat the crates right? I want to say goodbye to your sister and mother."

I agreed gladly and we parted at the hotel, with the promise that we'd meet at the train. I faithfully oversaw the loading of the equipment, never suspecting, in my feeling of importance, that I might not have been welcome company on his last call to Cornelia.

A little before train time, the loafers started straggling down to watch the train come in. But there were more of them than usual today, and as train time approached a small crowd was collected. They weren't the customary loafers, either, but solid men of the town. Mr. Dickson, dressed in his stiff black suit, strolled down in company with Mr. Rinker and Mr. Bennington of the hardware store. Soon, just before the train whistled, I saw Mr. Devoe, in company with Father, approaching. I edged over to stand beside Father, wondering why all these men were here. But there was nothing special in the air, just the desultory talk of men. I realized presently that this gathering was unplanned, that it was just the spontaneous gesture of our townsmen who were grateful for what Mr. Devoe and Mr. Dickson had accomplished.

When the train was ready to go, the conductor spoke to Father. He shook hands with the two men, and that started the goodbyes. When they were finished, Mr. Devoe looked around and saw me, and came over and put out his hand.

"Goodbye, Tim. I'm sorry we didn't get around to the fishing ." His hand was big and warm, and he smiled, but looking in his eyes, I knew he didn't enjoy saying goodbye any more than I.

I said goodbye and saw him and Mr. Dickson on the train, and then it pulled out. That was all. The men drifted in pairs and trios back toward town, and I started back, too, knowing what was wrong but not how to right it.

When Mother called us to dinner that noon, Father sat down and looked around, and then asked, "Where's Cornelia?"

"She's in her room, Charles," Mother said. "She didn't want any lunch."

"Why not?" Father asked. "Is she sick?"

"Just let her be," Mother said firmly, and Father,

after looking carefully at her, started talking about the mine.

That afternoon was bad. I had been lone-wolfing it so long I didn't know what my friends were doing. Harry Stotz and Joe Clark were camping up in Fire Canyon, Mrs. Stotz said; Phil Eagan had been gone three days visiting his aunt down the valley. I moped around, aimless, trying to pick up the threads of a life I'd lived before the Diver came.

The next day was worse, but at least it was different. Cornelia had had her breakfast before any of us got downstairs, because, she said, she was going to clean the house. She was grimly at it in the living room as we ate. I spent the morning with Davy Myers salvaging insulators from the light company dump, and came home at noon with three. When I walked into my room to put them away, I saw Cornelia had cleaned up my room. Everything was in a different place, and I made a quick catalog of my possessions. The box with the feathers I couldn't find. I looked carefully, and still couldn't find them, and my suspicion grew into certainty.

I boiled down the back stairs into the kitchen, where Father was chattering with Mother, who was helping Sophie. Through the back door, I could see Cornelia on the porch.

I ran past Father and halted in the doorway and said, "Where are my feathers?"

Cornelia, her face smudged and her hair wrapped in a towel, was changing mop rags. She didn't even look at me as she said, "I threw them away."

"Oh, darn, darn!" I howled. "Where are they?"

"I burned them with the trash."

I was stunned for a monent, and then I howled

again. "You knew I wanted them! You knew I was saving them! What did you—"

"What's this?" It was Father's voice behind me.

I whirled, and I was so angry I was almost in tears. "She burned my feathers! She knew Frank Eastman's uncle is teaching him to tie flies, so I could learn when he gets back. She burned them! Where'll I get teal wings, and mallard tails and pheasant wings! I traded for them, and they're gone!"

Father looked beyond me. "Did you burn them, Cornelia?"

"Yes—dirty old junk that smelled up his whole room."

Father just looked at her, an anger stirring in his eyes, and then he said, "I don't like unkind people, Cornelia, and that was unkind."

There was a moment of silence, and then Cornelia buried her face in her hands, and began to cry. She ran past me and up the back stairs, and we all heard the door of her room slam shut. Father was watching Mother, as if waiting for her to speak. She only shook her head, and Father said angrily, "Dammit, it *was* unkind."

"I know, but be patient with her, Charles."

Father said nothing; he reached in his pocket and pulled out a silver dollar and handed it to me, and stalked back into the living room.

Cornelia missed dinner that day; at supper, she was quiet, almost sullen, and went to her room afterwards. The next day, and the next, were no improvement. She had a quarrel with Sophie that morning, and it took all Mother's persuasiveness to keep Sophie from quitting. I got all this from Harold Engstrom, Sophie's nephew, because I was fishing that day. By this time, Cornelia and I weren't speaking, and that was something that hadn't happened since she was fifteen.

But all this was forgotten the following day, when I came home for supper, Father's paper under my arm. The door was open against the pleasant evening, and coming up the walk I could hear Father talking over the phone. "All right, Bert, we'll have to wait on word from Kansas City. They must be between Garden City and there. All right, do that, Bert, and, much obliged."

He was hanging up as I came in. Mother was standing in the hall beside him, and he turned to her and said, "Bert says the passenger agent at Kansas City wired they'd know by tonight."

"Know what, Pop? Hello Mom," I said.

Father reached for the paper, saying in deep disgust, "Where those two confounded blacksmiths are. The Emma broke down this evening."

"Mr. Devoe? Is he going to fix it again?"

"He'd better, or I'll sue the shirts off that pair of shysters," Father said.

"Wash up, Tim. Supper's ready," Mother said.

Cornelia was setting the table, and now she called, "Did you try the Denver passenger agent, Father?"

Father walked into the living room where he could see her. "No. They'd be gone from Denver."

"They were going to look at Pikes Peak. They'd have to stay over a day there, wouldn't they?"

Father didn't say anything; he just looked at Cornelia a long moment, as if he were struggling to keep his temper. Then he said, "Before I call Bert Embree again, tell me everything you know. Do you know the train he's taking out of Denver, the car number, the

Pullman number, the berth number?''

''Charles,'' Mother said.

Father turned to her. ''Ye gods, I've been home fifteen minutes. She's known we're trying to find them. Why didn't she wait until midnight to tell me, so we'd lose another whole day?''

''I don't care where he is!'' Cornelia flared.

''Well, I do!'' Father shouted. ''Is your head getting soft?''

He stalked to the phone and rang the station. There was no answer. He rang Bert Embree's number, found Bert and told him to wire the Denver passenger agent.

By that time I had washed up, and supper was on. Father came stalking to the table and sat down, and looked around him, at the meat, the potatoes and the sauerkraut. He picked up the serving fork and speared a piece of meat with a vicious gesture. ''I don't see why a man has to be at the mercy of incompetents,'' he growled. He looked at Cornelia. ''I'm not talking about you. I'm sorry I lost my temper. I'm talking about that pair.''

''He isn't incompetent,'' Cornelia said quietly.

''What do you call it?'' Father countered, the meat held high in the air before him.

''Two days ago you thought he was the finest man in the world.''

''The pump worked then.''

''It will work again.''

''You're absolutely right,'' Father said emphatically. ''For what I had to pay them I'll see they fix it. But why didn't he fix it right the first time? Does it take genius to pack a pump so it'll stay packed?''

''No more than it takes to fix the back screen door

that you worked on five separate times," Cornelia said.

"Please, please," Mother said quietly. She was angry too, I could see. She looked at us all and asked, "Are we a family, or are we kennel mates? Charles, you ought to be ashamed of yourself, and you too, Cornelia. This quarreling will stop *now*."

It did, but I think that was because the phone rang. Father answered, and we heard him say. "Yes, it's true. Yes. I'm sorry about it, too, but those things happen. Of course. They're on their way back."

That was the first of a score of calls that evening. Word had gotten around, and I saw that it annoyed Father deeply. He was sitting in the living room, half through his cigar and the paper, when I asked him, "When will he be here, Pop?"

"Who?" Father asked, looking up.

"Mr. Devoe."

Father shook out the paper and looked at his cigar. "In two days, I should think, if he can locate his equipment."

"Will the water be back where it was?"

"Yes." Father glanced beyond me to Mother, who was sewing at the end of the davenport by the table lamp. "I hope your sister is, too."

Mother just looked at him, and he went back to his reading. The phone rang again, and Father groaned, rose and went to the phone. It was somebody trying to console him. The phone kept ringing until I went to bed.

The following afternoon Father got a telegram which said: RETURNING IMMEDIATELY. DICKSON.; and all my excitement returned compounded. I got all my work done around the house, and I spent part of the dollar Father gave me getting a chain and ring for the knife Mr. Devoe gave me. All the time I was filled with an impatience that almost equaled Father's.

He and I met each day's train, and on the third day they arrived. Mr. Dickson got off first, and he and Father shook hands loosely. Mr. Devoe saw me and smiled and shook hands with me, saying, "Been fishing?"

I said I had, and then he turned to greet Father. Father's eyes were cold, Mr. Devoe's back stiff, and their handshake was brief.

"I'm sorry to have to interrupt your sight-seeing," Father said drily. "This time, I doubt if the rust will bother you."

"It might," Mr. Devoe said.

"I doubt it," Father said. "It can't collect much in five days."

"On the gland, you mean."

"That's what I mean."

"That gland is packed," Mr. Devoe said quietly. "It'll stay packed, too. It's something else."

"That's unlikely," Father said shortly, and he turned to Mr. Dickson. "Did you locate your equipment?"

"It's up front."

"Good. I've got the dray waiting. You've got your old room, and you can change while the pump is being hauled to the mine. The hotel bus is waiting."

Mr. Devoe regarded him thoughtfully, and then he glanced at me. "How's your mother, Tim?"

"She's fine."

"And Cornelia?"

"She's fine, too."

Father said, "We're all in tip-top shape this week,

Mr. Devoe, and I doubt if the town has seen many changes since you left. Now, would you care to come along, gentlemen? I'm hoping you can get to work this afternoon."

Father declined a lift to the hotel, saying he was going over to the mine. I rode to the hotel with Mr. Devoe and Mr. Dickson and the other hotel guests. I watched them change, and got Mr. Devoe's promise that I could watch this time too.

As soon as Mr. Dickson left to see about uncrating the pump, Mr. Devoe said, "What's everybody been doing, Tim? What's Cornelia been doing?"

"She's been sick and cranky, really," I said.

He'd been dressing. Now he stopped, and I told him how she'd burned my feathers, how she'd quarreled with all of us except Mother, how she wouldn't eat and how she wouldn't talk, except to fight. "She's just like a porcupine," I finished.

"Does she ever mention me?" Mr. Devoe asked.

"She told Father she didn't care where you are."

Mr. Devoe nodded and went on with his dressing.

Nothing happened that afternoon, because Mr. Devoe did not dive. Mr. Dickson discovered that the pump had been abused in transit and the two of them spent the afternoon fixing a pressure gauge on it. When I left for my papers, Mr. Devoe asked me if I would tell Cornelia that he would like to call on her tonight.

I told Cornelia this evening. He called on her and they went out together; Father, in the shortest of tempers, went back to the office after supper to work, since tomorrow was payday; Mother and I played rummy, and I went to bed early, so I could get up early to watch the repair.

Because Father worked late that night, we overslept the next morning. I was wild with impatience to be finished with breakfast. Mother hurried frantically to prepare it while Father, at his place, napkin in hand; drummed his fingers impatiently on the table. When Mother finally brought the coffee and eggs and toast in, Father said, "Where's Cornelia?"

"She was out late last—"

"I know that," Father said shortly, "but where is she?"

"She's not feeling well," Mother said. "Let her sleep Charles."

Father stood up, put his napkin on the table, pushed his chair back and started around the table.

"Where are you going, Charles?" Mother asked.

Father said grimly, "I'm going up to find out if my daughter is a permanent invalid," and stalked out of the room to climb the stairs.

Mother and I listened. We heard Father's voice, deep and rumbling, and then the sound of Cornelia sobbing. Presently, Father came downstairs and back to the table.

"Are you happier now?" Mother asked angrily.

"I didn't go up there to be made happy," Father said. He looked full at Mother, now, and in his eyes was an expression of utter helplessness. "What," he demanded plaintively, "has she got against being a farmer's wife?"

"The same thing I'd have," Mother said tartly.

I got to the mine late, but the hoistman put the cage down for me. It was like it was before, only Mr. Devoe was more quiet. He didn't joke with me like he had before, and he was almost sharp with Mr. Dickson.

Father came down in mid-morning, and I could tell he was angry because he'd had to wait in the shaft-house until Mr. Devoe finished his dive.

When the hoist pulled level with the station, Father gave all of us a curt good morning. Mr. Devoe was sitting on a crate and he greeted Father civilly.

"I assume your gauge is fixed," Father said.

Mr. Devoe nodded.

"And you've been down. What did you find?"

"That the packing is in place."

Father's face colored a bit, and he said stiffly, "Then I did you an injustice. What's the new trouble?"

"I'm not sure," Mr. Devoe said, "but I think the tappet working in conjunction with the rod and plunger is out of place. At least I can't find the set screw that should be there to hold it."

"Then let's machine one."

"That's being done."

"How long will it take to put her in shape? Another week?"

"Your pump will be working tonight," Mr. Devoe said.

Father smiled faintly. "I hope so. I don't like to keep you here any longer than necessary."

"And I shouldn't like to stay any longer than necessary," Mr. Devoe said. He and Father regarded each other levelly, each considering, interpreting the meaning of what the other had said. Then Father stepped into the hoist and signaled it up and was gone.

That was the way the second visit went. Nothing was quite right. Mr. Devoe did not call at the house that night, and Mother and Father took me with them to call on the Myerses. Cornelia stayed in her room.

When we got home, not late, there was a note in Cornelia's handwriting on the hall table. "Mr. Dickson called and said the pump is working." Father just snorted; Mr. Rinker had called him at the Myerses to tell him the same thing.

Sunday, of course, was always a bad day, and after breakfast Father announced that the whole family was going to church.

"Oh, Pop, why?" I protested. "Can't I just go to Sunday school?"

"You can, and to church too," Father said, and he glanced at Mother. "I would like to avoid calling the Lord's attention to the Bannings and to their pump, so I think you'd better stay the full program, Tim."

"Charles! Remember what you're saying," Mother said.

"But Mr. Devoe is going this morning. Can't I say goodbye to him?" I begged.

"If you can make it before Sunday school," Father said, and added, "I should think he'd be in church pulling for that pump, too."

"Charles, I will not have that sort of talk in this house," Mother said.

Father rose, saying, "Yes, dear. Tim, will you go wake Sleeping Beauty and tell her our plans?"

I wakened Cornelia, dressed quickly and ran down to the Mansler House. Mr. Dickson, dressed for travel, was smoking a cigar in one of the lobby chairs and chatting with a couple of townsmen. When I asked Mr. Devoe's whereabouts, he said he'd gone over to the Enricher to make a last check on the pump. I knew I could never make it to the mine and back in time for Sunday school and, miserable, I turned away from Mr. Dickson. Everything was wrong this time, and this was a fitting end of it. It seemed to me that none of us liked each other as we had before, and that a kind of blight had come upon our relations with Mr. Devoe. His knife was heavy in my pocket, reminding me of our last parting, underlining the wretched dissatisfaction of this one. It never occurred to me that Father, watching this go sour, had ordered the family to church so as to avoid further heartaches.

I went back to Mr. Dickson who, interrupted again, glanced up at me with open impatience.

"I have to go to Sunday school. Will you tell him goodbye?"

"Why, yes, certainly."

Thinking I would do my share to make all of this less unpleasant, I put out my hand. "Goodbye sir," I said.

Mr. Dickson's face altered; he smiled and shook my hand and said, "Goodbye, son, and good luck."

After Sunday school, I stood outside the church door until the family came. Cornelia was pretty and pale, and she smiled faintly as I stepped in behind Mother and Father and joined her for the ordeal inside.

Reverend Hardesty was just launched into his sermon when I heard the train whistle its approach to town. In fifteen minutes, it would be unloaded, turned around and heading out. I looked at Cornelia, and saw Father regarding her too. Her face was impassive; she seemed actually to be listening to the sermon. Father cleared his throat, crossed his legs and looked absently at the stained glass window.

It was Father who suggested the picnic up Fire

Canyon that afternoon, and all of us, Cornelia included, welcomed the idea. We hired a team and surrey, and, by early afternoon, with cold chicken and other food in our basket, Father's and my fishing rods under the rear seat, and all of us in old clothes, we headed up the canyon into a perfect late summer afternoon. Cornelia was quiet, answering when spoken to, volunteering nothing, and by the time we'd chosen our picnic spot, our spirits were beginning to sag. Fishing revived them, but when Father and I returned in late afternoon and saw Mother lying alone on a blanket, reading, we both felt guilty.

"Where's Cornelia?" Father asked.

"She went for a walk," Mother said.

When Cornelia returned, silent and cheerless, we set about preparing the picnic. Father tried to raise our spirits, but with little success. His attempts to tease Cornelia met with a wan and spiritless smile, and Mother kept watching her. I knew when Mother's smiles were on the surface, not felt, and they were like this tonight. We drove home in the dark, untalkative, each preoccupied with his own unshared thoughts, Father quietest of all.

Cornelia was up, finished with breakfast and was helping Sophie wash in the basement when we finished our breakfast next morning. Father, hat in hand, came in and kissed Mother goodbye, but instead of turning away immediately as he usually did, he hesitated beside her a moment, then said, "Do you think you could stand old Mrs. Moore for one evening?"

"Oh, Charles, do I have to?" Mother said.

"Pop, can't I eat at Davy Myers'?" I begged.

"No, I don't want to offend old Mr. Moore. I'd like a nice dinner, Margaret, and I'll want to talk over some business with Mr. Moore afterwards. You can always knit and pretend you're listening to the old lady. I'll even try to make our business short."

Mother only sighed, and Father, smiling faintly, went out. I don't remember what I did that day, except that it was like the other time after Mr. Devoe left; I felt lost and footloose, and I was late for a dinner that Cornelia fixed me in the kitchen with never a word of reprimand or scolding. I watched her while I ate, and realized, with sudden concern, that this wasn't the sister I once had. She was thinner, with a pinched look around the mouth, and she was beginning to move with the same, drab slouch of Sophie, who was fifty and work worn.

Our supper was pretty horrible—not the food, of course, but old Mrs. Moore. She had a voice like a file with which she dispensed lies and gossip with the abandon of a malicious child. Old Mr. Moore, who had a mechanic's love of a fact, talked under and around her in a soft, slow way, chiding her gently and picking up the pieces of destroyed reputations and putting them together again. After supper, Father and Mr. Moore went into the library; I got Mother's permission to go over to Davy Myers' until nine o'clock, and I ducked out.

Father and I walked downtown together next day, and when we reached the bank corner, where we generally parted, Father said, "Come over to the office a minute. I want you to run an errand."

Mr. Philips and Miss Carney greeted us politely, and Miss Carney stood up as we approached.

"I'll be ready for you in a moment, Miss Carney,"

Father said. We went into the office, closing the door behind us. Father hung up his hat, moved over to his desk, unlocked it with a key on his chain, rolled up the cover, and sat down. He wrote something on a piece of paper, folded it twice, swiveled his chair and handed the note to me. "Give that telegram to Bert Embree. Tell him I'd appreciate it if he got it out right away."

At the station, I found Mr. Embree at his telegraph key, and I had to wait until he was finished. Then he came over to the wicket and I gave him Father's note and the message. He unfolded the telegram and read it as I was turning away. I heard him give a short laugh, and I looked at him.

"Your daddy don't give that pair much rest, does he?"

"Who?"

"The diver and his partner," Mr. Embree said. "Well, tell your father they can't be past Denver this time."

"Yes sir," I said, and went out.

The Emma had broken again, I thought. When had it happened? And why hadn't Father told us? Was he trying to keep it from Mother? That didn't sound right, because Father trusted us. And didn't the town already know, and if it did, why hadn't the men Father met going to work spoken of it? The more I thought of it, the more puzzled I became, and as I walked slowly back into the town, my direction was unconsciously toward the Enricher office.

Once there, I went in and asked Miss Carney if I could see Father. He wasn't busy, she said primly, and I could go in.

Father was at his desk when I entered. He looked

over his shoulder as I came toward him and stopped beside his desk.

"Pop, did the Emma break down again?" I asked.

He didn't answer me immediately; he looked beyond me to the door, saw it was closed, and then regarded me. "Did you read that telegram?"

"No sir. But Mr. Embree told me to tell you that Mr. Devoe and Mr. Dickson couldn't be past Denver by now." A pause. "Did it break again?"

Father leaned back in his chair, regarding me steadily. "You don't know anything about it, Tim. Mr. Embree said nothing to you. Particularly, I don't want you to talk about it at home, in the family. Or anywhere else. Not a word, no suspicion of a word. You understand?"

"Yes sir."

He brought his chair off the tilt and said, "No, the Emma did not break down again. Now just be quiet and be patient, will you?" He smiled faintly, and still puzzled, I went out.

The two following days were agony, of course; neither Father nor I ever mentioned the telegram again, but my curiosity was a painful thing. If Mother knew about it, she didn't let on, and Cornelia never talked anymore anyway, so there was no use guessing about her. Davey Myers said he'd heard the pump broke again, but I pretended I wasn't interested anymore. Yet it was a mystery that grew more confusing by the hour.

It came to a head on the third morning after, when I was standing by the corner of the station, waiting for the train that I was sure would bring in Mr. Devoe. The train had already whistled, and I was staring down the track at the cottonwoods that screened the bridge when Father walked around the corner of the station.

When he saw me he halted, and we just looked at each other. He said then, "Well, I might have guessed."

"Can I stay, Pop?"

Father nodded assent, so that when the train pulled in we both strolled down to the coach as if this had been planned long since.

Mr. Dickson got off first, as usual, and when he caught sight of Father, he began shaking his head. "Damndest luck I ever heard of, Mr. Banning. The Emma's a sour pump; she's hoodooed," he said, accepting Father's hand.

"It looks that way," Father said briefly, and extended his hand to Mr. Devoe. There was a stubborn set to Mr. Devoe's chin, a certain wariness in his eyes, but Father only said mildly, "Getting tired of the country between here and Denver, Mr. Devoe?"

"I am that," Mr. Devoe said, and, sensing a strange friendliness in Father, he smiled briefly. Then he looked at me and said, "When you grow up, Tim, try to build a pump that'll work."

Father led the way to the waiting hotel omnibus, and the four of us got seats together. Mr. Dickson was already asking about the breakdown, but Father answered all his questions by "Rinker didn't tell me" or "You'll have to question Rinker on that." Mr. Devoe listened closely, frowning.

When we reached the Mansler House, the other hotel guest climbed down and went inside, but Father waited until all of us were down and the luggage was on the ground. Then he turned to me and said, "Tim, Mr. Devoe and I have some business at the office. You look after Mr. Dickson while we're gone." To Mr. Dickson he said blandly, "The men will take care of hauling your equipment. And there's no hurry about this. We'll have dinner at the house, Mr. Dickson."

He touched Mr. Devoe's arm and nodded toward the corner, and Mr. Devoe, puzzled as I was, fell in step beside him.

Mr. Dickson pulled himself together long enough to indicate his baggage to the driver, and then, his puzzled glance still on their retreating figures, entered the hotel. He registered, bought a handful of cigars, sent his bags up to their room, and then walked aimlessly through the lobby, with me at his heels.

He sat down in a lobby chair and, seeing me, started a bit as if he'd forgotten me. He waved to the chair beside him and I sat down and watched him light a cigar. The fierce scowl on his face was accentuated by his black eyebrows as he regarded me. "When did this happen?"

"I—don't know exactly," I stammered, and then, taking my cue from Father, I said, "You'll have to ask Mr. Rinker."

"Exactly. Where is he?"

"I—don't know."

He looked at me with a bottomless contempt and smoked with a baleful quietness. Suddenly, he shot a glance at me and said in his harsh voice, "Look here, young man. The Enricher hasn't changed hands, has it? Or do you know?"

"No sir, it hasn't."

He stared across the lobby; he looked at his watch; he crossed and uncrossed his legs; he went into the saloon, and came back again, a fresh cigar lighted. Altogether, it was one of the most painful half-hours I have ever spent. And curiously enough. the thing that was worrying me more than anything else was that Father had forgotten to tell Mother that he was bringing home two extra people for dinner.

When Father returned, he was alone, and there was some indefinable change about him as he approached us that I couldn't identify.

"Ready, Mr. Dickson?" he asked briskly. "Did Tim take good care of you?"

"Where's Andy?" Mr. Dickson asked.

"I expect he's waiting for us," Father said cheerfully. "Shall we go?"

The walk home was one of the most bewildering events of my life. Mr. Dickson was angry by now, and not careful about hiding it. Father seemed oblivious to him; he talked to me, he whistled, he stopped to chat a moment with Mrs. Brubaker on her front walk. He even got to reminiscing about the town to Mr. Dickson whose occasional side glances at him were filled with anger and despair.

Our front door, as always in summer, was open. Father opened the screen door, stood aside and let Mr. Dickson precede him into the house. I brought up the rear, so I didn't see the beginning of it. I only heard someone running, and then Cornelia was in Father's arms, hugging him. She didn't say a word, only hugged him, hiding her face in his shoulder. Mr. Devoe, I saw, was standing by the sofa smiling. I didn't even notice Mr. Dickson; I was watching Father and he said quietly over Cornelia's shoulder, "Get your mother."

Mother was in the kitchen, and I didn't even have

to speak. She simply looked at me, brushed past me and hurried into the living room.

"You're wonderful," Cornelia was saying into Father's coat lapel. "Wonderful, wonderful, wonderful!"

"Why is he?" Mother asked.

At the sound of Mother's voice, Cornelia broke away from Father and ran to Mother. Nobody had to tell Mother anything, she hugged Cornelia to her, and Mr. Devoe just stood there until Mother, her arm around Cornelia's waist, came over and stood on tiptoe and kissed him.

And then Mr. Dickson cleared his throat. He said angrily, "Excuse me, but—"

"Mr. Dickson," Father said jovially, "I've played a shabby trick on you. The Emma is working perfectly, and I'll be happy to pay the expense of your returning."

Mr. Dickson just glared at him, and said sardonically, "Excuse me again, but will—"

"You've just lost your best diver," Father said.

"And not to a farm," Cornelia put in.

Mr. Devoe said, "Old Moore has sold out to us, Jack—to Mr. Banning and myself." A slow smile broke on his face, and he said, "Come on, Jack. You'd have come to the wedding anyway, wouldn't you?"

Mr. Dickson stared at him for a moment, and then his face altered and he smiled. He came across the room to them, and congratulated them. "A machine shop," he mused. "What'll it be? Banning and Devoe, or Devoe and Banning?"

"Neither," Father said. He looked at Mr. Devoe and his voice was dry and thrusting as he spoke. "We'll call it The Independent."

A Cowboy's Christmas Prayer

by S. Omar Barker

I ain't much good at prayin'
  and You may not know me, Lord —
I ain't much seen in churches
  where they preach Thy Holy Word,
But You may have observed me
  out here on the lonely plains,
A-lookin' after cattle,
  Feelin' thankful when it rains,
Admirin' Thy great handiwork,
  the miracle of grass,
Aware of Thy kind spirit
  in the way it comes to pass —
That hired men on horseback
  and the livestock that we tend
Can look up at the stars at night
  and know we've got a Friend.

So here's ol' Christmas comin' on,
  remindin' us again
Of Him whose coming brought good will
  into the hearts of men.
A cowboy ain't no preacher, Lord,
  but if You'll hear my prayer,
I'll ask as good as we have got
  for all men everywhere.
Don't let no hearts be bitter, Lord;
  don't let no child be cold.

Make easy beds for them that's sick
and them that's weak and old
Let kindness bless the trail we ride,
no matter what we're after,
And sorter keep us on Your side,
in tears as well as laughter.
I've seen old cows a-starvin',
and it ain't no happy sight:
Please don't leave no one hungry, Lord
on Thy good Christmas night —
No man, no child, no woman,
and no critter on four feet —
I'll aim to do my best to help You
find 'em chuck to eat.

I'm just a sinful cowpoke, Lord —
ain't got no business prayin' —
But still I hope You'll ketch a word
or two of what I'm saying':
We speak of Merry Christmas, Lord —
I reckon You'll agree
There ain't no Merry Christmas
for nobody that ain't free.
So one thing more I'll ask You, Lord:
just help us what You can
To save some seeds of freedom
for the future sons of man.